He's Back

HE'S

Allen A. Knoll, Publishers
Santa Barbara, Ca

BACK

THEODORE
ROOSEVELT
GARDNER II

Library of Congress Cataloging-in-Publication Data

Gardner, Theodore Roosevelt.
    He's Back / Theodore Roosevelt Gardner II.– 1st ed.
        p. cm.
    ISBN 1-888310-11-1 (alk. paper)
    1. Second Advent–Fiction. 2. Jesus Christ–Fiction. I. Title.

PS3557.A7146 H47 2000
813'.54--dc21

                                                            00-037109

Text typeface is Electra Old Style Face, 12 point
Printed on 60-pound Booktext natural acid-free paper
3-piece case bound with Roxite B and Kivar 9, Smyth Sewn

An interview with the author of
He's Back appears at the end of this novel.
Free reading guides are available for *He's Back*.
Call (800) 777-7623 or email bookinfo@knollpublishers.com.

Also by Theodore Roosevelt Gardner II

fiction
The Paper Dynasty
The Real Sleeper
Flip Side
Give Gravity a Chance

essays
Wit's End
Off the Wall

children's
Something Nice to See

nonfiction
Lotusland
Nature's Kaleidoscope

And the Lord God
Formed man of the dust of the ground,
And breathed into his nostrils
The breath of life;
And man became a living soul.
　　　　　—Genesis 2:7

ANOTHER BLAST FROM GOD'S TROMBONES:

Frantic orthodoxy is never rooted in faith but in doubt. It is when we are not sure that we are doubly sure. Fundamentalism is, therefore, inevitable in an age which has destroyed so many certainties by which faith once expressed itself and upon which it relied.

　　　　　—Reinhold Niebuhr

ANOTHER TWANG FROM GOD'S GUITAR:

Jesus is coming
Look Busy

　　　　　—Bumper Sticker

And then shall they see
the Son of man coming in a cloud
with power and great glory.

—Luke 21:27

THE GOSPEL ACCORDING TO

FRANKIE FOXXE

Those who were on the
plane thought they were
going to die.

Lightning rocked the sky; thunder grumbled deafening roars. More than one passenger swore the lightning hit the wings and set them on fire. It being nothing short of a miracle that they landed.

It was unusual weather for Los Angeles. As one of the natives on the plane put it—"I thought it was the end of the world."

Later, when people heard who was on the plane, passengers remembered all kinds of things that didn't happen.

"I swear, it was absolutely Biblical," was my favorite.

"We were tossed like a tea leaf in a tornado," from someone with literary aspirations.

"A stewardess was screaming."

"All the flight attendants were hysterical."

"Everybody turned orange."

A man named Ben Boyle was thrust into the limelight by the Big Event. He's told his story so often on TV and in print that he's become a household name like Zapruder, the guy who took movies of the Kennedy assassination.

To have missed Boyle's tale you would have had to have passed the year in a bomb shelter.

On the off chance you summered (and wintered) under-ground, I'll summarize: Boyle was at the airport with his girlfriend and their little kid. They were waiting for a plane to Hawaii to start a vacation. The way he tells it, his girlfriend sees the guy first and her eyes about pop out of her head.

The P.A. system is announcing planes being canceled all over the place.

Ben Boyle follows her eyes to this guy coming off the passageway. He is wearing a white robe and sandals and has shoulder-length red-brown hair. His skin is dark.

No one saw anyone anywhere near that description getting on the plane; he wasn't on the manifest. The FBI checked every passenger and accounted for everyone except this stranger. Everyone was satisfied he couldn't have gotten in the passageway except from the plane.

Ben Boyle makes a bet with his girlfriend, and steps in front of the white-robed, dark stranger and says, "Pardon me, sir, would you settle a bet I just made with my girlfriend?"

Those eyes, Boyle said, just about laid him out, so intense were they. Boyle didn't wait for an answer, he was satisfied the eyes signaled assent. At the time, he hadn't thought the stranger might not understand English.

Boyle was barely able to get his question out. "Who... ah...are...you?"

The stranger kept those laser eyes trained on Boyle and without humor, without irony, he said, "I'm Jesus Christ returned to earth."

Ben Boyle lost his bet.

†   †   †

The whole beautiful thing was right up my alley. Frankie Foxxe by name, the Debunker of Myths by reputation. It is no secret I am nearing completion on the seminal work of Christian heresy:

Jesus Christ:
Man or Myth?
Christianity:
Truth or Fiction?

I am, I must be frank to admit, an ex-priest. Yes—I had been a real, honest-to-God lie-on-your-belly-prostrate-at-the-altar or-dained kind of priest. Yes, I was.

Gives you a bellyful of insight into the human condition, it does. Perspective. Lot of miserable souls out there for whom the Jesus we peddled was a savior in more ways than one.

I am no longer in that line of work. You might say I changed sides. I'd taken up the business of setting things straight, atoning for my misdirection. Telling it like it was—debunking myths—and, my, were there a lot of them.

Being an ex-priest is not like being an ex-judge or senator, where the title is forever. Once I mustered out of the corps, my name, Father Damien, stayed behind at the holy altar, and I was just plain Frankie Foxxe again—Debunker of Myths. That "Foxxe" is pronounced "fox"—those last two letters are just for pretention.

While the stranger in the white robes was deplaning in a Los Angeles thunderstorm, I was tracking TV's most popular evangelist, Ernie Jo Banghart.

The first thing I did when I got free of the priesthood—and I can't say it was an entirely honorable discharge—was to bone up on TV evangelists. What better venue for debunking the great religious myths? And the *ne plus ultra* was Ernie Jo Banghart, no question.

Of course, I despised him for the circus he made out of religion, but I did have a grudging admiration for his success.

That night, in Gulfport, Mississippi, I had my customary seat in Ernie Jo's Prayer Pavilion—eleventh row center. The first ten rows were reserved for the faithful who could be counted on to express bodily, and especially facially, their abject ecstasy for the television cameras at Ernie Jo's rousing exhortations. There were arm-wavers and grimacers, dancers and criers among them, and I didn't qualify—not the old Debunker of Myths. Why, Ernie Jo told me time and again, I could just thank good the Lord he let me in at all. But I wasn't a guy to make any waves to stand out in a crowd. My age, it could be said, was solidly middle. Somewhere between peach fuzz and crow's-feet. My driver's license said I had blond hair, but it wasn't as blond as it used to be. Blue eyes, too, as though my ancestors had been preserved by Adolf's ethnic cleansing. I was close enough to six feet tall to say I was six feet, and I damn well did. My metabolism was happy enough to keep me from giving the scale too great a pounding.

The Southern sky was torn asunder with lightning, just as it had been in Los Angeles.

"This ole terrestrial ball is takin' a real beatin'," Ernie Jo Banghart said from the stage to the faithful. "Whoooeeee!" Ernie Jo liked to salt his down-home vocabulary with some pretty substantial words that he knew most of his audience might not understand. He just wanted it understood he wasn't a total cracker. Of course, when it suited him, he turned the old cracker back on like a water tap.

The orange light flashed through the stained-glass skylight, a pastiche of Michelangelo's God holding out a beckoning hand to Adam—or was it a welcoming hand, or a saving hand? And if I hadn't known better, I'd have said all the worshipers turned orange.

The house, always packed, rain or shine, shuddered as one. No one looked up at the stained-glass God, whose visage took on a lugubrious quality as it was intermittently lit by the orange flashing light, then just as suddenly plunged into darkness.

The pavilion was brimful to the rafters with real honest-to-God down-home kind of folks who wouldn't know sophistry from Shinola; and they said there was no explaining Ernie's attraction. You had to be there right in the midst of the shoutin' and the stompin' and the music, oh, the music; then you could feel it, by golly, right down in your bones like nobody's business. There is nothing like it in the whole world. Nothing like it *a-tall*.

All eyes were on Ernie Jo, sweating under a welter of klieg lights and windward of the scrutiny of the television cameras.

Ever since before he had dropped out of high school, God had told Ernie Jo this was what he wanted him to do, and, Jesus be praised, he was doing it to the best of his ability—and that was, most of his followers agreed, simply the best on this sinful earth.

"OOOO ooo," Ernie said into the microphone he was gripping like a popsicle he was going to eat before it melted, you bet your life. "Seems lak God is talkin' to us—lak it's gonna be when He sends His Son back to us."

There was a cheer from the rain-dampened crowd. There

was plenty of free parking at the Banghart Prayer Grounds, but you couldn't get anywhere close to the auditorium door unless you got there two hours early.

Another crack of thunder shook the building. Ernie Jo glanced up at his stained-glass God, to see if He would give way.

God was holding firm, Ernie thanked the good Lord.

The Michelangelo knockoff had been Ernie's idea. Emily Sue, his wife whom he had snatched from the bosom of her family to be his blushing bride when she was but fifteen years old, had resisted the idea. In the first place, it was dangerous, she said, to stick stained glass so high in the sky. Not enough support. In the second place, it would be just awful symbolically if God and Adam came crashing to the ground in some storm—especially if some of their followers were sitting under Him at the time. And thirdly, she said, it was too reminiscent of Catholicism because wasn't the original painting on a Catholic church somewhere around the Vatican?

"I don't care," Ernie Jo said with his customary finality, "people recognize Him instantly as God and I want Him in my church. You got to admit, Emmy Sue, it isn't going to hurt us having Him up there watching over us."

"Even if the low bid to put Him there is almost a hundred thousand dollars?" she asked through a cocked eye.

Emily Sue was still a looker; everybody said so. She had a round face and a stalwart figure that was near perfect for draping the designer clothes she wore to such uniform raves. She looked like a teenager trying to act sophisticated in a grown-up world. And she was grown-up, all right. Why, that little girl from the bayou in her all-dressed-up-go-to-meetin' cashmere plum-colored couture dress was the chief operating officer of a 150-million-dollar-a-year company. It always embarrassed her when her Ernie Jo said she ran the show, but there was little denying it. She was running the business like nobody's business. And they were making money hand over fist, and she gave Ernie Jo all the credit for bringing in the shekels, but somebody had to supervise the spending of it, and that was she. It was just like any other mom-and-pop business, only the take was 150 mil the year.

Another dose of thunder rumbled the auditorium and some felt the earth was opening beneath them to swallow them up for all eternity.

"I was going to ask you to turn to your Bibles for today's message," Ernie Jo Banghart was letting his honey-fried Southern baritones flow into his hand-held microphone, "but," he looked up at the stained-glass God, "I think God is telling me otherwise."

A cheer rose from the floor of the hall until it drowned out the thunder.

"Glory, hallelujah," Ernie Jo shouted with a big smile, "praise God, but with all this goin' on outside, I'm gonna preach instead about the return of Jesus Christ our Lord to this trembling earth—GLORY, HALLELUJAH!"

The crowd of faithful were on their feet cheering, waving their arms toward the stained-glass God—reaching for His mercy on their sin-stained souls.

"'Cause if ever God told me to talk of the Second Coming," Ernie was shouting, "it is *right now!*

"GLORY, PRAISE GOD, YESSSS, LORD, HALLELU-JAH!"

You couldn't deny Ernie Jo was pleased with himself, and why shouldn't he be? He had the best looking wife of any, and that's a fact; and not only the prettiest but the best dressed, too. She wasn't drowning in makeup like somebody's wife he could mention; she never looked cheap.

And the audience loved Ernie Jo; oh, how they loved him. The smiles on their faces reached from Texas to Alabama, the ecstasy pounded in their hearts like a battlefield drummer, his beat quickened to the danger.

The Reverend Ernie Jo Banghart could do no wrong. God was in his corner and all was right with the world. And, Lordy, the way He was carrying on up there, something was afoot, and it wouldn't be surprising if it were Jesus Himself on His way back. Why, if you shut your eyes you could almost see Him where the heavens opened up, split in two by the lightning.

The trumpeters in the band onstage were playing a fanfare introduction to a musical interlude, and Ernie Jo picked up his guitar and began to sing one of his own compositions.

> "Jesus Christ is comin' back.
> He's on His blessed way.
> Confess your sins, save your souls,
> We're goin' home today."

He sang it three times, then had the audience join in for three more. Then: "Let's sing it one more time," and they did.

Ernie was self-taught on the guitar, but he liked to say he didn't know who to blame, the pupil or the teacher. He knew all the tricks and played with the flourish of one so secure in his own success that technique and talent never needed to be considered.

He was riding high; during one of the audience choruses he stopped singing with a self-satisfied look and cocked his ear to the faithful.

Onstage, a well-scrubbed vocal quartet carried the tune: two clean-cut, frizzy-haired girls, not so pretty they'd take any looks from Emily Sue Banghart, and two well-scrubbed young men who could have been thrown back a handful of decades and not been out of place.

Riding high he was, there was simply no gainsaying that. And it was no accident. Years of hard work, starting in tiny grubby tents and clapboard churches, spilling his guts to five or ten people. Laughing like a hyena, crying like a schoolgirl, emoting, dancing, *shouting*. He did it all and, "Blessed Jesus," he said, it paid off in handsome spades.

Of course he lived well, why shouldn't he? He was quintessentially successful. He had no stomach for denying his family the luxuries of a good, clean Christian life.

His standards were always high, and he held his colleagues to them. It didn't make him happy to have to expose a rising competitor for being an adulterer, he'd tell you that, but it was God's will and it had to be done. So, Ernie rode his high white horse before the television cameras, his own Excalibur safely sheathed but ready to do battle on any cancer he found on the Body of Christ.

Well, there was one down and only a half-dozen to go.

I checked the crowd. You never knew what casing the joint would yield a Debunker of Myths. There, toward the back of the auditorium, a young woman sat staring at the featured attraction. I remembered her forlorn face when all the fuss made the papers later. I'd bet it was her first visit to the Prayer Pavilion in Gulfport. She had come over from Mobile probably to see what her customer looked like in his environment. She had watched him on TV once, but she'd never made the trip, weekends being her busiest time.

She was a twenty-seven-year-old woman who looked forty-some, there was that much wear on her. I expect she had been a little afraid to come—afraid the holy women, and maybe even the men, would scorn her—would recognize her for what she was. But no one gave her a second look. Her slightly haggard I-gave-Satan-a-rough-fight look fit right in with this congregation.

She was settling in now, as though she were at home here under the big canopy of the Prayer Pavilion—shaped like an old revival tent.

She would have been thinking what a handsome man Ernie was. A little puffy, perhaps, but he was not yet fifty, and he looked miles better than most of her clientele. Personally, I'd put money on him being one of her kinkiest.

I saw her look over at Ernie Jo's wife, Emily Sue. The woman probably thought Emily Sue wasn't too warm-hearted where a man needed it most. Oh, she was pretty enough, all right, she just seemed so caught up with herself and looking right, and the business and all. I was sure she agreed with me: Emily Sue Banghart never had the first idea how to please a man.

More thunder rumbled the floor like an earthquake. I looked up at God and Adam and was relieved to see I was clear of the skylight. Ernie Jo was clutching the mike onstage as he had probably clutched something else back in Mobile—at the motel.

There were a lot of preachers on the microwaves, but there were no Bible-thumpers like Ernie Jo—it was a phrase made in heaven for him. And he was a Bible-waver—he had two hands and he needed the first one for the microphone. But what better to put in the second (after he had loosened his tie and top shirt button) than that holy of holies, the Holy Bible? And to wave it high in the air, his stubby fingers clutching it at the spine so its floppy black vinyl cover and white tissue pages would flap in the air—TV was a medium of pictures in motion.

And he would let rip with that honey-coated baritone voice that greased the coarsest skids.

"Gawd is speaking to us, friends, 'Oh, get ready for the Judgment Day,' He's saying—I can almost see our Lord Jesus coming on a cloud—oh, hallelujah, praise God—praise the Lord—open your hearts to Jeeesus—He's risen and He's coming again."

I couldn't say Ernie Jo wasn't sincere. But I couldn't swear he was, either.

The next day, I got Ernie Jo Banghart's magazine, *God's Guitar*, in the mail. The cover feature was "The Second Coming, Now or When?"

Belief is a protective garment; its
complete divesture leaves an
intellectual nudity that longs to
be clothed and warmed.

—*Will and Ariel Durant*
"The Age of Reason Begins"
The Story of Civilization, vol.
VII

THE GOSPEL ACCORDING TO

MICHAEL

"Call me a surfer dude,"
he said when I met him.

"Everybody else does."

Michael Lovejoy was just a kid, really—not yet twenty years old—a strange choice for a first strike, but the stranger moved across that slick, wet airport parking lot with Michael locked in his sights. It was as though he had blinders on against the more mature, more intelligent, and more affluent possibilities along the way. The Lord moves in mysterious ways. And maybe it wasn't so strange after all, when you think of Bethlehem and Nazareth and burgs of that throw weight.

Michael was slightly less than half my age, and it is difficult for me to remember myself being that age. I don't think I ever was. I picked up on my religion earlier. Twenty-odd years before I subsequently lost it. I'd been debunking myths since Michael was in kindergarten.

Michael rode waves, I read books. Michael had a lean, tan, muscular body and shining blond hair—physically, he was one of the creator's triumphs. If you believe in a creator, and I no longer do.

I confess it escaped me how a rational human being could keep interested in such a mindless pursuit as riding waves. Fun for a kid, sure, but shouldn't we expect a smidgen more of our adults?

Guileless he was, that was the word. Maybe that was why he was chosen. I didn't say gullible, but I wouldn't argue against it. Many are called, they say, but few are chosen. Only he had no idea he had been chosen for anything.

The way Michael tells it, he was in the L.A. airport parking lot, looking for his car and not that bummed out at the thought of not finding it. "It was a major piece of junk," he said. "Bought it from some druggie who probably ripped it off from some boneyard where old cars go to die of natural causes."

It was a Studebaker, the last-legs product of a company that died before Michael was born. You couldn't get parts for love or money, neither of which Michael had anyway, and he kept it afloat with tape, wire and kind thoughts.

The stranger didn't seem to care. He made a beeline for

Michael, passing over many with more reputable means of transportation.

As you can imagine, Michael's mom and dad weren't nuts about having him around the house now that he was old enough to have graduated from high school. Truth be known, as they say, Michael wasn't that nuts about living at home himself.

Amos and Andi were their names, if you can believe that. Both Ph.D.'s in theology. And what knocked Michael out was neither one seemed to believe in much. And they seemed to, by this time, believe less in Michael than anything. Oh, Andi might have entertained some vague hope that things would work out for her only son (their daughter was on her way to a Ph.D. of her own), but Amos had long since packed in whatever hopes he may have entertained.

So there was Michael, standing in the L.A. airport parking lot, staring at the horizon. He had just taken Jennifer, his best buddy's old lady (but not in any legal sense), and put her on a plane for Frisco after the funeral. Bart had just turned twenty, and he had taken one wave too many at twilight.

Michael blamed himself for Bart's death—as we often do when we are not to blame. Funny how it is only when we are truly at fault that we try to escape responsibility.

Jennifer had been bawling her guts out right up until she disappeared into the plane. There hadn't been a dry eye at the funeral parlor.

Understand, I wasn't there for a lot of what I am relaying, but then Matthew, Mark, Luke, John and the others who wrote the story the first time weren't there, either. I'm just writing what I was told—like the aforementioned gentlemen did. You might call it an oral tradition.

Michael Lovejoy had an inspiration sometime after he met Jesus—he was going to write it all down. Maybe make a book, maybe not. Maybe just use it like a diary to record stuff that no one would believe later if he told them.

Later he decided he didn't have the follow-through to see it to *completion. I tried to encourage him, but all I got for my efforts were his somewhat discombobulated notes, of which I have tried to make sense under these headings, "The Gospel According to Michael."*

The earlier notes were more complete, before he fell in love. I'm going to use his words whenever possible in his gospels.

The sun had just dropped over the horizon after frying off the rain clouds. I was checking it out at it as it went. Like I did four days before when my buddy, Bart, sank with it.

I saw these visions of Jesus on a cloud. His arms were outstretched at His waist, like in the stained-glass church windows, as if He were saying, "See what you did?"

Every night since it happened I had been paralyzed watching the last slice of the sun sink out of sight, and each night I relived the tragedy as though it might change something. And I asked Jesus, when I visualized Him on that cloud, why it happened. Jesus never answered.

I wondered if I'd ever get over the idea I could have done something to save my buddy.

We were at the beach in Redondo, Bart and me. Just south of where I stood at the airport, so the sun was sinking over the same edge of the ocean.

Me and Bart were like brothers under the skin. We could finish each other's sentences. We were tanned, macho dudes and the attention of the chicks didn't bother us. Only Bart knew how to talk to the chicks. I always seemed to get my tongue caught in my teeth. Bart was trying to help me over my painful shyness, but then suddenly, Bart was no more.

He looked like a god out there on his board with the sun dropping just so behind him like in a painting.

Then there was the crasher. Bart took the hit—something went wrong. It could have been a small screwup—a by-product of three-plus hours of pounding the waves that threw his judgment off—but when I looked up, I saw only his board that looked like a toothpick, bobbing pitifully.

I dove into the dark ocean, my arms frantically battling the monster current. I swam for dear life. I knew I shouldn't have left my buddy out there alone. I had to find him. I'd give him CPR and revive him. It was getting darker, and more hopeless, but, fueled by adrenaline, I battled those killer waves until I was totally drained. When I, at last, washed ashore, I felt something hard against my chest. It was Bart's board.

I was mad as hell that Bart was taken that way—so young—so many more revolutions of the earth, so many phases of the moon making killer waves.

What in the name of sweet Jesus was it all about? Was Bart being punished for some gnarly sin? Here was the purest guy being snuffed in his prime while murderers lived to a ripe old age. Could there be a God who let this happen?

Then I saw the peculiar stranger advancing toward me.

There were other people in the parking lot, making their way to their inert cars, but the stranger in the white robes ignored them. His eyes were fixed on me, as though I were the hope of the world or something, and the only soul in the lot. He walked like his sandals were on a track headed right for me. I had a sneaking suspicion I should get out of there fast.

I tried to move, but my feet wouldn't go anywhere.

The sharp hook nose rose below the soft, friendly, neat red-brown hair and sliced those hypnotic eyes like the wrath of Jehovah. The skin was like warm cocoa with a lot of milk.

The smile crept over his face like a sunrise and melted all the resolve I wished I'd had but knew I never would.

"Hello," the stranger said. The voice was mellow, soothing like the eyes. Cozy, like the hot pad you put on when your muscles are sore.

He coulda been in the movies, easy. Playing the good-guy parts—like in the late-night TV movies where there still were good guys.

"Hi," I gulped.

"You look as if you lost your best friend."

How did he know? I wondered.

"Where you headed?" the stranger asked.

"Looking for my car," I said, as though that answered the question. I turned away and suddenly remembered where my car was. The stranger was right behind me, stuck to me like he was a suction cup.

Trying to avoid his eyes, I ran my hand across the rear fender of my '54 Studebaker that was down to its undercoat.

I told the dark-skinned man: "I'm broke, man, flat. I mean, I'd love to take you to Kansas City, if that's what you want, but this piece of junk likes her gas and they're not giving it away these days."

"Get in," he said, "I'll get you some gas." It was as though he said, "I'm going to perform a few miracles here to catch your attention, then we can get down to business."

I shrugged. I had nothing better going on. Besides, I needed the gas.

After we got in the car, I asked, "Where to?"

"Hm—" the stranger pondered. "Why don't you point her toward the desert."

"Might be hot out there this time of year," I said.

"I can take the heat," the stranger allowed. "Can you?"

"If I have to," I said, and started the car. This is nuts, I thought.

I headed for the high ground above Hemet—the Idyllwild area. It would be cooler.

Maneuvering onto Century Boulevard from the airport, I felt my progress impeded by a lackadaisical Asian driver.

"Stupid Jap," I shouted like a burst of artillery. "Why don't you stay off the road if you can't learn to drive."

As I turned for the off-ramp, a dark-skinned man cut in front of me. "Black bastard," I yelled.

The dark stranger beside me said nothing.

We drove some miles in silence; I wondered how I could be so foolishly trusting of my strange passenger.

"Did you have a nice flight?" I asked.

"Hm? Oh, yes, very nice, thank you."

"Are you scared at all?"

"No—but there is a lot of praying in airplanes—you can feel it. And airports are thick with the relief of arriving passengers and anxiety of boarders—you can feel these moods, can't you?"

"I never thought much about it, I guess."

"There has always been fear connected with travel—even when it was by camel."

"I guess," I said abstractedly, checking the gas gauge. "But if we don't get some gas soon, we'll be in the market for a camel."

"Okay," the stranger said. "Pull into the next station."

"You have money," I asked, "right?"

"I said I'd get you gas," the stranger said with an effortless smile, "I'll get you gas."

"Hey, wait a minute," I said, a dense cloud covering my eyes then suddenly lifting. "You aren't going to rip it off, are you?"

"Rip it off?"

"You know—steal it."

The man smiled. "No," he said. "Thou shalt not steal."

"Yeah," I said, unconvinced. "Good advice."

"You working?" the gentleman asked me.

"Naw—some part-time stuff. Nothing permanent. I still live at home."

"What are you looking for?"

"Oh, I haven't exactly been looking. Something I can believe in; you know, meaningful. That's more important than the money...I guess."

"I have just the thing for you."

"You do?" I had to admit the stranger got my hopes up.

"I do."

"What is it?"

"I'll get to that—let's get the gas."

We were on a side road into Hemet when I pulled into one of those rundown gas stations you see in Depression Dust Bowl movies.

I had to blow the horn to raise anyone.

An overweight woman came struggling toward us. "Ooowee," she said, fanning her face with a flat hand, the flesh on her arms jiggling to and fro. "It's a hot one."

The stranger was staring at her. I looked at him and fidgeted in the seat.

"How much you want?" the woman asked.

Here the story gets murky. According to Michael, the stranger got out of the car and made his way—like he was floating, or walking on water—to the pump, where the woman hoisted the hose and put the nozzle in the tank opening without taking her eyes off the stranger.

Michael blushed when he told me, at the time he saw it happening it was almost a sexual motion.

The stranger whispered something to her and she got all glassy-eyed, and before Michael knew what was happening, gas was overflowing the tank and spilling on the ground. Like the Bible bit about the guy spilling his seed upon the ground.

Michael is taking it all in in the rearview mirror, waiting to burn rubber at the first sign of trouble. He doesn't see any money change hands, only the stranger putting his palm on her forehead and muttering something. When the stranger gets in the passenger seat with a benign look on his face and the woman makes her way up the driver's side, Michael smells trouble. He thinks she's going to ask him for money.

Instead, she gets to his window—which no longer rolls up—and looks across Michael to where the stranger is facing forward.

According to Michael, the woman had apparently all but fallen down in this trancelike swoon. Such is the hindsight memory—

like a Lourdes miracle or discovering the Shroud of Turin or a sliver of the True Cross. Suddenly she told Michael he was chosen of God to disciple God's son on his return to earth, and Michael thought she was loonier than a bedbug, but he drove off with the first full tank of gas he had since he bought the Studebaker. He hadn't learned much in his young life, but he did know not to look a gift horse in the mouth.

Back to Michael's notebooks:

We plunged into silence for a few miles, until the stranger asked me what was on my mind.

"This may sound funny to you, but I was thinking of religion—God and Jesus and all that." I glanced at the stranger. "Maybe it's your robes and all."

"Why should that sound funny to me?"

"Well, you know, I guess most people now look down their noses on religion."

"That so?"

"Yeah."

"Well, we oughta do something about that. When you look down your nose, you don't see very far."

"I know my parents do. I mean, here they are—they both have doctor degrees in theology, but I can't find any sign of belief in either of them."

"That so?"

"Yeah."

"So, what do you expect from religion?"

"I dunno—something to hold on to. Something that might explain this mess. And," I added, as an afterthought, "it would make my parents stoked. I guess I've been a disappointment to them."

"Oh? How?"

"I don't know. I didn't go to college—I don't even have all my high-school credits for a degree. I guess I drifted a little. You know how parents are. I didn't conform." My mind wandered back a few years. "My sister was the one they liked. She always did what was expected of her. She's the apple of the old man's eye."

"What makes you say so?"

"Oh, you know, like at Christmas. He thought it had degenerated into a commercial gift-giving orgy. But I was young—I liked stuff—and I guess the subtlety of his approach escaped me. Sis always made something for him: a necktie one year, a padded box for his cufflinks the next; and I was out at Thrifty Drug Store buying him some little trinket that he never looked at after he opened it. Every year after he'd open Sis's gift, he'd light up like a Christmas tree and say, 'Ah, the homemade gifts are the best.'

"I wanted to impress him with *my* gift—just once. So the next year, I was about eleven or twelve, I guess, I got a job delivering papers so I could save all my money and buy him something really impressive. He had been into stamp collecting, so I had this idea of getting him the top-of-the-line stamp-collecting book. I saw the most killer thing in a bookstore. It was the size of one of those giant Bibles," I said, with a sideways glance at the guy in the white robes.

"I earned extra money by selling more neighbors on the newspaper and increasing the size of my route. By mid December, I had enough money to buy the huge book. My mother tried to discourage me gently. 'Well, would Dad really want you to have sacrificed so much for him? And, is he really that serious about collecting that he needs a book this size?' I wouldn't hear of it. To me, it was the thought that mattered. And I didn't see how my sister, or anyone else, could top my effort.

"On Christmas Eve I spent two hours wrapping the big book. I took plain paper and with watercolors, and in spite of the fact I was a klutz with a paintbrush, I painted a picture of my father opening a big package on Christmas morning, with an enormous smile.

"On Christmas morning I couldn't wait to give the big package to him. Sis, who was fifteen at the time, had made placemats for the table with everyone's initials on them and a little Christmas tree on the bottom corner, but I was so excited, I insisted Amos open my gift first. He took the package from me, hefted it once or twice, saying, 'Um, heavy,' and set it on his lap.

"'Well, look at this,' he said, inspecting the custom-made wrapping. 'Homemade, just what I like. Is the gift homemade, too?'

"I swallowed a large chunk of excitement while my father carefully opened the package to preserve the custom-made paper. His eyes did open wider when he saw the big stamp book, but the enormous smile from his picture on the wrapping was missing. He was gracious but cool and said, 'Gosh, Michael, you shouldn't have done all this for me. I'm not a collector of this magnitude; in fact, I was seeing my stamp-collecting days coming to an end.'

"'Well, you'll just have to rejuvenate them,' Mother said.

"When he opened Monica's gift, Amos lit up, and the big smile from my drawing on the wrapping came to his face. 'That's my girl,' he said, 'that's what I like, homemade gifts.' I felt like I struck out again, as I had in so many Little League games when Father sat expectantly on the sidelines, hoping for a home run."

"Sad."

"I guess that's when I started to screw up. Drugs—cutting classes, spending all my time surfing." I shook my head.

"Women?"

I frowned. "I've always been freaked out about girls."

"Why?"

"I don't know. Rejection, I guess. I was very sensitive to rejection. I didn't want any more of it."

"You don't think the girls were just as scared?"

"Don't know. Guess I was too freaked to find out. Why am I telling you all this? I haven't told that to anybody. You're a stranger."

"I'm not a stranger. There are no strangers, we are all children of the same Father."

I looked at him through a cloud. "Yeah, your dad was like that, too?"

"I didn't mean it that way," the stranger said. "You want to stop to get something to eat?"

I couldn't help grinning. "Feeling lucky?" I asked him.

"You might say that."

My hand reached as if automatically for the knob of the car radio. I twirled the dial until I heard the voice of Ernie Jo Banghart saying: "No, sir, it's evil, plain and simple. Now I don't doubt the hand of Satan in there somewhere, but this man is a pornographic nightmare and he will have to be exorcised from the Body of Christ because, why, he is sucking Christ's blood just like a leech."

"Have you ever strayed from your marriage vows, Reverend Banghart?" another voice interrupted.

"No, sir, I never knew any woman but mah wife. I never kissed anyone else in mah life."

"Ugh," I said, turning to a rock-music station. "Types like that are lame."

"Why is that?"

"Don't they piss you off?"

"I don't know."

"Let me ask you something. I don't know how much you know about religion or anything, but don't you wonder what those cons believe in? Getting the dough to keep them on the air—or getting on the air to make more money?"

"Think it's all money, do you?"

"Lot of people think so, dude. You?"

"Judge not, that ye be not judged, I guess," he said.

"Hey, I just been spilling my guts to you, told you things I haven't told anybody. And I don't even know your name. What is it?"

"Jesus."

"Oh, yeah," I laughed. "Far out."

The Gospel According to

FRANKIE FOXXE

I always said if hell had a smoking room it would look like Rob Houston's lair at the *Gulfport Riptide*, comfortably off the main drag in Gulfport, Mississippi, which some residents modestly consider the Jesus capital of the world.

Rob, of course, is high among them.

There were also those who thought Rob was the spitting image of hell's major-domo, but, hell, beauty is only skin deep.

My boss is insufferable. I used to pray for a trust fund so I could tell him to shove it. That's before I stopped praying. The prayers went unanswered. That was one of the reasons I stopped praying. O ye of little faith.

Since I had been a priest, I thought I knew a thing or two about religion. But I knew next to nothing about the phenomenon known as Ernie Jo Banghart. How did he do it with his gelled bouffant hair and his crooked, used-car-dealer smile—closing in for the kill? He was *numero uno* by all counts, Nielsen ratings and the size of the collection-plate kill—three million a week—and in one-dollar to twenty-five-dollar donations mostly. "Mostly" is a word Ernie Jo would use. I, on the other hand, see myself as too educated to use "mostly" as an adverb.

Christianity's biggest myth was Jesus. And it was thanks to Ernie Jo Banghart that Gulfport was the Jesus capital of the world.

So it was no mystery why I wound up in Gulfport, Mississippi, reporting on a Z paper. Rob Houston called it a C paper, but he was flattering himself.

I wrote him a little piece about the high-school band cakewalk benefit right there in his smoky office. I suppose he was afraid I'd cheat if he wasn't watching me.

When he read it, he pronounced, as only he can, I had a way with words and he hired me. Because of that "way with words," which wasn't that special out of the context of that hick paper, he assigned me to the Ernie Jo Banghart beat, which he came to regret rather quickly.

I had not bothered to tell Rob I was a debunker of myths.

Instead of firing me or reassigning me to the high-school girls volleyball, Rob tried to change me—to win me over to the official stance of the paper, which was, to put it bluntly, to kiss the part of Ernie Jo's anatomy that he didn't ordinarily see. Having this power over me was more important to Rob than getting his desired results. The newsroom was full of amiable sycophants eager to do Rob's bidding. I was the challenge.

Rob Houston was a man who never met an affectation he didn't adore.

It sometimes seemed the stupider it made him look, the more he liked it. Take the cigarette holder, for instance. I honestly think he thought he was Franklin Roosevelt the way he clamped that thing between his teeth and jutted his jaw up in the air.

He loved to have audiences with his employees. These were easily the most painful part of the job. For Rob would ramble on, filling his room (and your lungs) with the cigarette smoke he was carefully filtering before it went into his lungs.

He'd tell you his lies that made him look like Attila the Hun or Rupert Murdoch, as the spirit moved him. But to hear him tell it, those worthies were in Sunday school as far as he was concerned.

He had these plaques and trophies around his office, but they didn't bear any scrutiny. They were for things like third place in some local duplicate-bridge tourney. The closest anything came to journalism was some honorable mention for advertising design in two-bit newspapers; of which the *Gulfport Riptide* was preeminent in this neck of the woods.

"Damnit, dingbat, what the hell is this?" Rob Houston liked to talk like Archie Bunker. Rob's personality was an amalgam of celebrities. He was wearing a cravat like Cary Grant, his nose and facial expressions were W.C. Fields. He was waving a handful of foolscap at me (my most recent submission) where I was seated on the supplicant's side of the editor in chief's desk. Rob's teeth held fast on his cigarette holder, the smoke worming its way up to his Jesus.

"Don't tell me," Rob said. "Let me guess. The great Debunker of Myths is outdebunking himself. Well and good, said the perfesser, but not on my time."

"Rob..."

Out came the cigarette holder. "Oh, don't worry, I'm on to you," Rob said in his Jimmy Cagney voice. "I knew you had hangups when I hired you—only you assured me you could work them out. I guess I was crazy to take on a guy with your background." Rob Houston jammed his FDR cigarette holder back in his mouth. It was Rob's theory that the further you were from the burning tobacco, the healthier smoking was.

He shook his head, burdened as he was, with a crushing sadness. "God help the Catholic Church if they have to take on losers like you for priests."

I fancied myself the *Riptide*'s ace reporter, but if you checked out the rest of the troops, you'd see I wasn't fancying much. So, it was all the more aggravating that I had to steel myself for yet another session where this world-class horse's ass was going to teach me another lesson.

Rob read from the copy trembling in his hand. His hands usually trembled for the same reason his nose was W.C. Fields red. "'Ernie Jo Banghart pounded his Bible and told the faithful that Jesus was coming back to earth for the second time. This is a remarkable prognostication from the nation's top-rated TV evangelist, since he has yet to offer convincing proof he was here the first time.'"

Rob Houston slammed the copy down on the desk between us, and glared at me, the author of that heresy.

The desk was piled high with trivia Rob squirreled away. Nothing was too insignificant to escape his hoarding grasp: old newspaper clippings, catalogs for office furniture he would never buy, tools, screws that fit nothing, Kleenex half used that he couldn't bear to throw away, used Post-its—for reuse. You get the picture.

In the newsroom of the *Gulfport Riptide*, the heat was starting to let up, which made habitation in the low-slung corrugated-metal building almost bearable. There was no air conditioning, it was a no-overhead operation.

But I was in the hot seat. Rob grumbled as he fished through

the piles on his desk for something to teach me a lesson—
"Blasphemy—you and your goddamn blasphemy." The smoke
coming at me smelled like burning garbage. Egyptian tobacco, no
doubt. Rob thought it was esoteric. I didn't smoke. I'd picked up
some good habits at my last employment and I was sticking to them.

"You mean *you* think Jesus is coming back?" I asked my editor.

"You got any idea how many of our subscribers are born-
again Christians?"

I rolled my eyes to affect boredom. "All of them?"

"You're right on the money," Rob said, "probably for the first
time in history. Ah, here," Rob came to the paper, opened it in front
of his face, found the page, folded it over and pushed it at me.
"There," he said, showing a full-page ad of Ernie Jo Banghart waving his Bible in the air, his baby-food-stuffed cheeks shining. "You
have any idea how much bread he puts on *your* table?"

My head swung into its sardonic nod. "All of it?"

"Damn straight. This one guy's advertising pays all your
salary and fringe benefits and leaves us a little left over to pay some
staffers who have the sense to know which side of the bread has the
butter."

"I always wondered about that expression," I said. "What difference does it make? You eat *both* sides of the bread."

"Funny, funny Frankie."

"Besides, if he pays you so much, maybe you ought to consider giving me a raise."

"Ha."

"It's been a long time."

"It's gonna be a lot longer."

"But seriously, Rob, believe what you want to, but Jesus is
gonna walk in here and yell 'Stop the presses!'? I mean, come on."

"Yeah, probably at deadline, too."

"Pheuuh," I let the air escape. Better to get rid of it.

"What got you this bug up your butt about Ernie Jo and the

Second Coming?"

"His magazine, *God's Guitar*—has it for a cover story this month. He's on the telly now saying the thunder is a sign the Big Guy is coming soon. It's hard to believe he believes it."

"You bet your ass he believes it, Frankie—so does every other godforsaken reader we got. These people aren't sophisticates. Not erudite, like you could be if you screwed your head on straight some morning. How many times do I got to tell you we cater to plain people with simple beliefs? This is not the venue for clever myth bashing. You're a *reporter*—a simple, lowdown reporter on a C paper in the deepest South. Stop trying to pretend you're a sophisticated New Yorker; I know better. You aren't even a sophisticated hick Southerner, for my money—any sophistication, you'da had a different dossier."

"Yeah, thanks, Rob."

"I know your story, Frankie, even the part you didn't tell me. Maybe it's time to start asking if you came here with too much baggage."

I shook my head. "Rob Houston, the great impresario."

"What's that supposed to mean?"

"You want to make an opera out of everything."

"Yeah, well, let me tell you one thing, and get it straight, Jesus, goddamnit—we are not screwing with the Second Coming in *my* paper. It is taboo—off-limits."

"Oooo," I said, "what happened to your 'very high regard' for the First Amendment?"

"It's undiminished, Frankie, undiminished. I know what you're going to say, but it's hot air. Look at the *New York Times*—look at any paper you think is great; they're *all* pulling their punches. And believe me, I know about punching—I was very nearly the light-heavyweight champion of the world."

I groaned. Rob Houston had very little truck with the truth. He wouldn't lie to spare your feelings, he wouldn't lie to cheer you up; he only lied in the time-honored cause of self-aggrandizement.

He could sit for hours, oblivious of deadlines, puffing on his FDR, telling of his exploits as a mercenary for the Israeli army (he wasn't Jewish and had never been to Israel)—or how he was the brains behind Henry Ford II.

I suspected Rob's *coup de grâce* in the fantasy world was getting his job as editor in chief of the *Gulfport Riptide* on the strength of his experiences as night editor of the *Atlanta Journal*, when he was actually a copyboy.

"Say anything you want," Rob was saying apropos of his strong commitment to the freedom of speech amendment of the Constitution, "but lay off people's religious beliefs."

"The Second Coming, Rob? Any way you could believe it?"

Rob shook his head, "Don't matter. Don't screw with the Virgin Mary, either. And I don't want to hear that it-wasn't-the-Almighty-who-crawled-up-her-nighty limerick again. You wear me out, Frankie—I'm not a young man anymore."

"It's a scam, Rob," I said. "You say Ernie Jo believes Jesus is coming back; I say no way, Jose. Ernie Jo Banghart would *die* if he were confronted with the real article. I'm telling you, there wouldn't be room for both of them on this godforsaken earth."

"Hm, godforsaken you say? That sounds to me like an acknowledgment of a deity. You going soft, Frankie?" He gave me the fisheye. "Maybe you want another shot at the priesthood. I'll bet you were a *godforsaken* priest!"

"Just a figure of speech," I grumbled.

"Our readers worship Ernie Jo." Rob didn't give up trying to win me over. "In a showdown with Jesus and Ernie Jo, I'd be very careful with my bets. Why don't you just do a nice story on the latest designer-V.D. epidemic? That's it, Frankie—give me V.D."

"No, thanks, Rob, you're not my type."

I dragged myself back to my desk. I wondered why almost every one of my ideas, including my Pulitzer nomination, began with a big nix from Rob Houston, editor in chief.

I was tired of trying to create scares of V.D. epidemics. Rob was an amateur at social engineering.

Back at my own cluttered desk, I was in my quitting mode, as I was every time I had to sit at the feet of that tobacco inferno, Rob Houston. I found I could listen to him for one or two minutes, but he could talk for hours.

I especially didn't appreciate his cracks about my history. I didn't share that with anyone, and I doubted that he knew half of what he said he did.

At times like this, I got a fever to send out résumés to real newspapers. Two things held me back: (1) my history, and (2) no way would I get a good recommendation from that savage, Rob Houston.

Ordinarily, a ringing phone griped me (don't like my work interrupted). Except after coming from Rob Houston, then I welcomed it.

The first ring hadn't ended before I said, "Hello?"

"Frankie? It's Rachel."

Rachel always told me who she was. It was a modesty shtick.

"That guy you work for is weird."

"You're telling me. What now?"

"He answered the phone. That place is so small the editor has to answer the phone?"

"He likes to keep his thumb down everyone's throat. It's a power thing."

"Well, he asks who's calling."

"Natch."

"When I tell him, he goes off on me about all this baggage you have and I should get your *history* before I get too involved with you."

I groaned. Could I, I wondered, work for anyone worse?

Rachel Brighton had been a student of mine in a night class I taught at the City College—Investigative Reporting. Augmenting the salary Rob Houston paid me was a dire necessity. Lot of women in the class, which was fine with me. Some of them (albeit not many) were actually interested in being investigative reporters. Most of them, I felt deep down, were more interested in finding a man. If he turned out to be an investigative reporter, so be it.

"Call me up sometime," she had said on the last night of class. She was a natural girl, no affectations, and though I had sixteen years on her, I called her. For some reason, the women weren't exactly standing in line. Perhaps I sent the wrong signals—with my history and all. But Rachel and I hit it off. She was bright, perceptive, fun to be around. She was quiet, she didn't push marriage, and every once in a while she got off a zinger that smothered me in gales of laughter.

I needed that, working for you-know-who.

"So, what is it?" Rachel asked on the phone.

"It?"

"Your history."

"Oh, it will disappoint you, I'm sure."

"Try me."

"I'll tell you sometime…" I tried to be vague, but she pressed.

"When?"

We made a date. I would have to consider my diversionary options. Our relationship was not yet at a point I felt comfortable spilling my guts to her.

ANOTHER TWANG FROM GOD'S GUITAR:

At the feet o' Jesus
Sorrow like a sea.
Lordy, let yo' mercy
Come driffin' down on me.
At the feet o' Jesus
At yo' feet I stand.
O, ma little Jesus,
Please reach out yo' hand.

—*Langston Hughes*
"Feet O' Jesus"

MILLIE BROSKY,

CHATTERBOX

I visited Millie Brosky in the hospital—mental— where she was still suffering from a nervous breakdown.

She was sitting in a rocking chair on a porch that was sheltered by large pine trees. She had that distant, vacant look of soothing medication in her eyes, and she spoke almost as though she were autistic.

She had been coping until the creepy Devil's Disciple who had used her innocence in the service of his lust had returned to apologize.

That's what sent her packing to the funny farm.

It struck me as a nice place to be—on that porch in a rocking chair, looking ahead at the tall pines. Rocking connoted contentment and one could have done a lot worse.

Millie spoke to the breeze, as though it were all just happening, but this was not at all like shooting the breeze.

When I saw them black jackets with them little red devils on them pouring through the door of the diner I waitressed going on three years already, I got such a lump in my throat I swear I'da choked to death.

And tonight I was in charge for the first time and, oh, Lord, the last thing I wanted was trouble and here it looked like I was in for it big time.

These savages who called themselves the Devil's Disciples were loud and nasty and they smelled something awful. Like they had all fallen in an outhouse somewhere.

When I heard their bikes on the highway, I prayed they'd go on into Hemet or Glory Pines or somewhere, anywhere but here. But I shoulda knowed better. We're so isolated out here, where else could they been heading that would feed 'em this time of night?

Soon as the first of them cleared the door, I smelled trouble—right after I smelled their toilet smell. They must of had some powerful hangups they could hang on their upbringing: a whore mother, drunk father—whatever—it's okay by me, long as they keep my place clean and tidy. I'm alone and I'm responsible. And the last thing I want is trouble.

You gotta understand we don't have much of a place here—

just a counter and a couple tables. Nothing fancy—just a hangout for a couple locals. Well, you shoulda seen them red devils, I calls 'em, they just took over the place. We were slow, that's why Randy, the boss, said I could handle it alone. So, it was just me and Sammy, the cook, but he wouldn't be no use with them savages. Even if he weren't afraid of his shadow. He was a short, fat man who sweat like a pig by the hot stove. I heard him groan when them red devils come in, but not so loud any of them would hear it.

Right off, I got this sickly feeling the way the devils looked at me. Like they're animals and I'm their dinner.

They'd have to be animals to look at me like that. Nobody else does—I still have a plague with these pimples and the makeup only goes so far. I don't have a lot of body to me even though I'm almost twenty-one—eight more months or so—my mother says I still look sixteen.

When I seen them looking at me, I wished I'd gotten on at the dime store instead, but I heard sometimes there were tips to be had at the Easy Eats diner and I needed the money bad. They did-n't want nobody under eighteen because they sold beer, but Randy, the boss, said he'd take his chances with the Liquor Board for a cou-ple months. Anyway, that's what I expect happened, because I sure didn't fool Randy lying about my age. I wasn't good at it at all. Like my mother says, "With Millie, what you see is what you get." So, here we are, short-handed, with a room full of these devils all yellin' at me like they's the only one in the place and I'm takin' orders as fast as I can, an' passing 'em on to get Sammy cookin' right away so he don't have to stand around.

First off I got coffee all around till it ran out and I hadda brew some more. But, Lordy, we didn't have the facilities for this kinda crowd nohow.

The devils started making dirty talk at me and I was so scared I knew I'd get the orders wrong.

There was this big guy at the counter and he looked like the boss of the devils so I tried to be real nice to him. I served him his coffee right away. Name was Charlie, he said. "No Charles, no Chuck, just Charlie," he said kinda sternlike. His face was all hair and it looked like his razor didn't have no blade in it. Even so, he looked like about the only one wasn't a real nutso animal an' I hoped and prayed to sweet Jesus that Charlie would protect me. If not Charlie, Jesus would be okay.

Then I hear this guy yellin' at me from one of the tables. "Hey, girlie!" he snapped, and I looked over automatically and I saw him waving a filthy hand for me to come over. He was smiling like no girl ever wants to be smiled at. His teeth were black as coal.

"Come an' set on my lap a spell," he called out so loud no way could I pretend I didn't hear him.

Oh, my God, my head was like I'd been in a cyclone, my armpits were a swamp—but I wasn't wet where he wanted me. I was stone cold there.

"Hey, you—slut!—get over here right now!"

I rubbed my hands on the sides of my thighs and worked my way between the foul-smelling Disciples to the corner table. I tried not to tremble when I stood before him, but I knew I wasn't fooling him. I was shaking like a leaf. Oh, why did Randy let me alone out here in godforsaken nowhere?

"'S better," the devil slurred his words as though whiskey had gotten the better of him. "I wuz afraid you wuz snubbin' ole Larry lak a snot nose. You ain't got a snot nose, have ya, girlie?"

I shook my head, then embarrassed myself by sniffling and drawing my sleeve over my nose.

A roar of laughter rose from them red devils, shaking the diner's salt shakers so they clanged together like a high-school cymbal player doing his thing.

"Come on, honey," he said, patting his smelly jeans—"set on my lap a spell."

I sniffled again and shook my head. I was fresh out of courage. "I got all these people to feed." I gulped for air.

"They'll wait on us. Come on, set a spell."

"I'm sorry, sir, I gotta work. We're short-handed. Truth be known, it's just me an' cook an' I got a real houseful. Randy couldn't a been 'specting so many folks lest he wouldn'ta left me here alone."

"Too damn bad, snot nose," he snapped, his arm whipping out to grab my arm and pull me down on his lap.

Sammy the cook was sweating and I could see he would be no good to anybody in my fix.

Sammy licked his lips a lot when he was afraid, and rubbed his hands on his chest, but did manage to get to the phone when he saw what the devil had in mind doing to me. But before he dialed, he stole a look at Charlie, who shook his head with the severe look of a school principal who was only doing what was best for you, and the phone slipped back into its cradle.

Next thing I know this pig's hands are workin' all over my body and I liked to passed out.

ANOTHER BLAST FROM GOD'S TROMBONES:

I had to look on while [the wild Indians] shot my precious husband dead, and in my sight my dear son Ole was shot through the shoulder. But he got well again from this wound and lived a little more than a year and then was taken sick and died. We also found my oldest son Endre shot dead, but I did not see the firing of this death shot.... To be an eyewitness to these things and to see many others wounded and killed was almost too much for a poor woman; but, God be thanked, I kept my life and my sanity, though all my movable property was torn away and stolen. But this would have been nothing if only I could have had my loved husband and children—but what shall I say? God permitted it to happen thus, and I had to accept my fate and thank Him for having spared my life and those of some of my dear children.

—Letter from Guri Endresen in Minnesota to relatives in Norway
December 2, 1866

ANOTHER TWANG FROM GOD'S GUITAR:

It always strikes me, and it is very
peculiar, that, whenever we see the
image of indescribable and unutter-
able desolation—of loneliness, poverty,
and misery, the end and extreme of
things—the thought of God comes
into one's mind.

—*Vincent van Gogh*

THE GOSPEL ACCORDING TO

JACK WHITEHALL

*You see this guy coming
toward you and you just
know he's going to tell you
what a miserable sinner he
is—and he looks it—
dumpy, dragging, deject-
ed.*

His portly face is a mixture of confusion and wonder—his nose is pointed in the direction of the nearest miracle. I'm just waiting for one of these religious types to tell me he's a happy sinner. Why should sin make you miserable? If it does, why sin?

Jack Whitehall was, in a way, my kind of guy. No artifice. As a Debunker of Myths, I was not what you'd call a real believer in faith healers, and Jack professed to be one; but to each his own, hey—whatever lights your fire. There are, after all, all kinds of faith, all kinds of illness, and all kinds of healing. So, who's to say?

Jack was a paid-my-dues kind of guy—and, yes, he was a miserable sinner, too—drinking, oblivious of the needs of those around him, unless he was slapping them with one of his group-insurance policies. His wife was especially overlooked in the needs department, and she'd had her share. So she just up and left him. Said she still loved him, of course, they always do, but said for his sake he'd have to pull himself out of his drunken slump and she was only what was popularly known as an enabler.

When Jack felt down in the dumps, he turned for solace to his Harley motorcycle. It was his first thought when he saw the front door close behind his wife and he knew she would be taking the car. So though he was unsteady on his feet, Jack climbed aboard that compact and efficient internal-combustion machine and headed down the hill.

His concentration on the road downhill was no less than when he was in the throes of one of his faith-healing sessions. The wind was in his face and it always felt good on the Harley. He knew he mustn't fall asleep. He'd go have a brew or two and commiserate with Millie Brosky at the Easy Eats. She'd probably be lonely this time of night.

Jack was slicing the air with the wedge of his face.

"Stay awake, buddy," he said to himself. "Stay awake."

Lately, Jack was worried:

I may have lost the touch. In the past I'd felt the power of Jesus on me—powerful strong. Lately, it just seemed drained out of me like I'd sprung a leak which I couldn't find.

I couldn't describe the feeling when I was healing. The lightning of the Lord shot through my body and onto some poor, sick soul, and those miracles happened—call them by any other name you care to, they are miracles.

My drinking was no miracle. I couldn't excuse it, but I could explain it. A lot of liquid lunches in the insurance game. I was a good salesman, the booze made me friendlier, and friendlier salesmen do better than uptight ones. Maybe booze gave me the courage to heal, though I certainly wouldn't want to attribute my successes to hooch. But it did free me up. I didn't think about it at all; see, it felt good is all I could tell you. Then it got to feeling so good I couldn't feel anything else.

I knew when I talked about healing by faith I heard the rumbles of doubt. Funny how no one doubted the drinking side of my character. But to me, there was no feeling in the world like feeling that power of Jesus pass through your body and into the body of some crippled sinner and to watch that unbelievable power make that person whole again. I'd seen it time and time again, and I could tell you firsthand you only have to see it once to fill your soul with the spirit of Jesus for all time.

I got that spirit of Jesus. But that doesn't mean I'm a perfect human being by any means. In fact, my wife was so fed up with me, she left me. And that just minutes before I got on my Harley and biked down to Easy Eats to drown my misery.

Well, talk about misery. When I got to Easy Eats, I saw all those chopped hogs parked outside and I could hear the devils raising holy hell inside and I had a premonition of what was going down, as they would say.

From time to time, I used to ride with these guys—they'd stop at my place sometimes.

The Easy Eats was my old stomping grounds, but my inadequate feet weren't stomping as I rocked through the door to holy bedlam. I had to steady myself with a hand on the wall when I got inside the door and the stench hit me.

Then I heard the ruckus at the table down at the end. I looked down there and saw a guy I didn't recognize without my glasses trying to have his way with that poor, innocent waitress and nobody was lifting a finger against him.

I was feeling no pain, what with the certain quantity of spirits I hastily swallowed to get me over the sadness of Stephanie leaving me like she did. If I'd had my wits about me, I'd have gotten out of there as fast as possible and called the sheriff. Instead, I stuck my nose in the thing as though I were fearless.

"Boys, boys," I shouted. "This is no way to carry on. Let the girl alone—can't you see she's terrified?"

"Snubbed Larry," someone yelled out in explanation.

"Come on, boys," I said, trying to be heard above the cackle of the merrymaking Disciples. "What if your Savior walked in here this minute? What would He think?"

"Man, we beyond saving," came another mirthful chime.

"No man is beyond the grace of our Lord and Savior, Jesus Christ," I said, moving on down to the spot where I now recognized Larry LaRue molesting poor Millie on the floor. "Our Messiah's due back anytime now, so it'd be to your advantage to shape up. What in the world do you think He'd think of you if He walked in here now? Larry?"

Larry looked up from his exercising. "This gotta be the last place Jesus gonna visit." And those bozos all had a cynical laugh.

Unsteady on my feet, I closed my eyes and folded my hands in prayer. "Dear Jesus, make Your presence felt in this den of iniquity. Visit the hearts of these sinners, show them the way, the truth and the light…"

Then I heard Charlie, their leader, call out to me from the counter. "Sit down, Jack—have a beer."

A seat had magically opened up next to Charlie. A bunch of the Disciples were standing by the door with their coffee cups cooling in their hands.

I staggered over to the counter, and hoisted my bulk up on that stool next to Charlie, there to lament my failure at spreading the Word of the Lord to the heathen.

"He's coming back, Charlie," I said. "I can feel it in my bones."

"Who?"

"Jesus."

"Jesus!" Charlie said, and laughed a blasphemous laugh.

God's Candidate

"**S**hall I do it?" he asked his congregation from the pulpit of his Arlington, Virginia, church, just a stone's throw, really, from the nation's capital. The heartbeat and pulse of this great land of ours.

Sure, he was Southern like all the rest of them. Willie Sutton said he robbed banks because that's where the money was. Well, the evangelists went south because that's where they did the Bible thumping.

He beamed from Mason to Dixon when he asked the question. He didn't have to explain it to them—they all knew he had been toying with a run at the presidency of his country—he just wasn't committed yet. He wanted it understood he wasn't playing hard to get, he *was* hard to get.

He looked a little hickish, alone in the pulpit, in his blue blazer—even with his Yale degree (how fussy can a divinity school be?)—even though his father was a senator. He was a well-fed man. Shortish, and broad in the shoulders, as well as the belly and, as I say, a hickish sort of face.

Those parts about fasting in the Bible were not as sacrosanct as the parts about feasting.

His wife was down front. He had impregnated her without benefit of clergy even before he was clergy, but he'd made an honest woman of her, there was no gainsaying that.

Of course, one of his fears about running for president was that someone would uncover it and try to smear him. Politics could be rough, he warned his wife, but she didn't share his ambition. If he had fears, they didn't show when he asked the congregation, "Shall I do it?"

Perhaps it wasn't the most uplifting of spiritual messages, and not everyone was so snowed by his charisma that they shared his giggly enthusiasm. Some were happy with him in the pulpit, but they had no concept of him as president. Oh, they supposed he was an upright, moral man with a decent head on his shoulders, but there seemed to be something vital missing. He had never been elected sheriff or to the school board or anything.

"Shall I do it?" he asked, and he was so transparently gloating that your heart went out to him and of course you answered "Yessss," though it didn't take an abnormal psychologist to realize the response was halfhearted.

So he ran anyway. But right from the start he put out the word he was *not* to be called a TV evangelist, he was a religious broadcasting executive.

He had to get some votes in the North, after all.

He finished second in the Iowa caucus, and that was hot potatoes, but that was about it.

A few states later he folded his tent and went back to his religious broadcasting, but not before he was raked over the coals for the hidden shotgun wedding and the settlement of a messy lawsuit over his alleged preferential treatment during the Korean conflict. His father was a senator, after all, and what good is that if you can't pull some strings once in a while?

He spent his time now looking for signs to spice up his prophecy concerning the imminent Second Coming of Christ.

—*Frankie Foxxe*
Religious Phenomena in the U.S.

The reasonable man adapts himself to the world; the unreasonable one persists in trying to adapt the world to himself. Therefore, all progress depends on the unreasonable man.

—*George Bernard Shaw*

THE GOSPEL ACCORDING TO

MICHAEL

My car was purring along on its first full tank of gas since I bought the junker.

Now it was really acting like a cat that had just been well fed. It was dark and cats like the dark. And for a minute I thought I was driving a Jaguar.

We drove in silence, me and this guy who says he's Jesus. But my mind was spinning. I thought it was some kind of trick. Somebody testing me out—the son of two unbelieving theologians. But then I thought, who would waste their time on me?

But who or what was this guy, then? If he really were Jesus, why would he be in my ratty old Studebaker with all the bastardized parts holding it together? Why would he zero in on a guy like me? Oh, I know the nuthouses are full of guys who think they are Jesus Christ, but the funny thing was this guy wasn't yelling Bible verses all over the place, and he didn't seem the least bit nuts.

I never was too religious myself, so I never gave a lot of thought to what Jesus would be like. One minute this guy seemed normal; the next he seemed to have this laserlike stare where he could take you apart with one glance.

Like now, I didn't say anything so he didn't, and I just felt after that bomb he had dropped, the next move should be up to him. Like if he wanted, he was going to have to convince me he was Jesus Christ. I didn't see why I'd have to convince him of anything. Not that I could.

I was in the middle of trying to figure out this guy when I heard him say, "Look here, fella—you want to give me a hand?"

I don't know what you'd expect from Jesus—I guess we expect all these hero types to have deep voices, but his voice was kind of high pitched and to me it took something away from him.

I guess high, feminine voices go with sensitive souls and I could accept Jesus as a guy who could sympathize with the down 'n out rather than one who could punch you out.

"Give you a hand?" I said, noncommittally. "Like, doing what?"

"Saving the world."

"How can I do that?"

"Come with me. I'll show you."

"Hey, but wait a minute. Why should I want to save the world? Save it from what?"

"Like it the way it is, do you? Think things are perfect? Think people treat each other all right?"

"Yeah, but that's not my line."

"What *is* your line?"

I dropped my eyes. He had me and he seemed to know it. "I guess I don't really have a line."

"Good," Jesus said, as though something had been settled.

"You one of these religious freaks?"

Jesus smiled. "You might say that."

"But I told you I don't have any money."

"Did I ask you for money?"

"Well, ah, no, ah, but I expect you will. Look at the TV evangelists. They take in millions." I frowned. "They say it costs millions to start a church."

"I'm not interested in starting a church."

"What *are* you interested in?"

"People," Jesus said. "People getting along better with other people."

"You can't operate without money."

Jesus smiled. "You watch too much television," he said.

"Yeah, and I can't stand those TV evangelists."

Jesus fixed me with his uncanny stare, his eyes gentle yet burning. "Like to put a stop to it?"

"Well, yeah, but, jeez, don't look at me like that, will you?" I was getting flustered. "I mean, come on, dude, how would I go about it?"

"We could give away what *they* sell."

"What's that?"

"Hope—in a word. You can branch out from there all you want—security, a good feeling, forgiveness, a father figure to tell them what to do. Love is where it's at, Michael. Love your brother, sister, mother, father, the whole world."

"You call that simple?"

Jesus smiled. "The *idea* is simple. This is a grass-roots idea. You start with one person—you—and you do some minor surgery."

"Surgery?" I shrank at the thought.

"We cut out the hate. Before you can love, you've got to rid yourself of hate. Make sense?"

"I...guess."

Jesus smiled again, clapping me on the back.

We had just pulled into the diner parking lot. It looked like the middle of nowhere, where the Easy Eats all-night diner stood just off the highway. Besides the motorcycles out front, there was only a pickup truck out back that looked like it hadn't picked up anything for a generation.

Easy Eats was a frame-and-stucco structure with storefront glass windows and a flat top that sloped down to the back like a steamed clam.

When I saw the neat lineup of Harley-Davidson bikes, I backed up the car.

"Where are you going?" Jesus asked me.

"Somewhere else," I said. "This place has a little trouble going down—"

"Let's go in," Jesus said. "See if we can lend a hand."

"Oh, no—I'm not fighting those psychos," I said. "Look at the cycles. There must be a hundred of them."

"There are ten to be exact."

"That's okay, they ride ten to a bike."

"Come on—"

"Now, wait. Figure this out—there are two of us. Ten bikes—they still have us five to one. How you gonna overcome that?"

"With love," he said.

"Take my word for it. The Disciples are not susceptible to love. Rape, murder, mayhem they're into. You go in there, you might not come out alive."

Jesus smiled at me. A wan, melancholy smile—not raucous, not condescending, just understanding. "Lot of people don't think I'm alive anyway. Some don't think I ever lived."

I hung back—letting Jesus lead.

When he opened the door the racket swelled like a sudden crescendo of the drums in a gung-ho military band. Then—that God-awful smell hit me and I thought I'd barf.

Be ye therefore ready also:
for the Son of man cometh
at an hour when ye think not.

—Luke 12:40

LARRY LARUE LIVE

Man, when I seen this sumbitch coming toward me, it just hit me like a ton of bricks.

There's no explaining, I wouldn't know where to start.

So, I let go of a few choice words. I mean, it was like I panicked when I seen him. Not that I couldn't have taken him with one hand tied behind my back, but there was something eerie about the bastard an' he just kept coming at me like it was preordained or something.

To make matters worse, the bitch I was pinning to the floor—she wasn't being cooperative in the least—puked all over me. My natural inclination was to laugh in her face. Imagine some pissant spilling her guts on a guy who smells like I do. But this black bastard in the white robes and the sandals was staring me down and nothing came out of my mouth.

I mean, Jesus Christ!—that's exactly who he looked like. Except for the skin color, of course. And you can bet I wouldn't be spilling my guts like this if I didn't have this revelation.

But gimme a *break!*—I saw this big-time judgment coming down on me for having a little fun with a broad. Well, she was snubbing me, and everyone knows no bitch gets away with snubbing a Disciple, and that includes the Virgin Mary.

I was a bull and she was the cow, but when I saw the white robes advancing and the Red Sea parting, I was nothing. That bitch, who got away, was whimpering in the corner like a whipped puppy.

Bastard stopped me cold. When I was just a kid, I had this vision—I won't call it a dream because it was just too real. But a guy who looked exactly like this stood over me and he didn't say nothing—just stood there like he was judging me—and I couldn't tell if he liked what he saw or not.

I knew it was Jesus and no one could tell me otherwise—not my mother—she insisted it was only a dream—or God Himself.

It was my mother got me onto the sin book. She was what you'd call a good woman in those days—all wrapped up in Jesus and suchlike, and she told me Jesus kept a sin book and every time I was bad—wham! right down in the sin book, and I'd have to do two good deeds to balance it out, because you never could erase a sin in the sin book.

I carried that sin book around in my head all through my childhood and it was burdensome. I sure as hell didn't want to fry in hell. But I couldn't get too worked up at the sound of heaven as my ma presented it. I was a bad dude and I'd never feel at home in any fairy land full of priests and prissy women.

I was killing an idle moment one day (my life seemed to have more and more idle moments), looking at Harley-Davidson motorcycles, when I caught a glimpse of a pack of Devil's Disciples.

There were three of them and a mangier trio I had never seen. They smelled to high heaven; tattooed all over hell's half-acre, the Devil's Disciples were real scumbags. I had found a home.

Now, the Disciples didn't take kindly to snubs from the womenfolk, and I wasn't about to let any bitch make me feel small, and this effing waitress had gone and made all kinds of silly-ass excuses for not responding to my natural instincts.

There wasn't no alternative but to show her who is boss by inserting my manhood. Hell, they all want it anyway, what's the sense of fussing 'bout it?

And just about that moment, this guy comes strolling in as though nothing was coming down and he looked straight at me, and I thought of the sin book for the first time in years.

Something was messing with my conscience and I didn't care for it. Who the hell was this guy, anyway? Someone who had to understand you didn't eff with the Disciples and live to tell about it. But I rolled off the girl. What the hell good was she passed out like that, anyway? Oh, in different circumstances I'd have had my way with her just the same, but this sumbitch was frankly driving me up the wall with his goddamned look.

"Ye are the salt of the earth," the guy said, like a weirdo. "Rise, my son," he said. "Sin no more."

Jesus! I had this unholy feeling this guy was Jesus. He looked a lot like those pictures you see around, only darker.

The place turned stone quiet as I stumbled to my feet. I

didn't like anyone screwing with my head like that, but I remember thinking, Jesus, this guy has power.

I wanted some of that.

And Jesus, when he came out,
saw much people,
and was moved with compassion
toward them,
because they were as sheep
not having a shepherd:
and he began to teach them many
  things.

—Mark 6:34

THE GOSPEL ACCORDING TO

SHERIFF
STONEY JESSUP

*That Sheriff Jessup is a
piece of work.*

He's built close to the ground and leads with his belly. He wears his Texas sheriff's sombrero inside and out to keep a lid on his pointy head. He is also plagued by boils, especially annoying under the collar. Not what you would call one of nature's miracles. Sheriff Jessup puts you off at first—he seems a little stiff—but once you get to know him, he's okay. He isn't devious or even complex. A man who lives by his strong faith, it being fostered by the Ernie Jo Banghart Miracle Ministries out of Gulfport, Mississippi—my hometown.

The sheriff lived alone with his dog, so communication with humans was a luxury for him, and when he finally told me his story, I thought that it would never stop. I have therefore taken some liberties, editorialwise, with Sheriff Jessup's recollections:

When things get beyond me in law enforcement, I just turn my troubles over to the Lord. He hasn't let me down yet. Long as your belief is sincere, you get a fair shake.

And I want to state right up front, I accept Jesus Christ as my Lord and Savior, and as Ernie Jo Banghart says, there just ain't two ways about that.

I grew up with a single mother, and the TV was my babysitter for many years. It was on when I got up in the morning and when I went to bed at night. I did my homework by it and ate most of my meals off a tray in front of it. I wasn't any kind of honor-roll student or anything, but I did my homework—as much as I could understand.

I owe a lot to TV—and I'm not ashamed of it. It was the program "CHiPs" that inspired me to go to work in law enforcement. It wasn't any need to shoot somebody, like you hear from a lot of cops. And Glory Pines suits me just fine. It's a quiet place—about twelve hundred citizens when you count the outlying suburbs in my jurisdiction and the summer folk whose empty houses need my year-round protection.

After awhile—a small town like this—you got so's you could recognize the sounds of the vehicles going by the sheriff's station where I lived upstairs (and worked downstairs). For instance, tonight I had no trouble making out the sound of Jack Whitehall's chopped hog—his Devil's Disciples-issue Harley-Davidson. Not that Jack was a member of that band of no-gooders, but he was awful friendly to 'em—they'd come on their caravans sometimes just to raise hell and he'd open his place to 'em.

So me and Fluffy are watching Ernie Jo on the VCR, with his Second Coming talk amidst all that lightning and thunder they had in Gulfport, when I hear the caravan, and it always puts me on edge. I've got the responsibility of keeping the peace 'round here and those devils'll be a challenge every time.

Well, just out of idle curiosity, I hoisted myself outta my chair in front of the TV to check out this current nuisance and I'm darned if I didn't see a couple of them riding double—and one of them had on these white robes like he was trying to look like Jesus. I don't have to tell you in my book that's blasphemy.

I hoped and prayed there wasn't going to be any ruckus up there at Jack's place. It was getting late out there and one man (me) against the Disciples was not a pretty picture.

I said a prayer: "Dear Lord, protect me and my dog, Fluffy, from any harm that might come to us at the hands of Satan and his Devil's Disciples. In Jesus's name we pray. Amen."

I always started and ended my day with a prayer. My tiny Pekingese was so accustomed to the prayer ritual that he suppressed all his social instincts and slunk over to his little pink quilted basket in the corner until my soul came back to earth. Fluffy had an uncanny sense about those things.

"Fluffiest dog I ever seen," I said when I first saw him at the breeder's, who supplied me with papers—a testament to the Pekingese's noble birth—together with certification that the dog's name was Oedipus Rex. I could have called him "Rex" and been legitimate about it, but the nickname "Fluffy" just stuck. Besides, Oedipus was some kind of foreign name and I prided myself in being a patron of things American.

I'd had a couple years in L.A. on a motorcycle and I frankly resented anyone not connected with peacekeeping presuming to ride one.

I couldn't concentrate on the TV, so I went over to my desk and picked up Ernie Jo Banghart's magazine, *God's Guitar*.

I sat down and stared at the inside front cover. There was a cop from Pensacola, Florida, giving a testimonial about how Banghart had saved his soul. The guy was a soul-saving partner of the Banghart ministry. For a monthly donation he had all the advantages that position implied. And HE HAD HIS PICTURE IN THE MAGAZINE!

He isn't any better looking than me, I thought, not with my cap on, and he isn't in charge of a department. Maybe someday I'll be asked to pose for one of those testimonials in Ernie Jo's magazine.

I looked in the mirror on the wall beside my desk. It was a rectangular piece of glass that somehow made me seem taller. I took a long look now and decided there wasn't any reason they couldn't use me in a testimonial.

I could hear the engines cutting out up at Whitehall's place.

Jack Whitehall was a drunk who called himself a faith healer; I knew the story and I wasn't comfortable mixing drunks and religion.

They'll be on me 'bout the noise, sure as shootin'. I knew that much.

The phone rang. I only had to listen a minute before I grunted and slammed down the phone. It was that busybody Filmore again, tattling on Mary MacDonald again. Freddie Filmore was jealous of her Johns is what he was. If Filmore weren't so cheap he wouldn't have to be jealous.

I pushed myself back away from my desk, giving Fluffy a gentle pat before I slid him to the floor. I stood up and squared my shoulders. There was always danger to consider in this line of work, though Mary never made a fuss.

I strapped on my Sam Bowie belt, leaned over and patted Fluffy once more for good measure and strode outside and down the hill to do my duty.

Out in the night mountain air, in my sheriff's uniform, I felt worthy of my niche. Mary was a nuisance, Filmore was a pain, but it put a little purpose in life, a little opportunity to perform my duty in the highest tradition of my calling. I felt good up and down my stiffened backbone.

I strutted down to the Filmore spread with my head high. In a small town like this, everybody knew every move you made, so I was careful to carry myself as a conscientious law-enforcement officer at all times.

Mary—used to be one of those "college cuties," a group of Santa Barbara college girls who satisfied student loans while satisfying randy men behind a modest house near the heart of town. Picked up a nice piece of change, Mary did, doing that. It was all under the guise of modeling and massaging, and nothing else had to happen unless the girl agreed.

Mary was a good-looking gal; that I wouldn't take away from her. So good-looking one of her Johns named Filmore fell in love with her. He had thirty-four years on her, and when he proffered the offer of cohabitation, she said no. He persisted and in time wore her down. He was wealthy enough so neither had to work, and they were to live on love in his mountain retreat in Glory Pines.

His divorce dragged on, and the physical passion gradually lost its juice, and both Mary and Filmore decided they didn't really like each other.

They lasted together just over seven years, and when Filmore told Mary to "Get out," with as much charm as those words imply, she decided she deserved better. Mary petitioned the courts for redress. In the meantime, she moved to the musty, dark and inhospitable guesthouse out back. A sympathetic judge, who was rumored to have pronounced her a gal who gave exceptional value, came down on Mary's side. He ruled the marriage was common law and Mary was entitled to a thirty-percent share of the Glory Pines mountain property.

After the verdict was rendered, Mary asked Filmore for her share, giving him the option of selling or paying her thirty percent of appraised value. Filmore refused, claiming he didn't have the cash and couldn't sell the property, the market being rather as soft as she was. So she announced she would stay in the guesthouse until he bought her out.

Gainful employment in the environs being rather scarce, and Mary not having a car, she had to catch as catch can, it was said, and she reverted to her former trade.

I was not stepping lively on this errand. I knew for a fact Mary was a fast worker and I had no desire to interfere with her livelihood.

I could feel in my bones that Mary was still occupied in the small house in back, so I sauntered, with military posture to be sure, up on the front porch of the Filmore mansion.

I was giving serious consideration to knocking when the front door flung open and I was greeted by Filmore, a rangy guy with gray beard stubble whose tonsorial habits had gone all to hell when he'd had the terminal falling-out with Mary.

"What in the Sam Hill you doing *here*, Sheriff?" Filmore said with unbridled aggravation.

"Thought you called in a complaint," I said.

"You know darn well the criminal perpetrator is out back in the guesthouse with her victim."

I nodded, as though Filmore had spoken wisdom. "Yes, sir, can I get you to sign a complaint?"

"Oh, Sheriff, since when do you need a written complaint to arrest a lawbreaker?"

"Procedures," I said stoutly, moving past him into the house. *Good Housekeeping* magazine wouldn't be taking any pictures here.

"Just go arrest her," Filmore barked.

"Not so easy. Got to have a signed complaint. I can't just go interrupting citizens in the sanctity of their homes. Need probable cause 'n all that."

"*Probable* cause? You know what she is! You got *positive* cause, now just you go out back and arrest her!"

I sat at the dining table and elbowed a space between books (auto-repair manual), magazines (*Field and Stream*) and unopened mail.

"You got a blank piece of paper?" I asked Filmore.

Filmore, strutting his disgust, produced the paper and I looked around the desk.

"A pen?" I asked.

"You have one right in your pocket," Filmore snarled.

"Oh, so I do." I took it out with deliberation and began to write.

"Let's see," I said, "what's the date today?" When Filmore told me, I argued until he rummaged the table and produced a calendar in proof.

"Oh, so it is. Now," I said, "what is the nature of your complaint?"

"She's a hussy!" he screeched. "You know that. God knows you've picked her up often enough, with*out* my signing any papers, I might add."

There was a rustling in the driveway outside. From the corner of my eye I could see an older gentleman making his way up the drive. That would be Henderson, and I couldn't imagine how Mary could imagine anything with Henderson.

Quickly, I finished the "complaint," and Filmore signed it without looking. "You've let him get away," Filmore groused, his lips turning like an angry kid's.

"Oh, well, sorry. I thought you were after Mary."

"Well, but you didn't catch her in the act."

"Have *you*?"

"I've seen enough," was all he could say.

"Well, thanks for your interest. I'll go back there and book her on your complaint. Hold her for a hearing. You'll appear, of course?"

Filmore tightened his lips and snapped a single nod. "If I have to."

Mary was waiting for me at the door. She had a wan smile on her lips. She was dark-haired, thin, medium tall and wore a sack dress that covered even the imagination.

"Hi ya, Mary," I said. "Got a complaint."

We walked side by side up the street. I never saw any need to cuff Mary. She was compliant to customers and cops alike.

At my station house, I said, "Going to have to book you."

She trotted out her wan smile again. It took all her effort. "Didn't Jesus say turn the other cheek? Forgive us miserable sinners?"

"Yeah, well, I don't need no lecture from you 'bout my religion. I got a job to do—now, I may not always like it, but I gotta *do* it."

Mary looked like her head was aching.

"You know, Mary," I said, trying to put her at ease, "you are a good-looking woman."

She batted her eyelashes like a coquette. "You're too kind."

"Why, I'll bet you could find any kind of work you wanted."

"Oh, I don't know, I've got an arrest record as long as your...(she smiled)...arm."

"Well, but...I guess if there is no money for bail..."

Her head seemed to be throbbing. Why did I try to make every time seem like the first time? Well, maybe this time she wasn't going to help me. It took me a minute to realize it. "So," I said, "do you have anything to barter?"

"Just what you see."

My breathing stepped up the pace. "I like what I see," I muttered.

Since Mary paid her bail, so to speak, I released her on her own recognizance.

Fluffy and I watched another half-hour of Ernie Jo Banghart, and I want to tell you, that man sure can preach!

Then the phone rang.

"Sheriff? It's Polk. You going to do something about these hell-raisers or do we all just have to live in fear for the rest of our lives?"

"You getting any noise?" I asked. I wasn't hearing any, but I had Ernie Jo Banghart on the VCR. Old Polk was a writer who didn't even have a TV. Not even a radio, as far as I could tell. A real kook. Ask me, if he had a TV he wouldn't be so sensitive to the least peep outta anyone.

"Sheriff, you know you can't get those slimes together without there being substantial noise."

"Yes, sir, Mr. Polk. I know how you feel. Unfortunately, the laws of this land of ours permit free association and assembly of all manner of persons, and unless you catch them breaking any laws…"

"Why do we have to have such riffraff around here in the first place? This is a *quiet* mountain community, repeat, *quiet*. We shouldn't have to put up with the likes of these animals. That's not what I pay my taxes for."

"I'll check it out," I said, and hung up. Sometimes humble pie was the only dish on the menu.

I wasn't too happy about strapping on my firearm and putting Ernie Jo Banghart on hold to go on this fool's errand.

I tucked Fluffy in under his blanket and off I went to do my duty.

When Charlie, the Devil's Disciples' so-called leader, answered Jack's door, I detected a different attitude from him.

"Why, hello, Sheriff," he said, smiling. "What can I do for you?"

"Got a complaint," I said, not returning the smile. In my line of work it was dangerous to let down your guard. I kept my hand on my side arm, just in case.

"Complaint?" he asked, perplexed. "What about?"

"Well," I said, "noise, I guess."

"You hear any noise?" he asked, cocking his head as though he were listening for some hard-to-hear sound.

"Just got to check out the complaint," I said, by way of explanation. "Doin' my job, is all."

"We just practicing our religion," Charlie explained, "freedom of assembly, you know, Sheriff."

"Religion, huh?" I can tell you I was mighty skeptical.

"It's just the Disciples, an', of course, Jesus."

"Jesus?" My back stiffened. "Why, man, that's blasphemy."

Charlie smiled and it wasn't one of his sarcastic smiles. "Come on in an' see for yourself."

Well, I went inside, letting them know right up front I was mighty skeptical.

Jack Whitehall's place was one of those country heaps, heavy on the lodgepole-pine post beams an' geegaws, with a fat, yawning fireplace that crackled and cackled at the least excuse. Native American rugs covered most of the floors (Jack would sometimes slip and call them 'Indians'). It was a big place. Four bedrooms in back and a large, high-ceilinged, airy living room, not so neat you had to worry about spilling some chewing tobaccy on the floor.

The place smelled of Old Spice aftershave lotion. Jack used it liberally. He'd forgotten that he first used it in an attempt to cover the alcohol on his breath. His wife hadn't been fooled.

I was always mighty uncomfortable in Jack Whitehall's home. It was an unholy mess.

Cleanliness, everyone knows, is next to godliness.

I surveyed the assembled souls. They were a motley crew. Ragtag, without any qualifications to recommend them as even suitable. But they seemed eager to hear what the man was saying. Amidst dirty socks, right on the floor, everyone was sprawled listening to this man in the white robes talking in a high, quiet voice.

Jack Whitehall was playing the host and a young boy was there who seemed lost. The Disciples were not smelling any too good. The Old Spice wasn't cutting the mustard.

I stood with my back to the far wall. It could be an ambush trap, but I was curious. The man was not Ernie Jo Banghart. There was no excited waving a Bible in the air, no drama at all, hardly to speak of, just quiet talk.

Over the fireplace Jack had an enormous crucifix with Jesus on the cross, almost life-sized. At closer look, the resemblance to the Jesus giving the talk was not that close. It was carved from a pine log by a local amateur chainsaw artist, who Jack patronized more out of charity than for the sake of artistic merit. The wooden Jesus had sharper, more angular features, was thinner with showier muscles and a sadder expression on his face. The wooden Jesus was the one I thought might say, "Why hast thou forsaken me?" while the new in-the-flesh Jesus you could imagine saying "Father, forgive them, for they know not what they do."

This so-called Jesus was talking: "Have you ever wondered about the meaning of existence?" he was saying. "Ever wonder how you could make a difference in the vast scheme of things? Yes, insignificant you. How *you* could contribute to the well-being of your fellow man? I'm going to tell you how.

"But first you will understand that great changes are not wrought overnight. That if you agree to help set this world right, you are going to have to work. You will have to steel yourself against failure. You are trying to change the nature of mankind which has been befuddled since the beginning of time. Changing thousands of years of behavior will not happen in an instant, no matter how much you believe in miracles."

There was a mumble of assent, but they seemed unsure if they were in the presence of a huckster or a visionary. Mostly, he seemed like the guy at the county fair. Glib, with a kind of rude charm, and I was uncomfortable listening so close as I did, when I thought I'd be better off finishing the Ernie Jo tape.

But then there were those infernal white robes. Surely this Jesus business was no more than a ruse to get attention. Whatever was his angle? When did the price of the merchandise surface? Like the guy at the fairgrounds, he built you up until you were just bursting with curiosity about how much the darn thing was going to set you back. He was such a skilled pitchman you believed his little machine was going to do everything from slicing your potatoes in the shape of those cute little curlicues to healing your bunions, and you just wished he would get to the price so you could plunk down your bills and get some relief from those blessed bunions.

"All right," the man was saying to the motley multitude. "What is the biggest difficulty mankind has?" A few of the brave muttered things like "Hunger," and "War," and "Crime," but the speaker cut them short.

"Hate," he said. "The absence of love. From time immemorial, man's inhumanity to man has been the biggest stumbling block to human progress. Religious intolerance, class hatred, nation against nation, brother against brother, husband against wife. There is a basic incompatibility that we must overcome if we are to see real progress in our earthly world."

"What's the scam?" someone asked.

"Scam?"

"Yeah, is this some kind of school where you pay tuition, or do we charge people for getting rid of their hate?"

"There is no charge."

"How do you get paid?"

"In satisfaction," he said. "A lot of intolerance and hate is generated in religion, too. There are towns where one faction crosses themselves with two fingers, the other with three, and they hate and distrust each other over that difference. This animosity builds and festers and quickly spins out of control. All of man's ills arise from hatred and intolerance. Why can't we overcome it? We all have it within our power. It takes no special equipment, no magic formula."

"So, how can we do it?"

"One on one. Of course, the first thing we must do is get rid of the hate we have."

"Hey, what about hating sinners? You want us to love evil people?"

"You don't love the sin, you love the sinner."

It seemed like a simple idea, really, but I know something about hate. It wasn't that easy to beat.

THE GOSPEL ACCORDING TO

ERNIE JO BANGHART

Brucie Banghart was a lad, it was said, who hadn't a clue.

I was pleasantly surprised to find that supposition fundamentally flawed. I was able to get some very nice information from him, which I have incorporated into the gospels of Ernie Jo Banghart.

In the many fights Brucie had overheard as a child between his folks, he gathered there was one thing missing in his conception: the consent of his mother.

Apparently, Emily Sue had, consciously or not, sought to emulate the Virgin Mary, when one night she woke up screaming and discovered Ernie Jo was at the end of his tether, abstinencewise.

Man is conceived in sin, and so it was with Brucie Banghart.

Ernie's people had let it be known that if his young teenage bride wasn't pregnant within a year, it would be a slur on his manhood — and what with Emily Sue's shy demurs, the pressures just kept building.

They have a name in the Bible for what he did, but it wasn't until modern times that it was considered a crime when a husband forced himself on his wife.

Oh, Emily Sue thought of leaving the brute, but she had no place to go. Her folks were not about to admit they'd made a mistake in giving in to Ernie Jo and allowing their precious fifteen-year-old to marry him. Then, as Ernie Jo's fame grew, so did hers.

"I wasn't no bigger 'n a polecat, I swear," Ernie Jo would say. "An' I'd had a vision 'bout me wrasslin' a bear an' folks tell me I was a sight fo' sore eyes, though I don't hardly remember myself." Then he'd start in on his story again. If God heard it as often as I had, I imagine he'd had his fill.

Ernie Jo started on that sawdust trail when he couldn't afford sawdust, and he shouted and he danced, taunted and cajoled his way to the top of Jacob's ladder, waving his Bible over his head all the while for all to see. He worshiped the Lord and His Word and made no secret of it. Later he could have bought enough sawdust to spread across the old U.S. and back, but he didn't need sawdust then, he got himself television, and television took him anywhere he wanted to go.

In those days, he came out of Biloxi, Mississippi, not old

enough to vote or even graduate from high school. You didn't need a college degree or seminary learning to praise the Lord, and, Lordy, as awkward as he might have been, he was living proof that the excitement of preaching was not something you could get from books.

They called it the sawdust trail in those days, because the sawdust they put down on the ground to soak up the rain or to keep the dust down stuck to the soles of your shoes and made a trail of sawdust from tent meeting to tent meeting.

You don't know what hot is until you've been inside one of those stinking-hot tents in the Old South. Ernie Jo knew he had to put on some show to get that sweltering crowd's mind off the heat. They were waving fans from the funeral parlor like cuckoo clocks and old Ernie Jo would gyrate like Elvis Presley, laugh like Phil Harris and cry like John Barrymore; sing like Johnnie Ray and dance like Gene Kelly. Nobody fell asleep when Ernie Jo Banghart was onstage.

In those days, taking up a collection was a noisy business because what there was of it was all coins. Small coins.

Ernie Jo and Emily Sue rode in a car you wouldn't even call a car today. It rattled as it chugged along the rutted roads that took them to the true believers.

Ernie Jo, the part-time preacher's kid, was a traveling university to those great-unwashed back-country folks. It was education for them, entertainment. Excitement. There was simply nothing else. It was a good message—you couldn't argue with it. God loves you—love Him back, He will forgive your sins. For, let us face it, we are all rotten sinners.

And when he made the call to the "altar" after the Lord's hell-fire 'n brimstone'd been delivered of him, clean as a hound's tooth, why, they stepped right up there, you better believe they did, because, sister, the man had charisma in spades, he did. And besides, it was just a short walk and all your sins were going to be forgiven in that little journey. "You are going to be washed in the blood of the Lamb, and that's the blood of Jesus Hisself, and I don't care how rotten you've been—how evil your thoughts—covetousness, jealousy, lust even, you *will be forgiven—and not only for now, not only the past infractions, but you will be forgiven for all time, until Jesus returns to the earth and scoops you up in His loving arms, presses you to His bosom and takes you along to the heavenly kingdom of God Almighty. So help me God! Hallelujah, oh, Lordy Jesus!"*

And on every swing through the bayou, he was like an insurance man collecting his residuals. Every time he reappeared, the crowds grew. They'd gas up the old jalopy and ride into town for three hours of the darndest carrying-on you ever did see.

And the women. Oh, the women loved him. He was such a good-looking boy. Careworn women, fingers raw to the bone with scrubbin' and all the chores they kept up to keep that poor family from falling apart, to keep working so they wouldn't have a moment to think how poor they were—why, by then he was sure enough something to look forward to, and whatever night he came through town, why, time would be made for those women to come on out to the tent for prayer and praise.

And it amused the women, Jesus be blessed! And the menfolk were not about to admit that their womenfolk needed amusing, but the menfolk started to notice as soon as they got home and went to bed there was a certain amorousness in the distaff that had not appeared heretofore, and perhaps all that absolving of sin had its place.

And Ernie Jo Banghart grew in the Lord, he grew in wisdom, and the fear of the Lord was in him.

He told how that loving God was coming back to earth, just like He did before in the body of Jesus Christ, and we'd all better get ourselves ready to receive Him in our hearts—for those who really believe are going to reign with Him and be swept to heavenly glory, and those who don't are going to fry in hell.

Lord, in those struggling years did Ernie Jo ever, in his wildest dreams, count out those pennies and nickels in the offering plate and think that someday his weekly offering would be three million dollars? Never in this world!

But the thing just took hold and snowballed like nobody's

business. *The audiences grew and grew, outgrowing the tent because there was just no show like him. He even took up the guitar so he could sing to his flock. Then he started with a backwater TV station somewhere well south of the Mason-Dixon and it just grew like Topsy.*

He never wanted anything for himself, he said. But before you knew it, he had his own jet airplane. And his main house cost just a tad over a million, and land in rural Gulfport, Mississippi, was not what you'd call high. There were a couple more houses: Palm Springs, Palm Beach, the Bangharts liked it warm in the winter, Emily Sue was conscientious about her tan, year-round.

But as good as he did, Ernie Jo wanted it understood right up front, he never sought any personal credit whatsoever. "I am just the vessel," he'd say over and over. "All glory and praise belong to Jesus. Hallelujah!"

†   †   †

After the call came from the sheriff out in Californy, I laughed so hard my sides split. I said to Emmy Sue, if nothing else, it was the best laugh I'd had in a long time.

What happened was this: this here sheriff out in a place called Glory Palms, or something, out in Californy, not that far from my Palm Springs place, but not anywheres near so exclusive; this sheriff calls me up out of the blue and says there's a fella preaching out there says he's Jesus Christ returned to earth.

Well, that was just about the most ridiculous thing I ever heard, but it did give me, as I said, a good laugh.

Brucie went back to his office to crunch some numbers and Emmy Sue stayed put. We were in my office and I don't mean to be immodest, but it crossed my mind now and again that my office— study, pastor's study, I should call it—was bigger than those early tents I preached in on that there so-called sawdust trail.

Yessir, this office, and all our buildings on my Miracle

Ministry grounds, I can honestly say I earned by the sweat of my brow. And we built the place one brick at a time—pay-as-you-go.

But now I had an unsettling feeling in the pit of my gut. This guy in Californy was obviously a charlatan, and if there is one thing the ministry of the Lord don't need, it's another charlatan.

"Emmy Sue," I addressed my bride over my desk—and it was a big desk. There was some talk awhile back that my desk cost $20,000, and wasn't that an extravagance for a minister of the gospel? Well, I just tell it like it is. It was a gift from a wealthy parishioner—who wished to remain anonymous.

'Course, that snoopy Frankie Foxxe asks if that wealthy donor knew he—or she—was giving me the desk, an' I changed the subject.

"Emmy Sue," I said. I called her Emmy though her real name was Emily. It was our private name—'course, I called her that on the air all the time—old habits are hard to break. "Just suppose, for the sake of argument, that this guy the sheriff told us about was the real Jesus."

"Oh, Ernie, that's preposterous."

"I know it is, but we're just brainstorming now. What do you think would happen?"

"If something was going to happen," she said, "I expect it would have happened already."

"And what would that have been?"

"I don't know; you're the preacher."

I was embarrassed to say, after all that preaching, after all that Bible study, I didn't know myself—not for certain.

"You know who's gonna have a field day with this?"

"Who?"

"Frankie Foxxe."

"Oh," she said, holding her head in misery.

"The old Debunker of Myths—" I smiled at that. "Self-styled, of course."

Emmy Sue waved her hand. There were some nice rings on

those fingers—but they weren't showy like some evangelists' wives I could mention.

"And when Frankie Foxxe turns on the spotlight, the glare won't make us look good."

Then I asked her the question I seem to have to ask over and over here of late: "Could I get you to run over to the house with me—get under the covers?"

"Oh, Ernie, I have work to do."

And that was it. Always work to do or a headache or just plain not being in the mood. She was still—going on thirty years of marriage—a very pretty girl. I counted myself a very lucky man to be blessed with such a helpmate. The Lord was good to me when He brought Emmy Sue and me together. But lately, a couple sayings have been turning over in my mind: Pretty is as pretty does.

Emmy Sue went back to her office and I wondered what went through her mind when she rejected me again and again. Was she at all cognizant of the fact that I was responsible for her being where she is today? Me and the Lord, of course, because nothing happens without the Lord's blessing. But there is not a single person in her family has it as good as Emmy Sue. Come right down to it, there ain't many in the whole world got it good as Emmy Sue, and she knows it. But when it comes right down to it, she turns a blind eye and a deaf ear to me. Now, I am against the sin of adultery as strong as any man, but, I'll tell you, sometimes the urge comes on so strong I'm beside myself beseeching the Lord for relief.

It don't do no good beseeching Emmy Sue.

That which is born of the flesh
is flesh;
and that which is born of the Spirit
is spirit.
Marvel not that I said unto thee,
Ye must be born again.

—John 3:6-7

THE GOSPEL ACCORDING TO
MICHAEL

I was out back of Jack Whitehall's place with Jack looking over the vast emptiness that lay still behind the house and barn.

It was like a multi-acre blanket of green-brown, keeping the earth in its place. It was a nice, clear afternoon; there wasn't any smog at this altitude.

"Jeez, you got a lot of land," I said to Jack.

"It's God's land," Jack mused. "I'm just passing through—not even a pinprick on the timeline of human history—and that's even less on the map of recorded time."

"But you own it, don't you?" I asked.

Jack shook his head. "There's a passage in Exodus that sums it up: 'The land shall not be sold for ever: for all the earth is mine,'" Jack said. "The Almighty owns it. I have my name on a piece of paper with the bank and I can use it for a while, then decide who to pass it on to—but it's all to the greater glory of our Lord Jesus Christ and it's going back to Him in the end."

"Charlie says you can heal people by praying," I said. "Is that true?"

"God heals. I'm the instrument."

"It really works?"

"You bet it works," Jack said, with a far-off look in his eyes. "The next time I feel the Spirit move me, I'll let you know."

I didn't tell Jack about my father's opinion of faith healers and evangelists and "folks of that ilk," as Amos called them. It wasn't very good—and yet this man seemed like he could be my father. I had this fantasy that someday I might change all that with Dad. Share my experience with him. Get him to see the light.

"What do you think of this...man who says he's Jesus?"

Jack didn't answer right away. Finally, as though it were a great effort, he said, "I like him."

"Yes, but do you think he is Jesus...I mean, the Jesus returned to earth? Do you think that's possible?"

A longer silence passed.

Finally, Jack exhaled, but he still seemed confused. "You are looking at a man who has a lot of faith. You might say when I was at my best, I lived by my faith. Now, I know the Bible says Jesus is coming back to earth, but I, frankly, never thought much about it. I was willing to consider it in the symbolic realm, like when we die, Jesus comes back to take us up or something. But as far as walking the earth like one of us..." Jack trailed off and shook his head.

"He asked me to sign on with him," I said. "Like being one of his disciples, I guess."

"Yeah," Jack said. "Me, too."

"You gonna do it?"

"Well, as I say, it's putting the old faith to the test," Jack said. "Way I look at it, what if he isn't Jesus? Have we lost that much? We can jump ship anytime we smell anything phony. I don't see the signs the Bible said we would see. On the other hand, you could stretch things a little and make a case. But," he paused, surveying his acreage, "time will tell."

"What do you mean, time will tell?" I felt gypped. "How much time? *What* will it tell?"

Jack Whitehall smiled. "I have a vision, Michael," he said. "I see this whole field covered with people—shoulder to shoulder—and Jesus is talking to them—softly—no shouting—and everyone is transfixed." He looked at me with a fatherly frown. "When that happens, we'll both know."

Jack patted me on my shoulder.

His next words were drowned by the roar of two dozen-odd motorcycle engines.

† † †

All those Devil's Disciples poured through Jack's front door with their girlfriends like they were on a safari, eyes darting all over as though they were looking for a two-headed hyena. It was the second wave of Disciples. Word was spreading fast.

Jesus was sitting on Jack's couch and it was like they didn't see him right away.

Then, one by one, their eyes seemed to click on him there on the couch, the white robes first, then the sandals, then the long hair. And the strangest thing happened—they went reverently silent when who he was registered in their brains, and they dropped down to a place on the floor as though they were sinking lightly in water. He had hypnotized them without doing anything.

All eyes were silently, expectantly on Jesus, who, without prompting, rose to face his audience, strewn all over Jack's living room like the dirty socks.

Jesus spoke so softly I thought everybody'd be straining to hear him. It was not necessary—his voice cut through the rank air in the room and focused all the attention on his simple words.

Jesus spoke far into the night. When everybody began to wind down, they filtered out to throw their bedrolls out on the field behind the barn, and Jesus joined them.

I dropped on Jack's living-room couch, unable to sleep for the second night. My brain was buzzing a hundred miles an hour. After Bart's death, despair had taken hold of me. I felt my life had no meaning. I was grasping for guidance, and now I'd found it. I couldn't tell my parents how I felt—they'd have given me a lecture on being strong. They always did when I felt especially weak.

Now for the first time in my life I felt like I belonged. Jesus was so thoughtful and considerate of me—he introduced me to everyone as the man who had brought him to Glory Pines. Not the kid, child, boy, guy or even *young* man, but *man*. Man! I felt useful for the first time in my life.

Listening to Jesus talk—sitting at his feet and hearing a message that made sense, it was like being hit in the face with a cold wave—it surprised you, but it woke you up, too.

A Bible lay open on the low table next to the couch—I reached for it and began leafing though it listlessly, stopping to read a passage here and there.

Each time I stopped, I read more, until I was totally into the whole thing. It took on this amazing, electrical meaning after I had listened to Jesus for hours.

I read for three and a half hours, until the sun came up and I dropped from exhaustion. I woke up some hours later with the Bible open across my chest. I never felt better in my life. It was like no matter what happened to me, I would always remember the poetry in the Bible; the common-sense philosophy seemed to speak directly to me. I began to see how things seemed to tie together in the book and in Jesus's talk. I saw things tying together in my life—giving it, finally, after all these nineteen years, some meaning.

Jesus passed through the living room on His way to walk in the woods. Brazenly, I stopped Him.

"Oh, Jesus," I said—I was so excited. "I've been reading the Bible—it's just about the best book I've ever read." I stopped myself. Did that sound dumb? "Well, I guess I haven't read that many, but, jeez, it's just full of this awesome stuff—totally cool. But I wondered something," I said and frowned.

Jesus looked at me with a question on His face.

"I mean, in the Bible, you say 'thee,' and 'thou,' and 'shalt,' and 'verily,' and stuff, and you don't say any of that stuff now."

"King James," He said. "I didn't talk like that, that's the British King James Version. I could, though—verily, thou must know nobody talks like that today, and I really hadn't thought to stand out like that. Verily, what dost thou think?"

I wrinkled my nose. "Better without it," I said.

I watched Jesus go outside through the big wooden-and-glass door Jack had on the side of his living room, and it was like beautiful butterflies had taken over my body, inside and out.

I understood for the first time in my life what people meant when they talked about being born-again Christians.

At last I would have something to talk to my father about. We could sit together for hours talking over the meaning of a few verses of Mark or John. Maybe a Psalm, the Revelations. That could take years.

And here I was, living under the same roof as Jesus Christ,

who came back to earth just as predicted time and again in the Bible. Why, the folks would be green with envy.

I couldn't hold off going to the phone any longer.

"Sure, son, go ahead," Jack said when I asked him if I could use the phone.

"Mom? Hi!" I knew I had more joy in my voice, more love, than ever before.

"Michael, where are you?"

"Up in the mountains, near Idyllwild. Mom—I've got the most awesome news."

"Well, good." Mother had a soft-toned, reasonable voice—in the higher alto range. She was always the one in the family who could be counted on to be reasonable. And she did encourage me sometimes—tried to say nice things. "You sound excited."

"Oh, I am, Mom, I am," I said. "I think I understand how you felt when you were my age."

"Felt?"

"Yeah, you know, when you decided to go to divinity school—or theology or whatever."

"What do you mean?"

"I mean—I've found God. And Jesus. Jesus is right here, Mom—He's changed my life already. I've been reading the Bible like crazy and it just makes me feel awesome."

"Well, good for you, Michael," she said, but she sounded confused.

"I've been born again," I said, full of excitement. "You've got to meet Jesus. Can you come up?"

"Jesus," she said slowly, as if trying to grasp a foreign concept. "What do you mean, Jesus?"

"I mean Jesus Christ is up here. He's come back to earth like I told you. I picked Him up at the airport and brought Him out here. He spoke to about fifty of us last night. He's electrifying—you gotta meet Him."

There was a long silence.

"Oh, Michael," she exhaled at last. "You don't seriously believe you met Jesus at the airport?"

"I've never been more serious in my life."

"Oh, Michael," she said in the tired tones of a long-suffering mother, one who has tried her best and seen only hopelessness for her efforts. "It's so preposterous."

But she couldn't discourage me. I didn't make this trip for nothing. There *was* meaning to it. God had at last touched my life. I didn't blame Mom for her disbelief. How could she know the power of this man without meeting Him? No one could have told me the wonders of Jesus if I hadn't met Him myself.

"When you meet Him, Mom," I said, "you'll change your mind." I hung up in the middle of her protest.

I was not going to let her bum me out.

Where it is a duty to worship the sun, it
is pretty sure to be a crime to examine
the laws of heat.

— *John Morley*

THE GOSPEL ACCORDING TO

ERNIE JO BANGHART

Whenever Ernie Jo Banghart gave me something sensitive — something that might not have put him in the best light — it served a larger purpose, which I didn't always foresee.

Like the two pastors who came to see him in his Gulfport office. Ernie Jo said they were trying to look serious, important and relaxed at the same time. It wasn't working. They just looked nervous — like there was something out of kilter about their mission.

Of course, when Ernie Jo was doing the telling, I'd have out my radar to detect his self-serving exaggerations. This tidbit, which I doubt he should have shared with me, was told as a good-humored prank:

J. Fenster Wald was one of the pastors. The J. was for John, a name with honored Biblical connections, but Fenster thought it too unglamorous for evangelical stardom. I could have told him he'd be better off losing weight than messing with his name, but that wouldn't be my place. He wouldn't listen to me anyway. I'm not getting off that easy with my own weight. We evangelists have big appetites.

Walter Jackson was the second of the pair, and they looked like they could have been in the movies in the twenties.

And, you will notice, they came to me, not the other way around. Either one of them, I was sure, would gladly kill for half of my audience ratings.

I thought the cordiality in their small talk was a mite strained, frankly, but there is bound to be tension when two aspiring neophytes come face to face with a star.

Well, it was Bobby Candle they come to talk about. I had my suspicions of Bobby Candle way back. Him and his wife were a team, and she was covered with makeup like it was head-to-toe. I had never seen anything like it in my life. I'd heard her called a bulldog in drag, but that's strictly off-the-record. But they put on a show, the two of them, and he had got a following. He was gimmicking up the Lord something awful — water slides and a palace for a midget who's dying of some dread disease. Now he had taken to selling time-shares at his version of Disneyland — why, it's like the man was selling used cars, and every now and then the missus would chime in with an 'Amen,' and suchlike. You just had to *know* Bobby was selling those condos ten times over.

My visitors were there to tell me he had sinned. Caught him with his pants down, and they were giving me chapter and verse.

"Why, ah don't believe a word of it," I said, astonished. "No brother minister in Christ would sink so low."

"We have documentation," J. Fenster Wald said, "affidavits." And he produced them.

I absorbed the scandal slowly. Then I sat back in my padded chair and frowned.

I shook my head and said, "What a shame."

I didn't suppose I ever managed to camouflage my distaste for Bobby Candle. I had referred to him in the past as that hen-pecked midget with the rolly coaster, in re: his Jesus Christ Loveland Playland. But the twerp could raise money, and his Nielsens were beginning to get within shouting distance of mine; not that I was bothered by that.

When my guests were about to fall off their chairs in antici-pation, I broke the silence: "What did you gentlemen have in mind to do with this..." I paused to fish for a euphemism, "information?" I pronounced with a raised eyebrow.

"We were looking for your input," Wald said with an easy familiarity he didn't seem to feel.

"Offhand I'd say we'd better tread with care," I said. "This could be a ball of snakes."

"Oh?" Wald didn't seem to understand.

"I mean, gentlemen, we don't want to go spittin' into the breeze with this thing."

"You mean it could backfire?"

"I mean, if we are proved wrong, we're gonna have a faceful of spit," I allowed. "Maybe even with a slightly different spelling." Everyone had a good laugh.

I stood up and said, "Excuse me for a minute, will you?" and I left the room like I was going to the bathroom. I gave them five minutes to incriminate themselves—not that I wanted blackmail ammunition, but it don't hurt to protect yourself—so my tape recorder was purring in my absence. When I got back, I said, "Let me pray on this, gentlemen. You have my word nothing will leak from me until we all agree the time is right."

My gentlemen callers seemed a little put out that I wouldn't sit there shooting the breeze with them all day. They had come over a thousand miles, but, frankly, I didn't see the point of blowing my whole day when there was nothing more to say.

When I heard the outside door close, I turned on my trusty tape recorder and backed it up. When I pressed Play, I heard Fenster Wald ask Walter Jackson, "Do you think Ernie Jo will double-cross us on this thing?"

"I think it's a safe bet he will," Jackson responded, and they both laughed.

So that's when I called you, Frankie.

The Gospel According to

FRANKIE FOXXE

I drove out to Ernie Jo's prayer grounds knowing the evangelist was going to spin me dizzy.

What is it that turns an ordinary mortal into a superstar television preacher? It's a lot more than luck. Some call it a gift, others a choice of the deity; charisma, sure, energy and enthusiasm — drive. I often caught myself wondering how much of the malarkey Ernie Jo spewed he actually believed. But I know this, he has to *seem* sincere to the great unwashed who send their crinkled dollar bills to him, who just adore the way he says, "I don't care what you send, that's between you and the Lord." And so be it, hallelujah, amen.

Ernie Jo had been jovial on the phone. He was just as jovial when he offered me the chair across his desk.

"Shoot, old Frankie, you know what Emmy Sue said when I told her I was calling you? She said, 'You're inviting the fox into the chicken house.'" He apparently found that amusing. We were sitting in the 747 airplane hangar he had dolled up for an office.

"What did *you* say?" I asked, and he was pleased I did — I could see it on his puffy face.

"I says, 'Well, I'm no chicken.'" And his level of merriment told me his motives for the meeting were important to him.

Natch, Ernie Jo wouldn't tell me *why* he wanted to meet me — he thought he was tantalizing. But since debunking myths was my bag, I couldn't say him nay.

And he was a sight for sore eyes.

Ernie in his Western-dude outfit, with the silky brown shirt with the flap doodles over the pockets and the pearly buttons, and the silky shoestring of a tie around his neck, all held together with a sterling-silver-hammered-out face of Jee-ah-zuz.

The pants were those oyster-white things with the brown piping that made him look fresh from an upholstery shop, the kind that specialized in the down-home look for celebrities. The I-may-be-rich-and-famous-but-I'm-just-one-of-the-folks look.

Way back, when I began taking after Ernie Jo, which was just after Ernie Jo had taken off with his guitar-strumming TV ministry and was jamming those Nielsen ratings right through the corrugated-iron roof, Ernie asked me, "Why you takin' on so? I ever done you harm of any sort what so ever?" And I had to allow as it was not at all personal, but "I am a Debunker of Myths," I explained.

Myself, I usually dressed like the crowd so you wouldn't see me. Long-dead blue jeans and a tee shirt with some smart-ass saying on it was de rigueur when I was on the job. But when I came calling on the Reverend Banghart, I wore my white ice-cream suit with the peppermint-candy-striped tie, the white wing-tip shoes and the sissiest damn pink shirt you ever saw. I did it to bug him. I knew how he hated queers and dandies, and here I was, dressing up as both. To frost the cake—as well as the host—I brought my white-covered vinyl, simulated-leather Bible. The kind Ernie Jo sold to the women in the audience on his camp-meeting tours for a hundred dollars. It was just nice for the gals because all the womanly stuff was highlighted in red; the stuff like obeying your husbands, and all.

Ernie Jo always wondered where in the name of Jesus I laid my hands on that Bible, but I never told him.

"I guess you wonder why I asked you to come out here today," Ernie Jo said, settling back in his outsized swivel chair. He liked to tip it back and interlace his fingers over his ballooning gut while he looked at the ceiling. A glass and pitcher of iced tea sat sweating on his desk.

"Oh, no," I said with expansive gestures, "I just figured you were going to release your financial statements to the press and you were giving me first shot."

We both had a good laugh over that, though it took some effort on Ernie Jo's part. "But seriously, though," the reverend said from behind his altar-sized desk, looking straight at me now, for emphasis. "I've nothing to hide on that score, Frankie, it's just that those things are so danged complicated, I don't hardly unnerstand them myself sometimes. We just got so much money comin' in from so many various and sundry sources, money that services so many needs and the like, I can't hardly keep up with it. I don't trouble myself with those nuts and bolts myself. I'm a saver of souls, Frankie, not a bean counter. You know I've always been aboveboard about my personal salary." He paused to snigger. "Far's I unnerstand it. My wife just takes my check and puts it directly in the bank, so's I don't hardly see it myself."

"And how big is that check?"

"Oh, after the taxes an' everything is taken out it, it's about eighteen, nineteen hunderd."

"A month?"

"Now, Frankie." He smiled that smile that always tickled his blue-haired worshipers. ("God never said you couldn't tint your hair a bit, never said nothin' 'bout lookin' your best being a sin.") "That's ever' week. But don't forget, I turn right around and give five *hunderd* or so right back to the church."

"Is that a donation? Tithing?"

"Not exactly. I pay them for my housing."

"Oh, yes," I feigned surprise, "that is to repay a loan they made you."

"Oh, something like that."

"Do you pay interest?"

"You bet I do. To answer your next question, if I recollect rightly, it's around eight, nine percent."

"Would four be more like it?"

"Oh, I don't know. As I say, I don't think about money—my business, my only business, is saving souls."

"Your wife and son are on the payroll, too, aren't they?"

"Well, they have major responsibilities here. It's not as though it's a handout or anything. You don't work for nothing, do you?"

"Oh, I don't know about that," I said. "What would you say your wife and kid haul in annually—a couple hundred grand?"

"I honestly don't know, but whatever we pay them they are well worth the price, I can assure you. Unnerstand we are running a hunderd-an'-fifty-million-and-some-change business here, and out in the private sector, why, you couldn't begin to touch executives for that kinda money. Why, they get year-end bonuses ten times more'n that."

"How about the house in Palm Springs and the one in Palm Beach?"

"Those I paid for outta my own pocket—and I use them for church business. Meeting prospective big donors and the like."

"And the airplane?" I asked.

"That is the same—and I have to fly all over the world for my crusades, and that is a tight schedule—and to check on our foreign missions and the like."

"No loans from the ministry?"

"No—oh, I think we had outside help—you know, a donation or two here—a loan there. Ask Emmy Sue—she's the bean counter here. I strictly save souls." He laughed easily.

I never took notes at these meetings—I didn't forget what I wanted to remember. I didn't have a tape recorder, because it inhibited the subject, and, besides, I wanted my subjects to be able to crawl out of some embarrassing hole by denying whatever incriminated them, knowing full well I could not make the defense that I had it all on tape.

I asked Ernie Jo about Thomas Kempis's *Imitation of Christ.* "He says the human effort to know is an insult to God. A sign of pride. What do you think, Ernie Jo?"

The preacher waved his hand. "Listen, the more you know about God the more you love Him. Knowing is no insult. What we can, we know. What we can't, we believe."

"Where is the evidence?"

"In nature. The trees all around you—the oceans, the sun, the rain."

"The people?"

"Certainly the people—the people most of all."

"Hitler? Stalin?"

"Well, now, He makes the people. What they do with themselves is out of His hands."

"I'd settle for a little less suffering."

"Yeah, all right, the suffering question..."

"Is the suffering of one abused child worth the pleasure of the rest of us?"

"Go on, Frankie—say what's on your mind. It don't matter none to me. I heard all the arguments before—there ain't nothing new, you hear? My God is a good God and the sin and suffering of this world is just to prepare us for the paradise of the next. So if you get right with Jesus now, why, you're gonna be in heaven in the life to come."

"So heaven is going to be free of sadness and suffering?"

"Bible calls it 'paradise,'" Ernie Jo said with a lip smack of satisfaction.

"Ever think it could bore you to death?—heaven, I mean—that is, if you weren't already dead. I mean, let's assume for a minute that what you say is true. God put incredible suffering in this world so we could know pleasure. And I assume you are including the monstrous murders committed in his name through the centuries, the mindless intolerance that still exists. So, now when those who are willing and/or able to acknowledge Jesus fly up to this heaven, why, there isn't going to be any more sin and suffering, only pleasure—but my question is, how will you know pleasure when you don't experience pain?"

"But who hasn't experienced pain?"

"In heaven?"

"No, on earth."

"So you mean everyone will remember earthly pain and suffering when they are in heaven?"

Ernie Jo nodded. "That's right."

"Okay, then how much unrelieved pleasure will there be in paradise?"

"Total."

"For how long?"

"Bible says for all eternity."

"I assume that wasn't written by someone who experienced it firsthand."

"Well, not firsthand, maybe not. But the Bible is the Word of God, Frankie— inspired by God. God spoke to those writers."

"Dictated the whole thing?"

"Might have done. At any rate, it wasn't just made up like no fiction."

"Does pleasure vary? I might find pleasure in watching water flow down in a stream. Someone else might revel in the companionship of lusty women. Will we all be served in heaven?"

"Well, I don't say carnal pleasures will be served, no. You know the Romans verse: 'The carnal mind is enmity against God.' I expect those souls will go to roast where they belong."

"So how do you envision this pleasure, as sort of a sweet repose?"

"I expect so. But you gotta unnerstand, Frankie, I don't have the specifics. These things are not ours to know. We will come to know them in good time—if we are saved."

"Are you saved, Reverend?"

"I sure am working on it."

"You have to keep working, do you?"

"You bet. Everybody does. You have to open your heart to Jesus and keep it open. You have to not only invite Him into your heart but you gotta keep Him there. I mean as a *permanent* guest."

"What about judgment, Reverend Banghart? You think a fair and honest God is going to damn some poor soul to hell—some poor soul he dealt an inferior set of brains—because he was too stupid to not do the wrong thing?"

"Ever'body has it in him to get right with the Lord. I seen it with my own eyes. The worst sort of criminal, and I meant the *worst,* can accept Jesus Christ as his personal Savior. That don't take a Einstein genius."

"But your God is going to exclude the Buddhists, Muslims, Hindus, Jews—anyone who doesn't believe in Jesus?"

"I'm afraid unless they see the light before they're called, that's gonna be their fate."

"But, Ernie Jo, you are talking about eighty percent of the world's population."

"I know it. That's why we make such an effort with world evangelism. We desperately want to bring the Word of God to these ignorant people—and I don't mean that 'ignorant' unkindly, I mean it in the sense of ignorance of the saving power of Jesus Christ. Once they are given the Word, why, they flock to Jesus by the *millions!*"

"But even millions is a pittance when you consider the world population is over six billion," I said.

"I won't give up until the whole world sees the light."

"How will it end?"

"With the Rapture. Those who got themselves right with the Lord are gonna be called up with Jesus. Those that don't gonna perish."

"But why would a God exclude eighty percent of his people?"

"I don't know all the answers. I admit to that. But you read the Bible, you'll see."

"Suppose I read the Koran, or the Talmud—will I see something else?"

"Maybe you will. But the Bible is the inerrant, inviolable Word of God."

"I know it sparkles with literature and poetry. As mythology, it's stunning. You could even make a case for a possible moral code, though I think it's a little too stringent and unreasonable in spots."

"Well, you think wrong, Frankie."

"And what about the Catholics? If we throw them out of the picture it looks a lot bleaker."

"Well, I got nothin' 'gainst my Catholic brethren, but they gotta be born again in Jesus Christ our Lord before they got a chance at salvation. The Mother Teresas of the world can do all the good works they want, and I give them all praise for it, but it ain't gonna get them no closer to heaven."

"Well, it just seems a logistical nightmare for your God. A lot of bookkeeping on who fits the mold and who doesn't," I said. "So how many souls you figure have been won for Christ?"

"No tellin'."

"Okay, but let's try to narrow it down. If we have six billion, and about a billion of them claim to be Christians. What percentage of those have got themselves right with the Lord—been born again, as you say?"

"I don't know for sure, Frankie. I seen the statistics, I expect you have, too. What do they say? Maybe twenty—thirty percent of so-called Christians are born again."

"But now we are down to say five percent of the world's population. Is that reasonable?"

"Reasonable? We're doing our best to raise it. That's why television is so impordand. We reach millions, worldwide."

"No, Ernie Jo, I mean, if I understand you correctly, your way is the only way. And yet you have a God that reaches only five percent of the world's population. The God who created the heavens and the earth, the sea and the dry lands, in seven days, the one who started with Adam and Eve, who sent the flood, the one who brought himself to earth as Jesus Christ, is only touching five percent of the world's population. Is that a significant God? He's only a five-percenter. Doesn't he want the other ninety-five percent?"

"Of course He does," Ernie Jo said.

"Did he create the other ninety-five percent?"

"Of course He did."

"And put in them the ability to reason?"

"Yes."

"Then how is it that ability to reason has led so many away from him?"

"Well, I don't know that it has. Our revivals bring us a very high percentage of those who are exposed to us. You talk about your five percent—why, we get seventy, eighty percent of those we can reach. That's why I'm putting on a big push for China. I want to save the souls of a billion heathens."

"But why should an omnipotent God need you or any of your fellow evangelists? Shouldn't man, having been created by this all-powerful God, be predisposed—or even programed—to accept and worship him gratefully for giving him life?"

"I'll agree it should be that. But you are not reckoning with one impordand factor."

"What's that?" I asked.

"Satan!" Ernie Jo expectorated the word. "The power of Satan to disrupt the work of God."

"Oh, Ernie Jo, really—you don't believe...?"

"Yes, I *do* believe. Don't you start tellin' me what I believe. I believe the Bible..."

"All of it?"

"You bet all of it."

"You know how many religions contain a flood story?"

"All the more reason to believe it."

"Do you realize, if you take that story literally, how much water would have been rained on the earth?"

"Forty days and forty nights steady rain—lot of water."

"Yes, and taking the measurements in the Bible it's enough water to sink a battleship—what would it have done to that little old ark?"

"Couldn't touch that old ark. It was steadied in the storm by the hand of God," Ernie Jo said, not yielding an inch. "Why, boy, there's more miracles wrought by the hand of God than you can shake a stick at."

"How do you stand on the Sermon on the Mount?"

"Foursquare."

"What about sex?"

Ernie Jo sat up. "What about it?"

"I get a lot of confusing signals from the Bible. Now, this

guy, this fellow pastor who you got bounced from the church for some kind of sex thing, what was his misdeed?"

"Why, he had a bunch of adulterous affairs."

"What kind of definition do you hang on that, Ernie Jo?"

"Well, he had women. Sex with women not his wife."

"How do you know that? Is that, I mean, something you saw?"

"Well, no, I didn't *see* it. But I didn't have to see it. Ever'body knows it."

"Anybody see it?"

"Well, you don't *see* things like that."

"I understand he denies it."

"Well, let him. We got the goods. I mean, we have the word of women involved."

"Could they be lying?"

"Nah. Not them women. Honest as the day is long. What would they have to gain?"

"So you'd trust a woman's word against a man?"

"In those matters, I would."

"Any kind of woman? Let's just say we have a minister on one hand and a prostitute on the other. Would you still go with the woman?" I let my eyes bore in on old Ernie Jo and his face showed the slightest flush.

"That might be different," Ernie Jo allowed.

"Now, surely, Reverend, God put these biological urges in man to prolong the species—either that or the species has been perpetuated *because* those urges are there. How long do you figure it would take the world population to die out if procreation wasn't a fun experience? Now, are you trying to tell me men following— you know, going—where those urges take them, that that is somehow contrary to the God that put the urges there in the first place? I mean, you seem to want it both ways. You say God is responsible for everything, and that's gotta include the sex urge. And yet you insist that at the same time God gives these urges, he wants them curbed."

"Well, it's Satan working against the Lord. And, oh, I can tell you Satan never lets up."

I could tell he was itching to get to the point, so I stopped the needling.

"This here special reason I called you here, why, I'm gonna have to seek your advice on whether to put this on the record or not. An' that's why I asked you to come. Because I trust your advice."

"Let me guess," I said. "You've got something on a competitor."

Ernie Jo frowned. "I wouldn't say competitor. We don't think of competition in the work of the Lord like you newspaper folks do. Now this...and it is apparently not only women this demon goes after, but men...and boys as well. There is solid evidence of ho-mo-sex-u-al behavior." Ernie Jo had a flair for emphasizing and stretching out the syllables in any word that might excite the passions of his audience, whether millions on TV or one in his Mussolini office.

"What, more sex? You called me here on more sex? It's such a tough area, Ernie, I don't know—you sure you aren't spitting into the wind, like you say? I mean, are you a hound's tooth yourself?"

He waved a hand of expulsion. "Don't worry 'bout me."

"I don't know, Ernie Jo, how far you want to take this sex business. Don't you have a sixty-million lawsuit against you for the last guy you tried to hang with this sex-scandal-sensation stuff?"

"That don't bother me none. I got him dead to rights."

"Oh, I don't know if that matters that much. You know what they say, Reverend, 'Boys will be boys.' So, I don't expect you'll shock any of the men that much. Oh, you may get some elevated eyebrows from the blue-haired grandma set, but are you sure you're all that squeaky clean yourself?"

Ernie Jo jolted upright. "I never even kissed anyone else but my wife—and I was seventeen when I'se married—she was fifteen. So, you don't have to worry none on that score."

I got a kick out of that. "When they ask you that question on

TV, kind of lay back in your chair if you can—and look bored. That is instead of jumping like you just did and protesting so hard. Be more believable, you do."

"Well, God is my witness and I don't need your advice."

All through the meeting, Ernie Jo seemed in a strange state of excitement—it was almost sexual.

He stood and shook my hand as any superior being who wanted to end a meeting would.

No sooner had I gotten to my car than Ernie Jo came barreling around the corner in his Lincoln Town Car and pointed it east (a star shall rise in the east, after all).

I didn't see any reason not to follow him.

Two wise men, heading east.

CLAUDE CULPEPPER

PRESENTS

Claude Culpepper didn't look old enough to be wizened, but wizened he was.

*His place was a page out of the Undistinguished Motels of 1947 book.
It was one of those places where they drew the parking lot first, then
stuck rooms on what was left of the land. Claude's place was quaintly named the "Restawyle Motel," and he rented by the hour.*

In his "office" window, the stick-on letters laid it on the line:

POSITIVELY NO REFUNDS!

*Claude was reluctant to tell his story, fearing I might make
trouble with the girls, their Johns, the law or the holies, as he put it.
But given the taciturn nature of his business and the garrulousness of
his nature, his nature won out.*

I got some a them stick-on letters over by the Wal-Mart and
assembled them in that particular order. I even spent an extra six
bits for that there exclamation point. That's because I had it up to
here with guys griping about the accommodations after twenty lousy
minutes when they booked the three-hour rate.

I told them until I was blue in the face they could have
booked for an hour, and I always told them there was positively no
refunds in case their eyes was bigger than something else. I always
been up-front, no two ways about it, but the girls wasn't the only
ones who noticed the difference in the Johns goin' in and comin'
out. And damn right I would book the room again if they vacated. I
don't picture any of their "dates" giving any refunds.

So, up went the sign. Well, it didn't do a lot of good. The
overly optimistic Johns still bitched and moaned, but now I just
pointed to the sign and saved a lot of breath.

Name's Claude Culpepper, and I been managing this place
for a mite over a dozen years. 'Fore that I was in housekeeping at a
place down the road about a mile, so I know the territory, all right.
In a way, this managing all-night traffic is easier than cleaning the
crud outta bathrooms, in a way not. The girls is okay, I got no problem with them, but the Johns who come around bitching to me

about the rates or some girl didn't please him just right, I gotta set 'em straight right off. I'm just a manager of the premises, I say, I'm not any kind of madam. You got a gripe, you take it to the girl direct. She's a independent contractor and I don't have the least responsibility for her. And I know the owner will back me up on that. He's one of those eye doctors in North Carolina, lookin' for a tax deduction for the place, and we have a deal. I keep the income after a certain amount, and that's how I happened to go into this renting-by-the-hour setup. But I tells 'em in no uncertain terms, that's all I do, rent rooms.

Seen some real beauties in my time—not the girls, the Johns. I knowed that TV preacher from a mile off—he couldn't fool me with his ridiculous disguises. But my lips was sealed. It's like a code of honor out here on Route 45.

I was always a good sport. Oh, when I was bored, I might listen in on the phone conversations, but mostly they bored me even more.

I got to admit, Rhonda, in twenty-nine, was one of my favorites. Pays without squawking, even makes the bed when she finishes. And her phone conversations is interesting enough to listen straight through sometimes. We have the old switchboard-type phone system at the Restawyle. The owner, he wasn't much for spending money on newfangled contraptions. "Keep the price down, Claude," he says to me. He calls me Claude; I calls him Doc.

The light on number twenty-nine lighted up on the switchboard and it was glowing at me like a dare. Rhonda would be using the phone.

I picked up and she gave me the number.

While I was dialing the number, I got this vision of her sitting on her made bed. I often had visions of my girls, I calls 'em. Rhonda would be straightening her nylons for her next visitor (she always dressed up after work).

She'd be sittin' there on that soft bed (years ago they was a mite harder, I reckon), swingin' the top one of her crossed legs, and with the one hand not holding the phone, she might be twirling them paste pearls she wore. I couldn't swear to it, but that's what I saw in my vision anyways.

There was a lot of wear on Rhonda, there was no hiding that. But, shoot, that was life. We all wear out sooner or later.

Like the stuff in the rooms was wearing out but we held onto it, long as we could. Like the switchboard. The rugs was avocado when the place was built—that was the in color. Then came dark brown. Well, they's both *out* now, but we still got 'em in various combinations, depending on where they wore out and such.

The doc wants to keep the walls that there mushroom color. Thinks you don't have to paint so often. That ain't exactly right, but he's sticking to his guns on that matter.

I could hear the springs creaking on Rhonda's bed in twenty-nine. 'Cause she'd been swinging her leg like that. She gets on me 'bout oiling them springs—but I can't cut them mattresses apart.

Well, this other girl picks up the phone says, "Hello." Friend of Rhonda's—another hooker. Thought I'd stay on the line a second or two—see if I could be of any assistance.

"Hi, Trixie, how's tricks?"

Trixie laughs. "Oh, Rhonda, you know my name's Priscilla."

"Yeah, but, Pris, I don't know. Seems too highfalutin', the line we're in."

"What's up?"

"I'm waitin' on the reverend. I expect he'll be along any time now. He's very prompt."

"How prompt is he after he's there?" Pris asked with a twerpy laugh.

"Oh, he gets his money's worth. Signs up for the hour and gets every minute of it."

Now Rhonda was laughing.

"What's so funny?" Priscilla asked.

"Oh, I hear him on the TV, callin' down the wrath of God on the adulterers an' fornicators. I mean, if that just don't take the cake, Trix, I don't know what does."

"Of all the nerve."

"Yeah. I swear I tolt him he looked like Ernie Jo Banghart, an' you know what he said? He said, 'A lot of people tell me that. My name's Jack.' Well, I call him Buddy, 'cause it's easy—I mean, I'm liable to slip with that Jack business an' call him Joe—or even Ernie....

"I gone out there to see him in action, out by Gulfport. It's him, all right. He puts on a good show, all right. Music and jawing like you never saw. 'Let's sing it one more time,' he'll say over and over until them folks, who is packed to the roof and back, be standing on their feet shoutin', 'Hallelujah.' I could blow that John sky-high if I was that kind of girl."

"He ought to be givin' you some huge tips—the chances he's takin'."

"Tip! Are you kidding? He used to try to always jew me down on my price. I tolt him in no uncertain terms I don't do nothin' for jes ten dollars, not even bare titty. I swear he's one of the cheapest I ever comed acrost," Rhonda snorted. "No, honey, he don't tip none. That man's gonna squeeze ever' nickel till it squeals bloody murder." She laughed and it shook the bed so it got to squeaking like a stuck pig.

"'N I gotta dress up the room homey lak for him. I bought a couple a pitchur frames 'the five-'n-dime. I tell him I'm only in this line o' work to make a home for my baby. Oh—there he is now, Trixie—I'll be talkin' to ya. Bye—"

I saw the reverend, as Rhonda called him, at the door. I wasn't paying much attention to the outside. So, there he is, got up like Teddy Roosevelt, and I expect Rhonda was in for a rough ride this afternoon.

Rhonda didn't answer the door right away and that made the reverend itchy, I could tell. Rhonda always said it heightens the excitement to let 'em wait a spell. The danger of getting caught, I guess, enters in.

I saw her jaw drop when she finally opened the door and saw President Teddy Roosevelt standing before her. She wasn't looking too young, but, Lord's sakes, what could you expect the life she led? Well, it didn't seem to cramp her business none. I'll bet she gave good value. Didn't come too dear like them high-priced girls over in New Orleans. She was the Wal-Mart of hookers, not the Neiman-Marcus. But, shoot, the act was the act. Most of 'em had their eyes closed anyways. Probably picturing one of them young movie stars.

While the reverend was in room twenty-nine, I noticed a guy parked across the street, keeping his eye on my premises. That was you, I expect, Mr. Foxxe. I knew the reverend wouldn't like that, but I didn't see it my place to raise no fuss over it.

Well, as you know, the reverend stayed the full hour, all right. It was uncanny the way he timed it to his TV show exactly. She was in a line where rapid turnover equaled higher wages, but she was no complainer. Not Rhonda.

The reverend came out and took off his disguise and threw it in the trunk of his car and drove off, a new man.

Soon's the reverend took off down the highway, Rhonda was back on the phone: "Take my word for it, Trixie, I could hardly keep a straight face. You know who he was today? Guess? No, Theodore Roosevelt. Honest ta God! He's got a stick-on moustache and a monocle and he's saying 'Bully' all the time.

"You just wouldn't believe it, Trixie, he's waving a big stick an' speakin' softly. Well, just between us, his stick ain't all that big. 'Course, I tell him it is—'Oh, Buddy, that's a big stick,' (she giggled) an' he jest drinks it all down like vintage wine. 'Call me Teddy,' he says. Lord knows who he'll be next—you never know from week to week who's gonna walk in the door. I'm waitin' for King Kong, I swear.

"Oh, and I almost forgot—he wants a threesome. Honest ta God. I told him I didn't know anyone here, but he's pushing me—well, of course, he'll pay—we get it in advance. I wrote a poem about that very thing:

If you don't get it when they're hot
You won't see it when they're shot.

"You'd never see a nickel—him bouncing outta here with all that guilt an' remorse," she giggled.

"He's a real showman, that one. Yeah, I think we could get seventy-five easy, maybe a hundred. 'Course, we gotta see it in advance—there ain't no substitute for that percentage in any other way.

"Oh, an' you know those pitchurs I put up to make the place look homey?... well, he picks the one of the kid up and says, 'Who's this, Rhonda?' An' I says, 'Oh, just a kid—' and he says, 'Your kid?' an' I just sort of giggled 'cause I got it over by the drugstore, ya know, but he seems real taken with it. So, darned if he don't say, 'You got a very pretty chile, honey. Favors you...'" She laughed. "Well, I swear I broke up at that, but he's dead serious, an' I'm laughin' so hard my sides ached. Honest ta God, I thought I'd split a gut. Oh, Lord, he asks me her name and I went blank. I couldn't think of a kid's name to save my soul. An' you know what? He only gets more interested. So I finally pull a straight face an' say, 'I don't mix my family in my profession, I expect you can understand that,' an' he puts the picture back down an' don't say nothin' more 'bout it.

"Well, Trix, I gotta run purify my kidneys. I'll catch ya later."

When God said, "Ha!
Let us make man"
And the elders upon the altar cried
"Ha!
If you make man, ha!
He will sin."

> —*C.C. Lovelace*
> *The sermon as heard by*
> *Zora Neale Hurston*

THE GOSPEL ACCORDING TO

ERNIE JO BANGHART

But Ernie Jo wouldn't be calling it a sin.

I saw him all ruddy-faced, sitting behind the wheel of his flashy Lincoln, and if he was embarrassed by what he'd just done, he didn't show it. I knew what he was thinking. Those Southern boys thought sex was only this in that, and the other in this, and that there in this here just didn't qualify. Not as a bona fide sin, anyway. No, Ernie Jo would be squaring it all with his God, driving back home to the bosom of his family in his Lincoln on Route 45:

You may be thinking that technically I sinned, but, Lord, as You well know, there was no intercourse involved and You said so Yourself in Your Bible that fornication was a sin, and so by the logic since You don't mention these other possible variations, why, I am still in good standing with You, Lord? That there's a question, Lord. Technically since I didn't enter her there where the children of God are made — that would be fornication, I know that much — and I'm not a fornicator, no way. But this other business — where she does some unearthly things to me — that's the question. When a wife turns cold, what's a man to do with his urges? Now, You know like nobody else, I love my wife like nobody else. And I always ask her first. But how much rejection can a man take? And I'm talking about a man in the public eye, a celebrity, if You will — and You know I get hundreds of chances of women, girls even, just throwing theirselves at me, offering to do "anything" I want. It's not easy to resist that, Lord. Not for a mere mortal. And some of them are real lookers, Lord. I know You been expecting more of me 'cause I'm a preacher and all, but, Lord, Lord, I'm a human being, too. And I'm just asking You, as a favor for all of my devotion in preaching Your Word, could You send me some sign about what to do when these terrible urges come upon me? I gotta have female contact. I get so worked up shouting Your praises, I just need that feeling you can only get with a person of the opposite sex — and I never did think anything of going after men and boys like some pastors I don't have to mention to You.

This is agony for me, Lord. You know I don't want to be a

bad man. You know I've devoted my life to Your service. I never forget my humble beginnings, Lord, You brought me up every step of the way. And the last thing I would ever want to do was draw Your wrath because I am misunderstanding some sin on a technicality. So, if I don't see no sign to the contrary, Lord, I'll just continue to assume that You aren't holding me responsible for no technical sin.

All glory and praise be to You, Lord, and Your only begotten Son, Jesus the Christ, whose second coming to earth we all eagerly await.

Amen.

ANOTHER BLAST FROM GOD'S TROMBONES:

It was, when you think about it, an insane place to build a city. If you want to drive around all those crazy hills, you'd better have awfully good brakes on your car because half the time it's straight down and the other half it's straight up. And now here was this black stretch limo—stretched beyond reason—slithering up and down those hills like it was nothing—a birthright even.

And the cops. They were swarming all over the streets. If you stopped long enough to add up all the pensions on the streets of San Francisco that night, you might be crushed by the tax burden.

And nobody was telling who was in that black boat. It wasn't clear if it was a big secret, or no one knew.

Was the president coming? Or some kook rock star?

One thing was obvious. It was someone somebody thought needed protection.

The grated iron mouth of the Fairmont Hotel garage opened and swallowed the limousine in one gulp.

Once those iron lips closed on him, the word leaked out that it was a famous reverend—come to address the faithful, with an eye toward keeping them faithful.

†   †   †

The reverend stood on the stage, behind a stonehenge of bulletproof clear glass. You could see him, you just couldn't shoot him.

Father, as he was known to the faithful, was delivering himself of a stormy oration. Standing beside him, not as bulletproofed, was his faithful interpreter of seventeen years. The messenger was expendable, not the message.

Out front were the children. Thousands of them collected here in San Francisco to get fired up with the wisdom of the ages courtesy of the man or god to whom they devoted their lives.

After a while the reverend couldn't tell them apart. They were all young and clean and shaved, with the same glassy-eyed stare. The glazed-over eyes were cultivated by the group as a symbol of single-minded holiness.

But after a week of selling flowers on the streets and in the bars sixteen hours a day, it was no longer necessary to cultivate the stare. It was there.

George was in the sixth row center. George was a group leader, five charges he had (four girls and a guy), and he was in charge of hawking flowers in Wisconsin in sub-zero weather. Four hundred and fifty thousand dollars the six of them raised for the father, the first nine months of the year. George him-self had done fourteen hundred dollars in one day.

Sixteen hours a day, seven days a week—six-teen hours if you made your quota. If you didn't, you put in overtime at the all-night saloons until you unloaded your load of blooms. Flowers wilt, people don't. But when your whole life was selling flowers, a couple more hours only made that holy glassy-eyed stare come easier.

Besides, a worn-out body and tired mind is

impervious to evil thought.

In the trenches, where they sold the flowers at five below zero Fahrenheit, they never questioned the chastity edict from their thrice-married messiah, going on a dozen kids.

"Be fruitful and multiply, replenish the earth and renew it" was, in this cult, an elitist privilege.

The father was shouting now. "Would you rather sleep, or work for God?"

"Work for God!" came the resounding reply.

"If I say work twenty hours or sleep?..." the interpreter matched the speaker's inflections. After seventeen years of speaking for the master, he was the master.

"Work twenty hours!"

"The world is full of evil, and evil must be tricked. We are making a new order. It is necessary to deceive the forces of Satan. It is a divine deception, sanctioned by God—for did not Jacob lie to Isaac? And did not God reward Jacob with making him the Father of Israel?"

"Yes, Father!" It was the roar of the mighty ocean that separated Korea from the United States, but nothing separated this Korean god from his American children—nothing except the interpreter and the bulletproof glass.

The lying came easy. It is often easier to lie than tell the truth—and with the understanding that lying is really the work of God, it is a lead-pipe cinch for the master and zombies as well. For what is there to prohibit the easy lie but the pangs of conscience. Once you get that out of your system it's all roses.

"If opponents of our church continue to persecute God's will, God will invite them into the Spirit world."

He said a lot more, and he got no argument. The exhaustion ploy worked like a charm, it always did. Of course, they were also too exhausted to understand what he was saying, so a lot of words floated under the bridge until he finished with "...and I say to you tonight, the Messiah has come again and he is here with us to guide us on our heavenly mission of unifying the world and driving out socialism."

A roar of approval went up. The zombies didn't realize they were cheering because the speech was over and they could go to bed; nor did these unseasoned in the reverend's theology realize when he spoke of the Messiah's return, he was talking about himself.

—*Frankie Foxxe*
Cults and Brainwashing in the U.S.

Well, you can all live for Jesus,
because he's coming back real soon.
No it will not be ol' Buddha
that's sittin' on the throne.
And it won't be ol' Mohammed
that's calling us home,
And it won't be Hare Krishna
that plays the trumpet tune.
And we're going to see the Son,
and not Reverend Moon.

—*Mark Farrow*
Oh Buddha

THE GOSPEL ACCORDING TO

FATHER FRANKIE

"Jesus Christ, Frankie, you were a goddamn priest."

The telephone sizzled on my ear. My thoughts had been drifting now and again to Rachel Brighton and here she was, calling with a bombast I found annoying.

"Who told you that?"

"The guy who answered the phone," she said. "He said, 'Don't tell me you're getting involved with that ex-priest?'"

"Rob Houston," I muttered. "He would."

"It made me wonder," she said. "Am I?"

"Are you what?"

"Getting involved with an ex-priest?" Rachel asked, then her voice turned excited again. "But, my God, Frankie—no wonder you wouldn't tell me your story. I'll bet it's just the tip of the iceberg."

"No, I'd say that was pretty much of the iceberg."

"But there's more. Like, why aren't you a priest now? Like, why are you so gaga about debunking religion? The cat's out of the bag, Frankie, tell me all."

I let go of a defenseless chortle. Rachel was, I thought, a rather straightforward kind of girl. Not at all what I was used to. There was a spark of life there, an engaging sort of excitement.

"The reason I'm calling," she said, "is I have some news I thought you might find interesting." She paused.

"Well, what is it?" I prodded her. It was not the best time to chat, I had a deadline and I had barely begun to think about the piece.

"I don't know," she giggled suddenly. "Now that I think about it, with this priest shtick and all, I don't know if I should have called you."

"Why not, Rachel?"

"You sound a little distant today. You angry I know you were a priest?"

"No, no, I have some work to do is all."

"Okay, call me when you're free."

"*Rachel, what's the news?*"

"Lunch—when you have time?"

"Okay—I'll meet you in a half-hour at Calypso Pork Rinds."

"Okay."

When I slipped the phone back in its cradle, I found myself strangely titillated. Not by what the news could be, but that Rachel had wanted to see me.

†　　　　†　　　　†

When your girlfriend tells you she has news for you, what's your first thought?

She's pregnant, right?

I couldn't work it out mathematically.

Of course, those thoughts lead me back to the Mobile motel, the quaintly named Restawyle, and by my calculation Ernie Jo rested there just awyle—very comfortably fitting into a one-hour TV, as well as his "hostess's," time slot.

Aside from the hilarious getup to hide from his legion of fans, Ernie Jo's visit to the Restawyle Motel bordered on insanity—when you consider how righteous he was about other flock fleecers who stray from his Biblical ideal. He'd already put his reputation on the line with that poor guy he'd accused of having "many affairs so repugnant to God and the Body of Christ that I'm embarrassed just to talk about them. But it is a cancer on the Body of Christ and I say remove it afore it spreads." The guy has sued Ernie Jo for slander, but he was stripped of his ministry just the same. Some thought the church organization a little hasty in taking Ernie Jo's word for it, and thought perhaps they were kowtowing to their Gulfport star at the expense of a shepherd with a modest-sized flock, but the deed was done.

Now Ernie Jo was about to spring the same trap on another of his fellow clergy, and here he was, in the identical activity himself. Lordy, as Ernie Jo would say, it boggles the mind.

I was only five minutes late for Rachel, a virtual record for me, and found her waiting at the table in the back corner.

I guess I had been stingy with Rachel with information about my past. Sure, it was selfish—I didn't want to scare her away. She was a modern take-it-or-leave-it girl about religion. We'd had many discussions about God, faith, beliefs, religion—and she always impressed me as a levelheaded agnostic, though she did say one day that she really wanted to believe there was some greater force out there than mere humans, who would get back at us if we screwed up. But other than a feeble hope for a god of retribution, who, if we are honest, we would want to punish our enemies more than ourselves, Rachel didn't believe any of those "stories" like Noah's flood, Jonah in the belly of the whale, the Immaculate Conception and the Resurrection. She also thought the rich would be first in heaven, if there were such a place, and not one of them would be stuck in the eye of a needle.

My kind of girl.

The meeting of my seat with the maroon Naugahyde booth set her in motion.

"I have this girlfriend, see, and her name is Jenny—and, well, frankly, she is throwing herself away on this creep—this Devil's Disciple kind of guy with the motorcycle and the smelly black-leather jacket and the whole bit.

"But Jenny's all right. We were friends growing up in school and all and we, like, kept in touch all these years—I'll call her one week, she'll call the next—no matter where we are we keep in touch.

"Last week I tried to get her in L.A., where she's living with that creep—and nothing. I couldn't get her for days. She forgot to turn on her machine or something— and I thought of you when she told me—get this—she spent the weekend with *Jesus Christ!* And he's black—like Indian or something. I mean, doesn't that just knock you out? So I said, 'Come on,' ya know, but she says, 'No, it's true, I swear it. You see it with your own eyes, you'll believe it, believe me.'"

"Jesus!" I said.

"You bet your life," she said.

I lapsed into a silence I could see was bugging Rachel.

"What are you thinking?" she asked, watching my eyelids compress in cogitation.

"I've a feeling if your friend's so gaga over this guy, he'll be worth seeing. Before you know it he'll have a hundred Rolls-Royces. Those black messiahs with the bedroom eyes could rule the world."

"But that's just the thing. This one preaches poverty. Riches of Spirit and that whole enchilada. Just like the Bible — none of that God-wants-us-to-be-rich stuff to justify the Rolls or the pad in Palm Springs."

"Lot of them start that way," I said. "It's a good hook."

"I suppose," Rachel mused, not convinced.

"I can do a story that'll wipe this guy off the face of the earth."

"Sounds combative, Frankie. He's preaching love. Is that so terrible?"

"Oh, I'll love him first. Build him up so the fall has some drama."

"Jeez, Father Foxxe, may I call you Father?"

"Cut it out."

"You haven't even seen the guy and you're taking on like a nutcase."

"Oh, I've seen him, all right, a hundred times over. His kind are a dime a dozen."

Rachel giggled.

"What's so funny?" I asked.

"I was just thinking Father Frankie is better than Father Foxxe, I'm going to call you Father Frankie."

"Very funny."

"So, how are you going to do this story, Father Frankie? By remote?"

"Cut it out, Rachel," I said, then furrowed my forehead. "I'll have to go out there and interview him."

"Maybe he doesn't give interviews."

"You kidding? Those fake messiahs are publicity starved. Whatever they get, it's never enough. This could be my big break. A national exclusive byline. Get me free of that idiot, Houston. I could syndicate the story. Be discovered by a *real* newspaper."

"You know what I think?" Rachel asked me.

"What?"

"I think you should start trading on your ex-priest status. Could be very big. A kind of P.R. hook—then you could say you were dating an ex-Moonie girl."

I opened my eyes. "Am I?"

"I don't know how else you could explain our traveling together across the country in search of the true Jesus."

† † †

When I got back to the *Riptide* after lunch, my boss, the bore of the Gulf Coast, called me in to tell me Ernie Jo Banghart was taking his circus (not his words exactly) out to Los Angeles for a weekend miracle.

"Just like that?" I asked.

He nodded, the smoke blessedly clouding my view of the man. "Do us a piece."

"Why's he doing this all of a sudden? We're talking five days to a weekend—he can hardly drive his props in that time."

"Ask him, dingbat. Use your pea brain once in a blue moon."

Rob spoke in such eloquent prose. I did realize he wanted me to do the story remote control, but I had an idea: wouldn't it be great if I could get him to finance my trip to see the mountain messiah?

"Rob," I said, with a sad face, "there's no way in the world I could go out there this weekend."

It set him thinking. I could guess the first words that came to his mind were, "I don't want you to go out there, dingbat." Perhaps he'd add, "One of Ernie Jo's services is much like the other." But instead, old Rob's smoked cerebellum was cranking its rusty gears.

"That so?" he said, with an inflated eyebrow. "Since when do you set the rules around here?"

"I'm just telling you," I said. "Not this weekend."

"Well, Jesus, *lah*-di-*dah*," Rob said, shaking his hand on the end of his wrist as though his fingers had just touched something untouchable. I knew I was getting to him. "You'll do what I tell you to do—what's so big about this weekend?"

"Personal stuff," I mumbled as though embarrassed.

"What personal stuff?" he pressed.

I shook my head. "Personal."

He shook his head. "Change it!" he bellowed, with a fist on his desk—and I heaved a sigh of defeat. The great man had bested me once again.

"If you insist," I said, and that was how Rob Houston and the *Gulfport Riptide* happened to pick up my airline tickets.

It is the test of a good religion whether
you can make a good joke about it.

—*G.K. Chesterton*

THE GOSPEL ACCORDING TO

SHERIFF STONEY JESSUP

I never heard anything
like it in my life.

They had to go past my place to get to Jack's place and the cars just did not stop. It was like a hundred miles of string unraveling up the hill from the flatlands to Glory Pines and on to Jack's meadow.

When I got to Jack's place and saw the hordes of people, I wondered if I shouldn't have worn my uniform. Probably better not. One lone peace officer didn't stand a Chinaman's chance against a mob. It's funny how so many people have a built-in resentment against cops.

I almost couldn't believe my eyes when I laid them on all the folks. It was as though a city had emptied out from some nuclear threat or something and they had all leaked out on the remote, quiet, mind-your-own-business kind of place—Glory Pines.

There was a number of Devil's Disciples out there, but they were cleaned up, so I hardly recognized them. There was the usual assortment of kids with rings in their noses, looking like some prize warthog or something, but I wasn't looking for trouble. I was looking for Jack Whitehall. But in this crowd it was like looking for a needle in a haystack.

I found Jack Whitehall guarding his door. I figured this so-called Jesus was in there and Jack was a self-appointed guard.

When I got up to where Jack stood, the first thing I noticed was there was no smell of alcohol about him. That was a first as far as I was concerned.

"'Lo, Sheriff," Jack said, and I didn't detect any edge on his tone. I thought he knew why I was sniffing, but he didn't say anything.

"Toilets?" I wanted to know. "Where you got the toilets?"

"You gotta use the toilet, Sheriff? It's in the house."

"The house? For this crowd? How many you got?"

"Two."

"Two toilets? You need a hundred of them."

"I'm sorry, Sheriff. We had no idea this many people would come here. Nothing was planned—no announcements or any-thing—it's just—a miracle."

"Then work another miracle and get some toilets up here or I'm shutting you down."

Jack surveyed the crowd, then the road and parking lot... "How long you figure it would take to get the toilets up here?"

"No idea."

"It's two hours from the freeway as it is, I hear."

"Then tell 'em to go home."

Jack smiled in spite of himself. "Sir," he said—and he didn't sound smart-alecky—"that's an announcement I'll let you make."

"Well, they're on your property and you don't have a permit. So, you move 'em off."

"Tell you what, Sheriff. Our best bet is you go back, put your uniform on, come back with your bullhorn and some real authority in your voice and see if you can clear 'em out. It's our best shot."

Jack was a laid-back guy. He talked like he was singing in a bar somewhere. It was soothing, all right, but it wasn't what I wanted to hear.

"Look here," I said. "I'll do no such thing. I'm ordering you to disband this unlawful assembly under penalty of arrest."

Jack checked the swelling crowd again and sighed. "Okay, Sheriff—why don't you come with me—put some authority into it."

"Not me. I'm outta uniform."

"Ah, yes." Jack moved over to the front of the crowd.

"May I have your—may I have—can you hear me?" He was yelling but the crowd didn't seem to be in the mood to quiet for anything short of the main event. Jack realized how hopeless it was, looked at me for understanding, but I just waved a hand for him to do his duty.

"Sheriff Jessup says our meeting today is illegal..." There was some booing from those who heard him. "Says we need more toilets for so many people," the crowd laughed, "and permits and what not, and he asks that you all disband. Go back where you came from and maybe we'll be able to plan the thing properly."

Jeers, hoots, boos. Jack shrugged his shoulders and walked

back to me. "Best I can do," he said. "Gotta leave the rest in the hands of the law."

Hang it all, I thought, and looked again at the endless bodies. I saw them as one big powder keg ready to blow. Lord, I wondered, what would Ernie Jo Banghart think if he saw this? "Don't pull this on me again, Jack," I said sternly, "or so help me I'll make an arrest."

"Yes, sir," Jack said. "Next time we'll get toilets."

"Next time? Oughtn'ta be a next time, you know what's good for you. Hell's bells, Jack," I said, man to man, "we got a quiet community here, you don't wanta be go making a circus out of it, do you?"

"Don't know, Sheriff," Jack said, "the Lord moves in mysterious ways."

That little episode brought home to me how little effect I could have when the outnumbering was so staggering. It gave me all the excuse I needed to leave Glory Pines. It was my day off, anyway, and the sign was on my door to call the next jurisdiction in case of trouble.

Still, I started to get nervous as I drove down the hill in my little sheriff's car and saw all those cars going up.

There just wasn't anything could keep me from an Ernie Jo Banghart revival meeting this close to home.

I can hardly see how anyone ought to wish Christianity to be true: for if so, the plain language of the text seems to show that the men who do not believe, and this would include my father, brother, and almost all my best friends, will be everlastingly punished. And this is a damnable doctrine.

—*Charles Darwin*
A passage in his autobiography
expunged by his family

THE GOSPEL ACCORDING TO

FRANKIE FOXXE

The Shrine Auditorium in Los Angeles had to be the kitsch capital of the world.

With a pair of contented camels on either side of the stage topped with Muslim minarets, you knew you were as close to heaven as you were going to get—if you happened to be a Muslim.

Ernie Jo Banghart would turn the place Christian in a hurry.

Rachel and I arrived early to ensure a good seat, but we needn't have worried. The house was surprisingly sparse.

In the foyer, a woman with a microphone was breathlessly making a news event out of the latest gathering. She was par for the local-television-interview scene. Ask enough mindless questions and sooner or later some jerk would say something she could glom onto for a fifteen-second bite.

The woman with the mike, made up to a fare-thee-well, was trying to stir things up by asking questions of those unmade-up souls among us, contrasting her striking TV beauty with their washed-out selves. Did they see some ominous portent in the dramatically reduced audience? Would the presence of Jesus adversely affect the Ernie Jo Banghart Ministries? But this was the hard-core faithful, and as near as I could tell, they all hewed the party line.

A pasty-faced citizen was praising the Lord and Ernie Jo Banghart for the TV crew as Rachel and I went down front in the auditorium, which must have had six thousand seats underroof. But, from the way the faithful were trickling in, you could tell it would be a washout.

On the arms of the aisle seats of the tenth row, were signs that said:

No children under 12
in the first 10 rows

We found a couple of seats between a white, frail woman in her eighties and a young girl who couldn't claim more than seventeen years, who was teeming with child and who sat with her hand on her belly, as though the music of sweet Jesus would pass on through the womb to the fetus. Beside her, her innocent-faced husband looked like he might have taken the wrong freeway exit and ended up here instead of Chavez Ravine for a Dodger baseball game.

Brucie Banghart, in a brown suit, with a pencil moustache, sauntered to the microphone mid-stage. He adjusted it up, then down, then tightened the screw. He had a sheaf of papers in one hand that he consulted from time to time, as though he were working up to delivering himself of a weighty oration.

"Welcome to the Ernie Jo Banghart old-fashioned revival. It's good to see ya all here today. How many of ya comin' t'morrah night?"

Most of the hands waved heavenward.

"Well, that's jist great. Now, I gotta special treat for ya folks as our thanks for ya comin' on out today. We got tapes an' we're sellin' 'em at a one-time-only special of two dollars."

The band was in the back of the stage, between some potted palms. It was the usual assortment of gospel rockers with a whole range of guitars, keyboard, piano, string bass, and the drums, oh, yes, the drums. The drums beat out the thumping rhythms that got the blood racing in this Jesus-loving crowd. Only the drummer was new. Rumor had it that the former drummer was guilty of getting the blood of the Reverend Banghart's daughter-in-law racing a mite too fast. Brucie's wife, Anita, was seated now primly at the piano, and whether or not she was pining away for the missing drummer, I couldn't be sure. But one thing I did know for sure, and that was everyone had a secret somewhere. That much I'd learned in my trade.

Over to the side of the stage were several rows of chairs. Brucie Banghart came from the microphone to the front row of these stage chairs and swung his arms over the empty chair next to him, chewing his gum and going over some computer printouts, trying to figure out what in tarnation all those numbers meant.

I leaned over to Rachel. "What do you think Brucie is trying to figure out on those computer printouts?"

She shrugged.

"I'll bet he's poring over those numbers, which are like

Greek to him, to tell his dad how much it costs them to put on the show. Then he'll know how hard to squeeze 'em for the offering."

Anita moved her fingers over the keyboard almost without effort in her high-necked blouse, red blazer and blue skirt. You could almost mistake her for a real-estate saleswoman. I tried, I really did, but I just could not see her stepping out on her husband. But my experience on the receiving end of the confessional taught me you couldn't tell anything by looks.

While I was watching Brucie, I wondered what kind of job he could hold down if it weren't for his daddy. A pole climber for the telephone company, maybe, but I doubted he had the coordination. An airline ticket clerk, or would he be able to keep all *those* numbers straight? He apparently didn't have any music ability or he might be in the band. No, I decided Brucie was a lucky boy.

The music had reached earsplitting proportions when I turned to case the house. It was pathetic, with about two thirds of the ground floor empty and the balcony bare. I'm sure the ushers had instructions not to open it until the first floor was full. It made for better photography.

"God, doesn't this insufferable pounding of this 'Jesus saving your soul' music get you down?"

"Don't listen to the words," Rachel said.

"But the music! How can you stand this music? It's been going on for over an hour."

"Oh, the music's fine," she said.

After ninety minutes of the rollicking, frolicking music, the people occasionally whipping themselves in a minor frenzy, waving their arms, kicking their heels, gyrating their bodies, the royal family began to trickle onto the stage. Mrs. Ernie Jo Banghart came on with her grandchildren, two little boys in cute little blue blazers and ties, neither one within spitting distance of eight. They sat themselves down a few chairs away from their father, whose concentration on the computer printout remained unbroken, while the mastication of his gum proceeded at a reliable pace.

Ernie Jo sauntered on, in the middle of a song, from stage

left. The polished quartet with shiny faces and happy prepackaged smiles were singing their hearts out for blessed Jesus, and Ernie was fumbling with his tie tack. He moseyed out again and made another entrance, as though he were just one of the boys in the band. He crossed to center stage, picked up his guitar, and joined in the merrymaking. When the music stopped, he came up to the microphone and said, "You know, this thing is worth about two cents and I can't find the other half of it, so that means I have a one-cent tie tack," and he giggled.

"Emmy Sue, I want you to come up here." Emily Sue made her way up to the microphone in her oyster-white Chanel dress with a gem-studded six-inch-tall belt wrapped around her.

Emily Sue was a woman who knew how to take care of herself, and though she had been married at fifteen, she had seen to it that life had been good to her.

"Emmy Sue," he said, "you remember that time we were in that motel and I forgot to bring my handkerchief from my pocket and you gave me that shoe mitt from that motel room?" Emily Sue smiled, her broad, winning, Southern smile, nodding her head vigorously. "Now, what am I gonna do about this tie tack?"

She said, "Well, get another one. They're only two cents."

I turned and whispered to Rachel, "Let's see if he mentions his ten-thousand-dollar Rolex watch."

"Now, you know," Rachel said quietly, "these people don't expect their preachers to be poor. It isn't seemly. They're interested in success. If God brings success to the preacher, He could to bring it to the parishioner."

"You know I couldn't do without you, honey," Ernie Jo was saying from center stage.

Emily Sue was beaming from ear to ear. "And you know I'm not going to let you do without me."

"Well, let's have another song," Ernie Jo said, and the band struck up to his arm beats. Ernie Jo picked up his guitar, hoisted his leg, planted his foot square center of the chair and strummed away and began to sing. Now, as the woman said to the interviewer out back, "You just gotta be there to feel it. There's no explaining what the singing of Ernie Jo does for people. It sure floods them in the Spirit of the Lord, for starters." This disappointing gathering of the faithful just went wild.

They were shouting "Oh, Jesus" and "Yes, Lord, God be praised." A woman cursed by being born into a class that couldn't afford orthodontia, paraded her overbite up and down the aisles, dancing, singing, her arms waving in the air, like a heavily sedated presidential candidate. I turned to Rachel. "Do you think they are ever going to get to the speaking service? I bet when the song is over, Ernie Jo says, 'Let's sing it one more time.'" After that, Ernie Jo said, "One more time," and again, "One more time," until he had said "One more time" five times and the chorus had been repeated five times.

Finally, Ernie Jo picked up his microphone, unbuttoned his collar, loosened his tie and rolled his shoulders up like a football lineman, poised for the tackle. "Oh, Lordy," he said. "Praise Jesus, there just ain't nothing like it.

"Folks," he said, "we've got something special for you today, our way of saying thank you for you all comin' out. We had this here special Bible made, two special Bibles really. Our regular one with the leather-like vinyl cover, and our smaller version for the ladies. Now, in this ladies' version we have all the women's passages high-lighted and annotated on the side there so you can see just what our Lord had to say to the women of the world. It cost us a lot of money to have these specials made, but that don't matter none. I only wish we could give one to every man, woman and child today, but I'm sorry we just can't afford it. So, for your donation of just a hunderd dollars or more, we're going to give you one of these right now. If you'll just come up here, formin' a line there in the center, and come up and wrap around here, I'm gonna shake everybody's hand here who gets one of these Bibles from us for your donation of only a hunderd dollars or more."

People stood up and headed for the aisle. A roly-poly guy in a rent-a-cop getup stood two rows in front of us and danced his way to the middle aisle to join the faithful with their hundred-dollar checks in hand or even just a wad of cash. They marched down to the orchestra pit to hand the money to Brucie Banghart. Rachel Brighton turned to me and said, "Oh, look, there's a cop for Jesus." I found out later that was Stoney Jessup, the sheriff of Glory Pines.

Ernie Jo pulled his guitar-strumming chair up to the lip of the stage, sat down and reached down to shake the hands of the Bible buyers, which were thrust high over their heads to reach and touch the hand of the exalted reverend where he reposed in his chair. He smiled only as Ernie Jo can smile. He sure was grateful for the donations, you could tell, but there were several functionaries in the orchestra pit keeping the line moving so as not to delay the service unnecessarily.

It was *carpe diem* time at the old Shrine Auditorium, and Ernie Jo was cashing in on the high emotional residue of the ninety-plus minutes of rockin' rollin' gospel hysteria. I estimated some two to three hundred faithful souls marched like lambs to hand over their hundred-dollar bills and their checks. Ernie Jo even took credit cards on the television, but I expect they ruled that out here as being too time consuming.

The donors' parade was dispatched in a tad under fifteen minutes. Ernie Jo stood up and said, "Well, I want you to know we appreciate it very, very much, and I say I wish we could give these away to ever'body here, but we just can't afford to do so. Now, my boy, Brucie, tells me it costs seventy thousand dollars to put on one of these crusades, and that's without any salaries whatsoever, just the transportation costs, the housing costs, and the rentals. Now, as you know, we don't charge admission, but we would appreciate it so very much if you would help us to defray some of these expenses in return for our coming here today. Our ushers will pass among you in just a few moments, and I won't tell you what to give. Just remember that what you give is between you and the Lord." When the bucket came to me I gave a dollar bill, folded over so someone might think it were a ten. Rachel passed the bucket on without putting anything in, and I noticed that about three quarters of the people in our row let it go by without making a deposit. It wasn't until the buckets of cash disappeared behind the scenes that Ernie Jo said to the faithful, "Now, will you turn with me in your Bibles, please, to—" and hunkered down for the day's message.

Ernie Jo had taken as his springboard text one of those verses about the waters coming down from the mountains and cleansing the souls of the earthly sinners.

There was some buildup about geography and the demographics of the time and what it all must have been like for the poor simple folk of the Bible.

The pitch rose perfervidly, then fell like a strong tide.

"And, oh, those waters, those waters, *those waters* will wash over you like the blood of the Lamb, and they will wash you *clean* and you will walk straight on the path of *righteousness* again—and be born *again* to our Lord and Savior, Je-sus Christ."

Ernie Jo trembled, he got down on his knees, he waved his Bible in the air and the pages fluttered like a flock of butterflies, and the audience was right with him every step of the way—on their feet, waving their own Bibles, dancing in the aisles, twisting their bodies in ecstasy.

"Oh, Lordy, Jesus, we miserable sinners—wash us all in the blood of the Lamb—cleanse our hearts and minds so we may be more acceptable to You in Your holy goodness and infinite wisdom—glory, hallelujah—praise God Almighty!"

It was one of Ernie Jo's peaks. There would be many in the "sermon" portion of the service, which rang in at just a touch under two hours. Peaks and valleys were his trademark. And it was not for nothing he had those ratings. No one did what Ernie Jo did better than Ernie Jo.

The Reverend Banghart sauntered across the stage; he walked like an Italian stud one minute and a tabby cat the next.

But when Ernie Jo walked the walk of Calvary, it was as though he were weighted down with the bulk of the True Cross, and he was like a bull moose, and woe betide any mortal who got in his path.

I knew Ernie Jo had to be vastly disappointed in the size of the crowd, he was used to standing room wherever he went, but whatever his feelings, he didn't stint on his showmanship.

There was no reading, no consulting notes. Ernie Jo would toss off a few Bible verses from the book in his hand, and that was all he needed. I'm sure he could have easily memorized those verses, too, but it gave him an excuse to hold his Bible for his exhortations, and that Bible in his hand gave him authority with his flock.

The marathon wound down with the inevitable altar call for the miserable sinners to come forward and proclaim in front of their fellow miserable sinners that from this day forward, they would accept Jesus Christ as their personal Savior, which would save them for all eternity. It was their ticket into heaven, Ernie Jo assured them.

"Now, this don't mean you gonna live perfect lives, ain't none of us perfect, but you take Jesus into your hearts now in front of your brothers and sisters in Christ and He'll be there for you when the time comes. I don't care what you heard elsewhere, good works is not the way to heavenly salvation—you got to be born again in Jesus—washed by the blood of the Lamb—and hold Him in your heart and mind and accept Jesus Christ as your personal Savior; now, folks, if you'll just come up here in the orchestra pit, I'll ask you the one burning question of mankind and I'll pray for you personally."

I couldn't tell the percentage of folks who dribbled to the orchestra pit who were legit and who were the ringers. Fifty-fifty at best.

Emmy Sue came to the edge of the stage and crouched down a ways from her husband. She pinched her eyes tightly closed and followed with the clamping together of her nylon-stockinged legs to minimize the impure thoughts in the pit.

After the ceremony concluded with hurrahs and shouts of hallelujahs, and another huzzah from the band for good measure, Rachel and I made our way backstage. A half-dozen souls separated us from Sheriff Stoney Jessup. We saw him receive a great bear hug from Ernie Jo. I picked up the tail end of the conversation when the sheriff said, "You be sure and let me know if there is anything else I can help you with." Ernie Jo expressed appreciation and claimed that he would indeed. The sheriff seemed like he was going to ask something else, but the request caught in his throat. When the sheriff moved to the side, Ernie Jo handed the returned Bible to a functionary, who returned the cop's hundred-dollar check.

"Well, well, well, Frankie Foxxe," Ernie Jo said, with a hale and hearty, almost sincere greeting. "What brings you to this neck of the woods?"

"Can you keep a secret, Ernie Jo?"

"Well, you know I can."

"I'm goin' to see Jesus."

"Ha ha ha ha," Ernie Jo could guffaw as well as the next feller. "Same old Frankie Foxxe."

"No, I'm serious, you oughta come along. Haven't you been predicting that he's gonna come back any time now? You could feel it in your bones, you said. He was comin' in our lifetime. Well, he's back."

"Ha ha ha ha. If I didn't know you better, Frankie, I'd say that was blasphemy."

"Well, what makes you think it isn't?"

"Ha ha ha. Same old Frankie. Haven't changed a bit."

"Thank you, Reverend. This is quite a show you put on here today—quite a show indeed. You give 'em an hour and a half of music and I thought you'd never say anything. What did the whole thing take, three, three and a half hours?"

"Well, we want to give their money's worth."

"Oh, you do that, I'll say that for you. Size of the turnout disappoint you at all?"

"Nah. I always say, Frankie, if I can reach one soul for Christ, I will be richly rewarded. We didn't advertise none. It was a spur-of-the-moment thing. Considering that, we did real good. Word'll get 'round. Tomorrow will be standing room only."

"Hmm," I said, needling him with my skepticism. "I'd like to get your reaction, Ernie Jo, on this fellow who says he's Jesus returned to earth."

"Nah, I heard, I heard tell about it. You know how many people think they're Jesus? Why, at any given time you could fill this auditorium with them. There's a lot of crazies around."

"But this guy might be the genuine article. I think you ough-ta check him out."

"No, no, no, no. There are no signs. You gotta have signs."
"What signs?"

"Well, read your Bible, Frankie. It tells ya just what's gonna happen—the trumpets, the angels, the earth is gonna shake. We'll all be called up in the twinkling of an eye."

"Well, maybe we misunderstood that. Maybe that happened and we didn't realize it."

"Ahh, same old Frankie. Tell me, where is this fellow hang-ing out?"

"Well, he's up in the mountains here—out near Idyllwild," I said—"sure I can't get you to go with me?"

"Love to, Frankie, but I gotta couple more services here. Then I gotta head back to Gulfport—but it's good to see ya again." He shook his head with a mocking grin. "That's a good one, Frankie," he said, but I could see he was worried. Then he passed on to the next well-wisher. Grasping the hand of some frail old woman, giving her a smile that reached from the Shrine Auditorium to the Coliseum. With the magnitude of Ernie Jo's smile, I pegged the dear old woman as a five-figure donor.

THE GOSPEL ACCORDING TO

FRANKIE FOXXE

"Over my dead body," was
the way I believe Rachel
put it, when I put it to her
the only way we'd ever see
Glory Pines was if we
could get off this parking
lot that used to be a freeway and rent a motorcycle.

We had to settle for a moped, and I had to leave double the deposit because the owner didn't think it would carry two of us up the mountain. When I told him that together we weighed less than some men (albeit real fat ones) and waved a hundred-dollar bill at him, he got religion, so to speak.

They were spread out over Jack Whitehall's acreage as far as the eye could see. It was a picnic-looking crowd, not a churchgoing contingent sprawled across the grass.

They had gathered here from word of mouth that spread like the flu from city to town, county to county—the word was that the Word was with him and this man was special. The air was warm with expectation.

The lucky ones who had made it to Jack's place at the top of the hill, and found something tenable to do with their cars, were scurrying to find a place close enough to see Jesus, without holding much hope for hearing him.

Rachel and I made our way to the field and saw the hopelessness of being anywhere near the speaker. I spotted a row of trees on a low hill on the far side of the multitudes, I took Rachel by the hand and we danced around the fringes until we came to a tall pine tree. I climbed it, then lowered my hands to pull Rachel up.

"Box seats," she said.

"Yeah," I said, "it's almost like being there."

"Jeez, you think we'll hear anything?"

"You see anything closer?"

She didn't.

It was a pleasant day, with a bright sun and cooling breeze—the leaves on the trees shimmering and catching the sunlight like crystal chandeliers.

I looked out over the mass of people on this field and tried to imagine they were forming some picture—like the computer-generated Abraham Lincoln or one of those Chuck Close paintings made with little squares of color. I tried to imagine it was the face of Jesus, then of Rachel. Then I thought I'd settle for a landscape of any sort, or a sailboat.

Nothing. It was just a huge mass of unrelated people, as logically arranged as spilt milk.

This crowd was America. Fat boys with pockmarked faces and wily kids running around waiting for something good to happen. Excitement. For some it was excitement enough to get out of a crowded, stuffy apartment into the fresh air. An outing. Who were these people out in the field below the trees? Auto mechanics, word processors, teachers, secretaries, anyone who wondered about the meaning of life. How to put it all together. How to explain the trees and flowers and beetles.

But where do you go to the bathroom when there are no bathrooms? And if you didn't bring enough to eat or drink you could starve to death till the road cleared. The mom-and-pop grocery down the hill was sold out of anything you could eat.

There were grandmas with white hair, some on the blue side, men in jeans, men in suits. Women in granny dresses, women in shorts and halter tops, designer jeans hugging their curvy rumps with a tenacity that beckons the boys to "Be fruitful and multiply, replenish the earth and renew it." Girls in prim dress, trying not to be too obvious about looking at the boys—young boys and girls trying to look bored.

And the males, from pre-teens on, will be watching those fabricked spheres as they undulate by them, building their own lust for multiplication.

For if God formed man from the dust of the ground and breathed into his nostrils the breath of life—that was his business. These boys had a different methodology in mind. And the girls who were generous enough to dress with the soul of the magnet would surely draw to them the eyes of the studs.

You were bound to get bumped in a crowd this size, and they were still coming. They never *stopped* coming. Over the rise at the top of the hill—up the road (God knew where they were leaving the cars), and sometimes they just appeared from nowhere.

Middle America, I'd say from the look of them. In spite of a few erudite faces—probably here with some sociological curiosity—they seemed largely undereducated and overfed and their curiosity was not of the intellect but of the emotional possibilities. Were they the truants from Ernie Jo Banghart's crusade? And how many of these spread out on this vast field, shoulder to shoulder with their fellows, truly believed? Were these the hard-core Christians or were they curiosity seekers? Were they open to miracles like Rachel was, or were they skeptics like me? What promise could bring so many people to an unknown field so many miles from anything that the cars could hardly move?

I remember studying Orson Welles's late-1930s radio program, *War of the Worlds*, in sociology class, and though they announced that the program was a dramatization, thousands of people fled their homes in their cars because they feared alien monsters were about to abduct them.

Was this a similar phenomenon? I was intrigued by the statistics. If ninety percent of Americans believed in God and sixty percent went to church, how many thought it was possible for Jesus Christ to return to earth and hold court in a grassy field in Glory Pines, California?

I asked Rachel what she thought.

"I don't know," she said. "The fundamentalists, for sure. What is that—twenty to thirty percent of Christians?"

"Maybe that's high. Half of the Christians are Catholics, and they don't push the return of Jesus. Too smart. Too busy keeping the flock in line for the confessional."

"Oh, Frankie, you're such a cynic."

"Thank you," I said.

"It gets old," she said, her face fading like a spent bloom. Then she brightened like an opening rosebud turning toward the sun. "Oh, but your thing was in the confessional, wasn't it? Tell me about it, will you?"

"Confidential," I said, hoping to turn her off.

"Okay, I don't need any names. Generalities—I'll bet it was fascinating. You know, hearing all that...stuff."

"Boring," I said.

"Come on, Frankie," she coaxed me with the slanted eye of the minx. "Did it turn you on?"

"Oh, my," I said in an effort to dismiss the thought, but the reality was sometimes it did, and more than once I suspected the women (of all ages) of deliberately trying to get me worked up.

"Come on, Frankie—"

"You don't want to know," I said. "Confessional is the hell of the priesthood. Listening to all that guilt spill out, sins and degradation, real and imagined—it was all so...depressing."

"So what did you do about it?"

"Tried to cope—unsuccessfully." There was a long silence between us—a rather sweet respite during which long-suppressed memories came to the fore. "There was this old Irish priest, Mickey McGinley was his name—letting him hang onto his job was an act of Christian charity."

"Fitting," Rachel said.

"He was my confessor. After the load got too much for me to bear, I spilled it all out to him. 'Oh, me boy,' he said—he had a pretty thick brogue, which I always suspected him of phonying for effect. 'Let me give you a tip. Don't listen—entirely. You catch the gist for the penance and tune out the details. It's good to have a few catch phrases at your disposal. For adultery I say, "Everyone gets lonely sometimes—" I find it's very comforting—to both of us.'"

"Jeez," Rachel said. "Priests are that cynical?"

"You don't know the half," I said. "'Anyway,' old Mickey said. 'Now, for example, Father, when you go blathering on about your impure thoughts, I tune you right out. *Every*one has impure thoughts, and most think they are the only ones to have such thoughts. I found it mildly titillating in the beginning, but when you've heard the same impure thoughts for over fifty years, it gets old, I'm bound to tell you. The good Lord gave us flexible minds—

minds open to all kinds of debris, and you shouldn't be surprised to find out some impurities will slip through the most rigid of filters. No, don't argue, Father, this fine-tuning out of the gory, boring details is a must or we'd all be in the loony bin, and then who would be left to hear confessions?'"

"He sounds like an interesting guy."

"Yeah," I said, looking over the crowd. "I remember one of my penitents, a young woman—couple kids and a no-good husband—to hear the women tell it, most husbands were no good, so I started tuning that out. This one I should have tuned in—she was lamenting her inability to please her husband. I threw in a catch phrase as soon as she caught a breath. I don't even remember what it was. Something trite, meant to be comforting—probably something about her husband pleasing her, or trying to, or does he, or something. I could tell by her silence she had never considered their marriage on an equal footing—she thought *she* had to do all the pleasing. Next thing I know, hubby's beaten the daylights out of her and I'm devastated.

"Father McGinley hears me out—probably sleeping through the details—and you know what he tells me?"

"What?"

"'Ah, Father, we mustn't interfere in the families. We can't make the rules if we don't play the game.'"

"Humh," Rachel said, then clicked her tongue.

I looked at her and thought, I must really care for her more than I realize, or I wouldn't have told her all that. I didn't tell her what I was thinking, but then I saw I didn't have to. The twinkle of satisfaction in her eye told me she was thinking the same thing.

Down below us, a young couple cradled a baby, first in his arms, then in hers. When the baby fussed, she hauled out an engorged breast and the child took it, offering mutual relief.

The young couple with their baby were becalmed in the vortex of the whirlwind around them. The young man beamed over the child at the mother's breast and gently stroked the downy blond hair. "You're going to see Jesus Christ," the young man spoke softly with a faint ethereal voice. "Our Lord and Savior," he said. "It will be a good, strong beginning for your life."

The young mother's eyes lifted from her child to her husband. They glowed with love and anticipation. "You say the nicest things," she said.

"You hear that, Rachel?" I said.

I don't think she liked my tone, for she shot me the most withering glance. "What about it?" she said with a challenging twist of her pellucid lips. "Oh, Frankie," she winced, "this is a beautiful thing. You want to sully the faith of the children? Why are you so negative all the time?"

How long, I wondered, until the young man realizes his wife has replaced him with the baby? Will he beat her, turn sullen, spew verbal abuse, or will he be one of the lucky few whose wives make room for them between the nursing and the diaper changing table? Maybe their strong belief in Jesus will help them. In her present mood, I decided not to share any of that with Rachel.

She looked lovely up in the tree. She was a rugged individual who looked frail. Her skin was translucent in the strong sunlight, her virtually nonexistent nose casting a faint, scant shadow on her angelic lips. Anticipation possessed her. Rachel seemed like a person who wanted, with an engaging painfulness, to believe.

Then for the first time I noticed television crews roaming with their cameras and lights. The privacy snatchers at work. I turned to Rachel. "First in war, first in peace, and first in the hearts of their countrymen."

"You got something against TV, too?" She asked in a manner so foreboding I didn't dare tell her the truth.

"Chewing gum for the eyes," I said, quoting someone, I forgot who.

"There are a lot of good things on television," she said, adding to the pile of our irreconcilable differences. "And this is going to be one of them."

I'm sure my jaw dropped as I looked at her. "You know that even before you hear him?"

She shrugged. "I have a feeling," she said, "a pretty serious, deep feeling. I can't explain it."

I looked at her as I would at any two-headed, no-nosed girl.

She looked back. "You were expecting a myth-debunking clone?" she asked with annoying aplomb. "I want to hear more about your priest gig." I ignored her. Perching in a tree is a good venue for ignoring someone. What I gave her was not enough. It is never enough.

Watching the TV crews made me think of how everyone had some purpose in his life, like these drones shuffling around on the grass, trying to disseminate the joys of the day.

Below us, the baby seemed to be sleeping on his mother's breast, when suddenly he jerked awake and began to whimper. The mother lifted the child over her shoulder in a graceful, practiced motion. The mother patted gently the child's back while the father looked on, with a smile of loving pride.

The baby began to cry, as though he were a turn-on toy. "Shh," said the mother, "Shh," said the father, but the baby kept on crying.

"Hush, little baby, don't you cry—" the father said softly, "Jesus is coming."

But the baby didn't stop his frightened and frightening crying. The child rejected the proffer of another breast; rocking, burping, patting were all for naught.

Just as suddenly as the wind-up crying had started, it stopped. It was as though the child sensed some calming influence. I looked across the field and saw "Jesus" suddenly appear as if from nowhere, his white robes fluttering in the holy breeze. You could hear the rustling of the pine needles against the cones. He wafted to the center of the throng as though he had been carried there effortlessly on that light, holy breeze. He stopped to face the crowd, with a line of stout-hearted pines behind him.

It was a blanket of people that sat silently, motionless, while the man spoke. He wasn't asking anything but to cut the hate out of their hearts, but I had the uncomfortable feeling if he had asked them to set themselves on fire we'd all be roasting in no time.

I watched him with my ferret-out-the-baloney eyes, and I was having a tough time. He was good, all right—I don't mean to suggest I thought he was Jesus returned—but for a motivational speaker, I couldn't fault him.

As he spoke, I was, in spite of myself, engaged in his subject. He was a superb pitchman—low-key, quietly dramatic tenor voice, hardly any gesturing, no histrionics. No razzmatazz. It was as though Ernie Jo Banghart had gone to Harvard and charm school simultaneously. There was an intelligence coming out of the speaker that threw me. If I had to speculate on what Jesus would have been like, had I believed there ever *was* a Jesus, I would, rather, have said he would have been more folksy, with a nice golden, honey-baked Banghart baritone voice without the twang. I did see him as laid-back, but this bird had a quiet intensity that grabbed you by the shirt and drew you up close to him, and said, "Listen up, this is important."

They sat in front of Jesus, bending the grass over for good. The bodies touched one another, there were so many of them. There didn't seem to be any of the pushing or shoving or territorial jealousies you would expect from the aggregation of so many strangers in one tightly packed place. There was, instead, a strange serenity. I can imagine a field of extras in a Cecil B. De Mille Bible epic where they are all instructed to look serene and stay calm, and where each of the thousand extras strove to please with his and her expression so as to make the shot successful, as well as to be invited to work again.

It was a big field. Almost football field in size. The farthest souls were on their feet for a better view. Rachel and I were up the tree on the twenty-yard line. Jesus was on the fifty-yard line.

It was a little eerie how he commanded such rapt attention,

without ever asking for it. No one had to say, "Quiet, please." No one had to settle the crowd. As soon as he stood there—appearing from who knows where—the audience sank into a hushed silence.

And up in front of the multitudes, the man who called himself Jesus was surveying the ocean of faces. The way he turned gently this way and that, as if to not miss making some eye contact with every living soul, you could almost say he was moving in mysterious ways.

The speaker's eyes, piercing and friendly, stimulating and comforting, passed down the lanes and byways of that gaggle of penitents. And those eyes could lead you right to your last supper, or into the bedroom, if need be. And they worried their way inside you and took hold of your heart and didn't let go, not if you turned away, not if you closed your own eyes. But the hold on your heart was not rough or sinister, not unwelcome; it was more a loving hug that left you at once breathless and euphoric.

The thing that might have been startling about seeing Jesus was how ordinary he was. And when he spoke you had the idea that he was smiling all the while, not laughing, mind you, but there was a smile in his voice if not on his lips. And he made you feel good with his simple, straightforward delivery which was no delivery at all, really, but a conversational engagement that lulled you to sleep almost while it excited you beyond experience. And he spoke to each one individually, as if pouring goodness from his heart directly into each of their hearts. His mercy flowed like an undammed brook, and no matter where he looked, his eyes were right on you, and you alone; from the last row to the first, he was talking to you.

To some he said, "I am the answer to your despair. Life has a meaning after all, and you are it."

To the Devil's Disciples he said, "The meek shall inherit the earth."

To others he said, "Ye are the light of the world..."

It was all familiar stuff, but spoken as if for the first time and heard afresh. Just as I was thinking these ideas weren't terribly original, he said, "Ideas don't have to be original, they have to be good."

And to me he said, "I am the genuine article. I dare you to find a phony bone in my body."

In our tree, I whispered to Rachel, "This is going to be some challenge for the old Debunker of Myths."

"Sh!" she said.

It didn't matter who you were, he had a personalized message for you. And it wasn't the flamboyant "go-to-hell religion" of the itinerant evangelists, or the soap-opera tears of the television superstar, or the "I-need-a-million-dollars-a-week-to-do-God's-work" evangelist. It was down-home and earthy. It was everybody's big brother—the guy who could shut down the bully next door by just staring at him.

As Jesus spoke he soothed the crowd. Everyone knew the Devil's Disciples were a pack of wild beasts. But they sat enthralled, lambs vulnerable to slaughter, because scratch any man and you will find the universal question buried therein, often ignored, often suppressed, often overlooked, but there nonetheless; the nagging, gnawing question, "What is the meaning of life?" For some reason the crowd assembled here today thought this man might supply the answer.

"'Why are you here, Jesus?' they ask me," he said. "'What do you want?' 'Not much,' I say, 'only to help make the world a better place.'"

"'What's the matter with it now?' someone will ask, and I say, 'I came back to make it better, not to criticize.'"

The laughter began muffled, then rose to course across the field and wave the neighboring grass in ripples of delight.

Jesus spoke without electronics. He spoke barely above a whisper, but there was no trouble hearing him in the last row—a row so far away in the crowd that Jesus appeared to them three inches tall.

"I believe we have within us the power to overcome animosity. I believe if we start with one second of peace in one person we can watch it grow to minutes and hours, days and weeks, years and lifetimes. Let us, you and I, spread this peace of mind to all mankind.

"Think about it. Is it a better way than we have pursued since man first walked this earth? Is love not preferable to hate, suspicion, warfare, greed?

"Much has been preached over the years in the name of religion, of various gods. This one simple idea often escapes notice. Love thy neighbor as thyself. Blessed are the pure in heart, because the pure in heart will not despise their brothers.

"What good does it do to love Christ and hate your neighbor? What service do you perform if you love mankind abstractly and are not be able to get along with your wife?

"You know the scripture:

'Thou shalt love thy neighbor,
and hate thine enemy.
But I say unto you,
Love your enemies,
bless them that curse you,
do good to them that hate you,
and pray for them
which despitefully use you,
and persecute you;
That ye may be the children
of your Father which is in heaven:
for he maketh his sun to rise
on the evil and on the good,
and sendeth rain
on the just and on the unjust.'

"That's Matthew five, forty-three to forty-five.

"I ask you little. Take off the shroud of selfishness. Look around you and you will see countless people who have been created just like you. They are different in some ways, but they are the same in so many ways. Think about your similarities. You are all in the same boat. The boat will sink without your goodwill. Don't count on the other guy to start the ball rolling. *You* fill your heart with love for your fellows.

"Think of one person you hate. Try to imagine him as an innocent child. Imagine his good qualities. Think of the struggles and barriers in his path of life—how hard his life may have been. Perhaps think he has had the worst of trials and tribulations that you yourself have had. Maybe worse. Visualize it all before you on a slate. Then wipe out the hate as though you were cleaning the slate. Tomorrow do the same with another adversary."

Nobody said it was a complex message. And yet something about its delivery sank into the souls of the congregated, moved them. Perhaps it was the simplicity of the idea, something they could readily grasp. Something that made sense, squared with their own ideas of sanity, of balance, of right and wrong. He was a salesman for the betterment of mankind. Is it any wonder some in the Jesus trade were so suspicious of him?

But no one in the audience stopped to argue. No one said, "Yeah, but, I'd like to see you live with my wife for just two days."

Instead, they vowed, almost to the man, to give it a try.

And when he had taken
the five loaves and the two fishes,
he looked up to heaven,
and blessed, and brake the loaves,
and gave them to his disciples
to set before them;
and the two fishes divided he
among them all.
And they did all eat,
and were filled.
And they took up twelve baskets full
of the fragments, and of the fishes.
And they that did eat of the loaves
were about five thousand men.

—Mark 6:41-44

THE GOSPEL ACCORDING TO

SHERIFF
STONEY JESSUP

On my way back, I had
the advantage of the red
lights on top of my sher-
iff's car,

so I could just pass—very carefully, of course—on the left. There weren't hardly any cars coming down the hill, anyway.

But what an unholy mess I found when I got back there to Glory Pines.

I'll be honest with you—there's never been a time in my law-enforcement career when I've been so ill at ease. My heartburn was kicking in, and the boil under my collar on the back of my neck was inflamed and I thought it would drive me nuts.

Sensing danger, I'd left my dog, Fluffy, at headquarters. I stood now on the edge of the swarm of people and bit my lower lip. I'd never in my life seen so many people collected outdoors like this—without the benefit of a stadium or some facility with hundreds of cops to contain pockets of trouble, should they arise. And here I was alone in an otherwise peaceful village with no history of anything like this. There was no police force in the world that could subdue a crowd like this, should it take it in its collective head to become unruly.

What could a speaker like this so-called Jesus do to a mob like this, should he decide to flip out?

The saliva left my mouth, lips and throat and seemed to drain into the palms of my hands. I stared at Jesus across the field, talking on as though he were oblivious to the potential for violence he was setting up.

This Jesus guy might be the genuine article and he might be an artful impostor, but I wouldn't give a nickel for the soul of anyone who stood up and doubted that this was their Savior, Jesus Christ, returned in all His glory to rule the earth.

And to me, that spelled trouble. Sooner or later, he's gonna be trouble.

And after this Jesus had talked so long, some of the listeners started to get hungry. They took out their apples and their sandwiches, and Jesus spoke of the parable of the loaves and fishes.

It was then the bread truck pulled up to the field just beside Jesus. The driver winked at him and said, "Help yourself."

ANOTHER BLAST FROM GOD'S TROMBONES:

Anything is possible, it can be said, if you believe in miracles. Perhaps God did create all organisms, including human beings, in finished form, in one stroke, and maybe it all happened several thousand years ago. But if that is true, He also salted the earth with false evidence in such endless and exquisite detail, and so thoroughly from pole to pole, as to make us conclude first that life evolved and second that the process took billions of years. Surely Scripture tells us He would not do that. The Prime Mover of the Old and New Testaments is variously loving, magisterial, denying, thunderously angry, and mysterious, but never tricky.

—Edward O. Wilson
Consilience

ANOTHER TWANG FROM GOD'S GUITAR:

Suppose I had found a watch upon the ground.... The mechanism being observed, the inference is inevitable that the watch must have had a maker; that there must have existed, at some time and at some place or other, an artificer or artificers who formed it for the purpose which we find it actually to answer.

—*William Paley*
Natural Theology

THE GOSPEL ACCORDING TO

FRANKIE FOXXE

I'm frank to say I'd never seen Rachel quite so giddy as she was after this Jesus finished his talk.

Immediately, a throng of people surged forward to surround him, and Rachel said suddenly, "Come on, let's get down there before there's no place to stand."

We jumped out of the tree and worked our way into the blanket of people who seemed, at any moment, would trample us.

They oozed over the small rise and vanished beyond normal vision. Rachel and I were a couple blocks from the master. It seemed like everyone in the audience was now in line.

"Jeez, Frankie," Rachel said, "at the rate he's moving them along, we'll be here forty days and forty nights, let's give it up."

I looked each way along the line and put my hand on her shoulder. "You know the debunking of myths is my life's work. The debunking of *this* myth may be my magnum opus."

"Well, he has no talent whatsoever for keeping the line moving. He should shake hands, say 'Have a nice day,' and move on to the next."

A short rotund woman on the far side of sixty turned around. "Isn't he just the most giving soul?" she asked Rachel. "He'll talk as long as you want." She rolled her eyes.

To pass the time, I turned to Rachel. "What do you think, Rachel, Jesus as a motivational speaker?"

I saw the old fumes building up behind her eyeballs. The eruption would be volcanic. "You and your cute quips."

"Think he's real, do you?" I needled some more.

"I think he's genuine," she said. "I don't see anything phony there, do *you*?"

"Hard to tell," I made that much concession, "hard to tell."

"Phonies are easy to tell," she said.

"Not always," I disagreed. "You think he could have come back to earth after two thousand years? You buy that?"

"I don't have all the answers, Frankie, and, contrary to what you might think, neither do you."

"See any way it's possible? This guy you see here lived two thousand years ago? Came back on an airplane? Los Angeles?"

"Miracles do happen," she said with more conviction than she could possibly have had. And speaking of being had, I was had by Rachel. She led me to believe she was a skeptic, and now she'd turned into a full-blooded fundamentalist. That, in my book, was dirty pool.

"You may not like the creation theory," she said, "but you haven't given me anything better."

I groaned. Then I was willing to let the matter drop.

She wasn't.

"Look at those trees," Rachel said.

I followed her eyes to a stand of pines across the meadow.

"Yeah?" I said.

"Where'd they come from?"

"Seed," I said.

"Where'd the seeds come from?"

"Other trees," I said, but I knew where she was leading.

"And who made the seed?"

"Well, I suppose it came out of that primordial soup in some form or other."

"Primordial soup, huh?" she said. "And where do you suppose that came from?"

"Ah, yes," I said. "These are the mysteries of life, Rachel. It would be so neat and simple to say a great God stood around five to fifteen billion years ago—stood in nothing, mind you, and said, "I think I'll create me a world." Boys and girls, creepy-crawlies, birds and bees, mosquitoes (so we might experience the torment of itching), and all those damn beetles. This is a guy who gave us dinosaurs and the giraffe, not to mention floods, famines, earthquakes, tornadoes, hurricanes..."

"Okay, enough already! You can make fun of it all you want, but I don't see any answers coming from you."

"Primordial soup," I said. "Evolution, my dear. Not all at once—one piece at a time. *Billions* of years, remember. Lots of time to work the green slime into algae and—perhaps a billion or so later—a tulip. Tadpoles to tree shrews to apes to people. Why would a sharp God waste all his time on intermediaries? And why not a bunch of Einsteins, and no serial killers? If there is a plan, it isn't very well thought out, is it?"

"*Skeptic!*"

"Okay, let's say God made it all—the seven-day trick—even before anyone thought in terms of seven-day weeks. Okay, then who made God? Did he make himself—maybe from the rib of a passing woman? Or is there a God's god who did the job? And then a God's God's god, and so on, ad infinitum?"

"*Atheist!*"

As the line inched forward to talk to Jesus, Rachel became edgy, like she wanted to solve all the dilemmas about the philosophy of religion before we got to him.

"Take dying, for instance," she said.

"What about it?"

"Everyone is afraid to die," she said. "It's scary if you consider it the end of everything. Then there is the fear of the pain. It could really hurt. Whatever you have that kills you, I mean. So, instead, people have hope. They think they are going to heaven—or someplace—to be with all the people who went before them. And they die expectantly, with hope in their hearts. Is that so terrible?"

She'd stuck me with a hard question. "Terrible?" I said, buying time. "Only if you consider self-delusion terrible. I guess it's only terrible if it leads to terrible results. Pie-in-the-sky heavenly salvation delusions may not hurt anybody if you don't have to kill those who don't share your particular myths."

She glared at me as only Rachel could glare. I think she took an advanced degree in glaring, she was so good at it. The guy behind us wasn't bad with the glare, either. He had a Santa Claus belly and bad breath and was glowering at me. From the look of the canvases for his tattoos, bulging out of the sleeves of his tee shirt (GOD IS LOVE), I considered prudence the best policy. I couldn't be sure in his case, in spite of his tee shirt, that Jesus's message about not hating anybody had hit his particular home.

"Can we talk about something else?" she said.

"I'm game," I said. "You start."

I think this was the beginning of her Ph.D. thesis, probably titled:

The Anatomy of the Facial Glare
In Interpersonal Mood Alteration

which was the most pretentious title I could come up with on such short notice.

"Rachel?" I asked her after a long, glaring silence. I gave in. I couldn't stand that accusative glare.

"Hm?"

"Were you really a Moonie?"

"Bet your life."

"What was it like?"

She scratched her nose. "Like the confessional, I guess."

"The confessional?"

"Boring. Selling candles twelve to sixteen hours a day, seven days a week. That's why I was surprised to hear you say the confessional was boring. At least you weren't dealing with drunks in bars."

"They'd come to me after the bar. How'd you get out?"

"Parents had me deprogrammed. I was secretly glad they did, but I kept up the pretense of resentment. I didn't want to erase *all* their guilt."

It was getting dark. The sun had faded behind the trees. Cars were moving down the hill with only slightly more alacrity than they came up.

Rachel turned to face me square on, as though she were trying to box me into something. "What would it take to get you to say you believe, Frankie?"

I laughed. It was, alas, a nervous, put-off laugh. She was

backing me against the wall.

"Believe?" I said. "Believe what? The whole enchilada? Virgin birth? You know, there is, I've heard, a strain of turkeys somewhere in New Jersey that reproduces without males."

"Every woman's dream," Rachel said.

"Yeah—anyway, all the products—the offspring—are female—which, I guess, makes sense."

"So, you're saying you could go for it if Jesus were female?"

"I'm speculating it might make more sense, is all."

"Hey," she said. "God is a woman—why not?"

"Used to be," I said. "The boys changed that some eight to ten thousand years ago. Read the Old Testament—all those 'false gods' were women."

She shook her head. "Not the way I see it. God the Mother and Jesus her only begotten Daughter."

"Well, maybe a couple centuries from now—the next millennium, maybe, but no way could a woman bring this off today—"

"Why not?"

"Because our leaders are men. We expect men to be president, to run for president. Some woman tries it, we'll listen politely for a short while, then switch channels."

"You are a male chauvinist *pig!*" she said.

"Not really. I like women okay, but face it, all these gurus are men. Hey, I'm not saying it is ethical, moral, reasonable or right, it just is."

"Well," she grumbled, "it shouldn't be."

I took that as a concession.

"Maybe it's because the women want men leaders. Think about it—the men were raised by moms."

"So were the women."

"Yeah, but men in the workplace seem to get along better with women superiors than women do. Women look up to men."

"That a universal truth, Frankie?" Rachel was no slouch.

"Well, okay—ask anyone—"

"Scientific proof?"

"Okay—I won't argue it. I don't have to—just look around you. Are *any* of the TV evangelists women? You don't even have to *ask* why not. That's not my point: my point is they just aren't. Can you imagine some woman pushing guilt-free sex and buying a hundred Rolls-Royces? No woman today could bring off a stunt like this Jesus."

"Stunt, huh?"

"What do you call it?"

"Call it?" she said. "I call it what it is—a beautiful experience, an ethereal happening that transcends our usual self-absorption. That's what I call it. And I don't care what you say, I wouldn't feel any different if he were a woman."

After two and a half hours, Rachel and I were close enough to Jesus to hear what he was saying. A man just ahead pressed a handful of paper money at Jesus.

"Oh, thank you," Jesus said, and I got a momentary thrill. Here, I figured, would be his downfall. "It is a kindness that warms my heart. But you keep the money. You may want to give it to the poor or find some other humanitarian use for it. I do not require money."

"But surely," the man said, "you have expenses that have to be met. Life is not cheap nowadays—and I want to do what I can to get your message across."

"Most generous of you. My message is simple and it is within the individual that it must work. It requires character, not cash, to be effective." Jesus handed the money back to the man. "You treat others as you want to be treated and I will have all the remuneration I need."

Back in the line, Rachel laughed when I said, "This duck is not going to be an easy shot."

It was then I got my first exposure to Michael. He was moving along the line to tell those patiently assembled that Jesus would speak to them all but it could take a very long time and if they had to get somewhere they might consider coming at another time. He said, "It would help speed things up if you could be brief in talking to Him because there are so many that want to shake His hand."

It was there while we were waiting in line that I struck up a conversation with the good-looking, tanned, blond kid, and he told me, awestruck, about his special relationship with Jesus.

I had no intention of being brief with Jesus. This was grist for my debunking mill. When we finally got to the head of the line, I stuck out my hand, "Hi, Jesus, I'm Frankie Foxxe from the *Gulfport Riptide*. I wonder if I could ask you a few questions."

"Sure, Frankie. Good of you to come."

"First of all, who are you?"

"Who do you think I am?"

"I don't know, that's why I'm asking."

"Who do the people say that I am?" Jesus asked, waving a hand at the long line of people waiting to talk to him.

"They seem to think you are Jesus Christ returned to the earth as they feel they were promised in the Bible."

Jesus smiled.

"Would you give them an argument?" I asked.

"Should I?"

"If they're wrong."

"Let me ask you a question, Frankie Foxxe," Jesus said. "Who are you?"

"Well, I'm not suggesting I'm anything special."

"Neither am I," Jesus said, smiling. "Remember Luke eighteen, eighteen and nineteen:

> 'And a certain ruler asked him,
> saying,
> Good Master,
> what shall I do
> to inherit eternal life?
> And Jesus said unto him,

Why callest thou me
good?
none is good, save one,
that is, God.'"

Jesus seemed to will his arms to float from his sides, palms up. "I am here with a simple message. Love your fellows. That's all. Let's wipe out hate. Can *anyone* find that objectionable?"

"Oh, I could make some debating points. What about Satan, the big bugaboo of the evangelists? Should we love Satan? What about those who are evil? Love 'em?"

"Love the sinner, not his sin," Jesus said.

"I know the airplane story, but where exactly did you come from?"

"I came from the Father. We all came from the same Father," he said.

"Is that a heavenly father or an earthly father?" I asked. "Because I'll buy that we all came from one or two of something which I am happy to call father—but some invisible guy in the sky? Where does he hang out? Where did he come from?"

"Or *She*," Rachel put in.

"I'll leave that up to you," Jesus said.

"You mean you are satisfied to have everyone here believe you are paranormal—that you were just dropped from the sky into that airplane? And this time around you just happen to speak English?"

"Oh, I think what they believe about me personally is not that important. If we can somehow get the hate from our hearts we will have accomplished my mission."

"So you aren't really Jesus?"

"Perhaps you aren't really Frankie Foxxe."

"I have fingerprints on file. I have a birth certificate, a driver's license. When I go on an airplane I have a ticket and my name is listed on a manifest."

"Those things are of this world, Frankie—I am of another world."

"So you really are a fairy or an angel or just some garden-variety extraterrestrial spirit?"

The Santa Claus with halitosis behind us was grumbling like an active volcano, and others picked it up. As it swelled to proportions verging on general anger, Rachel suddenly became afraid someone might decide to lynch me for blasphemy. She tugged at my sleeve. "Come on, Frankie, let's give someone else a chance."

"No, no, wait a minute," I said. "If we are going to love everybody, we've got to love even those who inconvenience us. Even anger us, right, Jesus?"

"Right."

"Not so easy all the time, but I'm game if they are," I said, looking up at the crowd snaking endlessly behind us, which now had self-consciously simmered down. "How old are you, Jesus?"

"I suppose I'm as old as I look."

"So if you were around here a couple thousand years ago, you are only in your thirties because that's how old you look? You aren't a couple thousand years old?"

"Oh, that's all a matter of how you count."

"So how do *you* count?"

"I don't count. It's not important to me."

Hmm, I thought. My expectations that I could quickly trip up this man and expose him as a fraud were not being met. This Jesus seemed to be a fancy-footwork artist who could dance around any question without a slip. I would put him down as very clever, but I wasn't fooled into thinking him genuine. I shot another arrow from my quiver: "As you were talking today about love and taking hate out of your heart, I kept thinking of the Bible passage that goes:

'If any man come to me,
and hate not his father, and mother,
and wife, and children,

and brethren, and sisters,
yea, and his own life also,
he cannot be my disciple.'

Luke fourteen something, I believe," I said.

"Twenty-six," Jesus said, and nodded gravely.

"A bit at odds with what you've been preaching today, isn't it?"

Jesus shook his head sadly. "So many translation glitches. The book has been through the mill, there's no denying that. I expect some scribe somewhere, making his case for celibacy in the clergy. It's such a tough sell," he said, and I could see he felt it in his bones.

"Yeah, okay. Let's talk God. Where? Who? How?"

"Look around you, Frankie. You tell me. It all came from a Cracker Jack box?"

"That's a question, Jesus, not an answer," I said. "Afraid to commit yourself?"

"God is in you, Frankie, believe it or not."

"That's nature," I said. "What is the nature of God?"

"Ah, what is the nature of nature? God is the nature of nature."

"Do you talk to him?"

"All the time."

"Did you come from heaven and were you sitting at his right hand?"

"Yes."

"What does he look like?"

"A lot like you, Frankie, but there is one significant difference."

"What's that?"

"He's not so skeptical."

"Why does he allow suffering? Is he falling asleep at the switch?"

"Why does everyone blame God for all of man's transgressions? He's not a puppeteer. He isn't sitting up there pulling everybody's strings. If He were, you wouldn't need me down here drumming up trade for the brotherhood of man. You wouldn't have to strive for perfection, you would have it."

"And it would be tedious, is that it? We wouldn't know good if we didn't experience bad. Isn't that the pitch?"

"There are six billion people buzzing around down here on earth. God would have His hands full controlling them all."

"Okay, then what's his job? How does he spend his days?"

"Want to find out firsthand?"

"Suicide you mean? Wouldn't that send me to the hot place?"

Jesus laughed. "Well, Frankie, if only believers get to heaven, I'd say you have a long way to go."

A cheer went up from the crowd and Rachel steered me away from Jesus, who, in parting, called after me.

"I hope I'll see you again, Frankie—love thy neighbor."

In spite of myself, I felt my heart pumping a mile a minute and a certain shortness of breath. It was a feeling I did not share with Rachel.

ANOTHER BLAST FROM GOD'S TROMBONES:

CARDINAL: I have good news and bad news.
POPE: Good news first.
CARDINAL: Jesus is on the phone.
POPE: That's wonderful news. What could be bad?
CARDINAL: He's calling from Salt Lake City.

Jesus said unto him,
Verily I say unto thee,
That this night,
before the cock crow,
thou shalt deny me thrice.
Peter said unto him,
Though I should die with thee,
Yet will I not deny thee.

—Matthew 26:34-35

THE GOSPEL ACCORDING TO

THE POPE

Vatican City: The pope
and his closest confidant,
a cardinal:

"Jesus," the pope said, "the man says he's Jesus?"

"Yes, Your Holiness."

"But surely thousands of people have thought they were Jesus. Psychotic delusions."

"Yes, Your Holiness, but this one seems different."

"How different?"

"Convincing. Not insane. Knows his Bible cold. Preaches only brotherhood and has an enormous following. *And* he takes no money!"

Silence. Long and edgy. The cardinal wanted to break it, but he knew his place. He could hear the pope breathing. It sounded like a death rattle. He would have to gently suggest the old man have the doctor look at his chest.

When the pope finally spoke, he took a deep, rattling breath and shook his head. "I am supposed to make a pronouncement," he said.

"Yes, Most Holy Father."

"And my word is infallible," he said, not really as a question, but not as gospel truth, either.

"Yes, Your Holiness."

"And our finances, you say..." he trailed off in pain.

"Slipping, Most Holy Father. Badly. Attendance is off, donations are down. We are especially hard hit in North America. We have so many expenses."

The pope nodded wearily. "So if I say he is the real Jesus, we dig our own graves..."

The cardinal nodded. "Seal our doom."

"But...could he be?"

The cardinal raised an eyebrow. "Unlikely, I should think."

"Yes, yes, me, too," he hastened to respond. "But," he said and paused. "Yes, the big but..."

The cardinal knew what the old man was thinking. Insurance. How many of their parishioners were in it for the insurance? Maybe their belief wasn't that strong, but they realized the possibility—what if they were wrong? Would it be better to go through the motions of belief in case there was something to it? And, he figured, the pope was making similar calculations at this very moment. Of course, was God a guy who could be fooled by someone faking it for insurance? Would God be fooled if the pope acknowledged the man in the desert of western North America to be Jesus—just in case he was? And how would God feel if the pope denied His true Son?

Or did the pope have doubts about the possibility of a man returning to earth after two thousand years? It was a test of faith, all right. The age-old conflict between faith and scientific possibility.

The pope rose from his throne. The cardinal noticed he was having more and more trouble getting up and walking. How long could he last under this strain? Would he want to live to preside over the demise of his Church after a two-thousand-year run?

"I don't suppose it would do to put it off—say we are praying on it?"

"With all due respect, Most Holy Father, it might appear His Holiness was unable to make up his mind."

"Yes, yes," the pope waved impatiently, "wouldn't be politic, would it?"

"No, Your Holiness."

Silence, but a silence without thought, for what else *was* there to think?

"Your Eminence," the pontiff said wearily, "I have always valued your advice and counsel. And I would not be surprised if someday—and not in the too distant future—you might succeed me."

"Perish the thought!" the cardinal said, agitated in his eyes and mouth. "May you outlive us all, Most Holy Father."

"Yes, yes, not very likely," the pope said. "Just the same, tell me, Your Eminence, what would *you* do?"

"Oh, Holy Father, I'm afraid I am a practical man with a woefully inadequate, pragmatic turn of mind. I would weigh the alternatives. I am afraid I would not have the courage to bring down the Church based on the pronouncement of one man."

"Even one whose every utterance is deemed infallible," then he added modestly, "to the faithful?"

"Even so," the cardinal said. "*Especially* so. With all due respect, and I am saying this as one who is not fit to wash the feet of the most holy father—I see two possibilities, both of them fraught with risk. It is, as I have heard on your American tour, a no-win situation. You say this *is* Jesus, how do we explain he has not been here to see you? And our income and attendance continue to slump. And he is giving it away."

"But I understand there is no ritual."

"No, Your Holiness."

"But the people will surely miss the ritual—the rosary, the confessional, the Mass, we have so much to offer."

"Indisputable, Your Holiness," the cardinal said. "And I don't mind overlooking that ingrate heretic, Martin Luther. As I recall, he made quite a name for himself doing away with our rituals. And so, the only realistic option is for us to deny him…this…" the word stuck in his throat. "…Jesus."

"Thrice, Your Eminence?" the pontiff said with a raised eyebrow. "Or will one denial do?"

"Oh, I should think once," the cardinal said. "Between us, Your Holiness, I've always considered a bodily second coming as something of a Southern Baptist phenomenon—in the United States—and what are those others called? Pentecostals. The tongue speakers. I don't think you'd disappoint many Catholics were you to say while this man who calls himself Jesus may do good in the world, you don't see any evidence that this is the genuine article."

"And if we're wrong?"

"Oh, Holiness, that's the risk. But think about it, I don't think this Jesus has ever even mentioned Your Holiness in any of his talks. I should think if he is not acknowledging your existence, let alone your great importance in religious history—the direct line from Peter, the Vicar of Christ—why, it might be a little awkward to say, 'Yea, this is verily the, you know, guy. The big one.'"

"And if we're wrong, we'll spend eternity in eternal damnation, roasting in hell's fire."

The cardinal thought the most holy father was getting carried away with the drama. "That is certainly one view of things," he said. "But, Most Holy Father, isn't our God a loving God? He doesn't hate, all that horror in Deuteronomy notwithstanding. Surely, He would not punish you for an honest mistake."

"Hmm." The holy father contemplated that and realized it was only a hopeful opinion.

"Why don't you pray on it, Most Holy Father? See if God will make known His wishes to you."

The pope smiled his wry, pixie smile. "Like those television evangelists do?" he said.

But he did it, he denied him, and satisfied himself, within the parameters of the urgency, that the great God above would not look askance at a pope for trying to save His Church.

THE GOSPEL ACCORDING TO
SHERIFF STONEY JESSUP

"Sheriff? This is Ernie Joe Banghart," he said into the phone.

I was pleased. It was so like the big man to be so modest. As if I wouldn't recognize Ernie Jo's voice. "How's it going out there in glorious Glory Pines?"

"It's a real nightmare," I said, trying not to sound too down. "It's nothing but one big traffic jam here. A real nightmare."

"Why don't you do something about it, Sheriff?" Ernie Jo said, putting me on the spot.

"I'm trying," I said.

"Seems like to me that impostor has got you all buffaloed out there in sunny Californy."

I didn't like that, but I didn't say anything.

"That man's a menace, Sheriff, he's destroying our ministry."

"Oh, sir, your ministry is fundamentally strong, I'm sure. There's nothing like it on this earth. I'm sure any setback will only be temporary."

"Well, I do appreciate that, Sheriff, so very much—your confidence in me. Yes, sir, I do so very much. The reason I'm calling you, Sheriff, and disturbing your peace out there in sunny Californy, we been thinking here on the humid Gulf about our prayer partners and our magazine, *God's Guitar*; and we were thinking, Sheriff, we would be honored if you would consent to us using your photograph in our magazine—it's all for the work of the Lord, you know. And as I say, having a man of your stature—of your importance—pictured there, would be a real feather in our caps here."

"Well, I..." I started to say but I choked up. Here was my dream and it was being offered by the man himself.

"You don't have to make up your mind right away, Sheriff, we got a couple weeks to deadline for the next issue, you just take your time."

"Yes, sir, thank you, sir."

"Now, Sheriff—you don't happen to have an eight-by-ten black-and-white glossy of yourself in uniform anyplace, do you?"

"I could get one," I offered.

"Good!" Ernie Jo seemed pleased. "Well, you take good care of yourself, Sheriff; let us know in your own sweet time."

"I'm flattered, sir," I said, "very flattered. Ah, how…I mean, do I have to commit…? I noticed in the ads what it says is how much the prayer partner in the picture is giving your ministry by way of a monthly offering."

"Well, that's up to you and the Lord, Sheriff. But now you mention it, there is something you might be able to help us with."

"What's that?"

"You being uniquely situated as you are, Sheriff."

"Uniquely situated?"

"Yeah—it's this so-called Jesus thing. You know how it's hurting us. You were at the Shrine out there in Los Angeles. I've never experienced such pitiful crowds. The man is simply a menace to religion as we know it. So, I was wondering if you had any ideas how to prevent this disaster from ruining us."

"Ah, no, sir, I don't," I said. "But as I say, I think it will pass in time."

"How *much* time, Sheriff?"

"I don't know."

"How much time you think we got? I myself don't know how long we can hold out at this rate," Ernie Jo said. "So, I was wondering, Sheriff, if you didn't have some weapon in your arsenal that might neutralize him temporarily."

"Weapon?" I didn't know if I'd heard him right. Surely Ernie Jo didn't want me to shoot Jesus.

"Yeah," Ernie Jo said. "I was wondering in particular if you had any jezebels out there who might seduce the sucker."

I was shocked to hear my idol talking like that. It was like I didn't want to believe my ears.

"Got anybody like that?" Ernie Jo asked again.

"Well, sir, I don't know if that would be a Christian thing to do."

"Don't you worry about that. The Lord has given me specific instructions to deal with this menace as I see fit. I was thinking you could lock him up in your slammer there, but I'm just not sure how that could work. Might backfire, you know, so I thought we could neutralize him with some sex scandal. It would have to be someone more or less arousing—someone he couldn't resist—you know what I mean, Sheriff?"

"Well, sir, I *don't* know if I'm hearing you right."

"You're hearing me right. I've cleared it with the Lord—you would be an instrument of the Lord, Sheriff, you have my word on that. It would just be a temptation. Our Lord was tempted many times by Satan—as you well know. If he really *is* Jesus, there shouldn't be any problem. But if he's just a human, why, I can't think of a better way to find out right up front."

Naturally, Mary came to mind. I even thought how I could wait until the next time Filmore called to complain and I had to book her again. This could be her bail. But I didn't know. I had a hard time accepting the idea as straight from the Lord. I didn't mean to suggest that Ernie Jo was scamming me, but somehow it still bothered me.

"Well, Sheriff, you still there?"

"Yes, sir."

"So, you be thinking about it, Sheriff?"

"Yes, sir."

"Good! I'll be talking to you—and, Sheriff?"

"Yes, sir."

"God will bless you."

ANOTHER BLAST FROM GOD'S TROMBONES:

2500 Marriages Arranged in Heaven

*T*wenty-five hundred couples dressed like the dolls on the top of the wedding cake were assembled, arm in arm, at Madison Square Garden in the heart of the melting pot of the world, New York City.

The couples were staring straight ahead. It was that vacant holy stare that the cult cultivated. The stare came from selling candles or flowers on the streets sixteen hours a day, seven days a week, and the few that understood the prophet's technique understood with that kind of work schedule and the droning indoctrination that followed, no cultivation of the stare was necessary. The stare was there.

They called him Father, and Father had arranged the marriages. After years of preaching that the worst sin of all was sex, he had decided the time had come to think about the perpetuation of the faith. And for that, he was constrained to admit, he had as yet found no substitute for sex.

Of course, the Immigration Service was becoming a real pain. He had all these foreign disciples—why, he was foreign himself. And while he didn't need U.S. citizenship, he didn't want to see his troops decimated by deportation—not in this land of milk and honey, this seemingly limitless market for flowers and candles.

Yes, Father knew best, and he had paired them up not only by size and weight, but with the considerations of citizenship uppermost in his mind.

U.S. citizens were mated with everyone else, many of the couples didn't speak the same language, but you didn't need many words to sell flowers sixteen hours a day.

He felt the power of the Almighty as he matched those names so the brides and grooms could say their marriage was made in heaven.

Everything was there for a top-notch ceremony: The 2500 brides and 2500 grooms, the exalted head of the church performing the ceremony en masse, the indefatigable interpreter, the bulletproof stonehenge glass so you could see Father without shooting him, and the press. Oh, the press. They were in clover—photographers snapping pictures like it was the final surrender of World War II.

And, by God, from the look of these troops, the analogy was not that remote.

—Frankie Foxxe
The Cult Culture

And Jesus said,
Somebody hath touched me:
for I perceive
that virtue is gone out of me.
And when the woman saw
that she was not hid, she came
    trembling,
and falling down before him,
she declared unto him before all the
    people
for what cause she had touched him,
and how she was healed immediately.
And he said unto her,
Daughter, be of good comfort:
thy faith hath made thee whole;
go in peace.

—Luke 8:46-48

THE GOSPEL ACCORDING TO

MICHAEL

"The instant I laid eyes on her, I knew she was the woman of my dreams" was the way Michael later put it to me with his newfound exuberance.

It wasn't that I was surprised to hear a guy go gaga over a girl; it was just surprising coming from Michael.

"My father might not like her—she's so different from Mom."
Mary was a little older than Michael, but he assured me that was no problem for him and he hoped it wouldn't be for her.

And, oh, yes, he spoke of being hit by a freight train, and other terrible analogies. The boy was smitten, no gainsaying that. Here's how it happened, according to Michael's notebooks, mostly:

The Devil's Disciples were volunteering as security guards around Jack's place. People came at all hours to see Jesus, and if it were left up to Him, He'd see them all, including psychos with guns and knives.

The Disciples passed on the requests to see Jesus to Jack, who screened them. Even so, He was seeing people practically non-stop all day—people came from all over the country. Cripples and sick people came to be healed. Jesus underplayed that, but I have seen more than a few amazing things. Even Jack was healing some. Not all, of course, but I didn't detect anything phony.

According to the newspapers, magazines and TV, the established religions didn't like it much. Too many people were getting the idea the answers were in how you treated your fellow man, and how money and wealth didn't matter. So church attendance was off and contributions to the TV evangelists were way off, making preachers like Ernie Jo Banghart mighty mad.

Jack's screening aside, there wasn't any way he could keep these two guys out. They looked like department-store mannequins. But they were modeling suits somewhere between undercover policemen and accident/injury lawyers.

They wanted to see Jesus, they said, as they flashed their FBI identity cards as though they had just finished a top-hat-and-cane tap dance. They held the pose—hands out and palms up, with the leather case dangling open at the end of their outstretched hands: *tah, tah!*

The agents called Jesus Hey-soos, and fired questions at Jesus like they were competing for most shots in their firing range.

Was he a terrorist? A communist? A spy? Homosexual? How did he get on the plane? Did he have contacts in the Middle East? How did he explain there were no fingerprints for him in their file?

Jesus answered the questions in good humor—"My contacts are not of this world..." But the agents didn't appreciate His humor.

"Who do you report to?" was the last question.

One answer. Jesus said, "Only to God."

The agents furrowed their brows, tightened their eyelashes and said He would be hearing from them again.

"I'll look forward to it," Jesus said cheerfully. The agents thought He was joking.

It seemed like only minutes after the FBI agents left that Mary came into my life. Only I wasn't the one she was visiting. Usually, Jack just turned anyone away he had the least doubt about. This time, he seemed torn when he said slowly to Jesus, "There's a woman you might not want to see."

"Why not, Jack? She is a child of God, is she not?" Jesus went to the door, and brought her into the room.

Mary's body was tight and compact. She had on a pair of sheer black tights and a skimpy skirt that fell short of polite-society expectations.

"Tell me your name," Jesus said.

"Mary," she said, smiling like it was a great effort. She was like a child, and I smelled a lot of scent as she brushed past Jesus into the living room and tried to look sultry. Her perfume overpowered Jack's Old Spice. She patted the seat next to her on Jack's couch. Jesus took the cane chair opposite. Mary frowned.

When I saw her it was like someone was beating on my heart with drumsticks. She didn't look like a movie star or anything, just someone who had seen all sides of life.

There was a touch of nervousness around Mary's lips—her thin hands were flying about her lap, ill at ease, as though she were not good enough to be here, as though she might blunder into some faux pas that would embarrass her.

I didn't have any idea anyone could seduce Jesus—or want to. But it seemed like that was what Mary was trying to do. And for some reason, that didn't turn me off her. It was easy to see what a struggle she was having at it—as though someone had a gun at her head and she was just going through the motions, scared to death she might succeed. I saw in her a poor soul desperately crying out for attention, and it reminded me of me trying to impress my dad.

"Don't you like me?" she said, as though she were reciting lines in a play.

Mary had the cutest little ears you'd ever seen—and dangling from each was some kind of bird in flight. One was headed front, the other back. Her eyes were large and soulful, they might have been almost any color, but they looked black to me.

"Of course I like you," Jesus said. "I love all God's children."

"Do you think I am one of God's children?" she asked.

"Everyone is a child of God."

She didn't seem convinced. "Why won't you sit next to me?" she asked, "...if you love me..."

Jesus smiled to put her at ease, but the frown on her forehead seemed to indicate a girl with an agenda that was not being served.

"My love is the love of the parent for the lost child," Jesus said. "What is your love?"

She watched Him through tears. "It's my *business*," she sniffled, and a small laugh came out of her. Like the laughter of long pain. "My business is love, but I've never felt it."

"Who sent you?" Jesus asked Mary.

She didn't seem surprised at the question. "The sheriff," she answered, without guile. She was a good person. She wasn't going to deceive this kindly man. She had a job to do and she had made her attempt, but it was easy to see her heart wasn't in it. But *my* heart was completely captivated.

"But why would you agree to it? Is he paying you?"

"Hah," she said, shooting the word in a blast of saliva.

"You didn't expect *I* would, did you?"

She shrugged her shoulders as if to say, "You never know."

I knew something was happening to me, and it was happening for the first time. I didn't know what to make of it. Why was I so attracted to her? She was probably ten years older than I was. All I knew was I wished she would sit as close to me as she wanted to sit with Jesus. There was something dovish about the way her body drifted—like my mother. But Mary's fingers were thin and pretty, unlike my mother's, whose fingers were gnarled by arthritis.

Seeing Mary in the same trap with Jesus I was in with my father drew me to her—I felt like we were siblings under the skin, but my stirrings were not anything like I'd have for my sister.

I thought about how my father thought I should have a girl to be a calming influence on me.

"How did you start this?" Jesus asked Mary.

"It's a living," she said. "I couldn't make near as much cleaning house."

"Are you at peace?"

"Hah, that's a good one."

Jesus looked at her, and the deep understanding on His face opened her like the floodgates and the whole story came pouring out through the tears and the sobbing.

It wasn't an unusual story. The distracted parents, the missing love and understanding. The falling into higher paying, not such Christian, work in college. Then on to Mr. Filmore and the end of that, and her necessitated return to selling herself to live. Nowhere to turn.

"You can turn to me," Jesus said. "And the Heavenly Father."

Jesus moved to sit next to His seductress and put His arm on her shoulder. She buried her head there and blubbered like a baby.

"The sheriff will kill me."

"Why?"

"I failed."

"No," Jesus said. "You didn't fail. You have saved yourself. From this day on your feet are on the path of righteousness, for His name's sake."

I could feel the fear and confusion lift from her soul. In the twinkling of an eye, she was restored to the innocence of infancy. She was one of God's children again. I wanted to reach out and hold her myself.

I started toward her, then stopped cold. Jesus looked up. He smiled, then excused Himself, leaving me and Mary alone in Jack Whitehall's living room.

Mary sat on the couch, with the most beatific smile on her face. I shifted from foot to foot before her, but she seemed preoccupied to the point of not realizing my presence.

I cleared my throat in an attempt to get it to form some words. But the radiant smile on Mary's face tongue-tied me.

Just then, Jesus strolled back through the room and observed my problem. "Oh, Mary," He said, looking the worn waif in the eye, "this is Michael." She seemed bewildered at the news there was someone else in the room. She looked up at my face and the smile faded from her lips.

"Michael," Jesus said, "this is Mary." Then He left the room as gently as He had entered it.

"Hey," I managed, with an awkward wave of my hand.

Mary seemed troubled.

I moved to the seat next to her on the couch. "Mind if I sit down?" I asked. I paused only a second. When I sat, she moved away from me, the smile flew from her face and her body stiffened as if the blood ran cold in her veins.

"That Jesus is some guy," I said, then swallowed when I thought I had made a stupid beginning. "I picked Him up at the airport. I brought Him here."

Mary shook her head.

"You don't believe me?"

Mary said nothing, tears forming in her eyes, "I'm sorry. I'm never going to do that again. For money. Only for love."

Maybe, I thought, someday you could love me...?

"You are a good boy, Michael," she said through her tears. "I am not a good girl."

When I opened my mouth to protest, Mary jumped up and bolted from the room. Before I could form the words in my mind, "Wait, don't go," she was gone.

What is wanted is not the will to believe, but the wish to find out, which is the exact opposite.

—*Bertrand Russell*

The Gospel According to

SHERIFF STONEY JESSUP

"Sheriff, my good buddy, it's Ernie Jo here.

How did it go?"

"Well, sir, I done it. I got the best we got to go over there with instructions to seduce him."

"What happened?"

"He didn't seduce. Saved her soul for the Lord."

There was a long and deadly silence on the phone and I was feeling none too good about it. Thinking maybe it would have gone easier for me to lie about it. But then I knew Ernie Jo'd go on the television and tell all the world, and he'd look bad because it wouldn't be the truth.

"No way I can go on the TV, Sheriff, and say you had even *partial* success?"

"Not according to what I hear. He felt sorry for her. 'Go and sin no more' kind of thing."

"Oh, Sheriff, this is bad news," Ernie Jo said.

"Yessir," I said. "Way I hear it, she give up the sinful life altogether."

"I heard that before," Ernie Jo said. "Time will tell."

"Yessir," I said. I was sorry to have to disappoint the Reverend Banghart, but there just didn't seem any way around it.

"Bad news."

"Yessir. Sorry, sir."

"There must be some girl in the godforsaken place who could do the job, Sheriff. I mean, he's a man, isn't he?"

"Well, sir, there could be an argument."

"What argument?"

"I mean, if he really were Jesus and all—"

"He's not!" Ernie Jo snapped, so loud I had to take the phone from my ear. "So what do you recommend, Sheriff?"

"Recommend? Why, I don't know."

"Lock him up, Sheriff. Get him out of circulation. No other way. Out of sight, out of mind!"

"Well, sir, in all due respect, he is very popular here, and I hate to think what would happen if we have these people turn into a mob."

"We got to take that chance, Sheriff, to save Christianity from total ruin. And, Sheriff, in all my talks with the Lord, this is the only conclusion I can come to. Your so-called Jesus is out to ruin Christianity by pretending to be something he's not. We can't sit idly by and just let that happen. I don't want that on my shoulders, Sheriff, do you?"

Well, I didn't suppose I did, but I still didn't know how to answer him.

"Do it, Sheriff!" Ernie Jo said like he was a marine sergeant and I was a raw recruit. "We're all counting on you. The fate of Christianity is in your hands."

Ernie Jo hung up the phone before I could ask him about when my picture would be in *God's Guitar*.

ANOTHER BLAST FROM GOD'S TROMBONES:

Jesus in America

The camera dollies with a young woman, attractive but not annoyingly so. She is on her way at a bright pace up the steps of a library building.

"I love to read," she says, "stories by great authors like Dickens and Galsworthy."

She opens the door and hops inside. The camera follows as she walks to the bookstacks.

"If I could read about only one person, I think I would choose to read about Jesus Christ. He is the greatest man who ever lived. And in this book," she holds up a compact-sized book, "you can read about how Jesus came to the Americas after His resurrection and talked with the people there. It is the Book of Mormon and we will be glad to send you a free copy if you will call the toll-free number on the screen. And we'll send you information about the Church of Jesus Christ of Latter-day Saints, too."

—*Television commercial*

Beloved, believe not every spirit,
but try the spirits
whether they are of God:
because many false prophets
are gone out into the world.

—I John 4:1

MORMON COUNTRY

Salt Lake City: It was a mix of apostles, bishops and high priests who met with the First President in the Salt Lake Mormon Temple.

There was so much excitement, it was difficult to tell who was talking.

"We're holding, but the unrest is palpable."

"The reporters are clamoring for a statement. They want to know our stand on this Jesus in California."

"What is our stand?"

"That's what we have to decide."

"We are on record as believing Jesus Christ already visited America after His resurrection. Doesn't that make this time harder to deny?"

"Not necessarily."

"I don't see an option. Denial is our only out."

"Like Peter?"

"Peter was a Catholic."

"But if Jesus visited America before…"

"Why would anyone hang around here if this man were the real Jesus? Why worship someone *in absentia* when the real thing is among us?"

"Because it is easier to worship an unseen god than a visible one. More is left to the imagination."

"What are the signs?"

"Can we really say definitely, 'This is He'?"

"I think we could deny it on the basis of Scriptures. 'All eyes shall see him,' and the like."

"Trumpets, clouds, the works? *All* eyes? Isn't that a little difficult now that we are convinced the world is round?"

"I just don't see how we can easily deny this with our history of belief of the same resurrection before. We said He came to America…"

"That's a point."

"But, gentlemen, if we err, which side would be more prudent to err on? I mean, do we say this is the real thing then find out it isn't, or deny it and find out we're wrong?"

"Shouldn't we factor in some math here? Mathematically,

what are the chances?"

"Slim."

"Exactly."

"But if one of our main tenets is Jesus came to America before, doesn't that make it almost imperative that at least we grant it is a possibility?"

"Joseph Smith found those tablets in New York. I'd feel a lot better about it if this Jesus had shown up in New York…"

There was some grumbling, followed by a knock at the door. An anonymous church staffer said, "The vultures of the press are ravenous. Can we tell them something?"

"Tell them we are deliberating."

"I've told them that. They smell blood."

"Tell them to go with their instincts."

"They did that, they'd be in here through the windows hounding you—"

"He came to America before…"

A vote was taken—

"Yea or nay? He is or he isn't?"

The naysayers had it.

"America…"

There was not a yea among them. Not even Mr. America.

Hamburger

"**H**amburger, he treated me like a piece of raw hamburger."

She had been a church secretary. Naïve, she said. So naïve she agreed to a plane ride from Kentucky to Florida to meet privately, in a hotel room, with the leader of her flock.

"When you serve the shepherd, you serve the sheep," he had said to her.

She was serving the shepherd raw hamburger.

After it was over he ignored her and said only, "So long," when he left the room after combing his bouffant hair just so.

An hour later on television he said he had had some awful good ministering that afternoon.

Sure, she watched the program; what else was she going to do holed up in that hotel room? But it made her mad.

But not so mad she couldn't be persuaded to make a financial settlement that paid handsome dividends to her pseudolawyer and left her some crumbs, with the stipulation that she keep her pretty yap shut.

She was twenty-one when she rendezvoused with the parson. They weren't so stupid to arrange anything with someone younger.

His wife had been cold to him. What were his options? But then he treated the girl like raw hamburger, that's just what he did.

She'd kept her part of the bargain for the few

measly bucks she got after the law student got his. She kept her pretty yap shut, all right, but someone else spilled the beans. Church politics. Out to get her shepherd. Well, she couldn't get excited, he deserved it.

And they got him, and got him good. Put him in the slammer for a little real-estate hype exaggeration to fill the ever-bigger collection plate.

A judge aptly named Maximum Bob thought forty-five years was about right, forty-five years of protection for society. The young lady, for her part, succumbed to a contract with *Playboy* magazine to tell her story (as heartrending as they could work out) and show her lovely body, and after all, as she put it, wasn't it time she started feeling good about her body again?

Penthouse had outbid *Playboy*, but they wanted to show more of her secrets. She opted for what she must have considered apropos for a church secretary: The salvation of her mystery. And the boys at *Playboy* kept their word, she kept her legs together in all the pictures.

As she told her interviewer, her experience with the reverend had been revolting, just sickening beyond words. But she was grateful to *Playboy* for giving her the opportunity to feel good about herself and her body again. Because the reverend had treated her like a piece of raw hamburger, yes, he did.

It was turning a lot of people into vegetarians.

—*Frankie Foxxe*
The Underbelly of Fringe Religion

A woman that feareth the Lord,
she shall be praised.

—Proverbs 31:30

THE GOSPEL ACCORDING TO

MICHAEL

I couldn't sleep all night,
thinking about Mary.

I thought of myself as one of God's forgotten children, and I thought of Mary in the same boat.

I got up at first light and saw that Jesus was already up and about. He was walking in Jack's field like He was lost in thought. Or maybe He was praying.

I went out, and as soon as I got close to Him, I pulled back. I didn't want to bother Him. A couple Devil's Disciples were sitting on a fallen log at the entry to Jack's place, awaiting the next wave of worshipers. The Disciples had cleaned themselves up some, but they were still totally mean looking. The thing about it was, if they said "No," to anyone, they didn't get an argument.

The sun was starting to come up behind the trees. It was making the sky orange. The dense pines looked like surfboards on edge with the orange light behind them.

Jesus turned to face me, and a broad smile washed over His face like He was really glad to see me. He made me feel so good with that smile.

"You're up early, Michael," He said as though it were a compliment.

"I couldn't sleep," I said. I must have blushed when I said, "Mary."

He nodded and that nod told me He understood everything. "Women are an enigma, you know." And He smiled again, that warm all-inclusive smile that made me feel like I was taking a mocher wave, head high, saltwater pricking my face and body.

"How can I find her?" I asked, sort of embarrassed to be bothering Him.

"I'd go to the sheriff's station," He said. "He knows everybody in town."

When I walked into the sheriff's station, Sheriff Jessup had his dog on his lap and was watching Ernie Jo Banghart strumming his guitar on Christian television.

The sheriff smiled knowingly when I asked him where I could find Mary. "She's five houses down the main road here. Little red shed down the driveway from a big log house in front." He took out from the middle drawer of his desk one of his tan business cards and gave it to me.

"You give this here to Mary. Tell her I sent you," he said, adding a wink of conspiracy.

I turned to go, when he stopped me with: "You the kid living up there with Jack and the fellow calls himself Jesus?"

"Yes, sir."

"You got any pull with the man?"

"Pull? I don't think so."

"I was just thinking it might be for his own good if he was to move on from here. A bigger place could handle the crowds better. More parking and such. Understand I'm as much for free speech as the next fellow, but this thing has got completely outta hand for the residents of this here community." The sheriff stretched out his syllables on the words he wanted to emphasize—*co-muh-nee-tee*. "So pass that on, will you?"

"I'll tell Him what you said."

"Los Angeles be better—even Palm Springs—Frisco, Phoenix—any of those places could handle the crowds. It's way too big a burden on Glory Pines."

He seemed to want to talk some more, so I waited. But he didn't say anything, just sat there petting his dog on his lap and staring at the TV.

"You'd rather watch that guy on TV than listen to the real Jesus in person—almost in your backyard?" I asked, not smartass, or anything. "Just curious," I added, so he'd get the idea.

"You're too young to understand about loyalty," he said quietlike, without taking his eyes from the screen.

I was kind of insulted, but I didn't have an answer. I was loyal to Bart, but he was gone. I thought I was loyal to Jesus, but in terms of time, it wasn't a good test.

"Man makes you feel good when everything seems hopeless," the sheriff said, shaking his head at the thought. "You don't

HE'S BACK

jump ship for the latest fad in religion."

"You think Jesus is a fad?" I asked him, startled at the description.

"I expect he is," the sheriff said, watching Ernie Jo put down his guitar as the song ended. "In terms of time, why, Ernie Jo has it all over your man. What's he got here now? Not a lot of real time. Ernie Jo's been preaching the Word for over thirty years." The sheriff twisted his mouth to the left side of his face. "An' I expect if your man don't kill it—" He nodded at the screen, where I saw a close-up of Ernie Jo's face screwed up, making a pitch for funds.

"The need has never been greater," I heard Ernie Jo say.

"If'n your man don't kill it, Ernie Jo's got another thirty in him, easy."

"But," I argued, "Jesus has been around two thousand years."

"Not in the flesh, he hasn't," the sheriff said, stroking the dog, still nestled contentedly in his lap. "Not in the public eye— under scrutiny. That's the real test." He shook his head sadly. "No telling about folks and their being so fickle. Reverend Banghart is on very hard times, I'm afraid, and it's all caused by your man and his gimmicks."

"Gimmicks?"

"Oh, you know what I mean. Love, don't hate..."

"That's a gimmick?"

"And don't take money. Why, boy, that's just naïve. Even a kid like you knows that's not realistic—not by a long shot."

On the screen, Ernie Jo was winding down his pitch.

"See, I'll tell you something about loyalty," Sheriff Jessup said, swiping a finger across his face, under his nose. "I got this here dog, Fluffy, and he's loyal to me and I appreciate it," he reflected. "Don't see how I could live without it. Loyalty is very important in this world—" Then he paused to think a moment. "I suppose we'll take it for granted in the next—" And his eyes rolled up toward heaven.

"So, loyal as Fluffy is to me, I'm loyal to Ernie Jo Banghart—

it's just that simple. And you want to know something, kid?"

"What?"

"It feels real good."

I wanted to get down to Mary's place, but I felt the sheriff had invested some time and thought in me. I felt I should sit there awhile and while I was at it, I might understand what he saw in Ernie Jo Banghart.

For my taste, he was too emotional, the way he waved his Bible around and strutted back and forth across the stage and even got down on his knees. But I could see why some people would go for it. It was dramatic—like a TV soap opera. I just couldn't imagine anyone preferring this actor to the real Jesus. But then, maybe the sheriff was right and I didn't understand loyalty.

Ernie Jo Banghart was preaching *against* Jesus, but Jesus wasn't even mentioning Ernie Jo in His talks. Still, it seemed to me we were heading for a showdown between Ernie Jo and Jesus and I didn't see how anybody could side with this lame TV dude, but looking at the sheriff watching the screen so intently, I had to concede there were things I didn't understand.

"Well," I said after a few minutes, waving his card, "thanks a lot."

"You tell him what I said," Sheriff Jessup said. The dog's ears perked up when I left.

I can't even remember how I got to the door of her little shed behind the log mansion, with tall pine trees all around. I heard a noise inside. My heart jumped at the sound. It brought Mary to life. I could see her in my head—feel her in my heart. I wanted to touch her.

Somewhere I got the courage to knock. Nobody answered. Perhaps I had been too gentle, but from the size of the place, I thought a deep breath could be heard front to back.

I knocked a little louder.

It seemed like forever before Mary opened the door a crack. I could only see about two inches wide of Mary from head to foot.

She was wearing jeans in place of yesterday's miniskirt, and a simple white sweatshirt instead of the tight, silky, low-cut blouse. My heart raced. She was *so* rad. It was a great effort for me to chuck out, "Hey, Mary, it's Michael."

"How did you find me?" Mary asked, not very happily.

"The sheriff told me where you…"

"I don't do that anymore," she shot back, and slammed the door.

This time I wasn't going to give up without a fight. "Do what, Mary?" I yelled through the door. "*Mary*," I yelled louder. "Do *what?* The sheriff didn't say you would *do* anything."

"Not so loud," she pleaded.

"Then come on out!" I yelled at the top of my voice.

"Be quiet, will you?" Mary said through the door. "I can only stay here if I don't make any noise." The door opened two inches. "What do you want?"

"I want to talk to you."

"I'm no good to talk to. I'm only good for one thing, and I'm no good for that, anymore."

"Well, how do you know you're no good to talk to if you won't talk to anybody?"

It didn't seem to be an argument she had considered.

Mary took the chain off and slowly opened the door. "I can't talk here," she said. "Can we go for a walk?"

"Sure," I said, stoked at this first little victory.

We walked a short way under the tall pines. Tension built in the silence. I soon got the idea I could wait till hell froze over before Mary would say something.

So I blurted out, "I couldn't sleep last night thinking about you."

A soft groan came from Mary. "Why would you think about me?" she asked.

"I don't know why. Man, it's so frustrating. You had this most beautiful smile. Then when you met me, it turned to sadness. I have to know why. What is so bad about me that made you so sad?"

"It is not you, Michael," she said.

"But I saw it with my own eyes," I said. "One minute happy, the next very sad." I added facial gestures to copy my memory of hers.

She didn't respond except to give tiny sighs.

"If it wasn't me, what was it?"

"You were just…I don't know, normal, maybe. A reminder of my ugly past. I mean, I had forgotten it was there for a minute, after talking to Jesus. But then you were like reality, and that's something I can't handle," she trailed off.

"Why?"

"Because," she said, stopping, and turning to look me in the eye, "I'm a whore."

I flinched.

"That is," Mary said, "I was until I met Jesus."

"What did He say? What did He do," I asked, excited, "to change you? I've seen it so often, but I don't understand it."

"I don't understand it, either," Mary said. "I guess it was just the feeling that someone cared for me as a person. And, believe me, I wasn't so likable—I was even there to seduce Him." She gave a small laugh, which moved me, though I knew if I stopped to think of what she had done, it would have grossed me out. I guess that was the thing about love—it blinded you to a lot of stuff.

"But why would you want to seduce Jesus?"

"The sheriff sent me. He's in cahoots with that evangelist. What's his name? Baghard or something."

"Banghart?"

"Yeah," she said. She was talking like she was in another world. "Things going hard for the evangelistic trade with this Jesus around. I mean, they've been making a mint promising Jesus, so when He shows up, there isn't anything left to promise. And besides, He isn't asking for money, and the others can't get on without it, so they're getting desperate. You know, if Jesus is really back, who needs the evangelists? Just go right to Jesus."

"You think He really *is* Jesus?"

"I don't know why a girl like me would know," Mary said. "But I'll tell you this, He's something."

"Yeah."

The smile had returned to Mary's face, just talking about Jesus, and I was hot all over again. I just couldn't imagine this girl as a hooker.

"Dude," I blurted out, "I did everything I could to mess up my body. Drugs, you name it!"

"Me, too."

"Why is it so many of us?"

She shrugged. "Can't cope, I guess. Took the easy out. Didn't bother to try — not like they had to when it wasn't so easy to screw up your mind with smack."

"Yeah," I said. "I wonder if it isn't because so many of us grew up without religion. No fear of damnation if we screwed up."

"Maybe," she said with a short nod.

"So what are we going to do, Mary, try to save what's left? Try to make the most of what we didn't trash?"

"If there *is* anything left."

I reached for Mary's hand. She pulled back. "Oh, Michael — don't you understand?"

"Naw."

"I can't. I may want to, but I just can't. You're just too..." she reached for the word..."innocent." And the tears came, and before I knew it she had run off again.

I had so much pain walking home, I crawled into bed and pulled the covers up over my head. Now Jesus, Jack and I had our own rooms in Jack's house. Jesus had spent the first few nights in the barn, but after a few sleepless nights, because of all the demands on Him from all kinds of visitors, He moved into the house in self-defense. The Disciples stayed in the barn. Jack was supporting everybody. He must have been a killer insurance salesman in his time. After I settled in the bed, I began thinking. Deep down I thought Mary liked me. She never really came out and said she didn't like me. All she said was she wasn't good enough. Can you say you're not good enough for someone you don't like?

I found myself tossing and turning, trying to find the right approach to win some time from Mary. But I didn't want to bug her. Suddenly it occurred to me that I could write a letter—that way Mary could read it often, if she wanted to, and think about it on her own time—and answer me, if she wanted to, and not, if she didn't want to.

The only thing was, I was a lame letter writer. If I wasn't careful I could wreck the whole thing with a bunk letter.

I got up and found some paper and started writing ideas in short sentences. Then I made complete drafts—seven of them before I thought that at least it shouldn't offend her, and might even give me a chance to win her over for some more talk.

Dear Mary:

I am writing you this letter even though I am no good at writing letters, I am less good at talking to you in person since you always wind up running away from me.

Why do you always run away? I would never hurt you. I care for you too much. I care even more after our walk that was much too short.

You seem to feel shame, but so do I. Who is to say which shame is worse? Jesus has helped you and He has helped me the same. Can't we at least talk some more? I don't expect anything from you, just to be with you. It makes me feel so awesome.

If it is okay to see you again please put a ribbon or cloth or something on your door handle. I will come by every day until I see it. If it is never there I will still come by because I won't give up hope that you will change your mind.

I won't bother you again though because I care for you too much to make you mad.

With best thoughts,
Michael

I delivered the letter in the middle of the night and slid it under Mary's door, then tiptoed away.

For the love of money
is the root of all evil:
which while some coveted after,
they have erred from the faith,
and pierced themselves through
with many sorrows.

—I Timothy 6:10

JACK...OF ALL TRADES

One morning at three, I sat bolt upright in my bed and realized for the first time I hadn't had a drink since I met Jesus.

I wasn't conscious of any subliminal forces, it just happened without me knowing it. I'd just been so damn busy, I hadn't even thought about it.

And I hadn't thought to hate Stephanie for walking out on me. I couldn't deny I had it coming.

Oh, Lord, if you could have seen what they did to my place. It wasn't surprising, all the people we put through here. I look out in the morning and I can't believe my eyes. I used to have to cut the grass in my field for fire prevention. The crowds had flattened it so it was too low to cut.

It looked like it had snowed Styrofoam and McDonald's wrappers. I had to hire a big cleaning firm to clean up after every one of Jesus's talks—he doesn't call them sermons. It was costing me a small fortune to keep the place shipshape for all those events, and I wouldn't be averse to some financial help from the public— especially from the folks who come here and litter my grass.

But, I love his talks.

I am a Christian—born again. I try to hold no prejudices. I don't use my middle name or initial because it is Edward, so that makes me a J. E. W. You wouldn't believe the abuse I took as a kid—it stung me so bad, I scratched out my middle initial whenever it appeared where anyone could see it. Notebooks, baseball glove, report cards.

The worst thing the kids said to me was, "You're a Jew and the Jews killed Christ."

The reason I bring it up is, this New York Jew—the cliché, stereotype—I can't help what he is. I don't mean any disrespect, but he—that is, his name is Saul Berkowitz—and he's been hounding me to get Jesus to sign an exclusive contract with his TV outfit, and I'd have blown him off out of hand, but he is so persistent, and the numbers are just staggering. I talked to Jesus about it; he, of course, said he wasn't interested in money, blah-blah, but with the numbers Berkowitz was talking, I couldn't resist, so I had him come out to Glory Pines. But first, I asked Jesus how he felt about Jews.

We were in my living room, and it was cold enough to have a fire in the fireplace under the chainsaw wooden Jesus, which I felt peculiar about. I mean, I know it was just a wooden impression, but it was different enough from my visitor to be off-putting. He didn't seem to mind.

"Jews?" he said. "Why, no different than anyone else. Why?"

Well, I must have reddened, because he cocked his head at me like he was sorry for my predicament. "There's the story—you know, about the Jews killing Jesus—ah—you?"

"Preposterous," he said. "Not true at all. And even if it were—what are we saying? Two or three Jews two thousand years ago represent all the Jews in history? Is everyone living today responsible for slavery? The white man's burden," he said, and smiled.

So that cleared the coast for Saul Berkowitz, as far as I was concerned.

I didn't have to call him—he called me daily. I tried to discourage him, but told him I thought Jesus would sit still for his pitch, anyway. I, of course, was secretly hoping he'd take the money. It certainly would go a long way toward improving my outlook about things.

Saul Berkowitz had a long, black limousine drive him here from the L.A. airport. He was a short, squat guy with a balding head and a belly on him that put the sheriff to shame. Whatever there was of his neck wasn't visible above his collar and tie. He was one of those guys who thought a cigar lent him macho, and he used it like a stage prop: drawing deeply, exhaling smoke rings, toying with it, examining it, waving it.

Jesus regarded Saul with an intriguing fascination as he made himself at home on the love seat facing the fire. Jesus sat perpendicular in a cane-backed chair.

"Well, ah, Jesus," Saul began without fanfare, and with just a touch of doubt in addressing him that way. "You've made quite a stir—and that's not easy to do in this jaded country these days." He checked Jesus for a reaction. If he saw any, he did better than me.

"You're the biggest thing to hit the airwaves since O.J. Simpson offed his ex and her boyfriend." I winced at the odious comparison. A faint smile came to Jesus's lips.

"The reason for my coming out here—across the country—is to get you interested in a plan that will solve all your problems with the stroke of a pen."

"Problems?" Jesus raised an eyebrow and looked at me shrinking in my seat. "I don't have any problems, do I, Jack?"

"Well, no...not personally. No."

Jesus looked back at Saul.

"Ah, Jesus, you must understand it takes money to run an operation like you got here. Jack will verify that," he said, tossing his cigar hand in my direction. "Am I right, Jack?"

"A fair amount," I mumbled.

"Jack was telling me what a production this is and how he keeps you out of the grimy day-to-day details of the thing. As it should be, as it should be," he was reassuring someone, perhaps himself. "And you have so many TV crews out there— we could eliminate all that and make room for more of your flock."

"My flock?"

"Just a manner of speaking, ah, Jesus. We're very interested in you, Jesus, you're a hot property right now, and you know what they say, 'Strike while the iron is hot.'"

"Who should be doing the striking?" Jesus said. "You or me?"

"Well, ah, both of us. Both of us. I'm prepared to offer you a hundred million dollars for a one-year exclusive."

"My, that's a lot of money, isn't it?" Jesus said.

"Well, I think so," the promoter said. "In my humble opinion."

I expect Jesus was trying to be polite by not rejecting the proposition out of hand. "What would be expected?"

"Nothing you aren't doing now," Saul said. "A few speeches a week—whatever you feel like, and we'd do the rest—broadcasting to an audience we'd estimate upwards of fifty million people."

Jesus smiled. "And I wouldn't have to sell your product, or anything?"

"No, but now you're talking *real* money. You want endorsements, and, believe me, the sky's the limit—" The cigar seemed to freeze in place as though it had taken on a mind of its own. "If you'll pardon the expression."

"You say exclusive—" Jesus said. "Does that mean what I think it means?"

Saul looked perplexed. He began sniffing the smoke from his cigar as though he might draw a genie from it. "Well, yeah, forsaking all others, you might say. You wouldn't expect us to lay out that kind of dough and let others hop aboard the gravy train for free?"

"But isn't that contrary to my message—exclusion?"

"Not the way I see it. We're not hating anybody here, Jesus— anybody can see your show. We aren't excluding any audience. Jesus, we're available all over the world now."

"Everywhere?" Jesus said this not as a skeptical question but as a semi-awed musing.

"Practically. Oh, there are hamlets here and there that might not be hooked into cable, but we're talking hick city."

"Hick city?"

"Yeah, you know—out in the sticks."

"Not really. Living in the woods, you mean?"

"Remote areas."

Jesus nodded. "Like Glory Pines?" he said.

"I'd be happy to check that for you—if you're interested."

"Oh, I think we're all right as is," Jesus said. "The exclusion of anyone is not among my priorities—and the money—well, I just couldn't even imagine it. It sounds a little corrupt to me."

"Jesus Christ!" Saul Berkowitz said. "I can't believe my ears. You'd turn your back on one hundred million? Why, Ernie Jo Banghart would *kill* for a fraction of that amount. He has to *pay* for his TV coverage."

"Maybe you should make your proposition to him."

Saul frowned. "Not the same," he said.

"Same message," Jesus said. "Different approach."

"Yeah," Saul said, recognizing defeat. "Different. Listen, Jesus, you want I should get the powers that be to sweeten the pot a little? Maybe we could goose the bubble—a signing bonus or something."

"Oh, I guess not—remember, thou shalt not live by bread alone."

"Alone, yeah, but try living without it."

Jesus smiled. "I'm trying," he said.

"I want to tell you, Jesus, you're making a huge mistake. I've been in this biz for thirty years or more, and I ought to know. Nobody is asking you to do a thing different. You just go on as you have been—only instead of a dozen TV companies out here underfoot, you'd have only one. We'd be doing you all a favor—besides the money."

"Sounds good to me," I said, and I knew I shouldn't have.

"Bet your life. What do you say, er, Jesus?" Saul was pressing. "Have the contract right here—" And he whipped it out of his jacket like a matador with a cape. "Can't go wrong, believe me. Your biz is religion, mine's TV—take my word for it, it's a good deal."

"I believe you—"

"Oh, ho, wait a minute," Saul said with a frown. "Are you saying you *don't* believe me? You want me to go back, get them to sweeten the pot?"

"Oh, no..."

"Because I'm authorized to go to one fifty if it would do the deal. Here, let me scratch out the one hundred mil and put in one fifty—and you can put your John Hancock on the bottom line here—take your time reading the fine print—it's all boilerplate, anyway."

I am afraid my eyes were bulging so hard, they were about to drop out of my head at the ease of that fifty-million-dollar addition. Based on my experience in the insurance biz, I'd say Jesus could have goosed Saul up to three hundred million without even trying.

But Jesus would have none of it. He was polite, but firm—"Thank you for coming all this way," Jesus said. "I'm sorry Jack didn't tell you I don't take money. Gives you a bad taste in your mouth—the message gets buried. You know all that, Jack, don't you?"

I hung my head, then made an effort to nod, chastised.

"You're making a big mistake," Saul said again. "Change your mind, you know where to reach me—" And he started out the door, then turned back. "Oh, yeah, promise me one thing, will you? Anybody else makes you a better offer, give me a chance to top it, will ya?"

Jesus smiled and looked at me to help him out of the soup.

"Yes, yes," I said. "Thanks for coming—sorry," I added, and I *was* sorry. Boy, was I sorry.

After Saul Berkowitz left, Jesus turned to me and said, "I'm sorry, Jack—that would have been quite a bit of money for you, wouldn't it?"

"Not for me—well, I could have taken a small percentage of it for expenses, but the money was for you—"

"You know, I don't want to keep you from taking his money—or anyone else's—but you would understand if it came to that, I'd move on."

I nodded, mute. What could I say?

After Jesus went out for a walk, I imagined what it would be like with Jesus a star of his own commercial television show. He'd be talking about ridding ourselves of hate and something would interrupt him, like this guy with a pounding headache or maybe some babe putting on pantyhose.

One hundred fifty million dollars up in smoke. What was

the result?

All TV crews were nonexclusive, so they had so many television crews underfoot you could hardly move on my place anymore. *And* they were all making a fortune because they were selling airtime hand over fist to the headache people and the pantyhose babes, and they were getting the programming free.

People are flocking here to get healed. There's been no talk whatsoever from Jesus about healing, yet they just seem to many people to go together. Jesus is skittish about it. Doesn't want to get started, he says, there'd be no end to it. I do what I can, and many go away claiming they are healed just being in Jesus's presence.

Even though the thing has mushroomed beyond the imagination, I can't really complain. The experience of having Jesus here could not be bought with all the money in the world. He is simply a fabulous person. Is he really Jesus returned to earth?

As the man said, good question.

All day and into the night, Jesus is giving audience to pilgrims—and they are coming to my place. I can't help but feel like a celebrity. But seeing Jesus in action is a lesson you'll never get going to church or watching Ernie Jo Banghart rant on TV.

They all seem to bring tales, in one form or other, of people they couldn't help hating. Jesus looks straight at them, his eyes burning with compassion, and whatever magic it takes he has, and he tells them not to hate—it only destroys the hater, not the hated. Compassion, understanding, being the larger person are all arrows in his quiver.

A few days after the Berkowitz scene, I was out in the field, supervising the cleanup crew after yet another of Jesus's talks to the multitudes, when I heard the footsteps behind me. I turned and it was Michael. I could have guessed. Even his footsteps had turned morose.

"Can I talk to you a minute?" he asked.

"Sure," I said. "Anytime."

"You know about girls," he said, making a simple declarative statement that I didn't find so simple.

"What makes you think so?"

"Well, you were married..." he said, as though that were proof positive of a mysterious wisdom.

"Lot of people married," I said with a chuckle. "Lot of them divorce. I wonder if any man knows anything about women."

Then he told me about his note and the ribbon on the doorknob. "She hasn't put any ribbon out," he said, "and I check, like, four or five times a day. Did I make a mistake taking that note to her?"

The answer, of course, was, how should I know? but I knew that would not cut the mustard, so I turned philosophical.

"Oh, Michael, men and women are so different—and so changeable. Women are loving and passionate one day and sullen, self-absorbed creatures the next. The only thing I know about women is we can't do without 'em."

"Do you think Jesus can help me?"

I looked over to where Jesus was across the field talking to the Devil's Disciples. The question didn't float like a leaf, it more or less sank like a rock.

"I've prayed to Jesus to get Mary to put the ribbon out—to talk to me at least. If only I could talk to her, I could convince her, I'm sure."

I nodded. It was a poor substitute for an answer.

"I mean, He *is* the real Jesus, isn't He?"

The question lay between us like a sleeping snake. One false move could be deadly.

"There's the question, Michael. There's the question. What do you think?"

"Me? I'm convinced. Almost from the beginning. I know it's a little weird, the plane bit and all, but when you know Him it kinda erases all doubt."

I nodded again. "Ah, it would be truly wonderful if only it were that simple. It could be, I suppose, a colossal hoax. The biggest one ever perpetrated. Evangelist Banghart thinks he's going to ask for money, get rich and disappear. He could make a fortune, just passing the hat at one of his gatherings. Why, I've seen him turn down, I don't even know what it adds up to—with the TV and the tabloids, hundreds of millions? This without even asking."

"Exactly!" Michael said. "Do you believe He was here the first time around?"

"Oh, yes, definitely."

"And did He say He'd come again?"

"Yeeesss," I grudgingly admitted.

He looked straight into my eyes. If I didn't know he was such an innocent, I'd have thought he was trying to intimidate me. "So? Now you see Him face to face and you have more trouble believing than when you just read about it?"

"You don't?"

"No. I have less trouble believing what I see than I have believing what I read. So what do you think, Jack? Real—or fake?"

I shook my head. "I'm ashamed to say it, Michael, but I can't make up my mind. I am impressed, yes, but *convinced?* Not yet. I guess I'd like to see a bona fide miracle. Bring someone back from the dead—or heal the sick. If I can do it, he should, too."

I could see Michael was disappointed. Those who believe relish company. I had always been a believer, but this guy Jesus really put me to the test.

"My dad's made a study of Bible history—all his life. I wonder what he would think if he met Jesus."

"Let's introduce him," I said.

"Oh, Dad would never come up here," he said.

"Let's go to him."

"Really? You think Jesus would go?"

"I think Jesus would do just about anything you asked him."

"Really? Would He get Mary to go?"

Oh, the engaging innocence. It really warmed my old heart. "Let's ask him."

Two minutes later, I was back in the house and had not had a chance to propose the trip to Jesus.

There was a knock at the door. It was the sheriff, hat in hand, with a long face.

"Jesus here?" he said.

"Sure is, Sheriff," I said. "Come in."

I went out back and called to Jesus. "Sheriff Jessup wants to see you."

Jesus came across the field, then into the house. "Hello, Sheriff," he said.

"Yes, sir," the sheriff said. "Jesus," he said, with an awkward twist of his hat in his hand, "I'm going to have to ask you to leave Glory Pines."

Jesus raised an eyebrow.

"He bothering someone?" I asked.

"Yes, sir, he's bothering just about everybody in town. You have to know it's a nuisance having so many crowds around."

"He doesn't ask for the crowds," I said. "They just come."

"I know it. But if he were someplace else, the crowds would go someplace else and we'd have a little peace around here."

I thought of sixteen ways to argue with the sheriff. Freedom of assembly, freedom of religion, freedom of association, free speech, etc., but Jesus just said, "I see your point, Sheriff, so it will be time to move on."

"You don't have to do that, Jesus," I protested.

"I don't want to stay anyplace I'm not wanted."

"But where will you go?" I asked.

His smile was heavenly. "Wherever God sends me."

ANOTHER BLAST FROM GOD'S TROMBONES:

The Virgin Mary Revisited

A devout young Catholic girl died an untimely death and was whisked to heaven, where she encountered, naturally enough, Saint Peter.

The saint made her an offer, the granting of one wish.

"You mean—anything?" the girl responded, bursting with excitement.

"Anything," Peter said.

"Could I talk to, oh, jeez, I've always wanted to...could I talk to the Virgin Mary?"

"Sure," the gatekeeping saint said, "easily done. Just step over here behind these unused harps and stare off at that cloud." He pointed to an orangish-pinkish puff of moisture in the heavens.

The child did as she was told, and suddenly there appeared a blue dot which enlarged until she saw standing before her the Virgin Mary in a blue habit.

"Oh," the girl said, overcome with throat-choking emotion, "oh, I've always dreamed of this day. Tell me, tell me if you will, if you can, what was it like to be the mother of the Savior of all mankind?"

Mary wrinkled her brow. "Vell, to tell you the truth," she said, "ve vanted a doctor, but you take vat you get."

—Frankie Foxxe
Religious Humor—The Oxymoron

THE GOSPEL ACCORDING TO

MICHAEL

Jesus did it!

I think Jack should consider it a bona fide miracle that Jesus got Mary to come out and talk to me. It was like a sunrise after forty days and forty nights of rain.

Ever since that first night at Jack's, I'd been reading the Bible a ton. It was so full of wisdom! I remember Jack telling me the things in the Bible were true, not because they were in the Bible, but they were in the Bible because they were true.

Me and Mary talked about this on our first walk around town. After she came out of hibernation, was the way she put it.

"It did me good," she said. "Self-psychoanalysis."

We were heading away from Jack's place and the crowds of people that always collected there to catch a glimpse of Jesus—the bolder ones tried to talk to Him, and much as Jack tried to protect Jesus, He was busy all day and into the night, encouraging people, one-on-one or in small groups, to stamp out hate. And whatever shape they came in, they always went away uplifted.

Love was on my mind as we slipped into the woods and walked close so our shoulders occasionally bumped. Each time we touched—on the sly like that—my heart jumped.

"Everybody should take some time to think about themselves," I said.

She gave a short laugh and said, "Some of us do nothing else."

Mary looked different today in the bright sun. Before, she seemed burnt out, nervous, skittish. And still I had been crazy about her. Now she looked rested, alive, even energetic—her hair sparkled in the sunlight, her eyes were clear—it was like a giant crane had lifted the burden of her past from her shoulders.

I mentioned it to her.

"Sure," Mary said. "And I have Jesus to thank. The way He talked to me—nobody ever did before. To think this much goodness could come out of that devil's errand I was sent on." She shook her head, as though she still couldn't quite grasp the idea.

We found a path along a narrow stream, with clear water

reflecting the trees as it tumbled among the rocks. We stopped and stared at this mirror of nature and another wonder of God's good works. After a shared moment of silence which seemed so intimate to me, I asked her, "Do you think He's really Jesus?"

"Oh, yeah," Mary said, her eyes sparkling from the sun on the water. Her dark eyebrows could keep overhead sun from her eyes, but couldn't stop the reflection from the stream.

"The same man who was here before?"

"Yeah, sure," Mary said. Then she explained: "I don't know what I believed before. I guess I didn't think about it much after I was a kid in Sunday school. My mom used to dress me up like a china doll when I was a kid—on Sunday, for Sunday school. She never went to church and my father just slept in. So it was a drop-off thing. When they split, that stopped, and I remember missing it for a while. I never had any reason to get dolled up like that after I stopped going to Sunday school.

"About all I remember is two rows of chairs in an alcove off a larger room where the adults were. And the felt board where the teacher, this dowdy woman, stuck cutout paper figures of Jesus and Mary and Joseph and God knows who else on, and told us stories I never understood. I guess I didn't think much about Jesus after that.

"My parents' divorce was not a happy thing. I can remember my mother washing dishes over the kitchen sink, tears just pouring down her face, her shoulders shaking, and muttering, 'Oh, God, why did you do this to me?' But this man is no ordinary man. You can see it just by looking at Him. He's gentle, kind, caring, almost motherly."

"Well," I said, "but could He just be a special person without being Jesus returned to earth after two thousand years?"

"I don't know," Mary said, turning her pretty face to look at me. "I don't know how we can ever know. But He doesn't seem like a liar, a cheat or a con man, so why would He say He's Jesus if He's not?"

"Yeah," I said, losing my focus on her, "that's the thing."

"Now, if a guy like Ernie Jo Banghart told me he was Jesus, I'd say, 'No way.' But this man, this Jesus has made such a difference in my life," Mary said, "if He told me He was Queen Elizabeth, I'd believe it."

Suddenly, I felt her hand take mine, and my pounding heart bounced up to my throat and I couldn't get any sounds through my voice box.

And then we were walking again, leaving the tiny village, full of visitors, behind.

I was so happy walking in the woods, by the stream, hand in hand with Mary MacDonald, that I had this burning feeling to share my joy with Amos and Andi—but even as I thought of it, I realized how ridiculously premature it was. You didn't go running home to the 'rents after a first date.

While all these words were gurgling in my throat, Mary said, "I'm so happy, Michael. With you in the woods like this. It's like I'm being given a second chance to lead a decent life—dare I say a Christian life? It's like I'm being lifted off my feet and I'm floating toward your goodness, and all the badness that was me is being left behind."

She looked at me with eyes that burned through my modesty. "Is it all right for me to say that? Do you think I can ever live down my past?" she said, as though her well-being and future were caught up in my answer.

"The past is gone," I said, finding my voice, "it is no more. The future is never certain. All we can know is now."

"You're right," Mary said, and suddenly we were hugging, and I felt a warmth between us like I had never felt before. Our souls were meeting between our bodies and we were being transferred one into the other and back again.

When I finally felt the earth beneath my feet again, I blurted out, "I want to take Jesus to meet my folks. Would you go along?"

Mary's eyes turned moist as they locked on mine. "Oh, Michael," she said, "that's the nicest thing anyone's ever asked me.

Do you think I'm ready?"

"Of course you're ready."

Her smile turned the whole world to love. "Then, yes," she said. "Yes, yes, yes, yes, yes, yes, yes!"

† † †

As soon as I invited Mary to visit my folks I had second thoughts. I remembered how brutal my dad could be to friends of mine—how he'd ask them tons of questions to show them up, to make them feel stupid. Oh, Dad would never come out and say they were stupid, he'd just set some verbal trap, and when they fell into it, he'd sit back and smile.

Mary reassured me she'd been through worse things.

I wondered.

† † †

I'd hoped Mom would answer the phone, but no such luck. It was Dad with his forced friendliness—the self I'd learned over the years to suspect.

"I've met a girl," I said hopefully.

"A girl, eh? Serious?"

"Well, enough so I'd like you to meet her."

"That's serious," he said, raising his voice in mock excitement. Everything Amos did seemed to be mocking something. "So when do we have this pleasure?"

"When can you see us?"

"Let me check with Andi," Amos said, then the muffled sound in my ear told me he was ridiculing my request to Mom.

The hand lifted from the mouthpiece and Amos spoke into the phone.

"How would tomorrow night be for you and yours?" he said.

"Excellent!" I said.

Then when I added, almost as an afterthought, that Jesus would also be coming along, Amos paused, then said on the phone, "Well, won't that be something?" and I knew Amos planned mentally to merrily burst my balloon with one quick bullet.

† † †

I grew up in suburban Los Angeles, in a ranch house. They called them ranch houses because they had that thrown-together, rustic look you often found on a ranch. But now there were a great many more ranch houses than ranches. It made for a "cute" house that a lot of people found livable. You could put your muddy boots in front of the used-brick fireplace and it was like they belonged there. Everybody didn't think they were cute houses. Some even called them raunch houses.

Mom and Dad were at one with their house. They were both carefully turned out, almost like life-sized dolls. Flawless, as though at any moment they might be called upon to teach a class in some offshoot of religion, and they would be ready.

And the ranch house in tractville America would set them off just a bit from the common stucco box with the rock roof, aluminum windows and slab-sided hollow-core doors.

So the ranch house was an alternative for those who wanted a spark of uniqueness without the cash for flat-out originality. And face it, teaching was an altruistic calling.

Amos and Andi made their ranch house homey; with pictures in silver frames, with shelves of books, with rustic furniture that matched the used-brick fireplace.

There were no reminders that the two of them had Ph.D.'s in theology. There was no picture of Jesus, no footstool-sized Bible sitting on an oak stand, open to some especially meaningful Psalm.

It could easily have been the home of two college professors, which was exactly what the Doctors Lovejoy considered themselves. Their "theology" was above the masses. Their interest was in Biblical history, myth and tradition and ethics and morality—but from above, looking down at the big picture of all faiths, not as participants.

Sis was up north taking a Ph.D. in psychology. Another Dr. Lovejoy-to-be—setting an example I could never follow.

Dad had laid a fire in the used-brick fireplace for his guests. It wasn't that cold, but fires were welcoming, especially in ranch houses. Was laying a fire, I wondered, anything like laying a trap?

"I'm so very delighted to make your acquaintance," Dad said as he clutched Mary's hand in both of his.

Dad's smile froze as he shook Jesus's hand. "Well," he said, "I've heard some pretty miraculous things about you, delighted you could come."

"Perhaps the miracles have been exaggerated," Jesus said.

That checked the smile on Amos, midstream. "Perhaps," he said.

Mom brought her friendly smile with her from the kitchen and shook hands with the guests, and it looked like the arthritis in her hands was flaring up again. I was bummed about her pain in those crooked, bumpy fingers. Then she hugged me. "It's so good to see you again, Michael," she said.

I read on Mom's face her approval of my guests. It was like she was pleasantly surprised. More and more, Jesus seemed to look like those old paintings of Him. Of course, He was a lot darker in real life.

"Well, it was nice of you all to come," Mom said, with her generous smile.

"It is an honor," Jesus said, "to be in the home of two people so devoted to religion."

"Ah-hem," Amos cleared his throat obnoxiously, "Biblical history and theology," he corrected.

"Dad had a summer as a minister," I offered.

"That I did," Amos conceded, "that I did. And it was my last."

"Why was that?" Jesus asked.

"Oh, you don't want to hear that," Amos said, stroking his new goatee.

"Why not?" The amazing thing was how at ease Jesus was with anybody—a Ph.D. or a Devil's Disciple. He just naturally fit in anywhere.

"It's such a long, involved thing."

"Why don't you tell it while I finish making dinner?" Andi suggested.

"Well, all right," Amos said. "Find yourself a comfortable chair, and don't be embarrassed if you fall asleep." Dad didn't need much encouragement to talk.

Mom disappeared to the kitchen, unconsciously massaging her fingers, while we all settled in, and Amos began: "I had just graduated from the seminary and I was invited to take a small church in upstate New York for the summer. It was a picturesque little town, one of those places that appealed to artists and writers. I got there in early June and the pastor needed a vacation badly because his only son had disappeared in April and the hope that they held that he would show up was fading.

"Naturally, I got an earful of speculation from the congregation. Drugs and homosexuality were hinted at. The police chief came down hard on the boy's friend, an older married man who used to pal around with the boy in the pool hall. The chief couldn't accept that the friendship was natural. He thought the boy had just dropped out from drugs and the older man knew where he was and was protecting the boy with his silence.

"The chief didn't let up on the boy's friend. I suppose he felt a lot of pressure to solve the thing.

"This friend's wife came to see me and begged me to talk to the chief. Her emotional stability seemed precarious. She was a frail, nervous type, and she told me how hard these suspicions were on her and her husband. Because it wasn't only the police chief who harbored these suspicions, but others in town as well—people need answers.

"The next thing I know, the boy's friend has left town. The chief smells a rat and goes after him, thinking, he said later, the man would lead him to the boy, or at least provide some clue.

"The man turns up dead in a motel room, with a bullet hole in his head. The chief declares it a suicide. The chief declares the case solved. Still without the body, but he theorizes that the man killed the boy in a lover's quarrel, disposed of the body, and shot himself when the burden of his guilt became too heavy for him to bear.

"The pastor returned very shortly after the man's body was found in the motel. He told me he had spent his summer trying to track down clues from his son's college friends and teachers in the Boston area. He had come back empty-handed.

"I went on my merry way and not long thereafter I heard that the dead man's wife had gone to counseling with this minister. She asked him if when she died she would be reunited with her husband in heaven. He said yes, she would, so she killed herself."

Amos paused to let it sink in.

"Did they ever find the boy?" Mary asked.

"Aha!" Amos said with a smile on his lips that did not spell happiness. "They did find him. In the fall, when the leaves fell from the trees, they found him a mere half-mile from his house, in the forest, hanging from a leafless tree."

"That's what turned you against the ministry?" Jesus asked.

"You might say that was a contributing factor," Amos said.

"Soured you on religion in general?" Jesus asked.

"Narrow-minded religion. Silly, blind faith. Stupidity."

Jesus nodded.

"That's not our kind of faith," I said, defending Jesus.

"I'm glad to hear it," Amos said.

Mom announced the first course, a fresh fruit cup, and herded us all to the table.

When Mom set the fruit cup down in front of Jesus, His eyes widened. Mom's fingers were gnarled and funky before Him. Jesus looked from the fingers into her eyes.

Mom wasn't one to ask for sympathy—or to complain about aches and pains. She quickly sat down.

Spoons raised over the colorful fruit, Amos said, "Just what is your kind of faith? Hey-soos, I'd be interested." That weird pronunciation was Dad's way of saying he couldn't accept Jesus.

"Love thy neighbor," Jesus said.

"That sounds simple enough," Amos said. "What else?"

"If we ever achieve that, we can think about going on. My mission now is to eradicate the hate so many harbor in their hearts for those who are different than they."

"We're all different."

"Exactly," Jesus said.

"It may look easy, but it's a tall order. How will you go about it?"

"Teaching—example."

"What's the gimmick?"

"Gimmick?"

"Yeah—what's in it for you?"

"Satisfaction."

"Tangible, I'm talking."

"Just satisfaction."

"Dad," I spoke up, "Jesus doesn't pass a collection plate. He returns any money that's sent in. He just turned down one hundred fifty million from TV."

Amos's eyebrow went up. "How do you operate?"

"With volunteers."

"How do you eat?"

"We manage somehow," Jesus said. "Of course, we don't eat like this," He said, gesturing at the rack of lamb being placed in front of Him.

"Ah," Amos said, approving his wife's offering, "the sacrificial lamb."

There were compliments for the cook, followed by small talk.

"So tell me, ah, Hey-soos," it was amiable Amos steering the conversation back to pushing Jesus, "is there a God for Christians and another for Jews?"

"One God for all peoples."

"Buddhists, Muslims, Hindus…Zoroastrians?"

"Yes."

"So in a battle between Hindus and Muslims, whose side is He on?"

"God doesn't take sides. Whose side are you on when your children fight?"

Dad smiled his controlled smile. "Very nice answers you have. Where did you study?"

"With the rabbis in the temples."

"Oh? Oh…oh, ha ha," Amos broke into a guffaw. "I see, you mean two thousand years ago?" And he roared with laughter again.

"Dad," I said quietly, "a lot of people have tried to prove Jesus is bunk. Newspapers, the FBI—they called Him 'Hey-soos,' too—nobody can do it. He's changed my life—and Mary's life—why can't you just accept it?"

"You mean like Oscar Wilde saying, 'I can believe anything as long as it is incredible'? Well, I don't accept the preposterous, that's why."

Jesus smiled. "Or Thomas Browne in the seventeenth century said, 'To believe in only possibilities is not faith, but mere philosophy.'"

"Ah, touché," Amos said. "The *Religio Medici*, I believe."

There was a silence, which Amos seemed to finally want to break. "From what to what?" he asked me.

"Huh?"

"He changed your lives, from what to what? The last I heard, you were an up-and-coming surfer. What are you now, a university president?"

"Oh, Amos," Mom rebuked him lightly.

But this only gave him an added incentive. "He brought it up. I'm just asking for the specifics. But on second thought, I am willing to forgo specifics. Does this 'change' include the spectra of gainful employment of any kind?"

"Have I asked you for money?"

"No. No. Indeed you haven't. May I assume, therefore, that it is coming from some legitimate source?"

Why did my father always talk to me like he was addressing an audience he was trying to impress with his cleverness? I made a sound through my nose without answering.

Amos Lovejoy turned to Mary. "And how about you, young lady? Has your life changed also, as he said?"

"Yes." Her eyes were modestly downcast.

"And how about your parameters?" Amos asked her.

"Excuse me?" Mary said, looking up. The word was unfamiliar to her.

"How were you changed?"

"Spirit. My spirit was…well, I'm not good with words, I guess."

"No, no, you're doing fine. It was a spiritual thing, you say?" Amos encouraged her.

"Yes. A peace came over me like I guess you have to experience to understand."

"And do you have a job, young lady?"

I laughed uncomfortably, trying to derail the Amos Lovejoy Freight Express. "My father isn't really as materialistic as he sounds."

"Is that your answer, Mary?"

"She's between jobs," I said.

Amos arched an eyebrow, as though pay dirt had been struck. "And what was the last job?" he asked.

"She was in a service business," I said, trying to get to a new topic. "People-oriented—not so different from what you do, you know."

Mary smiled. Amos raised a hand. "With all due respect, Michael, for your superior powers of intervention, I was addressing the young woman herself. The question was raised about her former employment. You know we aren't snobs here. This is an ultraliberal household. If she was a waitress, she will not fare any poorer in our estimation than if she were a Supreme Court justice. But really, Michael, can't we let the young lady speak for herself?"

There was a moment of silent tension in the Lovejoy dining room. Squirming, fidgeting, light coughing. The cruel smile on Amos's face did nothing to lessen our nervousness. Finally, Mary, God bless her, took the bull by the horns:

"I was a whore," Mary said, looking Amos in the eye for the first time. The effect could scarcely have been more gratifying. Andi gulped and shot her napkin to her mouth, as if to hold back vomit from passing her lips. Amos's smile froze on his bluish lips.

"I see," Amos said through rigid, grinning lips. "Mary Magdalene revisited. Charming."

"Oh, but, Michael," Mother said, "not to be indelicate, but aren't you afraid of disease?"

I tried to smile bravely, then I put my arm around Mary's shoulder. "I love Mary, and nothing else matters to me."

Mary cried softly as Mom and Dad looked at each other in that silent warning communication they knew so well. I just wanted to crawl under the table with Mary and bail. Mom moved more slowly as she passed the desserts, a cute little cherry tart on each plate. She wore a frown of worry as she set each tart in front of her guests. When she got last to Mary, Andi paused, as though she suddenly felt she shouldn't be serving the girl.

"So," Amos said to Jesus, "how do you plan to go about your struggle with ethnocentrism? Seems to me large donations would come in handy."

"Do you think you can fight bigotry with cash?"

"Could give you a leg up," Amos allowed.

"But the wealth of spirit really is enough."

"That's good to hear," Amos said, "but you're a long way from a consensus in the religious community with that one—and speaking of the religious community, tomorrow night I'm the keynote speaker for a national Christian convocation in Los Angeles." Amos got a twinkle in his eye as he winked at Jesus. "Interested? All the leaders of the faith will be there. I think I could wrangle a speech for you if you'd like that. Maybe we could even consider a resolution of some sort—you know, a kind of endorsement—that we believe you are Jesus returned to earth."

"Oh, Dad," I said, "your tone of voice isn't very optimistic."

"No? Well, I'm perhaps speculating from my experience with the group. Pretty conservative, theologically, I'd say, but maybe you can sway them."

Jesus smiled—and when He did, it always seemed totally genuine—in contrast with Dad, whose smiles always had an edge to them.

"So, what do you say, Hey-soos, game?"

Jesus looked at Amos for a long time, as though He were trying to see beyond the taunting smile—to get into Amos's head before He made His decision. I don't know if He figured him out or not, but He said, "Sure, I'd be honored."

This smile of Dad's, along with the jerking of his head to military posture, signaled his ultimate self-satisfaction, and it didn't take a genius to realize the reason for it: he intended to make a fool out of Jesus at the convocation.

"What is your idea of religion?" Jesus asked Amos. A silence fell on the diners.

"Oh, I don't know. Filling needs, I suppose."

"Housing, food, clothing?"

"Spiritual needs, perhaps—emotional."

"For all kinds of people, Dad?" I asked. "Or only Episcopalians?"

Amos glared at me.

"What about the good people," Jesus asked, "who live for their religion, live by their faith, who interact better with others because of their faith?"

"I suspect those are few and far between," Amos said. "But I'm not saying honest belief is bad, though I don't think there is all that much of it around. Belief is wrong—unfounded—but not necessarily bad."

"How do you tell the honest from the dishonest?" I asked.

"When it gets usurious, that's bad. When one guy enriches himself on the frailty and gullibility of others, that's dishonest. Religion is myth," he said. "You've got to be careful how you play it. When you pass it off as God's truth, you are on thin ice. The guys that really gall me are the TV evangelists. A more scummy bunch you should never meet. That Banghart character is the worst."

"Do you think a world free of hate is an obtainable goal?"

Amos shook his head again. "Not possible."

"Do you think it's worth going after?"

"Waste of time."

"But those convinced in the meantime; wouldn't that be an improvement?"

"A drop in the proverbial bucket, Hey-soos."

"I'm disappointed to hear that," Jesus said. "I was hoping you would help us spread the Word."

"How would I do that? Quit my job and buy a pair of sandals?"

Jesus smiled. "You don't need the sandals, and you can do it in your job. It would seem that, teaching the history of religion, anti-ethnocentrism should fit quite nicely."

"Perhaps." You could tell Amos was not convinced.

"Why did you decide to teach Bible history, considering your feelings about religion?"

"Intellectual curiosity drew me to theology in the first place—as it pertains to historical behavior. The churches seem to peddle the pap that we are all sinners, lah-di-dah, so we should try to do better if we can, but since we are 'conceived in sin,' well, there can't be much hope, can there? Hope for what? you may ask. Going to heaven?" Here Amos lifted both hands and wiggled two fingers of each to let everyone know the word "heaven" was in quotes.

"Going to heaven is the big carrot on the stick. Be a good boy or girl and you'll be rewarded with paradise. Never mind what that is, it's going to be good. Well, why do we need the carrot? Why can't we just do the moral and ethical thing because it's the right thing to do?"

"How do we know what right is?"

"Oh, no," Amos smiled, "we aren't falling for that. We don't need the Ten Commandments to put us on the straight and narrow. We do our business without hurting our neighbor."

The dinner was over and Mary and I were itching to get out of there.

Jesus jumped up to help Mom clear the table. After the dishes were all in the kitchen, Mary and I went to say goodbye to Mom.

Jesus stood at the sink with Andi. He had Mom's two hands in His. He rubbed the joints of her fingers and closed His eyes—and that's all He did. No shouting, no audible praying, even, just a slow, gentle rubbing of her fingers.

I could see Mom was embarrassed. She wasn't comfortable holding hands with this stranger. Andi didn't believe in spiritual healing any more than Amos did.

Then Jesus brought Mom's hands up to His cheeks—one on each, as though they were lovers in a moment of tenderness.

Suddenly, Mom gasped and Jesus let go of her hands. She withdrew them and looked into Jesus's eyes before looking at her hands—palms up at first, then she turned them palms down. Then, flexing the fingers slowly, she gave a little cry and quickly retreated from the kitchen. There were tears in her eyes.

We followed Mom into the living room, where, speechless, she held her hands in front of Amos, fingers extended. Then she wiggled them with a squeal of joy. I looked to Dad for his reaction. Jesus had healed Mom's arthritis.

"Jesus, Hey-soos," Amos said, looking up from his easy chair to Jesus. "Are you a faith healer on top of it all? Mark one up for your side. But believe you're a two-thousand-year-old man reincarnated, or resurrected?" He tightened his lips and shook his head. "No way, Jose."

Killer! I thought. That would give Amos something to chew on when he introduced Jesus to the Christian convention.

There were tears in my eyes when I hugged Mom and said goodbye. Mary was sobbing, too. Jesus looked slightly embarrassed when Mom hugged Him impulsively. Dad just looked dumbfounded.

Then gathered
the chief priests and the Pharisees
a council,
and said,
What do we?
for this man doeth many miracles.
If we let him thus alone,
all men will believe on him:
and the Romans shall come
and take away both our place and
nation.

—John 11:47-48

THE GOSPEL ACCORDING TO

FRANKIE FOXXE

Ordinarily, being admitted to the convocation of Christian clergy was a simple matter of showing up.

When word got out the group of ministers would be taking up the issue of "Jesus," everybody wanted to come, and I had to do some tall talking to squeeze into the press balcony; the *Gulfport Riptide* being not exactly the *New York Times*.

It was a grand collection of ministers of the gospel. Men in dark suits and a smattering of women in darker suits. The hard core wore clerical collars. They all seemed businesslike and prepackaged friendly. They were assembled in the downtown Los Angeles Dorothy Chandler Pavilion. The contrast of the crystal chandeliers and the plush burgundy seats to the weather-beaten venue of the Ernie Jo Banghart crusade, the Shrine Auditorium, a few miles south, was startling. Here were none of the loud greetings you might find at a meeting of the Rotary Club, but there was a buzz in the room—not a roar. Back-patting took the place of backslapping.

It was a secular auditorium that held the holies. Sacred edifices with more modest aspirations weren't this large. Oh, several TV ministries could oblige them, but that wasn't in the cards. Or perhaps the ministers felt less inhibited if their disagreements took place outside the house of God.

They were not quite as pompous as the priests of my acquaintance, but they were in the running. Imagine the burden of professing a holy life. You have to look friendly and inclusive to your fellows, but you can't let your guard down. Say your inclination is to utter a stream of blasphemous profanity—it wouldn't go over.

The word had spread like a prairie fire that Jesus, in quotes, was to appear, so the assembled holies had to add another dimension to their demeanor—a blasé mask for their excitement. Ernie Jo Banghart and his cohorts were not the only ones affected by the phenomenon. The mainline churches noticed a continuous drop at collection time, and demoralizing sliding in attendance after an initial spurt to see what the Church as an institution had to say about this person who seemed to be distilling millennia of polemic into the simple avoidance of hate.

Amos Lovejoy stood at the podium, center stage front, and

smiled a professional smile at the brethren (and, do we say sistren?). Most of the assembled important clergy were below his feet, virtually all below his head.

Amos looked like he was feeling good and uneasy intermittently. "Ahem," he said, as if trying to subtly quiet the multitudes. It took some effort but he brought them under a semblance of control. The smile flashed, then faded.

"Ladies and gentlemen," he said, "don't make me regret I didn't get an introduction to quiet you down." The smile pulled his muscles so his neck was a network of TV cables. "The good news," he raised his voice, "is I'm not going to speak about Biblical history tonight. As some of you know, in my hands it can be pretty dreary stuff. No, the prepared text is in the ashcan—because," he paused with a dramatic tilt of his head, the gray hair held in place by a dollop of hair gel, "I have met the man called Jesus."

He had their attention. There was a titter of uncomfortable laughter from the cheap seats.

"I'm sure there isn't a man, woman or child with eyes and ears in his head who has not become aware of the man who calls himself Jesus.

"Those same eyes and ears are on us, ladies and gentlemen, waiting for our response. Organized religion, they call us. What does organized religion have to say—is he or isn't he?

"The millennium is here. Many have predicted a second coming, and here is this man to call our bluff. Do we embrace him, or ignore him? The lay people seem to have embraced him. The clergy has been more wary. Of course, that might ring a bell historically.

"But in the here and now, we can no longer be content to theorize. We are faced with a dilemma of unprecedented proportions in our lifetime. I have my opinion, of course, which I will share with you when the time comes—and the time is at hand, ladies and gentlemen, the time is at hand. I am proposing we bite the bullet, so to speak, and issue an edict to the public on this man who calls himself Jesus—who says he has returned to earth. He is, or he isn't. If he isn't, we owe it to our congregations—and the world at large—to set the record straight. I don't have to tell you how much abuse could flow from a situation like this." Amos wiggled two fingers of each hand, in the quote sign, "'Jesus' himself will make an appearance and speak to you. Judge for yourself. Of course, it has been said, 'Judge not, that ye be not judged.' But we can't afford that Biblical luxury. So with all eyes upon us, let the debate begin." Amos threw out his right arm as though welcoming the bearded lady at a two-bit carnival.

There was a hubbub in the auditorium. Robert's rules of order were employed. The first order of business was whether or not television cameras would be permitted in the auditorium during the debate. It was an issue that had never come up at these meetings, there having been no interest in televising the convention before.

Cherub-faced Herman Walzer spoke in the affirmative. He had a little congregation in Kentucky someplace. The Southerners always were more gung-ho than those sticks-in-the-mud from the North. "Ladies and gentlemen, we already admit the press to our conventions—yea, in the past we have had to virtually beg any media to give us coverage. Now that national attention has been thrust into our laps, we are wondering if we shouldn't play coy. Never before has this body had the opportunity afforded to it now. We have labored in virtual secret, lo, these many years, and, Lord, you know we have nothing to hide. Let us put our souls on the table. I'd venture to say the pure hearts here are unanimous."

The light was bouncing off Herman's cherub cheeks like Christmas lights off golden Christmas tree balls.

"Think too, brethren, on the face we show the world. Is it to be one that says you cannot be privy to the workings of this group— representatives of congregations all over the country? Though we represent you, we don't trust you to understand these proceedings and we are ashamed to have you see us in action.

"I believe, along with Martin Luther, that we should demystify Christianity. Make it accessible for all to see. It can only strengthen us in our holy crusade to win souls for Christ."

I saw some of the assembled wince. "He's sounding like an evangelist," said a parson in front of me.

"Ernie Jo Walzer," muttered a man behind me.

There was a collective squirming of the faithful. "To those who want to treat our meeting like a gathering of accident/injury lawyers, rather than the Christian clergy that we are, I quote our Lord from Luke eleven, forty-six, 'And he said, Woe unto you also, ye lawyers! For ye lade men with burdens grievous to be borne, and ye yourselves touch not the burdens with one of your fingers.'"

Walzer looked across the faces in the auditorium and I looked with him. The preachers looked like so many pearls being agitated by sand in an oyster.

"Where are we going to stand on this phenomenon? Interest in our religion is at an all-time high. The reason for it is in our midst. Let us have a full and open debate on this miracle. For it *is* a miracle.

"Our cause is just, our hearts are pure. Brothers and sisters, let us not hide our light under a rock."

Robert Pierson spoke for the opposition. He was a man who filled his dark-blue suit to overflowing. The lights were a little warm for him and he took to wiping his brow with a white handkerchief. Reverend Pierson had a large flock in an Illinois college town.

"Delegates and friends; Mr. Chairman, I rise to speak for our Lord and against the mammon of TV cameras intruding on these sacred proceedings. Are we here for serious, thoughtful deliberations, or do we want our innermost thoughts and debates tailored to a television audience—held up to scorn by talking heads and spin doctors—when sanctity and reason should prevail?

"I think you will agree with me that the matter before us is of such a serious nature that it must not be treated as a TV sitcom. Let not our arguments be swayed by what we've come to think of as the will of the television audience.

"You and I are not sent here to be television celebrities. We are sent here to do the Lord's work. Was there television by the Sea of Galilee? Was the Resurrection put on instant replay?

"Many of us have frowned upon television-celebrity ministers. Yes, and I would not have dared say that had there been TV cameras and lights shining on me. Let us decide the question first. In serious, private deliberation.

"Some of you may be afraid to buck the modern trend of mass media in every corner of our lives. Afraid if we shun the circus atmosphere, we will be branded as elitists. But as our Lord said unto them, 'Why are ye fearful, O ye of little faith? Then he arose and rebuked the winds and the sea; and there was a great calm.'

"Great calm, friends, or turbulence? The choice is yours."

I judged from the applause meter in my head that the nay contingent had the stronger voice. And when the vote was taken, my intuition was borne out. The ayes lost it by a wide margin.

What no one was willing to say was the whole concept was dynamite. The ministers were going to debate the possibility of the scriptural prediction that this was Jesus returned to earth, as promised—and, as most of the assembled clergy thought, probably symbolic. He is here with us all the time and requires no special personification to make Him credible. But then, who was this man in the white robes?

This was, for the old Debunker of Myths, manna from heaven.

We were like canned sardines in there. I heard someone who was being squashed in the aisle say, "Where is the fire marshal when we need him?" There was a near riot outside to get in through the doors that were finally, and too late, locked.

Amos Lovejoy did the honors, introducing Jesus to the convention.

"Ladies and gentlemen, the moment we've all been waiting for. The man called Jesus—" And Amos stood back and with a flourish lifted an arm to stage left, which I thought smacked more of ridicule than of welcome. It was the bearded lady of the carnival again. The barker had done his job and it was time for him to slip out for a beer. But Amos didn't slip anywhere—but to his seat in the front row, where he pasted his eyes and ears on his performer.

Jesus seemed to float toward the podium—his white robes billowing just so. That was one of the amazing things about him, he walked like a lighter-than-air balloon. My first thought was he must have had a full-time laundress to keep his robes so white.

He looked at ease with himself, this man some call Jesus, some call the stranger, some call that man. Believe me, I looked for the slightest trace of the charlatan in him and found not a scintilla of nervousness about him, neither was there any condescension. Just a straightforward, looking-in-your-eye earnestness.

Jesus: "It was kind of you to ask me to speak at such an august gathering. Your sophistication is new and exciting to me...this time.

"Am I Jesus, returned to earth, after two thousand years? Some say yea, others, nay. They quote Scripture and claim the signs were not all there. Whenever the real Jesus comes, there will be no doubt. Everyone will see Him—everyone will believe."

Jesus raised an eyebrow. "Would that be wonderful? Imagine a world where no one doubted. Doubters will always be among us. They keep us on our toes.

"Jesus or no? Does it really matter? It doesn't to me. My message is simple. Let us turn our efforts to the eradication of hate.

"There are so many people now—six billion and rising. Communications are advancing, so we can learn of hate throughout the world in seconds. We can learn of others who differ from us, whom we can pity, ridicule, torment. Hate.

"So call me Sam Bast from the Hemet auto body shop, or call me Jesus, it matters not to me. But let us all join hands in hope and prayer. Let us rid the world of hate.

"Love thy neighbor as thyself."

You could hear a pin drop while Jesus spoke, softly high-pitched. You could imagine what was going through the assembled minds. This was not a bunch of Ernie Jo Bangharts who took the Bible literally. These were the middle-of-the-roaders who spoke of symbolism and metaphors. And today they had had their beliefs sorely tested.

Jesus finished his speech to deathly silence. The audience didn't seem to know he was finished. It was like Christianity's Gettysburg Address. Jesus left the stage much as he had entered it. It wasn't until minutes after he was off that the applause began with a single clapper and then it swept through the room.

Though I thought it was a pleasant little speech, I wasn't prepared for the electrification of the troops that was happening before my eyes. I caught a glance of Amos Lovejoy, in the front row. He wasn't smiling.

I wasn't sure of the cause of the tumultuous reaction. Some were genuinely moved; I'm sure some probably felt he was the real thing. Others seemed to be on their feet for a better view and simply expressing approval for Jesus's unassailable words. That was the thing about the teachings of Jesus, they were, for the most part, unassailable.

†   †   †

The ministers were milling about, still in an advanced state of agitation. A solid pack of them were surrounding Jesus. They seemed to be talking a mile a minute and he seemed to be doing most of the listening. Amos Lovejoy made his way nervously to the podium again. There were mutterings from every corner of the auditorium. I felt Amos had appeared too soon. The delegates wanted to digest what they had heard before the break. They had seen the man in person. How many really believed he was Jesus was hard to tell. From my soundings, I'd say very few of these professionals who made Jesus their life's work thought he had come back, and yet this

Jesus had an aura about him that could not easily be overlooked. There was a definite pull when he talked—more refined than a carnival huckster, more down-home than a Harvard professor. The fundamentalists like Ernie Jo Banghart seemed to have more trouble believing this was the genuine article, though they professed more conviction Jesus would return bodily.

Lovejoy stepped aside as the sergeant at arms swung his gavel dramatically to quiet the crowd. It was a thankless and hopeless task. It was a full ten minutes before the murmuring subsided sufficiently to let the speaker be heard.

"Ladies and gentlemen," he said. "Ladies and gentlemen— I will be the first to admit the speaker before me does not present an easy act to follow.

"Some of you may be taken aback at my use of the word 'act.' It is not an act, you will say, it is sincere and from the heart. And I will say to you, yes, I thought he was sincere, and, no, I cannot argue with his hypothesis—the world would be a better place if there were no hate in it.

"Now, I am a Biblical historian, and I am hard-pressed to fit this gentleman into Biblical history. What is his history? None is offered. We are told the FBI doesn't even know who he is. Has no fingerprints on file. He has done what some might consider miraculous things.

"So let's not lose our heads over this person. And I say 'person' because he seems to be a person, though I can't swear to it.

"Now, we have this resolution on the floor, and I can only advise caution. Let's not go off the deep end and shout to all the world our considered opinion that this is in fact Jesus returned to earth—as some will tell you He promised, and if He promised it, why couldn't He fulfill it? And what better time than the millennium—a two-thousand-year interval? Very neat and tidy.

"I will admit, while we don't know anything of his history, neither has anyone disproven his claim.

"I am reminded of what that great American, Ben Franklin,

said. He said, 'The way to see by faith is to shut the eye of reason.'"
Amos Lovejoy, I noted, was the only speaker who didn't quote the
Scriptures.

"By no means do I mean to denigrate faith. I only say we
must go into this debate with both eyes open.

"I submit to you, the wait-and-see stance is the only one we
can reasonably adopt. I recognize the arguments that will be and
have been made: a gathering of clergy such as this should be able to
make up their minds on a matter as central to their theology as this.
Don't be fooled!" he blustered and thundered. "Imagine the embar-
rassment if we stick our necks out and we are wrong! Fools—we'll
look like fools.

"Be reasonable in your deliberations. Don't give us a resolution that says to all the world we are fools. Keep your heads! We may
need them someday."

Herman Walzer carried the burden for the believers. He
seemed proud of his calling and privileged in his role as spokesman
for Jesus.

"Are we ministers of the gospel or are we skeptics? Have we
not professed to believe the Word of God with all our hearts? Are we
to confess that we—specialists in our field—don't know Jesus when
we see Him?

"What is our evidence?

"This is not a man as we are men. There is no record of His
beginnings on earth. There are miracles or miraculous happenings
attributed to Him. He got off a plane in Los Angeles, but He was not
on the manifest—He just appeared.

"Trumpets? Thunder? How literal must it be? If we had to
script His return, could we do it better? Believably so?

"I say we are fortunate to be on this earth at this time in our
religious history. It is an opportunity that crosses our path once in a
few thousand years. Now is not the time to equivocate; I for one
accept with pleasure this opportunity to stand up and be counted. I
see no harm in this man, only good.

"What will it take, my brothers and sisters, to convince you? If you still doubt, ask would you have been convinced the first time around?

"Does He need to be crucified and resurrected again to convince you?

"Doubting Thomases, join me in voting aye on the proposition. Do not let this cup pass from your lips.

"Those early Christians took a stand. And now it's our turn. Let us not be weighed in the balance and found wanting."

It was like a political convention. Body temperatures rose to compensate for the missing cigar smoke.

Though emotions were high for a gathering of this sort, I expected the result of the vote to be pretty much the same as the TV vote, with those who wanted the TV coverage coming down on the side of Jesus; and those who wanted privacy would be in the anti camp.

The final phrasing of the edict was the cause of major disagreement. You'd have thought they were considering a papal bull. The hard-core minority proposed:

We consider the man called Jesus to be the historical Jesus, returned to earth for His thousand-year reign, as prophesied by Scripture.

An equally hard-core minority on the other side proposed:

While we do not profess to know the exact nature of the man currently calling himself Jesus, it is our opinion that he is not the same man as the historical Jesus.

The majority fell between the two positions. But the final edict was far from a majority consensus. Debate raged over single words and punctuation. For with those devices, you could make it sound like you really did believe he was Jesus returned, or you thought he was an impostor, and too many of the delegates feared rejecting him outright. His message was admirable, but they had to guard against being hoodwinked.

The resolution was hammered out in a closed-door committee session, without the intrusive scrutiny of the TV cameras. Followed by the spinners spinning among the crowds of media mavens lest we misinterpret the meaning. It reminded me of that cute saying: "Please don't think you understand what I said, because what I meant to say may not have been what you thought you heard me say."

I could just imagine the argument that went on as they hammered out these innocuous words:

Resolved: This convention of Christian clergy, having given due consideration to the matter of the identity of the person who claims to be Jesus Christ, returned to earth as He promised, hereby resolves to support him in his Christian endeavors while continuing to investigate his true identity.

There it was. Pretty harmless. And still the debate was heated. When the votes were finally tallied, even that tame resolution lost by a two-to-one margin.

Mysteries are not necessarily miracles.

—*Johann von Goethe*

THE REVELATION OF

JACK WHITEHALL

You don't know pain until you've had a heart attack.

That's all I can tell you. That, and the fact that I was sure I was a goner. The pain shoots up your arm like an electrical charge and you can't do anything to stop it.

Charlie of the Devil's Disciples called the paramedics and they took me to the Palm Springs Hospital.

Somehow, I don't know how, word got to Jesus at the convocation. And, bless Him, He came back. I think the sawbones had given me up by the time Jesus arrived at the hospital. I was slipping in and out of consciousness and my memory of what happened is vague, but I remember Jesus standing over me at the bed and His eyes burning into mine, His hands on my shoulders, massaging gently my muscles, and then I opened my eyes wide and suddenly I felt good, like I had been lifted up on the wings of an angel and I was flying high over the mountains, and I felt so euphoric for a minute that I thought I was dead and I was seeing from a heavenly, hereafter perspective.

But I was alive. He had saved me. I had the proof I needed. I was now certain this was the *real* Jesus Christ, who'd returned to earth to save us sinners.

As you get nearer to the end, your mind turns to what's left— how much, how long. But when this kind of thing happens to you, it exaggerates everything. You think now every moment counts. The minutes are too precious to waste on pettiness, on worry, on self-absorption...on hate.

That little muscle that pumps blood to the rest of your body is an amazing thing. It pumps day in and day out, every moment of your life without missing a beat. But, when it decides to quit, there's no tomorrow. And there's nothing tells you how important tomorrow is like a heart attack.

One minute I thought I was a goner. The next thing I saw Jesus bent over me, whispering words I couldn't even understand.

And then I was new. Whole. Cured. Why is it a man like me who heals others by faith can be so skeptical that he would ever be healed?

They Shall Take Up Serpents

Shoot, no, the boys is not refinded, but they's believers, and ain't nobody gonna tell them it ain't so about them snakes and the strychnine. Why, it is so, right there in the Bible, for all to see for theirselves: Mark 16:17-18: "And these signs shall follow them that believe; In my name shall they cast out devils; they shall speak with new tongues; They shall take up serpents; and if they drink any deadly thing, it shall not hurt them; they shall lay hands on the sick, and they shall recover."

And they's only two more verses and that's the end of the Gospels Mark, and that came right outta the mouth of the Lord Jesus Christ Hisself.

So you jes come on down to one a them there so called mountain communities anywhere in the Appalachians bordered by Ohio and Florida and see for yourself. It's a real test of faith—separates the men from the boys—the believers from the non-. And I don't care if thirty-five died from the slithery copperheads in one year and five more from drinking battery acid and stuff, them victims didn't have the true and strong belief in the Lord or they wouldn'ta died, it says so right here in this here Bible. And that's from the mouth of the Lord Jesus Christ Hisself.

And I besides don't care if they wanta pass all the laws they care to outlawin' our religion. It is plumb against the Constitution of the U-nited States to interfere with my religion.

Why, them serpents is descended from the Garden of Eden altogether, and it's they caused all the trouble in the first place. So we's gonna show this old world we ain't afraid a no serpents.

—*Frankie Foxxe*
The Underbelly of Fringe Religion

He hath shewed thee, O man,
What is good;
and what doth the Lord require of
    thee,
but to do justly,
and to love mercy,
and to walk humbly with thy God?

    —Micah 6:8

THE GOSPEL ACCORDING TO

FRANKIE FOXXE

Rob Houston, editor of the *Gulfport Riptide*, strolled the corridors of the pressroom like a lion on the hunt, his head bobbing from side to side in search of the most tasty meal, his nicotine-yellow teeth gleaming with saliva.

When he spotted me at my desk, he stopped, took his cigarette in its holder from his mouth, then tossed his head in the direction of his office, as if to say, "You—inside."

I followed my boss to the office that set him apart from the less exalted.

Houston's mouth was set in that tight position of disdain when he motioned me to sit in a chair. As always, the room was a smokehouse, and Rob was the smoked ham.

His voice and his nose were W.C. Fields. "Got an assignment for you," my editor said.

I looked up, my dashing eyebrow cocked in query.

"Jesus Christ," he said.

"I gave it to you," I said. "You don't like my stuff?"

"Bland," Rob Houston said, flicking an ash that he seemed to find offensive from the end of his cigarette.

"He's a bland guy. He's no Ernie Jo."

"Ah," Rob said, bringing his flat hand down on the desk with dynamite force, then wincing with the pain it caused his arthritis. "That's just your damn problem. You're obsessed. You've got an obsessive personality and I don't mind telling you it's a disorder. Now, have you noticed any changes in the paper lately?"

"Can't say that I have—but you know me, Rob, I don't read it that much."

"Yeah, some team player."

"Oh, it's not that, Rob; I just can't get worked up about the Daughters of Rebekah's bake sales."

"Well, damnit," the palm came down again with a crack of defiance, and a gasp of pain. Rob apparently didn't have much of a memory. "You better damn well start getting interested in our product here. I may be old-fashioned, but I still value such unfashionable commodities as loyalty to one's employer. You just think you are too damn good to read my paper."

"Okay," I shrugged, "I'll read it. You going to give me an exam about who made the winning touchdown at the high-school game?"

"No, goddamnit, I'm going to get you to write a real story about this Jesus character. A hard-hitting story. Oh, I know you can do it, because you've done it on old Ernie Jo until I'm so bored I want to puke. So what you would notice if you ever read the paper was Ernie Jo's ads have dwindled to nothing. So I called him to see why he wasn't happy with us."

"I'll never guess."

"I believe you're right. You don't have the mental apparatus to figure it out. Well, Ernie Jo was just as pleasant as could be and he explained that this ersatz Jesus was raising holy hell with his collection—out of which, you might be able to grasp if you had the brains of a seven-year-old, he paid for those full-page ads he *used* to take in my paper. Ernie feels, and I can't fault him, that your articles about him have been unjustly critical, a situation he says he can take all right. What he says is starting to crawl under his skin is that you are bringing this fake Jesus to these pages with kid gloves, and so Ernie Jo says, and I can't fault him, get ersatz Jesus to take some ads."

"Very funny, Rob," I said. "Where would he get the money? He takes no collections."

"Ernie Jo further wonders why—if you are the skeptic of skeptics—the great debunker of myths you say you are—why aren't you going after California Jesus with a chainsaw like you go after poor Ernie Jo?"

"Three-million-a-week poor," I reminded him.

"And we used to get some of it." The flat palm slammed the desk again, his face contorting with the pain of the hit. "Why aren't you going after him?"

"I am, Rob. But listen, you go hear him yourself. He's a tough nut to savage. He asks no money, only that you love your fellow man. How would *you* savage that?"

"Well, surely you don't think he's Jesus Christ returned to earth?"

"Surely not."

"Then *say* so."

"Why is that so important?"

"Damnit, damnit, damnit!" His hand went for the table again, but stopped short. "It's only a matter of our survival. You want a paycheck?"

"I wouldn't be opposed."

"Then *earn* it, damnit! Now, get your ass back out to California and do the hatchet. God knows you can do the hatchet like nobody else," Rob said, smoke obliterating his eyeballs. "He's a fraud and a fake. I know it, Ernie Jo knows it and *you* know it. The thing that just blows me away is your miserable failure at demonstrating it. Debunker of Myths? You're not even a mild skeptic where this guy is concerned.

"Well, lemme tell you something, hotshot—you go out there and do the job this time or there is no tomorrow for you here. You don't bring home the bacon this time, it's back to the monastery with you. You go back to celibacy and all of womankind will count their blessings."

She'd learned a new word before the service that night.

Fellatio.

The reverend was startled that she had never heard it. Oh, she was conversant with the gutter version, all right, but as he said, "For one so sophisticated, you sure are innocent."

There he was, up on the stage in the dusty tent, preaching away as though nothing happened, and she was sitting with her hands folded on the lap of her dress, prim and proper, as though nothing had happened.

She thought anyone looking at her might think she were pure and innocent, a middle-aged grandmother in a blue cotton frock with little mushrooms on it, pumping on the outer limits of that category, but still good-looking—the reverend had said as much.

But no one could read her thoughts and her thoughts were not on the sermon. Her thoughts were on the reverend. She knew she wasn't his first infidelity. She knew someday he would announce it to the congregation like he had with all the others. She knew it was supposed to mean she was giving up her self-centered esteem for the socialistic good of the group. But after all she had been through, she still wanted to believe she was special to him. Otherwise she'd have to think she was a slut, and she didn't want to think that.

She thought she ought to listen. He was liable to ask her about the sermon—if he ever talked to her again, he'd seemed so put out that fellatio was not among her crude skills.

There he was, all dressed in his Western leisure suit, with the ever-present sunglasses, using that foul language again. He used it all the time and she realized she should have gotten used to it, but she still hadn't after almost two years.

"We're all niggers," he was shouting. "There's the black niggers, the Indian niggers, the Spanish niggers, the Chink niggers and the honky niggers. Whitey don't understand Jesus was a nigger, too.

"An' if there was a God he'd be a nigger, too. They treats us all like niggers. I'm talkin' 'bout them cap-it-tall-istas. That's the most evil system in the world. Exploiting all my people, makin' slaves outta them. Niggers! But there ain't no sky god, I'm tellin' you that right here and now. I'm gonna prove it to ya'all."

The reverend leaned back as though he were about to be thrown off a bucking bronco and, putting his hand beside his mouth for further amplification, shouted, "FUCK YOU, sky god."

The reverend paused a moment, then his body began to quake with a case of the giggles.

"You see that!?" he exclaimed with ill-concealed glee. "Did he strike me dead fo' my disrespect? You bet yo' ass he didn't 'cause for the one simple reason that there ain't no sky god."

He cocked his head to the sky again. "You turn Lot's wife into a pillar of salt for a lot less'n 'at. Let's see you do it to me. Come on now, show me yo' stuff. I say again, fuck you, sky god! 'cause you ain't. I is, an' you ain't. The Bible say a man with hair black as a raven gonna lead his chilun—you ever seen hair blacker'n mine? Huh, have you?"

"Noooo, Father," they roared.

In the midst of the roar, Sarah thought she heard a popping sound—like a pistol shot. She looked around but saw no one with a gun, no one retreating past the guards who were stationed at each exit to keep the faithful faithful.

She turned back to the stage to see a badly acted look of astonishment on the face of their "Father". His hands were massaging a red substance into his chest.

"I've been shot!" he cried. "I told you they'd try to assassinate me. Well, they tried, but I'm the only God you ever saw who was shot and closed the wounds hisself."

He giggled again. "And don't get no notion no sky god done this. Jesus Christ died on the cross, remember that. No sky god healed him. He couldn't heal himself. An' don't you worry none 'bout any Jesus comin' again to harass you, 'cause he didn't come from no sky god in the first place."

—Frankie Foxxe
The Cult Culture

THE GOSPEL ACCORDING TO

SHERIFF STONEY JESSUP

The man called Jesus broke our agreement.

He came back to Glory Pines in spite of telling me he wouldn't. Jack Whitehall was his excuse. Jack had a heart attack and was in very bad condition, so I guess Jesus thought he could do him some good by breaking our agreement.

So Jack got well, don't ask me to credit it to this strange kind of "Jesus." So, okay, I was willing to let that go, if he'd packed up after this so-called miracle. But, no, he stayed and gave more talks at Jack's place.

What with the so-called miracle with Jack attested to by doctors, the meetings with Jesus got completely out of hand. My hands were tied. It wasn't that I *wanted* to arrest the man, I had serious doubts about it. Ernie Jo was on me about it—about how if things continued like they were, why, the Ernie Jo Banghart Ministries would have to fold, and I frankly couldn't imagine getting through life without Ernie Jo Banghart—Jesus or no Jesus. And things got worse and worse in Glory Pines as this so-called Jesus got more and more famous. It was my duty to bring him in to restore some semblance of order for the good citizens of Glory Pines.

I brought it off using my native intelligence, while the household was asleep. I navigated wide around the sleepy Devil's Disciple sentry, using a back road to Jack's place, then a path through the trees that wasn't guarded because no stranger to those parts knew it was there. I pointed my gun at the sleeping Jesus before I gently woke him, but the man went with me without making a sound. He even had a slight smile on his lips. He could have caused a real scene.

One of the nice things about a small operation was the convenience of everything. Why, here I could put this prisoner in my cell and then book him while I was all comfy at my desk.

"I guess we should get the booking formalities over with," I said, pulling out of my middle desk drawer the standard booking form. "Who are you really?"

Jesus smiled from his cell. "I would say you have me in here because you *don't* believe who I am."

I didn't like that. "No, seriously, I'd appreciate your cooperation. You got a better chance of getting out of here sooner if you cooperate. State your full name, please."

"Jesus."

I let out some breath. "Occupation?"

"Right now I seem to be a prisoner." He saw I found no humor in the remark. "Oh, just put down itinerate preacher."

"Address?"

"I've been staying with Jack..."

"Yeah, yeah—permanent address."

"Nothing has been that permanent." Jesus frowned. "I don't suppose 'heaven' will do?"

"Come on, now—you from the Middle East or where?"

"I guess it's at the right hand of God the Father or nothing."

I looked up into my prisoner's face. I couldn't see if he was putting me on. "But come on, that's preposterous."

"You aren't a Christian man, Sheriff?"

My back stiffened. "I am too," I said. "I'm proud of my religion."

"But you don't believe there will be a second coming of Jesus?"

"Well, I do so."

"Well, I'm here."

"Sir, that is blasphemy, and I don't take it lightly. I don't let anybody joke about my religion," I said. "You don't look like any Jesus to me."

"Why not?"

"Well, because you're not white, for starters—and I mean no offense by that."

"Naturally not. No offense taken. But if you believe the story, Sheriff, God is my Father. Now, in a world that is eighty percent dark skinned, would you be surprised to find that God had some color? Or that I inherited it?"

I stared blankly at Jesus. It was something I had never considered. Oh, maybe I visualized a swarthy complexion once or twice, but it was never more than a white man with a good suntan. I frowned. "Then how come the Christians are mostly white?"

"Oh? Lot of Spaniards—South Americans, Mexicans, Africans. Most of your blacks in this country are Christians. When you think about it, there aren't that many white people around. North America, Europe, Russia and some of Australia and New Zealand is about it, wouldn't you say, Sheriff?"

I had to say that it set me thinking.

I got up to stretch my legs. Then I went to the cupboard in the kitchen, took down a can of dog food, lifted a can opener from the drawer below and opened the can. I dumped the contents in a dish on the floor and Fluffy came trotting over for a feast, his whole body shaking in happy anticipation.

I sat at my desk and watched Fluffy lap up his chow. I got a kick out of the dog enjoying his eats so much and I didn't care who knew it.

"Nice dog you have there, Sheriff," Jesus said.

"Thanks, mister," I said. It wasn't easy for me to come up with a form of address for this prisoner. I didn't want to capitulate to the charade and insult Ernie Jo, but I didn't want to be disrespectful, either. I was not about to leave my bases uncovered.

"All Pekingese dogs are fluffy, but this here one was fluffier than most," I said. "When he looks up at me with them little brown eyes, I tell you honestly there is just no resisting him."

"Pekingese is a Buddha dog, you know," Jesus said.

"Nah." I shook my head. "Not this one. This here Fluff's a good Christian dog. Why, while I sit here with the TV turned on to Ernie Jo Banghart's Ministry of Ministries, I oftentimes catch Fluffy beating time to the music with his tail. I mean, he is just enjoying the daylights outta that *Christian* music. Singing 'bout Jesus an' all."

"Think he understands the words, Sheriff?" Jesus asked.

"Couldn't swear to it, mister, but I wouldn't be a-tall surprised."

"Where'd you get a dog like that, Sheriff?"

"Down in Hemet they got this kennel specializes in pure breeds—Pekingese, golden retrievers, poodles, I don't know what all. This was just the fluffiest dog they had. Doggie Dog's the name of the place—isn't that cute?"

"Yes, it is," the prisoner said, and it didn't sound like he was making fun.

"So tell me, mister, just what kinda religion you got?"

"Not too far off from your own, I expect."

"Now, you don't have to be so cagey. Unnerstan', you don't have to answer none of these questions you don't want to. Nothing official about this."

"Happy to talk to you, Sheriff. You know I am here preaching the brotherhood of man."

"Knowed a lot of brothers in my time that couldn't get along with each other."

"Exactly so. From the beginning, Sheriff—Cain and Abel— no one can get along. We find differences and let them annoy us. Before long, they destroy us."

"Well, to my way of thinking, discrimination is one of the keys to life. You gotta discriminate ever'day. Whether it's buying apples in the market or goin' through two applicants for the same job."

"Ah, yes, apples are one thing. People you don't like because they are different than you is quite another."

I scratched my nose. "What about freedom of association? I gotta 'sociate with folks I don't care to?"

"Why don't you care to?"

My shoulders felt like a bullock when I tweaked them. "Ain't nobody gonna tell me to like what I don't."

I was more than a little riled up, and though it was past my ordinary bedtime, I knew I couldn't sleep. I had an Ernie Jo show in the VCR I hadn't watched yet, and I thought this would be a good way to pass time with my prisoner, besides which, I wanted to get his take on my idol.

"You want to watch the Reverend Banghart with me, mister?" I asked. "I can turn the set the other way if'n you don't."

"Be glad to watch it, Sheriff."

I turned on the set. Then I positioned my chair to set it between the television and Jesus, who watched from his cell, over my shoulder.

A spinning ball of fire dropped from the heavens on the small TV screen and spun around center-screen until three golden G's emerged. They separated and formed the words:

Great Gospel Gathering

Another ball of fire traversed the screen, leaving in its smoky wake:

The Reverend
Ernie Jo Banghart

This dissolved into the smiling face of the reverend himself. In an instant, the camera pulled back to reveal the famous Ernie Jo pose: foot up on a stool, guitar resting on the raised leg, strumming away. Backed up by the four polished-faced singers and the boys in the band, Ernie Jo was singing his heart out:

"My Jesus is coming soon
He's been to Calvary
He's seen our moon
My Jesus is coming soon

Yes, Jesus is coming home
To hearts who open to Him
My Jesus will enter in
My Jesus is coming soon

He'll bring us perfect love
He watches the sparrow and dove
He moves great waters and oceans' foam
My Jesus is coming home

Oh, Lord, I'm gonna be ready
Oh, Lord, I'm gonna be ready
My heart will be free of sin
When I open it and let my Jesus in.

"Let's sing it one more time," Ernie Jo said, and they did. Five times, until the picture faded from the screen and then Ernie was on the library set he always used for his offering requests. It was the oak bookshelves with the white silk flowers in blue glass pots, knickknacks, a statue of Jesus (that was white!) and some books upright and some lying down.

Oh, I expected they could have filled the shelves with books—even books on religion—if they had to. But most of us cared for only one book, the Holy Bible, and Ernie Jo ofttimes said that one book was all he needed because it contained all the truth of the world, and all the knowledge a body would ever need.

Besides, Ernie Jo said the people who gave him the real trouble were those who read too many books. The "in-tell-lec-tu-alls," as he called them on his shows. And so he kept the "library" shelves to a respectable five or six books, all Bibles.

"Friends," Ernie said in a head shot looking straight at the camera, "I want to speak to you today straight from the heart. We have never been at a more dangerous crossroads in this ministry. Satan has sent us the greatest challenge of our entire lives and we desperately need your help, and, believe me, I am sincere when I say that.

"As you well know, there is a man in California who calls himself Jesus and who preaches on a mountaintop, and the only remarkable thing anyone can say about him is that he hasn't asked for money.

"Yet. And that's a big 'yet.' Friends, I would love to preach on a street corner, and I have. Why, I started preaching down on the town square when I weren't no more 'n grasshopper high. I would *love* to do it again, believe me. You all must know by now I don't want any financial gain for myself, but these progrums are costly. If I was to set up on the street corner and forgo teevee, why, I probably wouldn't reach most of you who cain't go to the corner for one reason or the other.

"Well, now is your chance to let us know just how much this progrum means to you. I don't care what you give, that's between you and the Lord, but I ask you, I beg you, give just as generously as you can. Checks, money orders, the address is on the screen. And if you have a Visa or MasterCard or Discover card and you could just go to the phone now—or after the progrum's over—and put your donation on your credit card, why, we could gain access to those funds right now which we need so very, very much.

"Please send what you can, whether it be fifty dollars or a hunderd, or a thousand or ten thousand, or just twenty-five dollars. We will thank you so very, very much."

The screen burst again into the fire and three G's. Then it dissolved to Ernie Jo Banghart, face front, Bible in one hand, portable microphone in the other.

"Folks, tonight I hope you'll forgive me if I depart from my usual order of things to talk about something I'm sure is on all of our minds. Something that seems so innocent yet something so orchestrated by that great demon of demons: SATAN!

"Now, a lot of well-meaning people, some of our own congregation included, have been, I'm very sorry to say, deceived by this man. They have been deceived into actually believing this is Jesus Christ returned to earth."

The audience laughed. Ernie Jo could be nasty in a poke-funny way.

"Now, believe me, and I don't mean to be humorous, but

nothing would give me more personal pleasure than to greet the real Jesus on His return. But, friends, our Lord said, many impostors will come in my name, many false prophets claiming to be the Savior.

"Now, we've had them before, and we've survived them. For some reason this man has gathered a following unlike those street-corner soap-box orators of old who claimed *they* were Jesus Christ.

"And I ask myself—Why?

"And I ask Emmy Sue—*Why?*" With each repetition the golden baritone built to an exciting climax.

"And I ask Brucie—*Why?*" And the audience groaned for him, the hopeless sounds of bafflement, of approval of Ernie's scorn.

"And I *asked* the Lord—*Why?*" Pacing back and forth across the stage for this litany, Ernie Jo now hunkered down until he simulated a beast of the field in total obeisance to his God.

Ernie Jo stood up abruptly. "An' you know what my Lord answered?"

"Nooooo," the crowd responded. The camera caught the angry congregation with their lips pursed around the oooo's. But it focused across the front rows now, not the usual full-house pictures, because now the balcony was virtually empty and the last rows of the downstairs were sparsely populated.

"My Lord answered me in THE NEG-A-TIVE!" Ernie Jo shouted. Emmy Sue was beaming her approval from her seat behind him on the stage. Their son, Brucie, was there beside his mom, but he was staring straight ahead, as though he were seeing an unpleasant vision on the far waters of the Gulf of Mexico.

Emmy Sue sat there looking like a cover on one of them fancy magazines. She was so nicely turned out you wouldn't hardly believe she was a minister's wife. And you could tell she only had eyes for Ernie Jo—she sat there watching him all the time, like she was just hanging on his every word.

"I know my Jesus and I glory in Him," Ernie Jo was saying. "To Him I give all power and glory, hallelujah! The blood of the

Lamb washed me clean!"

"Hallelujah," from the audience.

"So I ask you today, what does this man who calls himself Jesus talk about?" Ernie Jo asked the faithful. "Saving sinners?"

"Nooooo," they roared in unison, Emily Sue leading them with wide-mouthed O's, coupled with vigorous shaking of heads.

"The infinite mercy of the Father?"

"Nooooo."

"The Lamb of God who takes away the sin of the whole world?"

"Nooooo."

"Saving souls for the *real* Jesus Christ?"

"Nooooo."

"Being washed in the blood of the Lamb?"

"Nooooo."

"The Resurrection of our Lord and Savior the *real* Jesus Christ?"

"Nooooo."

"The Resurrection of the body and the life everlasting?"

"Nooooooo."

"No, he don't. He's a impostor as sure as I stand here, and it is just a mystery to me why so many is following him. He's drawing a lot of attention from God's legitimate work here on earth, he's hurting the legitimate preachers and congregations all over this country, and this man has got to be stopped so we can all get back to the real work of saving souls for the *real* Jesus." Ernie Jo was pacing, he was bobbing, he was shaking his fist, waving his Bible. He was being the lovable Ernie Jo that millions of us people used to send money to to show our appreciation.

Then Ernie Jo Banghart stopped dead in his tracks and faced the camera, square on, waiting with grim-set jaw while the camera zoomed in for a closeup.

"But, friends," he said severely, "I'm going to let you in on a little secret." The corner of his mouth pulled in, satisfiedlike. "The contacts of this ministry are far and wide. We have friends in high places. And one of those places is Glory Pines, California, where this so-called impostor Jesus decided to make his fuss.

"No, I cain't say his name, for reasons of privacy of the individual, but we have a distinguished prayer partner out there in Glory Pines who, if I recollect rightly, is having his picture taken at this very moment to be included in our magazine, *God's Guitar*, giving testimony to just what this ministry means to him. So you will have a chance to recognize him in due time, if you are a subscriber to our magazine. This prayer partner has been working with this ministry to solve the many problems this fraud has caused this, and all, respectable ministries. I can't be more specific than that, or else I'd let the cat out of the bag.

"The Lord Jesus Christ be with you, and your spirit," Ernie Jo said— "and that's the real one I'm talking about. I look forward to hearing from you, with a donation from your heart for just as much as you can spare, to see us over this low spot in our ministry. Remember, what you give is between you and the Lord, but I ask you, I beg you, give just as generously as you can. I'll thank you for it so very much." Then Ernie Jo was wiped off the screen with the three balls of fire.

Whew! That was my first reaction to that national-TV attention. Then suddenly the back of my neck burned. "That's *some* preacher," I said to the screen.

"Think I should change my approach, Sheriff?" Jesus asked.

I turned around. "Why?"

"Your man seemed to criticize me on theological grounds."

"Well, Ernie Jo's got his ideas, that's true," I said. "Pretty set in his ways."

"Good ways?"

"Oh, Lord, yes. The best."

It was pret' near four in the morning when I got some shut-eye. There wasn't no way I was going to leave this character alone down here, even though he was locked up, so I just got as comfortable as I could in my chair behind my desk and took myself a snooze till a little past daylight, when I heard some commotion outside.

I pulled myself up and went over to the window, where I saw some people milling about. There weren't any signs of them getting unruly yet, but I knew in my bones it was coming. I had to do some tall contingency planning. That's when I remembered the trench under the place.

It may not cover all theodicy
Or make him popular among the
seraphim,
But "If God were true," my Zander
said to me,
"He wouldn't make people not believe
in Him."

> —*Howard Nemerov*
> Zander on God

THE GOSPEL ACCORDING TO

FRANKIE FOXXE

My timing was right.

I got to California just after Sheriff Stoney Jessup threw Jesus in the slammer. I got a flight to the Ontario airport, rented a car, and made it to Glory Pines in record time.

I met the lad, Michael Lovejoy, at the entrance to Jack Whitehall's place. He told me Jesus was in jail and Jack Whitehall was down the hill looking for a lawyer with some angle to release him. In the meantime, they didn't want to turn the visitors into a mob, so they weren't telling anyone where he was.

Sheriff Jessup had not wanted to let me in the door. That much was obvious. There was quite a crowd milling around outside and though they looked peaceful, I could understand the sheriff's nervousness. Apparently, a number of the pilgrims had suspicions about where Jesus was. I'd put the crowd at about one hundred, but three of them could trample Sheriff Jessup to death. Besides, newspaper reporters Sheriff Jessup didn't need. But he could count his blessings. Most other reporters gave this story a short shrift. TV ate it up, and some seemed to write their pieces from the TV. I had the in because I made it the first time on the moped when no one else could get to Glory Pines, and other reporters and papers picked up my pieces. If I hadn't been so busy, I might have made a business out of it, but it was *carpe diem* time for the old Debunker of Myths: once-in-a-lifetime opportunity.

At the jailhouse door, I told the sheriff I had come all the way from Gulfport, Mississippi, and I had a very close relationship with Ernie Jo Banghart.

There was just one thing:

"You aiming for one of them real flattering pieces?"

I winked at the sheriff and whispered, "You keep a secret?— my boss wants me to crucify Jesus all over again. My boss sides with Ernie Jo Banghart. Advertising, you know. So any flattery in my piece will go to you."

The sheriff set up a chair for me right outside Jesus's cell, then settled back at his own desk to eavesdrop on the interview.

"What are you doing here, really?" I asked Jesus. "What do

you want?"

"To make the world a better place."

"How are you going to do that?"

"Start small. If we can keep brother from turning against brother, man against man, nation against nation, we've got a good beginning."

"That stuff in the Bible?"

"How about 'Love thy neighbor as thyself'?"

"What else?"

"Oh, there's Romans thirteen, eight: 'Owe no man any thing, but to love one another: for he that loveth another hath fulfilled the law.'"

"Yeah—another?"

"'Be not overcome of evil, but overcome evil with good,'" he said. "Romans twelve, twenty-one."

"Jeez, J.C., you *are* one of those guys who knows all the numbers. Very impressive."

"Not that impressive for a guy in my line." He smiled, and I shut my eyes to steel myself against J.C.'s impossible charm. "Could you do that for any verse in the Bible?"

"I'm game to try it."

I picked the Bible off the sheriff's desk. I leafed through it, stopping here and there, looking for a remote passage to my liking. "'And when the disciples saw him walking on the sea, they were troubled, saying, It is a spirit; and they cried out for fear.'"

Jesus smiled. "Matthew fourteen, twenty-six. Easy."

"Okay, let's get a little harder. 'And I brake the jaws of the wicked, and plucked the spoil out of his teeth.'"

"Job twenty-nine, seventeen."

"Hm. 'And there were four leprous men at the entering in of the gate: and they said one to another, Why sit we here until we die?'"

"Second Kings seven, three."

I was reading with a vengeance now: "'For without are dogs,

and sorcerers, and whoremongers, and murderers, and idolaters, and whosoever loveth and maketh a lie.'"

"Revelation twenty-two, fifteen."

The really uncanny thing, I thought, was this apparition answered almost without thinking, as though he were a high-speed computer. That set me thinking. What if this Jesus were only a highly developed robot—the product of some mad scientist, developed in secret as an elaborate ruse?

"Well, I don't care what you say, J.C., that's quite a trick."

"If thanks are in order, Frankie, please consider them given."

"Now, there seems to be some sloppy omissions in the gospel narrative, Jesus. Like what were you doing from three to thirty?"

"But the important things are there. If they had gone into all these little details, you wouldn't be able to lift the book."

"Couldn't they leave some other stuff out? Maybe the more preposterous stories in the Old Testament, for example—the whale eating Jonah, then spitting him up? All that human sacrifice for a vengeful God, who, in New Testament hands, becomes loving?"

"But the Bible is not a biography of me. There may be too much of me in it already. You know I am only an instrument of the Father who art in heaven—all glory be to the Father. I am frankly not comfortable with this 'glory to Jesus' talk. I never sought the glory. I told stories, others have told stories; I healed the sick, others have done the same. I didn't heal all the sick, I didn't bring everyone back from the dead."

"Why not?"

"I guess the power was not granted by God—who, as you know, moves in mysterious ways."

"Isn't that a bit of a cop-out? Aren't you supposed to be God incarnate in man? And if not, are you really Jesus, the Christ?"

"It is not for me to convince you. If you are lacking in faith, I can't convince you. Now let me ask you a question, Mr. Frankie Foxxe. Do you find fault with the Bible?"

"I don't know where to begin. I don't think there is sufficient proof there ever was a Jesus. If there was, what he did and said was probably extremely remote from what is recorded in the Bible. Virgin births and execution by nonbelievers, then resurrection of the hero figure have been hallmarks of dozens of religions throughout the world for millennia. If God gives me a mind and allows me to make rational choices, then I must conclude there is no evidence for you or God. And if I simply believed in him by blind faith, I would be insulting him by misusing the mind he gave me."

"Your sophistry is intriguing," Jesus said. "You believe, then, it all started how?"

"Well, hold on, I don't know. Nobody knows. It's a marvelous mystery. But simply because I don't know, I don't have to be forced to subscribe to a myth."

"Do you find fault with the moral code?"

"If you are saying the Bible and Christianity originated these rules—this moral code—I doubt it. Morals were around long before the Bible. I suspect folks never thought it was right to kill their fellows—even killing animals gave them pause. Of course, your Old Testament buddies weren't above cold-blooded murder of their own kids to appease this loving God of yours, but I guess he wasn't so loving in those days. Then there was all that bloodshed in the name of religion. A strong belief in one's religion seems to breed oppressive intolerance, doesn't it? The inquisitions. The Muslims, the Hindus, the Serbs—nobody can tolerate differing beliefs."

"Ah," Jesus said, "you are full of the old overworked doubts tonight, aren't you? Certainly you can squeeze bad from good. This is in the nature of people. It is not in the nature of God."

"Are you repudiating the Bible? God knows every feather that falls from a sparrow? You've said some pretty preposterous stuff yourself if we are to credit the Bible."

"Perhaps I was misquoted."

"Could it be anything else? No reasonable person claims that the gospels were written by anyone who knew Jesus—and the earliest written evidence we have is some four hundred years after Jesus is supposed to have walked the earth. I don't suppose I need point out the fallacy of God waiting until two thousand years ago, then depositing you in that bleak unpopulated desert. What was he trying to hide?"

"Had to be someplace," Jesus said. "Sometime. I'm back now and we are near a big metropolitan area. One of the biggest in the civilized world. Does that convince you?"

"Do I *have* to be convinced? That's another question."

"Or *could* you be?"

That made me smile. "You may have me there. I used to be. Never missed church or Sunday school. Prayed like a demon. Made deals with Jesus. I would trade good works—kiss his picture that was in a drawer somewhere—in exchange for favors. The bigger the favor, the more the number of kisses."

"What kind of favors?"

"Hard to remember. I think it was largely altruism. I had the idea it was wrong to pray for yourself—like, to get the baseball glove you thought you had to have. But I have a suspicion I went over the line once or twice. Like I'd say, 'If it is your will, dear God, could I have a baseball glove?' I had other superstitions. I walked by the church to go to school. I had a lot of respiratory ailments, but I wouldn't spit on the church property."

"What changed you?"

"Well, you may not believe this—and I don't brag about it— but I was a priest."

"No!" Jesus said, and I heard an echo from Sheriff Jessup behind me. I had forgotten about the sheriff. "Why should that change you?"

"The more I read about religion, the more I doubted it. It just seems that has to be the case with anyone. So who reads more, or is more knowledgeable about religion, than our theologians—our religious leaders? A paradox. Those who should instruct surely have less belief than those who seek instruction. Then there was the confessional. I listened to all these tales of woe, and what struck me was how common it all was. We not only dumped all this guilt on people, we made them spill their guts to us about it. Made them all feel like they were unique, miserable sinners when they were just the norm. We were in the business of serving the rich—that eye-of-the-needle talk was a ruse, a sop thrown in for the poor. For it is the poor that all this stuff is directed at. Keep from slaughtering the rich. Heaven will be their reward—and in case it isn't—they will be too dead to notice. The important thing is not to upset the applecart here on earth."

"Belief," said Jesus, "is a fragile thing. We do our best," he said, shaking his head at my apostasy. "We don't win everyone."

"But it's the whole spectrum of the religious establishment. From the television preachers and the tent revivalists to the faculties of our theological seminaries and even the pope. You hardly have a believer among them. Doesn't that bother you?"

Jesus smiled. "It is just as before," he said, "I have only the people."

I looked him in the eye and he gave me back a look as good as he got. But if he *was* so intelligent, he would be the first to acknowledge that what he was claiming was impossible.

I moved the discussion to sex—always a good topic in the context of religion, I thought.

"What about sex, J.C.?" I asked him.

"Private."

"Well, okay, cop out if you want, but give me a little insight into your view of women."

"I like them."

"A couple things bug me, J.C.—one is Adam and Eve, the other is when you were supposedly on the Cross—that whiny 'My God, why have you forsaken me?' seems a little out of character."

"Oh?"

"Yeah. Here you are, supposed to be the Savior of all mankind—who had predicted his impending death—who didn't bother to argue his case and who, the next thing you know, is a cry-baby."

"You ever been crucified, Frankie?"

"Only verbally."

"It smarts."

"Well, I imagine it does…"

"You wouldn't soon forget it."

"But, I mean, here you are, this macho figure, and you are taking a little suffering anything but like a man."

"Well, I didn't write the book, you know."

"But you are God, aren't you?"

"Maybe you are working that a little hard. I am God, sure, but so are you. God is in man. Read through the fluff, Frankie— God is in all of us. And tear any of our flesh and bones with nails and watch us whimper 'Why did you do this to me?' People whimper at a lot less than crucifixion."

"Now you say we are all gods. Not very inspirational, some of us. Then take the Crusades and such—down through the centuries, millions have been slaughtered in the name of Christ."

"You think we're proud of it?"

"They quoted their Bibles all the way."

"Anyone ever misunderstand anything you ever wrote, Frankie?"

"Fair enough," I conceded. "But I can't attribute even one death to something I wrote."

"But is your readership on par with the Bible's?"

"Oh—but the whole world could read everything I ever wrote without inciting them to kill—"

"Day in and day out, Frankie? I wonder. Soon Frankie Foxxe cults would spring up under every rock. People who almost worshiped what you wrote—some who tried to live by it. Others would find it nonsense. Arguments would break out—people would be suspicious of those who didn't agree with their interpretation of your words. Next thing you know, animosity, hate, boiling anger, bloodshed. Then should we hold you responsible?"

"Of course not..."

"But they would. Debunkers of myths would be out debunking old Frankie Foxxe. And why not? Hadn't millions died in bloody battles in his name? No matter old Frankie never meant for his readers to be divided in warring camps of those who believed what he wrote against those who didn't."

"Let's talk Deuteronomy, Jesus. All that stuff about stoning to death your son, and your wife if she disbelieves. That a loving God?"

"They *were* a little extreme in those days, weren't they?"

"I'll say. These literal fundamentalists should have a hard time with that stuff, but they just pass it off. 'Inerrant Word of God,' they say. That so?"

"I'll take your word for it. Before my time."

"So you can't affirm or deny that the story of Adam and Eve was made up to effectively kill the female deities?"

"Well, they were substituting the father for the mother."

"And to do it they decided to blame everything on the women. They really made a fool out of women with that story—blaming Eve for leading Adam astray. She was only made from an insignificant part of him by the writer's reckoning—a lousy rib—"

"It was a good rib."

"Preposterous on the surface. Absurd if you look any deeper. Man came of woman, it was never the other way around."

"How do you know, Frankie?"

"Common sense. You do not reproduce by cutting out a rib and letting it fester."

"Even if you are God?"

"Oh, Jesus, come on. You can't dignify that argument. I won't even try to embarrass you with it. You know what really bugs me?"

"What?"

"Adam and Eve had two sons. No daughters. Was there asexual reproduction in those days? Did the boys plant their seeds in their mother?"

"With God, all is possible," Jesus said.

"But why did they have to mess with things—what was wrong with a female deity?"

"I'd have been a girl," Jesus said, teasing me.

"Yeah, with a female God—Daughter of the Mother. Mother, Daughter, and Holy Ghost. What do you think?"

"These days, people don't go around dumping on women because of the Adam and Eve story."

"Oh? We got rape and all kinds of other sadism. Most of the crimes committed on others are by men. Virtually all of the crimes against women are by men. I'm thinking if the women were in charge it might be more peaceful."

"But for the women to be in charge they would have to overcome those who wanted to be in charge, and that takes force. Mrs. Gandhi and Margaret Thatcher were both saber-rattlers."

I smiled the smile of grudging admiration—"You know, J.C., I'll never believe you are who you pass yourself off to be. I have grave doubts that a guy like you lived the first time around. Maybe the myth had a tiny basis in fact. Every other guy was named Jesus in those days. But to believe that you lived a couple thousand years ago and came back again is simply preposterous. Yet you are obviously a very bright, well-spoken guy. Of course, how you could speak such perfect English when your language was allegedly Aramaic is impossible to fathom. But the thing that bugs me is: why? Why would a guy as bright as you try to bring off this stunt?"

"So what do you think, Frankie? Why would I?"

"A lark. It's all I can figure. And, believe me, I love it. It only shows how ridiculous the whole thing was anyway. I mean, they all said Jesus is coming soon, get ready, send in your nickels and dimes. So you appear out of nowhere and *they don't believe it!* I could have predicted it."

"But how long could I play out a lark?"

"As long as it plays, I suppose. I, for one, don't think there is going to be any thousand years in you."

"Seems a long time."

I grinned and shook my head. "The real kick in the pants is you know so much. That Bible-verse trick is really something."

Jesus smiled and shook his head.

When I left Jesus, I looked back at Sheriff Stoney Jessup. His mouth was slightly ajar. Then, I noticed for the first time, I was dripping with perspiration.

ANOTHER BLAST FROM GOD'S TROMBONES:

It'll Take More than Krazy Glue

$\boxed{T}$he leader of the breakaway African-American Catholic Congregation celebrated Good Friday this year by organizing a burning and a mock burial of images portraying Jesus Christ as white. "Set yourself free," Bishop George Stallings of the Imani Temple told a predominantly black group of several hundred people at Freedom Plaza in Washington, D.C. "We have come to bury the white Christ. If you want to see what Jesus looked like go to the mirror."

Stallings burned a portrait of Jesus with long blond hair and light skin. Similar icons, including representations of Christ on the Cross, were placed in draped coffin. These are images that "oppressors" have pushed on blacks, Stallings lectured, adding that his followers should seal the coffin with Krazy Glue so that no one can "pry it open."

On Easter Sunday, Stallings presided over the unveiling at the Imani Temple of a portrait showing Jesus as a black man. His purpose in all this? To correct the "misinformation" that Christ had Aryan features and a European background. "People say that's being racist," he said. "But they want to control you.... Reclaiming the true Jesus is searching for the truth."

—Chronicles

Pilate therefore,
willing to release Jesus,
spake again to them.
But they cried,
saying,
Crucify him,
crucify him.
And he said unto them the third time,
Why,
what evil hath he done?
I have found no cause of death in him:
I will therefore chastise him,
and let him go.
And they were instant with loud voices,
requiring that he might be crucified.

—Luke 23:20-23

THE GOSPEL ACCORDING TO

SHERIFF STONEY JESSUP

When I hied myself out of there, the sheriff looked out the window and saw how the agitators were coming thick and fast, and they carried signs of protest:

FREE JESUS

*   *   *

JESUS FREE

*   *   *

JESUS SAVES
SAVE JESUS

Then someone started to chant "We want Jesus," and others picked it up, "We want Jesus," until the whole crowd rocked the mountaintop as if one voice of an omnipotent God chanted, "WE WANT JESUS."

I saw Frankie Foxxe out there stirring up the crowd. I expected he was getting material for his paper that would make me look bad. Inside, my dog, Fluffy, was exhibiting signs of inner turmoil. He pawed over the floor with jerky movements. His nose twitched in suspicion.

The phone rang. It was Polk—that writer who had the bug up where things should only come out of—about the noise.

"This is ridiculous, Sheriff. They've been at it for half an hour. Can't you do something about it?"

"Yes, sir." I took a backseat to no one where butt kissing was concerned. Not where my constituents were concerned, I didn't. And proud of it. "I'll see what I can do."

I hung up the phone and went to check out the window. The crowd had swelled, since the last time I looked, to beyond the boundaries of my vision, and though I couldn't see the fringes, I was sure they were still coming.

I saw the dreaded but unmistakable jostling of a camera crew insinuating its way up to the front, near the door. It was only seconds before I heard the door handle turn. My heart raced. I was glad I had locked it. Not that I had any illusions about that flimsy lock keeping out any part of the determined crowd, but I just, frankly, didn't feel like opening the door and facing a camera crew—or maybe inciting the crowd to storm the place and free Jesus.

"KAN-TV. Open up. We want a statement."

"You'll have to wait."

"How long?"

"Just wait," I said, and picked up the phone to dial the highway patrol.

"Folks can't get in an' out," I said after identifying myself and my jurisdiction. "It's a real safety hazard...must be five, ten thousand. No, sir, I'm not exaggerating. If I could have a couple cars it'd sure help out...yassur."

When I hung up the phone, I took the ballpoint from my breast pocket, the one that had "Hillside Motors" stamped on it in gold. The one they gave me for patronizing them with my car work. I began composing my statement for the press and the crowd. I always had trouble writing, and today, I had it in spades. I wanted to sound firm and in control without setting off a riot. I wouldn't last two minutes in a riot.

It took me a full thirty minutes to work up, and rework, my half-minute statement. Then another ten minutes to rehearse it in front of the mirror. Jesus watched me from his cell and even offered a few pointers on delivery. Told me it would be best if I could memorize it, but I thought it would be too risky.

At last I was ready. I checked the mirror once again for the regularity of my uniform—I didn't want to face the cameras looking sloppy—then I stepped outside the door, closing it with my hand behind me. While the crew got the cameras ready, I asked the cameraman, "Any way I can get a tape of this?"

The cameraman tried to hide his smile. They love to ridicule law enforcement. "Sure," he said. "We'll send you one."

There was a roar from the crowd when I stood out on the

front stoop and the camera lights were switched on, bathing me in this holy glow.

I cleared my throat and glanced at the card in my hand. I was sorry to see it was shaking. I tried to control the trembling hand and a flash of pain shot to my face when I realized I could not. How would it look to this mob? Five thousand to one and I looked scared. I was not scared, of course, it's just I wasn't a public speaker.

My throat gurgled. "I have a statement to read," I said, hunched over the low microphones. "I said, I have a statement I'd like to read if you all could quiet down a bit."

The crowd quieted from front to back as the word was passed: "Sheriff has a statement."

"I am holding a black male..." And the audience erupted with laughter.

"Blackmail," the crowd shouted. "Blackmail, blackmail, blackmail," the chant was taken up by the assemblage. Behind me, the phone was ringing and I could hear Jesus saying "Telephone, Sheriff—you want me to get it?"

"Blackmail, blackmail, black...mail..."

"You want me to finish?" I shouted into the microphone. But it was no use. They weren't quieting down. The man with the camera on his shoulder said, "Go ahead and finish your statement, Sheriff, for the TV audience."

I tugged at the knot of my black necktie; it seemed especially tight. I cleared my throat and started again.

"I am holding a male Negro of indeterminate age." I looked up into the camera and tried to smile. I didn't think it came out so good. "His identity has yet to be established." There were boos from those in the front of the crowd who could hear me while the "Blackmail, blackmail" chant was dying in the background.

"Does He call Himself Jesus Christ?" a young man who had known contacts in the Devil's Disciples asked.

"His true identity has yet to be established," I repeated.

"What's the charge, Sarge?" another lad with similar affiliations inquired.

"Disturbing the peace."

Everybody laughed at that. Standing in front of that hostile mob was not the best experience of my life. "Now you all go on and disperse, you're impeding the orderly flow of traffic in my jurisdiction. I've called in the highway patrol to restore this thoroughfare to passable conditions, so if you all don't want any hassle I suggest you disburse right quick."

There was a roaring boo from the crowd that shook the foundations of the little jailhouse behind me. I made a snappy turn and retreated to the sanctuary of my headquarters to seek the comfort of Fluffy and await the highway patrol.

"You did all right, Sheriff," Jesus said from his cell.

"Well," I wondered at the seriousness of the compliment, "they didn't move none."

"You worried?" Jesus asked.

I dropped into my chair and the air came out of my lungs with a hissing sound.

"They try anything, I expect I'd just draw my gun on you. Way they feel 'bout you, you'd be good as gold as a hostage."

Jesus smiled. "You give me too much credit, my son," he said. "But my people are peaceful people. You have nothing to fear."

Fluff jumped up on my lap and I caressed him behind his floppy ears. He liked that.

"I've seen mobs get outta hand," I said. "Nothin' no one can do to stop 'em—only takes one crazy to incite a mob—so there's no tellin', there's just no tellin' a-tall."

"Put your faith in God," Jesus said.

"Hmm." I considered that statement. "Mebee," I said. "Leastways, gonna be a long night."

Outside, a new chant was taking hold on the crowd.

"Give us Jesus, give us Jesus, give us Jesus…"

By the time the highway patrol arrived with two cars and radioed for as many cars as could be spared to help, I had logged seven calls from good citizens of Glory Pines who wanted to use the road and either could not move, or were afraid to venture into the mob.

The patrolmen were ten years younger than I was and their neat moustaches didn't fool me a bit.

The taller one seemed to be the spokesman. His name, he said, was Donny. He had sandy hair, a nose that looked like he had given up boxing just in time, and the facial expression of a dead man.

"So what's coming down here, man?" he asked.

His tone put me off. I had sent for help, not for an inquisitor.

"Just like the roadway cleared, as this crowd is impeding the orderly flow of traffic," I said.

"All well and good," Donny responded, "but what's the cause of the gathering?"

I threw my thumb over a shoulder to indicate my prisoner.

"The nigger?" Donny asked, astonished.

I blushed at that. I didn't want anyone accusing me of racial prejudice.

"What're ya holding him for?"

"Thinks he's Jesus Christ," I whispered.

"So what's new about that?" Donny was constitutionally unable to whisper. Jesus smiled in the background. "You running a nut house here, Sheriff?" Donny inquired, full blast, "or a jail?"

I pulled at my tie again. I guessed that showed the highway patrol how nervous I was. Lord, how I wished I'd had bigger, more private quarters. I cocked my head to the mob outside. "Lot of 'em don't think he's so crazy," I said softly.

"So what're ya holding him for?"

"Disturbing the peace."

"Phewew," the highwayman spit out, raising the humidity in the room. "Jesus Christ," he muttered.

"Yes, sir," I said, "that's who he thinks he is."

"Well, Jesus, Sheriff. He's a black man."

"Well, I know that." I was getting a little ticked and had half a mind to say so. "Look, will you just clear the road?"

"Is this some kind of a gag?" Donny wanted to know.

"No, sir." I felt I had put the proposition clearly enough.

"We can clear the street, sure," Donny said, "and we will, but keeping it clear is another matter entirely. Now tell me something, Sheriff..."

"Yes, sir?" I simply didn't like his tone. Fluff sat in the corner and he didn't look happy about it, either.

"You have all these people blocking the street before you had this nut in jail?"

"No, sir. That is, not here," I hastened to add, "but we had other problems. Terrible traffic problems. Tie-ups, backups. You boys helped out with that."

"But you didn't have citizens blocking traffic with their bodies, did you?"

"*We want Jesus,*" roared through the closed window.

"No, sir."

"So let him out," Donny said, shrugging his shoulders as if to say, "you idiot."

"Well, we can't just buckle under an unruly mob." I thought it was important to make that point.

"Why not? You're holding him on tissue-thin goods. You can't hold him more than a couple days on what you have. Just get your ass out there in front of the TV cameras again and say you are releasing him on his own recognizance. If he really is Jesus Christ, you won't have any trouble. If he isn't, your troubles will be over."

"I don't know..."

"Well, think about it, Sheriff. We're going out there and we'll clear a lane for the cars, but we can't stay here forever. We just don't have the manpower." With a look over at the cage to the black man, Donny frowned before he turned back to head out the door.

"Jesus, look at the doggie," Donny said to his sidekick.

"Never saw such a sissy-looking mutt."

That made me so mad, I clenched my fists.

"Buddha dog," the sidekick observed, and they were gone to do their business.

While the highway patrol was outside attempting to bull-horn the mob into submission, I was fiddling with my pencil at my desk. I couldn't deny the highway patrolman had made some sense. Perhaps I should have released Jesus and taken a chance he would get the picture and move on, or the fad would just peter out, or some other evidence might come to light discrediting the mystery man in my holding tank.

The phone rang. I picked it up on the first ring. "Glory Pines. Sheriff Jessup speaking."

"Hel—*low*, Sher—*iff.*" I didn't place the voice until it said, "I seen you on the television just now and I just wanted you to know how personally grateful I am to you for standing up to Satan and that mob of thugs and gangsters. It is a most impordand service you are performing our Lord. I expect when the real Jesus comes He will also express His gratitude to you."

"Well—thank you, Reverend Banghart."

"Yes, sir, I liked what I saw on the television. I was just saying to Emmy Sue that we were going to be mighty proud to have you make us a testimonial for our faith partners."

"You did?"

"I'm so very pleased you haven't let us down."

"Well, ah, I mean, thanks."

"Keep up the good work, Sheriff. And whatever you do, don't let them con you into letting that phony loose."

"Well...I..." I started to say, but he'd hung up.

The noises outside told me that the highway patrol was not having that easy a time clearing the road. A groan from a crowd that size set my teeth achattering. I could feel the impending assault in my bones. And I frankly didn't care to be around to be trampled to death in the stampede to save this so-called savior—"Save the Savior"—I could hear the battle cry before it began.

I was seriously considering releasing the man when Ernie Jo Banghart had called. Ernie Jo stiffened my resolve, all right, but it was my resolve to use the tunnel to get the man outta there before it was too late—and to get away from the telephone and Ernie Jo's prodding.

The tunnel had been started by a vagrant I had picked up in Glory Pines littering the streets—not literally littering, but littering with his unkempt person. Keeping the town neat and tidy for its citizenry was my strong point.

The man, Rodger Vickers, by latest alias, was not playing the game with a full deck of cards. And he began digging the tunnel almost under my nose, and I was going to stop him, but the idea amused me.

The dirt piled up in his cell and Rodger covered it with his coat—a moth-eaten item he had picked up on his tours of the trash receptacles. The cell soon filled with dirt and the coat was inadequate to cover all but a small portion of it.

I asked Rodger, "Where did all this dirt come from?"

Rodger shrugged. "Maybe washed in from the rain."

"Hasn't rained in two months," I said.

The prisoner threw up his hands. "Well, whatever it come from, you oughta get it outta here. This here sink hole isn't fit for human habitation."

I was watching a television program when the solution came to me. It was a story about an elaborate escape from danger through a series of subterranean tunnels, and I could visualize my making a fast and mysterious getaway through the very tunnel that this nutcase was building with a spoon.

"Rodger," I said, "I am in agreement that the dirt can't stay in your cell. When the pile started growing, I was frankly hoping it would magically disappear just as it had so mysteriously grown. But that was not in the cards."

"No," Rodger agreed.

"I guess all that's for it is we take it outside and spread it around for a flower bed."

"Yeah," Rodger perked up. "That's an all-right idea. How you gonna get it out?" He was outfoxing the chief chicken in the henhouse and he just couldn't hide his satisfaction.

"I'm not going to do it, Rodger." Rodger's face fell into a watery puddle. "You are."

"Me? Why me? That's alotta work. You can't abuse me, I know my rights."

"Okay," I smiled like a clever cat. "I guess I could move you to another cell, where you'd have more room."

Rodger licked his lips. "Tell you what, Sheriff—I'm game. If I don't have to move too much at a time. I'm not as young as I useta be, so I can't work too hard, you know: lumbago and all."

"I understand. You can do it at your own pace."

And he did. And when the tunnel was complete, Rodger disappeared. So thrilled he was with his escape that he never again darkened the groves of Glory Pines. I knew that I could have driven him to Mexico City and Rodger would have returned to Glory Pines. But this escape was final.

So, I got my tunnel. I replaced the floorboards so I didn't have to worry about anyone discovering it. But just to be on the safe side, I laid down a concrete manhole with an iron cover locked into place.

"Okay, fella," I said to Jesus, "time to evacuate." I checked the mob outside. From the way they seemed to be boiling over, it wasn't any too soon to get out of there. I took a crowbar from the closet, unlocked the cell, handcuffed Jesus to the bars of the cell and pried up the floorboards. With my key from this giant key ring that some said made me look like a world-class night watchman, I unlocked the manhole cover, then unlocked the handcuff on the bar and locked the other end of Jesus's cuff to my own wrist.

"Let's go," I said. But try as we might, the two of us chained together could not pass through the narrow passageway. Rodger had not excavated his tunnel for two.

I came out of the tunnel and Jesus got up from his knees.

"Ain't gonna work," I said. "We gotta go separate." I locked the cell door. "I'm gonna go first—I'm gonna trust you to follow or I'm gonna come back after ya. So no funny business. Come on, Fluffy," I called to my dog, who came scurrying after me. "You close up after you in the hole—" I called to Jesus. "Put them boards back, best you can."

Jesus went along with it.

"Now you jest follow me," I commanded.

"Where he leads me I will follow," Jesus said.

"Attaboy."

A large stone had been placed on the hole at the end of the tunnel to camouflage it from a prying public.

I put my shoulder to the stone and rolled it away (and I was no angel).

We came out in the darkness behind the jail. As soon as Jesus emerged from the hole in the ground, I clamped the cuffs on him, and on myself, so we were, for our temporal purposes, as good as Siamese twins.

I led Jesus the few steps to the barn. I opened the door and we climbed into the waiting Jeep. We could hear the restless rustling of the crowd on the other side of the jail. From the sound of the crowd and the barked orders from the highway patrol bullhorns, I thanked God I got clear of the place in the nick of time.

The engine of the Jeep hopped to life. When we cleared the barn, we left the Jeep to close the barn door. I thought it prudent to cover our tracks as best I could. I did not turn on the Jeep's lights until we got to the main road.

We got to the cabin after two and a half miles on the main road and another three interminable miles up a rutted dirt road that bounced the Jeep like a marble on a washboard.

I had not come to this remote cabin in the woods because I was a coward. But I knew that prudence was the better part of valor.

In the cabin, I locked Jesus's handcuffs to a roof-supporting post and dozed off.

When I awoke, I was startled to see Jesus asleep unfettered by the locked handcuff. Was it a miracle? I reached for my pocket and found the key where I left it.

I sat up, staring at Jesus until he awoke.

I pointed at the unlocked handcuff. "How did you do it?"

Jesus smiled. "One of my easier miracles," he said. "I got the key from your pocket."

"And unlocked it?" He was stretching my faith. "And put it back?"

Jesus nodded.

"Why didn't you take off?"

"I didn't think you wanted me to."

"Jesus!" I reached for the open lock and the handcuff.

"You think that's necessary?" Jesus asked me. "I could have gone..."

I shook my head. "I'm not pushing my luck."

"Well, how about only locking me up when you are going to sleep?"

I considered that proposition, taking in some mountain air. Finally, I shook my head. "I'll consider that while you're locked up." And I fastened the handcuff to the post and snapped the lock shut, then checked my pocket to see that the key still safely there.

I settled back facing my prisoner. "What's it like up there?" I asked Jesus, nodding my head toward the sky. I was playing Jesus's own game, not letting on I didn't believe for a minute he was who he said he was.

"Are you asking this question of a free human being or a prisoner?"

"I'm just trying to get your slant on it. If you are who you say, you oughta know the answer."

"But knowing the answer and being moved to share it might be different matters."

"Yeah—but let's say you are divine. How come you're still my prisoner?"

"'Come down from the cross,' eh? I think I showed you how easy it was to break out of your bonds."

"Let's see you do it now that I have the key."

"To invoke faith in the faithless?"

"Well, okay. You throw off those handcuffs while I'm watching and I *will* let you go."

"With you as a disciple?"

"But, I'm…" I choked on the words.

"Unworthy? Well, aren't we all?"

"I wasn't going to say that." I could feel the heat at the back of my neck on that one.

Jesus smiled. "What *were* you going to say, Sheriff?"

My face heated up. "Nothing," I said. "You know, if I was convinced you are who you say, I might let you go."

"On the other hand, if I am who I say, I wouldn't need your help, would I? I could call on someone who could turn you into a pillar of salt."

That got me. Was there *any* possibility?

We sat in silence for an eternity. Jesus had closed his eyes and it made me wonder if my prisoner was talking directly to God, and if so, did I figure in the conversation?

"Gee—ah, sir, I was just, ah, wondering," the speech was coming difficult to me. "What sort of thing might happen, that is assuming you are who you say, you know, and someone, well, someone didn't believe you?"

"There are legions of nonbelievers," Jesus said.

"Yeah, well, what do you think might happen to them in the hereafter?"

"Are you one of them, Sheriff?"

"Well, sure, I guess, I don't know."

"You want to know what the odds are?"

"Ah, yes, sir—"

"Heavy, Sheriff. The odds are heavy."

"Hm," I said. I didn't like it. "So what could happen? I mean, is your God really a jealous God who comes down really hard on guys who, you know, don't toe the line?"

"You surely toe the line, Sheriff?"

"Well, that's just it. I think I am toeing the line, but maybe, then, you know, I could be wrong."

"Always that chance."

"What would happen, like, say I was going along, following my conscience on the thing, and I suddenly up and died and found out I had been wrong all the time?"

"Are you thinking you might be wrong, Sheriff?"

"Well, ah, not really, but there's always that chance—I mean, you seem a nice enough fella, but I was expecting..." I trailed off into an uncomfortable silence.

"More fireworks?" Jesus helped me.

"Well, yeah. Trumpets, the heavens rent with lightning—"

"There *were* trumpets. And there is lightning *all* the time— every minute or so."

"Hm, but what about all the dead being taken up along with the believers? I didn't detect any rapture."

"Maybe you don't believe the right stuff, Sheriff."

"Yeah, that's what I'm wondering. What about the thousand years—you gonna do that? Give us a thousand years? And what about destroying the Antichrist? Where's that?"

"Makes a good story," Jesus nodded.

"*Story*? You mean it's not true?"

"True?" Jesus said. "You have any idea how often the tale was told before it was written the first time? And how many people revised the original, then revised the revision to suit their causes?

Why, I'm surprised they got my name right."

I winced at that. "Well, what *is* true?"

"I am true. You are true. Beauty and goodness are true."

I told Jesus, in no uncertain terms, that I expected more specifics.

"Everybody does," Jesus said. "Parables and miracles have spoiled you. You really think there are certainties in this world? Neat-and-tidy answers to all the mysteries, if you only had the key?"

"But the Bible is very clear on these matters. How can you account for the fact that you are who you say you are when there isn't any scriptural authority to back you up?"

"Sheriff—these stories were written long after I was gone. I didn't write them. You have to allow for some excesses in zeal, some slippage in facts through the centuries. Why is that so important to you? Wouldn't you be satisfied to live a good life and see the rest of mankind trying to do the same?"

"Yeah, but where do we find out what the good life is? I say it's in the Bible. Do unto others, that stuff."

"Unassailable."

"So you mean you didn't walk on water and raise the dead?"

"That's a long time ago. I'm having trouble remembering last week."

"Yeah, me, too."

†   †   †

It just wasn't what I had in mind when I signed up for law enforcement—wrassling with religious controversy. That shouldn't be expected of any cop. I shoulda brought the TV. Time was starting to hang a little heavy on my hands. I was supposed to be in charge. But there were considerations. Like food, especially. Now what was I going to do about that? We had to eat. But how could I be seen in the market? They'd want to know what happened to this

Jesus guy. How could I get back without being followed? Then I'd have a riot all over again.

"Ah, sir," I began formulating thoughts as I spoke, "I was just thinking about maybe it was time for some food. Only I don't know as it will be too easy to get. I mean under the circumstances and all."

"That's all right, Sheriff," Jesus said, "I'm used to fasting."

"Yeah," I muttered, "I'm not."

Jesus smiled. "I can see that."

My lips were feeling dry. "You got any ideas for it?"

"Guess one of us would have to go for it."

"Yeah." I sighed. The weight of the world was on my shoulders. The long silence that followed seemed to amuse Jesus but it aggravated me.

"I was just thinking," I said, feeling my lips with my tongue, "how nice it would be if you worked one of them miracles and made some bread from this here stone."

Jesus smiled again. "That be to my advantage, Sheriff?"

"Well, it would give you something to eat."

"I'm not hungry."

"Hmm." That put me in a funk.

"Why don't we analyze this thing?" Jesus suggested.

"How's that?" I was keeping my options open.

"You are in a bit of a fix. If you could make a case that it was necessary to move your prisoner to a hideaway, you might be accused of not feeding him. I'm no expert, but it seems to me, in this society, people are forever looking out for the rights of the accused."

"Don't I know it!" I lamented. "So I'd just tell them you said you didn't need food."

"And you might find someone to believe it, if you had the strength to tell the story after all those days without food."

"Oh," I said. "Oh."

I held on just as long as humanly possible. One blessing about being in this hideaway was there was no phone and no television for Ernie Jo Banghart to put the pressure on me. I reasoned that I wouldn't mind starving myself into unconsciousness, and the same for the prisoner, but I just couldn't do that to Fluffy. So, I unlocked the man's cuffs and we got in the Jeep.

And it was in the nick of time, too, that we gave up our asylum, for the mob had stormed the jail, found it empty and started to fan out, combing the area for Jesus.

They were less than a half-mile from pay dirt when our Jeep approached them.

Six of them jumped in the path, in front of the Jeep.

I jumped out with Fluffy under my arm. "He's all yours," I said. "Now, if you'll just clear the path, I'm gonna get meself a cheeseburger an' fries."

As Jesus left the Jeep, the people parted and I jumped back in and headed down the hill.

ANOTHER BLAST FROM GOD'S TROMBONES:

Other complex mental operations, while engaging regions over large parts of the brain, are vulnerable to localized perturbation. Patients with temporal lobe epilepsy often develop hyperreligiousity, the tendency to charge all events, large and small, with cosmic significance. They are also prone to hypergraphia, a compulsion to express their vision in an undisciplined stream of poems, letters, or stories.

—*Edward O. Wilson*
Consilience

ANOTHER TWANG FROM GOD'S GUITAR:

I do not think Jesus Christ ever existed.

—*Napoleon I*
To Gaspard Gourgand at St. Helena

THE MAGNUM OPUS OF

FRANKIE FOXXE

Jesus Christ: Man or Myth? Christianity: Truth or Fiction? By Frankie Foxxe

Countless volumes have been written about this figure known as Jesus Christ. Most of them seem to take for granted that he actually lived. But the evidence is scant. All this speculation is based on the only written record we have—the Gospels in the New Testament of the Holy Bible, ostensibly written a generation or two after this character was supposed to have roamed a small portion of this earth. None of the gospel writers had actually ever seen Jesus. People often confuse those writers with disciples of the same name, but they were not the same people. The four existing Gospels, Matthew, Mark, Luke and John, contain a myriad of duplication, and could easily be distilled into one book.

To believe that St. Paul knew Jesus, you have to accept the Resurrection as fact, because the Bible says St. Paul heard the voice of Jesus *after* he was reportedly resurrected. Not, at any rate, a strong acquaintence.

We don't know how many times the gospels were altered, exactly how the translations took place or how skilled the translators were. If a work of fiction went through so many mutations, what are the chances the final version would resemble the original?

These stories were kept alive with an oral tradition—mouth-to-mouth, like resuscitation. If you've ever played "Operator," or "Whisper Down the Lane," you know how a message transmitted in minutes, by perhaps eight or ten people speaking the same language, can get garbled; it will give you an idea what a period of forty years and different languages can do. Couple that with the less than subjective hand of the clergy, and it might not spell mother—unless you want it to.

There is only one secular reference to the historical Jesus in ancient writings—Flavius Josephus, who was born after Jesus was supposed to have died, and wrote around 100 A.D. There was a note in one of his posthumous writings referring to a prophet named Jesus who wandered the desert, preaching and doing good works. But this observation may have been the handiwork of an ambitious monk, translating the Flavius Josephus work, who added that sentence (the only one found in secular writing of the period, remember). Since no mention is found anywhere else among the historians of that era, a persuasive case can be made that if there truly was this astonishing miracle-performing prophet on earth, someone should have known about it, and commented on it in writing.

Then the question of, why then? Why there?

Fleshpots and dens of iniquity flourishing in cities throughout the world, and the Almighty God sets his Son down in a sparsely populated desert? Why? Because the citizens were less sophisticated? Because communication with the outside world was virtually nil?

Why then? Of all the disastrous periods in history, why over seventy thousand years after man as we more or less know him started "sinning" on this planet were we graced with a "Savior"? What were those poor, beleaguered desert nomads being saved from? It was a hardscrabble existence at that time and place, and there was precious little time or energy for sinning.

All prior religions, and there were many, were, and are acknowledged today as, mythology. Is Christianity exempt from that judgment? On what basis? It has borrowed from Zoroastrianism, Hillel, even Buddhism and others; from a dozen moral codes. Divine paternity and resurrection were staples of ancient religions. Why is it that this mutation on dozens of predecessors is taken as fact rather than fiction?

The late philosopher Bertrand Russell said, "You didn't give us enough evidence." What evidence is there? None. This divine child was born under circumstances copied from other religions — then he disappeared for some thirty years until he resurfaced to perform sundry miracles like raising people from the dead and feeding the multitudes on a couple of loaves of bread.

Then God the Father called him home in the most painful death imaginable, hanging from a cross, with nails through his hands and feet.

Why? We're told he died for our sins—and presumably for the manifold sins of those who went before. But, what good did it do? Are people sinning less because of it? "Not," as the man said, "bloody likely."

So, this crucifixion cleared the way for God to forgive man's moral and ethical blunders. It was, Ayn Rand said, the sacrifice of the ideal (Jesus) for the unideal (the rest of us). The logic of the hypothesis has always escaped me. I can't fathom how the great unwashed are supposed to grasp it. Was God saying, "Give me the best you have—I'll kill him—and in gratitude for your giving him up, I'll let you off the hook forever"? Doesn't that sound like the reasoning of a totalitarian dictator?

So, who will make it into heaven? Only the elect (if you are a Presbyterian), only those who "believe" (if you are not), only those who do good things (if you are a Catholic) and those who have not played the game will vanish from the face of the earth. And if you happen to be a Christian, eighty percent of the world will vanish, leaving you a lot of elbow room.

Is this the act of a loving God?

It is amazing how many interpretations there are of the Second Coming, and how each person is convinced that his logic is infallible.

Now this Jesus out in the mountains above Los Angeles says you have to use your brain. He says the tribulation is really a personal thing, but I asked him, "Are you saying you're not here? Was your prophesied return only symbolism?"

"Poetry," he said.

I don't see any arguing that the Bible is poetry, especially the soaring King James version, but the fundamentalists say if you are going to doubt one word of the Bible, there's no stopping you from doubting everything.

Jesus says, "Look for God everywhere."

Yesterday I saw what looked like two young Hispanic domestics with two infants. Standing a few yards away from them at this bus stop was a young man, perhaps twenty-eight, thirty years old, and he was looking at those children. And the look I caught in his eye, just passing in a car, spoke volumes of love, of envy, of heartbreak. He seemed to say without speaking that this was the highest endeavor of which man was capable. A magnificent result produced with a minimum of effort. And yet, I knew that none of those thoughts were in this poor boy's mind, because it was easy to tell that he had some mental and/or emotional handicap laid on him, no doubt, by a God who makes men in his image, who creates all men equal.

The God of Love has instilled in this poor soul the ability and the capacity to love, but has inconveniently left out the fundamentals. The mind has been so confused that it can't grasp the simplest meanings of existence. It can't cope with the rationale of the complementary sex and why he just doesn't seem to appeal to any of them.

Now, a long time ago, someone, probably a loving relative, told me that these things happened because they were God's way of making us appreciate what we of sound mind and body had, appreciating it as a blessing from on high. But the question, why were these poor souls singled out? never found an adequate answer.

If it is necessary to create poor souls like this young man to prove the existence of God, is it worth it?

I heard a fundamentalist proclaim three hundred prophesies of the Old Testament were literally fulfilled by Jesus in the New Testament.

But they don't allow for writing one to fit the other.

The success of any religion depends on people taking it seriously. Look at the Muslims—fanatics, a lot of them. Their religion is about half as old as Christianity, and when Christianity was only one thousand years old, there was a lot of fanaticism. Remember the Inquisition and those nice Crusades?

I am always suspicious of people who seem intelligent going along with religion. Are they real believers, deep down, or are they just hoping to keep the poor, uneducated from revolting? Or maybe give them hope that otherwise eludes them in life?

The other bug is the apparent lack of any perspective about Christianity—a relative newcomer on the religion map. Let's just say, for argument's sake, man is roughly seventy thousand years old. Christianity is two thousand years old. That's a drop in the timeline of history.

So, to profess that Christianity is the one true religion stretches credulity. We should not fear mythology. Put into perspective, it could save a lot of prejudice, animosity and hatred.

Now this man appears on a mountaintop in a quiet California town and says he is Jesus Christ returned to earth. His mission is simple: rid the world of hate.

He is a gentle soul, almost feminine in his presence—like a Father *and* a Mother God. There is something magical about him. I can see why he has so many devotees. His quiet, unassuming manner makes you *want* to believe.

Everyone wants a dad to tell him what to do. To take care of him. We grow up with dads, most of us, and when we leave the nest, there is a void. This Jesus easily fills that void.

From time immemorial we've had our gods—people want to humble themselves to a superior being. We have always needed someone to look up to—to worship. And as many myths as I have debunked, if, and that's a big if, I had to believe in something, I could do a lot worse than to hitch my wagon to this man's star.

Religion fills a need, or it wouldn't be so successful. I suspect that those of us who resist the pull of faith in the supernatural fancy ourselves stronger creatures for it. But are we? Aren't we all in the same spiritual soup?

Religion has always been with us. Women had babies and they thought the baby came from God—a woman god, most likely.

Well, it's all about sex, anyway. Immaculate Conception, virgin birth—keep those women from being touched. As though that were desirable. The big switch from the female to the male deity. It may have grown out of the Church's need for accountability for all those illegitimates roaming the countryside. Nobody knew who their fathers were.

Church sermons are often about adultery and coveting thy neighbor's wife. Though I've had some neighbors' wives any red-blooded American boy could not help but covet.

There is little talk of murder or stealing—those people aren't sitting in the pews. But sex—parishioners have some truck with that topic.

I don't have to mention the kind of trouble celibacy causes among the Catholic clergy.

Am I softening in the presence of this latest addition to the panoply of religious icons? Unlike TV evangelist Ernie Jo Banghart, this—dare I call him Jesus?—is not preoccupied with sex. He says man's ills can be reduced to the all-pervasive hate, and if we can rid ourselves of this simple emotion, the world would be a much better place. The trouble, he says, is not too much unbridled love, it's hate.

In spite of my cynical nature, I like that. There is beauty in simplicity.

There is one thing that cannot be denied. That is that the mysterious man currently walking the earth, passing himself off as Jesus Christ, is a very clever, well-spoken fellow. The old Debunker of Myths finds only fissures, no cracks, in the facade of this man who is taking the world by storm.

†   †   †

This piece, brewing in the still of my mind for some time was picked up by the Associated Press and found its way into hundreds of papers, including the big ones. My byline was there for all to see, including that gasbag boss of mine, Rob Houston.

He wasn't happy about it. Not only was he disappointed that the tone wasn't more heavy-handed (when you were talking ham hands, Rob Houston had no peer), but he was out of joint to see my name appear in so many world-class papers, without any credit given to his precious *Gulfport Riptide*.

As a result, I heard from Rob Houston the sweetest words he ever uttered:

"You're fired!"

I was at home when the phone rang, bringing me news of yet another irate customer. This one I cared about.

"What are the fissures, Frankie?" Rachel stormed on the phone.

"What's that?"

"Fissures. I thought your article on Jesus bloody terrible. Supercilious. I agree with you on Banghart, but you are reaching on this one."

"Rachel, surely you don't think this guy is really Jesus?"

"Well, I haven't seen the slightest proof from you that he isn't. What *are* the fissures?"

"Jeez, Rachel."

"Come on, what are they?"

"Just a figure of speech."

"Aha! You don't *have* any fissures. You are debunking thin air. You know what I think?"

"What?"

"It's time somebody starts debunking you."

Methuselah lived 900 years,
Methuselah lived 900 years
But who calls dat livin'
When no gal 'll give in
To no man what's 900 years?

It ain't necessarily so,
It ain't necessarily so,
De t'ings dat you liable
to read in de Bible,
It ain't necessarily so.

> *—Ira Gershwin*
> Porgy and Bess

THE GOSPEL ACCORDING TO

FRANKIE FOXXE

I knew Ernie Jo Banghart wanted something when I heard I was invited to be on the TV program at his behest.

Why else would the evangelist risk exposure to my cynicism at his activities?

Ernie Jo's head bobbed with an I-couldn't-agree-with-you-more wobble when I asked him about it in the studio before we went on the air. He had his Bible under his arm. Was it an amulet for him? A talisman?

"Emmy Sue said I was crazy," he said with that jovial, jowly grin. "But they asked me for my suggestions of someone to take the dim view and I said I just did not know a dimmer person than you, Frankie."

"Thanks," I said.

Then he leaned forward—like he was leaning into one of his brimstone barrages which he would start with hushed tones and build to "Alexander's Ragtime Band." "'Sides,' I told Emmy Sue. 'The devil you know is better 'n the devil you don't know.'"

We were on the stage of the Phil Allen talk show. Talk, talk, talk. We were waiting for our time to begin. The camera crew was hustling about and the lighting technicians were scurrying around setting the lights so we'd show up in homes around the country, more or less as we appeared in real life.

I was not happy I was bracketed here with Ernie Jo Banghart, but the other participants were Amos and Andi Lovejoy and their son, Michael. A glance in their direction now and then gave me the impression it was an uneasy alliance.

The boy, Michael, seemed terribly nervous. His eyes darted all over the place, as though he were looking for the nearest escape hatch. Father Lovejoy, fiftyish, looked much as he did at the convocation of Christian clergy, but he seemed to stroke his Vandyke beard more often.

Andi, his wife, was poised and somewhat self-possessed, but I didn't see any indication to doubt she deferred to the big cheese.

I considered introducing myself and Ernie Jo, but I had this funny feeling I wouldn't be thanked for it.

The reluctant glances the beard shot at Ernie Jo were not

broadminded. The couple were a couple of Ph.D.'s in theology—he the preeminent Biblical-history scholar who introduced Jesus at the Christian convocation in L.A. I had a feeling the beard didn't suffer Ernie Jo Banghart gladly. I wondered if he had seen any of the evangelist's Bible-study programs on the Christian Network. Unlikely. But if he did, say he had an academic interest, I would imagine he had some rather stark interpretive differences.

This little walking ad for family values was standing together. The father looming large—like the outsized banana in the bunch.

Lot of those kids with important fathers wind up on the suicide pile.

I hoped Michael wasn't that fragile, but looking at him here didn't give me a lot of confidence. He seemed more confident in Glory Pines.

Whenever I saw a father-son combo like this—and I saw a lot of them from the business side of the confessional—I wanted to scream, "Kick him out of the nest, Big Bird!" I later came to believe that Poppa Bird had done his share of the kicking, but the kid had trouble learning to fly.

Phil Allen came roaring onstage at the last minute, like a stock car coming from behind to lead the pack of also-rans.

A blow-hard by nature, Allen made hasty introductions. We all shook hands and forced smiles, except Amos Lovejoy refused the hand of Ernie Jo—letting it hang in midair as proffered while a saccharine smile inflated his shadowy lips.

Phil had not so much a voice box as an arsenal of little explosives, as though his thoughts originated in the barrel of a machine gun that intermittently jammed.

Phil sat us in our seats like a guy with *gravitas*, who took life one serious step at a time.

He sat the five of us behind a table, in front of a five-foot-by-five-foot picture of the nation's Capitol building. It was framed to look like a window. I considered it a capital offense since Allen himself seated himself off to the side, behind a desk of his own—much snazzier than our plain table.

Phil Allen offered us no hints of what we were going to talk about on the show. All in the sense of spontaneity, no doubt. If the host was better prepared than the guests, it made him look better.

When the little red light on the camera went on, and the guy pointed at him, Phil Allen pasted a grim smile on his face and said, "Welcome to 'The Burning Issues.' Well, ladies and gentlemen, our planet has never seen anything like this before in history. The influence of this one man who calls himself Jesus on all our lives has been nothing short of astonishing."

Phil Allen was not a slouch at hyperbole.

"Thousands upon thousands of folks have made the pilgrimage to a small village in the California mountains called Glory Pines. They take with them their hopes and aspirations, their search for meaning, and virtually unanimously, they come away refreshed and satisfied that the arduous trip was worth the effort.

"People have gone to Glory Pines to be healed and have reported miraculous healing just by being there.

"Hundreds of millions have seen him on TV—he won't make personal appearances—we invited him here today, but he declined. His only appearances are through the televising of his sermons in the meadow in Glory Pines, California.

"His message couldn't be simpler: Do away with hate. Love thy neighbor as thyself. Start with one and let it spread across the world. Is it working? Well, in my experience, it is. Shopkeepers who I never thought had a smile in their repertoire are smiling, Chicago policemen are telling people to have a nice day, and there's even a rumor of a New York bus driver saying good morning to a passenger. There are, apparently, witnesses to this unprecedented kindness, but as yet, the rumor is unconfirmed."

We all got a chuckle out of that one. It soothed the nerves.

"We are fortunate to have in our studio today experts on theology, eschatology, the Parousia and the Apocalypse. Our subject:

Could the man in the California mountains, the man who has created such a stir in religious circles, the man who says he is Jesus, really be Jesus the Christ? And how can we tell the genuine article from the fake?

"Let me introduce my guests to the audience.

"On my right, Ernie Jo Banghart, television evangelist whose Nielsen ratings tell us he is the most viewed religious figure on the airways."

I could see Amos Lovejoy blanching.

"Next to him are the mom-and-pop of intellectual theology, Amos and Andi Lovejoy. Both have doctorates in theology—Amos teaches Biblical history at USC, Andi is dean of students at UCLA. A little friendly rivalry there.

"Next, Frankie Foxxe, the self-styled Debunker of Myths.

Neat, I thought. He got the facts out with a little twist of the belittling knife.

"Frankie," he went on, "serves as a buffer between Mom and Pop Lovejoy and their son, Michael, who may be on the other side of the fence on this issue.

"We're glad to have you all with us. Michael Lovejoy is the new Jesus's personal representative. Perhaps that would be a good place to start. Why do you think Jesus declined the invitation?"

Michael spoke first. "He is not a man to seek publicity or exposure. It's not His way. The first time around, He spoke to maybe thirty thousand people. He has easily exceeded that in Glory Pines already. But I think this is proof of the sincerity of the man. I mean, He has turned down serious cash because He isn't looking to make a fast buck." Michael glanced at Ernie Jo Banghart.

"What is he pursuing?" the moderator asked.

"He's just asking us not to hate anybody."

"How can he accomplish that in hiding?"

"He isn't hiding. People know where He is. Thousands and thousands of people find Him every day."

"Reverend Banghart," Phil Allen turned to the evangelist,

"do you believe that Christ will return to earth?"

"Yes, I do. It says so right in the Bible." He held up his Bible for all to see.

"And you believe…?"

"Literally."

"Everything in the Bible is to be taken literally?"

"Yes, I do."

"Then the question we are all waiting for your answer on is, do you believe this man is Jesus Christ?"

"I do not."

"Why not?"

"The Bible is very specific on how Jesus will return. A blinding light will flash across the heavens. The entire world will light up. There will be angels, He'll come on a cloud, trumpets will blare, the earth will shake, come on the heels of wars. And I say, the way things are going, a nuclear war would be a very good sign to look for."

The moderator broke in: "You mean, all of those things would have to come to pass exactly that way before you would believe it was Jesus?"

"Yes, sir. That's what the Bible says."

"Is there room in the Bible for various interpretations?"

"This is the Bible," the Reverend Ernie Jo Banghart declared, waving the book in his hand. "The Word of God we're talking about. Ain't no room for doubt."

"What about that, Dr. Lovejoy?"

"No, I don't think so. It is the word of men who wrote it."

"Inspired by God?"

"Well, insofar as you could say any action of man was God-inspired."

"Exactly," Ernie Jo Banghart said, waving his Bible. "Every action of man is inspired by God. Not a hair falls from the head of the smallest sparrow that He doesn't know about."

"Must be a pretty busy guy," Lovejoy mused.

"Frankie Foxxe, you call yourself the Debunker of Myths," said Phil. "You want to debunk this one, or has he sold you on his holy persona?"

"I thought you'd never ask," I said. "My take on it swings all around the court. One minute I think he's the biggest swindler who ever came down the pike, and I've seem some doozies.

"But then I'm knocked over by something he says or does, and I can't get a grip—I mean, he's not an easy debunk job. But I'll tell you the thing that gets me more than anything is the reaction. I mean, how many guys are there roaming the earth today claiming to be Jesus Christ? And a few women, too—an offshoot of feminism, I guess. Why don't they get the play this man does? Because most normal people's reaction to a guy who says he's Jesus Christ is to lock him up in an insane asylum. There isn't much of that with this man, and that's a bona fide mystery. But the other side of this piece of silver is not one mainstream establishment religious body, not one fundamentalist preacher says he—or she—believes this is the genuine article. I have the feeling they all just wish he would go away."

"Now let me ask our theologians to explain millennialism and the various types of belief that surround the Second Coming of Christ," said Phil. "Andi Lovejoy, could we hear from you? I think this might have been one of your specialities in school."

"Thank you, Phil. I did spend a good deal of time studying millennialism. There are three main divisions. First of all, the word 'millennium' means a thousand years. The word itself never occurs in the Bible, but the thousand years are mentioned in the Book of Revelation six times. Premillennialism is the oldest of the various millennial views. It holds that Christ will reign on earth for one thousand years after He comes back. So the word 'pre' refers to Christ being there before the millennium. This is the most literal translation of the Scriptures. You're going to have the Jewish nation restored and a thousand years of heaven on earth, practically, with the righteous dead being raised to enjoy this wonderful time on earth; the wicked dead will not be raised until after it's over."

"Is this belief currently held by any substantial groups?" the moderator asked.

"Well, it was the most ancient and the most literal view, but there are substantial numbers who still hold with this idea now.

"Amillennialism is the most popular, I suppose, of the millennial views, and it dates back to Augustine in the fourth and fifth centuries, and it's the view held by the Catholic Church, or at least it was at one time. It holds that the present age is the fulfillment of the millennium. There are other views that hold the millennium is being fulfilled by the saints in heaven, not by the rest of us on earth. They think there won't be any more millennium than there is now, then when Jesus comes the second time, which they believe will happen, it will be the end of earth as we know it—in an instant, in the twinkling of an eye.

"Some believe the Second Coming is not really an event but it's the spiritual presence of Jesus. It eliminates the millennium completely, and it is the liberal viewpoint of the day."

"That's fascinating," Phil Allen said with a burst of bullets (tah tah tah tah tah). "You said there was another. What was that called?"

"Postmillennialism. This is the idea that the whole world will become Christian and brought to submission to the gospel before the return of Christ. In this theory, Christ returns *after* the millennium. Therefore, we call it postmillennium. There are a lot of varieties of this, some very close to amillennialism. This view is favored by the people who find it is a rather literal fulfillment of the Old Testament promises of a kingdom on earth of righteousness and peace."

Dr. Amos Lovejoy said, "It was this view that caused a number of people to be publicly burned as heretics."

"Yes, and this view is not commonly held today," Andi said. "And the remaining controversy is between amillennialism and premillennialism."

"What do you think, Michael?"

"I think He's here. He's back. And He's going to rule for a thousand years." I wished Michael could get the nervousness out of his voice.

"Have you seen any evidence that the dead have been raised?"

"Well, raised where? Would we know if the dead were raised to heaven? I think they have been."

"Ernie Jo?"

"With all due respect to these other folks' views, I think the Bible's quite clear. When the real Jesus comes back, the dead will be raised and walk the face of the earth."

"And the Lovejoys. What is your personal feeling about a second coming of Christ?"

Amos Lovejoy spoke. "I believe that the Bible is a symbolic rendering of a religious ideal, in that the intention is that we should all live good lives, as though we are being judged by some deity, some almighty being. But I don't believe that Jesus Christ will come again and walk on this earth."

"There is nothing that could convince you that this man who is here now and claims to be Jesus Christ actually is Jesus Christ?"

"That's right. Nothing could convince me of that."

"I understand," the moderator continued, "this man knows his Bible cold. Ask him anything, he can place it, chapter and verse. Since there are literally thousands of verses, don't you find that uncanny?"

"I do," said Michael.

"Nah," his father broke in. "It's a parlor trick. The first thing anyone contemplating this kind of charade would commit to memory."

I saw Michael look at his father with a look that told of a lifetime of disappointment. Only now, it was the son disappointed in the father. "Dad," he said quietly, "why don't you tell them Jesus cured Mom's arthritis?"

Amos turned Chinese-lacquer red in an instant. Air was building in his throat, forcing his Adam's apple to dance. A vein stood out on his temple and pulsated. Amos Lovejoy was speechless.

His wife sensed his distress, and was about to step in on her own, when Phil Allen addressed her—"Is that true, Mrs. Lovejoy?"

I could see her dilemma. Her husband was glaring at her as if that glare would forbid her to answer. Michael was pleading with his eyes. Did she go with her husband or son? Her politic response surprised me.

"My arthritis subsided while this man who calls himself Jesus was in my house. I don't believe in miracles, but I do believe in coincidences. Perhaps it chose to heal itself."

"Well, but..." Phil was sputtering, "didn't this Jesus perform any incantations simultaneous with the healing? Any prayers? Laying on of hands—was he *there* when you felt relief?"

"Well, yes, he was."

"How exactly did it happen?"

Andi looked from husband to son and back to Amos again. But she knew she was on the spot—if she didn't tell the truth, Michael *would*, and they would *all* be embarrassed.

"I was in the kitchen, after dinner. Jesus, that is, the man who claims to be Jesus returned, I guess in postmillennial mode— he took my hands in his—pressed them to his cheeks and closed his eyes. Perhaps I shouldn't tell this, but it felt like the touch of a lover."

"Was he praying?" Phil asked.

"Nothing that I heard. Then he gently let go of my hands and..." Andi stopped to look at her husband. There could be no doubt in her mind he was humiliated and wished nothing more than for her to shut her mouth. But, of course, Phil Allen would not sit still for it.

"And what, Mrs. Lovejoy?" Allen prodded.

Andi picked up her hands and held them in from of her face

as though she were experiencing the miracle for the first time. "It went away," she said softly, wiggling her fingers and marveling all over again.

"Your arthritis went away?" Rat-tat-tat from the machine-gun moderator.

Andi nodded.

"And you told no one of this until today?"

She nodded again.

"Another groundbreaking exclusive on 'The Burning Issues,'" Phil Allen crowed. Phil Allen was such a bore, but I think, thick as he was, he sensed the tension in the Lovejoy family and he turned to the evangelist. "Reverend Banghart?" he said. "Do you believe this new Jesus can perform miracles—like curing Andi Lovejoy's arthritis?"

"No, I give him all credit for it. It is an impressive show, all right. Unnerstand I never did see this firsthand, but I hear tell of it, and if it is true, it is mighty impressive. But," he dropped his mouth in sorrow, "I've seen amazing feats like this before, an that don't, in and of itself, make him no authentic Jesus."

Amos seemed flushed and flustered as he cut in to speak: "It was my son there, Michael, who brought this Jesus character to my house. I am afraid I must dissent from that opinion expressed by my son. The arthritis coincidence notwithstanding, I was not snowed in any sense of the word. Oh, as cons go, I will admit, he's one of the best—he makes a good impression and all that, but Jesus Christ? Come on!"

"Michael, how do you respond to that?" Phil Allen asked.

Michael seemed to be blushing. "Well, ah, people, I guess, have different ideas about religion and things. I was never religious—we didn't have much at home. But when I met this—I don't know—something happened. I can't explain it, I was just knocked out when I saw how other people reacted to Jesus. He really has this divine thing about Him.

"My dad has devoted his life to religion—he has a Ph.D. in

theology, but he doesn't believe in God. He's a doctor of nonbe-lievers."

There was uproarious laughter from the studio audience — surprising both father and son. Michael's face registered the surprise, but Amos's face was tormented in anger.

"That's outrageous," Amos sputtered.

"No," the moderator interrupted, "let him finish the thought."

"Well," Michael said, sheepishly, "I didn't mean it to be funny. I'm just saying, well, religion means different things to different people. I don't have my dad's education and experience or maybe I'd be a skeptic, too."

More laughter. More anger on Amos's face. It was clear the audience was seeing this exchange as a comedy show, and were delighting in the comic relief.

But the really strange thing about this exposure on national television was Michael had become a celebrity overnight and he was sought all over the country for his opinions. Not so strange, when I think about it. That's the way American celebrities are made.

The only time Amos's phone rang, it was some close friend commiserating with him on how bad the kid made him look. Amos was livid.

...insult and injury were the possibilities of any day. Some ardent Christians snatched Jewish infants from their mothers' breasts and forcibly baptized them. If there were no ignorance there would be no history.

—*Will and Ariel Durant*
"The Age of Louis XIV"
The Story of Civilization, vol. VIII

THE GOSPEL ACCORDING TO

ERNIE JO BANGHART

I hear there's an old naval saying, "The rats are the first to leave a sinking ship."

Now, I don't want to say my ship was sinking exactly, but times had never been tougher because of this Jesus character who was causing such headaches to all of us.

I don't know which was worse, all my followers, who stood in line to say goodbye and to praise me for my wonderful progrums and how much I meant to them, or those who just deserted without so much as a how-do-you-do.

The layoffs this so-called Jesus caused me to make of the staff were so very painful for me. But it had to be done—the money just wasn't there. We kept on a skeleton crew of the most faithful and most senior members of the staff, but we had our troubles meeting even that reduced payroll.

Then to top it off—as though I hadn't hit the bottom hard enough—one of my longest term employees came in to see me on a Friday afternoon, and there was just no mistaking the hangdog look on her face.

Well, she told me, it wasn't easy for her to join the rats.

"How long you been with me, Elsie?"

"Going on pret near twenty-two years, Reverend," she said, standing before my desk with her Sunday dress she must have worn just for the occasion.

"And you're going to turn tail and desert me in this time of need? Why, I cain't believe it—not of you, Elsie, you were always the one we could count on. I mean, I seen this congregation dwindle to next to nothing, and that's all right, ever'body has fair-weather friends, but you, Elsie?" I just shook my head in wonderment. "You were the last person I'd expect of desertion."

"Oh, Reverend, you're making me feel terrible," she said.

"That makes two of us."

"It's just the mister and I want to see what this is all about in Californy. We always wanted to go. We haven't hardly been out of Mississippi, and, well, this was an opportunity we just didn't want to pass up."

"It's like a knife in my back, Elsie."

"I'm sorry, Reverend," she said, hanging her head like she was ashamed.

"But, Elsie, the man's an impostor. You believe me when I tell you that?"

She was twisting a handkerchief in front of her matron's belly. I could tell she wasn't happy about it. "The mister," she said. "He's been keen to go, and I told him you wouldn't like it. We seen him on TV—this Jesus, you know—and, well—the mister, especially—liked what he saw. He just thinks it's a once-in-a-lifetime opportunity—and I don't know but what there isn't near the work logging on the donations, because there aren't all that many nowadays, and the mister, he allowed as how I'd be doing you a favor, what with all the layoffs you've had to do."

"We didn't lay you off, Elsie. You were one of the best."

"Yes, sir. I appreciate that."

Well, there wasn't nothing more I could say but, "Good luck. Godspeed, and be careful you don't get swindled by that charlatan."

Things have frankly never been worse for this ministry, and that seems to be true for most ministries I know of. It got so bad, I was starting to think God had deserted me. I was grasping at straws to save my ministry from complete ruin. I realized, as I saw Elsie's back slogging out my office door, I had to play my ace.

I told my secretary to get Frankie Foxxe on the phone.

Ask, and it shall be given you;
seek, and ye shall find;
knock, and it shall be opened unto
you:
For every one that asketh receiveth;
and he that seeketh findeth;
and to him that knocketh it shall be
opened.

—Matthew 7:7-8

THE GOSPEL ACCORDING TO

FRANKIE FOXXE

I'm embarrassed to say
how much I missed
Rachel after she gave me
the bird for my *Jesus
Christ: Man or Myth?*
piece.

It was almost like she had become a die-hard fundamentalist.

I started looking for her everywhere. When a car passed by me in the street, I thought it was hers. When the phone rang, I hoped it was she. If someone knocked on my door, I just knew it was Rachel surprising me in a thoughtful gesture of love and desire. Of course, it never was.

She was angry about my Jesus-debunking piece and the fact that I hadn't given her the gory details about my ignoble exit from the priesthood. And so it was red-flag time in the old bullring.

I was back in Gulfport, getting together my meager belongings for a move. The center of gravity for myth debunking had tilted west and I was going to tilt with it. Rachel was my one loose end that I wanted to tie up—so I swallowed my pride and called her.

The first thing she said after I said, "Hello, Rachel," was, "Are you ready to come clean and tell me what it is in your past that gives you this thing about Jesus?"

So we met at my place. Not an inspiring venue for the decorator-conscious among us. It was furnished mostly with reading matter—books, magazines, newspapers. A man, I learned as a fairly young man, could only read so much, but that never served as an inhibitor to buying. I find that just living among written matter gives me a feeling of erudition—a conversance with intelligence, as well as a spur to catch up with all I've accumulated.

My collection was diverse but it leaned toward the myth-debunking function I had taken on.

From *The Quest of the Historical Jesus* by Albert Schweitzer to *Jim and Tammy*, a biography of the ubiquitous Bakkers—the TV evangelist who went to the slammer for bilking his fans—I had everything I could lay my hands on—in addition to all those I had read from the library.

In between were *When God Was a Woman* by Merlin Stone, *Science and Health* by Mary Baker Eddy, the *Book of Mormon*, Robert Lindsey's *A Gathering of Saints*, bios of Jimmy Swaggert, Falwell, Oral Roberts, dictionaries, concordances, encyclopedias.

Okay, you might say I was obsessed. Rachel thought I was.

I cleared a path to the couch for Rachel. She was deadpan when I opened the door and she marched in right past me and sat on the single chair. I was rather proud of myself that both seating implements were free of the print media.

I always rented furnished places for the quick getaway. I had this aversion to roots. Roots were okay if you were a rutabaga.

Sitting in the squat, dirt-brown chair, Rachel looked like one of the early queens of England—Elizabeth—Mary, maybe. Regal-imperial.

The squat, padded chair, designed, no doubt, by someone looking at a cardboard box and keeping his imagination in check, matched the squat, squarish love seat. I could see the sign in the window of the Apartment House Furniture Emporium out on the highway—

Love Seat & Chair
$99.95!

The queen's eyes followed me as I moseyed to the love seat. I had kind of hoped Rachel would sit there, but I should have known better. She was in the stiff-upper-lip mode, allowing for no nonsense in the touchy-feely department.

As soon as my gluteus muscles brushed the love seat, she said, "Start talking."

I sucked in some air but it didn't relax me. I wondered why I was even considering doing this bit for anyone. It was a sign of how far gone I was on Rachel. Love is, I suppose, confidences, and you could only hope your confidences weren't misplaced. "I am really not keen on having this blabbed around," I said kind of mealy-mouthed. "Rob Houston is a gasbag and he wants you to think he knows all this, but he doesn't…"

"I'm not going to tell anyone," Rachel said—an official dictum from her throne.

"Okay," I said, wanting to believe her. "Okay."

"Okay," she parroted me. It was not going to be easy. She wasn't in the mood for any diversionary tactics.

"I was in love in high school with a girl named Carol, a dazzling girl. It was mostly her personality, not her looks. I mean she was attractive okay, not a raving beauty, but she had this real fun way about her. A real live wire, you know what I mean?"

"Am I a live wire?"

"Hey, I'm not with her anymore, am I?"

"Guess not."

"Anyway, I was a year ahead of her and I went from our New Jersey high school to college in Wyoming. More for the skiing than the education, I guess. Anyway, Carol followed me out there the next year, after she graduated."

"She liked to ski, too?"

"Very funny. We were both Catholics. Everybody assumed we would be getting married. I had this old-fashioned notion that sex was for marriage only. I mean the real intimate stuff, but Carol didn't share my inhibitions. Some of these notions were self-absorbed from my religion, I guess, though I wasn't really a fanatic—went to Mass most of the time that skiing didn't interfere, but you wouldn't put me on any top-ten list of the most religious people you knew."

"So what happened?"

"She broke it off. I think it was her frustration over the sex thing. I wanted to wait. She said that was okay, but here I was, graduating, and she was ready to get married, and I guess I wasn't as ready. She told me she wanted to party more than I did and I was the most perfect person she ever knew, but she couldn't be that perfect. She transferred to Seton Hall after I graduated, found a man more to her liking—got married, had some kids, got divorced."

"The American nightmare," Rachel said. "What happened to you?"

"I was devastated. I had just taken her for granted. We'd

marry, play golf, ski, I'd put in some time at my father's textile business when I wasn't too busy having a good time. I was so stunned, I could only halfheartedly try to talk her into staying. She had no trouble sensing it was halfhearted, so she took off."

"Poor Frankie. What did you do?"

"I moped around for a while. For some reason I was reluctant to go back home to Jersey and face all those explanations. I guess I was so distant that I overreacted by signing up for the priesthood." I spoke quietly, as though I still had trouble understanding it.

"Celibacy—didn't bother you?"

"I'm telling you, I was a basket case. I was completely turned off by women. It wasn't the most rational decision of my life."

"So how come you aren't a priest now?"

I shook my head. "The old priests tried to tell me I was making a mistake. Rebounding from romantic failure was the worst reason for joining up—had the highest failure rate. But I was stubborn. I argued. I would show them. And I did. I got to lie on my belly on the floor, arms outstretched, in abject prostration to the almighty deity and give myself, my life, to God. The great, wondrous, mysterious, mythical good God above."

"Amazing!"

"Father Damien. You like it?"

"Oh, wow. So how'd you escape?"

My lips curled but they didn't form the words.

"God, Frankie," Rachel said, "you didn't get a dishonorable discharge, did you?"

"It was dishonorable, all right. I can't deny that—but it was voluntary." I stopped short.

"Tell me," she pleaded.

I stammered a moment, then said, "I don't know, Rachel, no one knows this story but the two principals."

I looked at Rachel to be sure that here was a person I could trust with my story as well as a person worth telling it to. It was a commitment to a future—a relationship—and I had been burned before—a hundred percent of the time—both times. I really didn't have the trust I needed, how could I? I had trusted before and failed. The wounds had healed all right, but in the process I had developed impenetrable scabs. But I also found that keeping it to myself all these years was stultifying and I thought telling it to Rachel now, whether or not she would in the long term prove worthy of the investment, might be liberating.

I stumbled at first and thought I must be sounding like a babbling idiot, but Rachel was rapt and gentle in her sympathy.

"There was a woman," I finally managed.

"Of course," she said softly.

"She was, I thought at the time, the most beautiful creature God ever made. She came to me for confessional and counseling. Her husband was a philanderer, he mistreated her. All clichés now, I guess. But there was this instant chemical attraction. I could not get her out of my mind from the moment I first saw her." I stopped and stared off into space and Rachel must have known I was visualizing her all over again.

"What was her name?" she asked quietly, trying to get me back on the track.

"Oh, it doesn't matter. It wasn't long before we were touching. I brushed her hand and she reached out with her other hand and held my hand to hers. Before you knew it, we were kissing in my rectory office and hoping the housekeeper wouldn't barge in. If she'd had any suspicion, I suspect she would have. It wasn't long before I went to her home for lunch and had my first real love. I was almost thirty years old. It was the most fantastic thing. Instantly, the celibacy vow seemed the cruelest, most demented piece of religious chicanery in a long history of repression. The Catholics, you know, are the only major sect in the world practicing this brand of inhumane repression."

"I know."

"I simply could not get my mind off her. There she was, in the forefront of my thoughts, even when she was out of sight.

"Were you ever in love, Rachel—I mean the head-over-heels, gaga kind of love where you knew it was right, right, right, even if it wasn't?"

"Sure," she nodded. "Followed a guy to Japan once. Told my folks I was crazy about Japan, but I couldn't stand Japan; it was expensive and crowded and the women were fifth-class citizens."

"Well, that was me," I said. "It was right, right, right, even though I was a priest who took a sacred vow of celibacy and she was a married woman—no one could tell me it wasn't right. The sun was warmer, the sky bluer, the air crisper. God was in his heaven and all was right with the world. Right, right, right.

"Then I started going around singing these sappy love songs. You wouldn't believe it."

"Yes, I would," she said.

"Her husband was very wealthy and she managed to get him to loosen those purse strings, so our parish was the lucky recipient of his (and her) largess. But she also used a lot of that lucre to dress to kill. There was never any question of her identity—even if you didn't see anything but her clothes. You should have seen her sitting in the congregation with her coal-black, luminous hair and the flashing, haunting eyes that never left my face. Imagine trying to preach a sermon under those conditions."

"How old was she?"

I frowned. "She was a little older than I was."

"How much older?"

"Does that matter?"

"It might."

"About ten years. But her figure was perfect," I protested too much.

"Does 'about ten years' mean fifteen?"

I smiled at her perception. "Okay—fourteen. But you don't think that bothered me—or should have?"

"Oh, no—sorry—go on."

"She was so exquisite I could hardly breathe when I had to

speak about her."

"Did your colleagues know?"

"I'm sure they figured it out sooner or later. I was totally consumed by her. I don't know if that was because she was totally consuming or because I had so little experience with intimacy, but I am not a guy to get emotionally carried away by *any*thing, a guy who never considered suicide, but I'll tell you, if she had asked me to shoot myself, I would have."

"Oh, Frankie."

"Yes, yes, I'm not proud of it. I thought time would make it easier for me—that our love would diminish—but the more I had of her, the more I wanted. And the real beautiful thing—the thing I could never get over—was that she felt the same way about me."

"How do you know?"

"She told me. But even if she hadn't, it was clear enough in her...actions. Well, I couldn't go on like that. Sneaking around to her house and worrying her husband would surprise us. I wanted to marry her. She said she wanted to marry me. I resigned from the priesthood. Defrocked myself. I couldn't be a hypocrite any longer. When I told her I had quit the Church to marry her, she got suddenly cool and distant. How would we live? she wondered. She wasn't willing to part with her substantial meal ticket for a life of poverty. To me, poverty was nothing once you kicked chastity."

"Poor Frankie."

"Yeah. You can imagine if I was devastated with my experience with Carol, what this must have done to me. I had no money, I had nothing, nowhere to turn. Nowhere to live. I couldn't eat."

"What did you do?" Rachel asked.

I laughed the laughter of despair. "I couldn't very well join the priesthood as I did the first time, could I? I did nothing. I took the car with me and lived in that until I pulled myself together. Cleaned myself up after several months, started driving aimlessly through the South working odd jobs, begging food, anything I could. Fate, I guess, led me to Rob Houston. Only a guy like that would hire a guy like me."

"What happened to the woman?"

"Oh, she started over with another priest. I guess it was the challenge of the chase with her."

I was winded. Telling my story exhausted me. I must have reminded Rachel of a lost little boy, for then she blessed me with her very best ministerial skills.

ANOTHER BLAST FROM GOD'S TROMBONES:

They have moved me to jealousy
with that which is not God;
they have provoked me to anger
with their vanities:
and I will move them to jealousy
with those which are not a people;
I will provoke them to anger
with a foolish nation.
For a fire is kindled in mine anger,
and shall burn unto the lowest hell,
and shall consume the earth with her
    increase,
and set on fire
the foundations of the mountains.
I will heap mischiefs upon them;
I will spend mine arrows upon them.
They shall be burnt with hunger,
and devoured with burning heat,
and with bitter destruction:
I will also send the teeth of beasts upon them,
with the poison of serpents of the dust.

—Deuteronomy 32:21-24

I think I know enough of hate
To say that for destruction ice
Is also great
And would suffice.

> —*Robert Frost*
> *"Fire & Ice"*

THE GOSPEL ACCORDING TO

MICHAEL

God smiled down on me from heaven, and putting me with Jesus is His most special favor in the world.

I never wanted it to end. That song "Jesus Loves Me" kept looping through my head.

Jesus loves me! This I know,
For the Bible tells me so.
Little ones to Him belong;
They are weak, but He is strong.
Yes, Jesus loves me! Yes, Jesus loves me!
Yes, Jesus loves me! The Bible tells me so.

Since my TV appearance with my mom and dad and Banghart and that reporter, I've been in constant demand on the talk-show circuit and I go as a stand-in for Jesus. He always tells me I did so well. He knows how to make a person feel good. One program is pretty much like the next and I can answer the questions in my sleep.

They always bring up my dad, as though they want to trick me into making fun of him. I try hard to avoid that trap. I just say my dad and I are different and try to promote Jesus's don't-hate-anyone message.

There was a knock on the door. Jack answered it. It was one of the security guards to announce that my father had come to see us.

I jumped up and said, "I gotta bail."

"Why?" Jack said. "Shall I send him away?"

"He's going to freak—he doesn't like all the publicity I get—thinks it makes him look bad."

"Apparently, he wants to see you," Mary said, quietly.

"Yeah, but I don't want to see him!"

There was a sudden commotion at the door. I looked up and saw my father wrestling with the security guard—the Devil's Disciple man was a lot younger than Amos.

Jack turned from me to Jesus with a what-shall-I-do? look.

Jesus said softly, "Honor thy father and thy mother that thy days may be long upon the earth."

I gave in.

When the fighting subsided, Amos straightened up, brushed himself off, more, it seemed, to restore his dignity than from any real need, then marched into the room.

It was obvious Amos was trying to breathe fire from his nostrils, but the only one he succeeded in scaring was me.

"There you are!" Amos exclaimed as though he had found me hiding somewhere. "Just the man I want to see." Then, as an afterthought, he turned to Jesus. "And *you*, too! It's high time we get all this nonsense out on the table."

"What...?" my words stuck in my throat.

"*You*, young man," Amos said, his face like a rubber mask of menace, this finger thrusting at me, "I'm sick and tired of seeing you on the TV saying how stupid I am."

"I don't say that," I protested, my skin heating.

"That I'm intolerant."

I didn't know what he was talking about. "I didn't say—"

"Don't tell *me* what you said. I'm your *father*! I heard it with my own ears."

"But, Dad, I didn't..."

The first blow from Amos's fist glanced off my jaw.

"Oh!" Mary's body jerked as she leaned forward to get up, the bulk of Amos blocking her way.

Without taking my eyes from my father—my hands raised in a defensive stance—I asked Jesus, "What should I do?"

"Turn the other cheek, Michael."

I turned my cheek, but it was more of a turn toward Jesus to see if He was really saying that seriously than it was a humble gesture.

Wham! Amos's fist cracked across my other cheek, sending me toppling to the floor.

Mary screamed when she saw me hit the floor. "Call the police!" she shouted.

Jack Whitehall went to the phone. It was a long time before I heard him say, "Need you over here, Sheriff... A fight, Sheriff—a bad one... I think you can handle it—with your gun... Sheriff! if I could handle it—I wouldn't have called."

When he hung up, I was groggily opening my eyes from my position on the floor. Father was standing over me, winded, still snorting his agitation.

I opened my mouth to speak. The faint words were preceded by a low gravel-scraping sound. "Honor thy father..." was all I could manage.

"Nice words, Michael, very admirable. But it'd be a lot better if you could put them into practice."

Amos looked like he was going to pounce on me right there on the floor, when he heard Jesus say, "Peace be with you, brother." I could see Dad was mad about that. I was beginning to think I had rotten luck to be in the airport parking lot when Jesus came through.

Amos turned on Jesus and was about to swing at Him when Jack stood between them.

Since Jack was as large as Amos, my dad couldn't dance around him so he could get his hands on that guy who was saying "Peace be with you..."

The sheriff came in carrying his dog. "What seems to be the trouble here, Jack?" I could tell he was trying to put some macho in his voice. He stood like a tough guy, but it was a little funny with that fluffy dog under his arm.

As soon as the sheriff's dog saw my big father standing over me, he started barking his head off and leaped out of Sheriff Jessup's arms and streaked across the floor, homing in on my big dad's ankle. With one ferocious chomp, he sank his teeth into Amos's flesh, causing Dad to let out a yelp; at that moment, he drew back his foot, with the little dog clinging to him for dear life, and with all his wounded strength hurled that little dog across the room, the little dog taking a hunk of Dad's flesh with him. Fluffy flew like a dust ball against the wall. There was a thud of the dog hitting the wall and the crack of his neck breaking.

A high shriek from the sheriff thrust him like a shot to the place where the dog had slid down the wall to the floor.

Sheriff Jessup fell with Fluffy and scooped the bloody fur in his arms and cried without shame.

The lawman looked up at Jesus. "Make him whole," he said, pleading. Jesus moved to the sheriff and put His hand on Stoney's shoulder. It was a tense moment—full of expectation—would Jesus raise Fluffy from the dead?

"He is with his maker," Jesus said. "It is God's will."

Jessup seemed to think about that for a second, then, shaking his head, cuddled the bloody dog to his cheek.

"He's all I had in the world," he whimpered. "You might just as well turned my gun on me, Mister—you take my dog from me." The sheriff spoke as though he were already dead. "I don't know what came over Fluffy. He's never done anything like that before."

Sheriff Jessup's hand drifted dreamily to the pistol in its holster by his side. His eyes fixed on Amos, whose own eyes instantly showed the terror of his thoughts. It looked like he wanted to take off, but he winced with pain when he tried to move. The sheriff took out his gun, but waved it around, as though he couldn't make up his mind about whom to shoot, Amos or himself.

"Now, Sheriff," Jack Whitehall said, reaching for the gun.

"No—" the sheriff said. "I never was anything to anybody except Fluffy. Now he's gone…" He turned away from us and put the pistol to his head.

"Sheriff!" Jack shouted, and grabbed Sheriff Jessup's arm. Sheriff Jessup pulled it away.

"Somebody got an anesthetic?" Amos moaned. He was nursing his ankle where the skin was obviously torn by a tiny set of teeth. There wasn't much blood, but Amos probably had visions of dying from rabies. "Isn't someone going to call a doctor?" All his life Dad was a hypochondriac.

"I'll get you some peroxide," Jack said, keeping his eyes on the sheriff's gun, now in an indifferent position on his lap. "I think you're going to live."

Mary nestled up against me after I got off the floor and returned to the couch, keeping an eye on my father and another on Sheriff Jessup. I was relieved to see that the late Fluffy had put my father out of commission.

Jesus was by the sheriff's side, crouched down on his level, speaking soft, soothing words in his ear.

"I'm lost."

"You are not lost in the Lord," Jesus said. "God loves you and so do I."

"Oh, oh…"

"Come with us, Sheriff. We *need* you. Help us spread the Word."

"What?"

"The Word—the war against hate."

"I *hate* him," he said, pointing to Amos. "He killed my dog and I *hate* him!"

"You certainly are entitled to some strong feelings," Jesus said. "But hating Mr. Lovejoy isn't going to bring Fluffy back. Hating only drains you of energy—of love. Fluffy is with God the Father now. You are holding him in your bosom, while his soul flies to the bosom of our Lord."

"You think so?" The sheriff's eyes were wide.

"I know it," Jesus said.

"If only I could believe…"

"Believe, my son, believe."

Not that which goeth into the mouth
defileth a man;
but that which cometh out of the
    mouth,
this defileth a man.

—Matthew 15:11

THE GOSPEL ACCORDING TO

FRANKIE FOXXE

Ernie Jo Banghart called
a press conference.

He called me first. I wasn't surprised at that or the subject matter. I'm not sure Ernie Jo got the word I had been fired. I was working freelance now, for a lot larger papers than that Gulfport rag. I didn't know if my newfound eminence in the field could hold, but I was enjoying the thrill of the ride in the meantime.

Ernie Jo stood in his favorite light-tan suit before a battery of microphones. His face was as long as Job's. He was sending the signal by body language that what he was about to say pained him to no end.

"Ladies and gentlemen of the press," he began, "this is not a happy occasion for me. I stand before you not by choice, but out of a sense of duty to my brothers and sisters in Christ. I do not revel in the task, and I honestly wish this cup could pass from my lips. But, then someone else would be compelled to do it, because, well, folks, simply because it has to be done to cleanse the Body of Christ once and for all. I tried to think of someone else to bring you this news, but as I thought over my fellow clergy, I just couldn't think of anyone I'd wish this unpleasantness onto. So I am biting the bullet myself. And, as I say, I take no pleasure in it, believe me."

Ernie Jo seemed like a man out of his element, which was, of course, waving his Bible in the air while dancing across a stage spouting like a sperm whale about *the waters gonna cleanse your soul*, and getting right with the Lord. Here it was Ernie Jo getting right with the opinion shapers. The boys and girls who could burnish his image, hoist him to his pedestal where you could tell he thought he rightfully belonged.

But he didn't realize what a weight he had become. How it would take more concerted lift than this meager bunch could manage.

"And it does pain me so very much to say it, but I am here about a fellow minister of the gospel who I wish would have known better than to do the things he has done, and I mean that sincerely."

It was a sadness, this charade. Ernie Jo was desperate. There wasn't a man, woman or child anywhere who could look at him and not see despair. But he was putting on the best front he could: jolly, jovial, smiling through his furrowed brows.

"Bobby Candle has been for many years a positive influence in the fields of Christ's ministry, with his wife, Billie Jean, to good Christians everywhere.

"I know he means well, I am convinced of that. Though his style of preaching is not my way of doing things, I don't respect him any less for it."

Ernie sucked in his cheeks then ran his tongue on the inside of his right cheek, as though seeking relief from a canker sore.

"But certain transgressions have come to mind that just cannot be overlooked any longer. Those others who are members of the Pentecostal Union of Churches want to nip this in the bud, so to speak—and we want to take care of it ourselves, rather than having some strangers get involved."

I groaned to myself. Get on with it, Ernie Jo. Everybody here knows what you are going to say, we're only here so we can report it. Enough already!

Someone in the back of the room shouted, "What'd he do?"

"I'm getting to that," Ernie Jo said. "I'm getting right to it." He smiled the cat-with-the-canary smile and I couldn't help but think he was mighty proud of himself. Ernie Jo thrived on attention.

"Well, folks, Bobby Candle, he's got some voracious appetites, I'm sorry to have to tell you. And it's not only for women. No, sir, it's boys, too." Ernie Jo stretched his long face. "It pains me, it really does, that a minister of the gospel could stray from his sacred marriage vows like he done." Ernie Jo shook his head in sadness. "Now, I suppose you're going to ask next what proof do we have. Well, I'll have to say that the proof is just about as irrefutable as you can get. We have signed affidavits, notarized statements, and we have just so many of them that these transgressions cannot be doubted.

"So much as it pains me to do so, in behalf of members of

the Greater Pentecostal Ministries, I am asking Bobby Candle to step down voluntarily and have the powers that be at headquarters appoint a pastor to tend his flock until all these unpleasantries can be sorted out." He paused to show us his face and posture were like those of a guy who'd bet a bundle on the losing team. "I'll entertain questions, if you have any." That was big-hearted Ernie Jo talking.

No one was fooled except Ernie Jo, who was trying mightily to fool the troops into thinking him a white knight—Dr. Christian exorcising the cancers from the Body of Christ—which was Ernie Jo's own metaphor for his heroic actions. But he came across only as a little man trying to save his skin by drowning his buddy. Talk big, look small.

"Would you be available to take over Bobby's congregation, Ernie Jo?" a man in the second row asked.

Ernie Jo put on his wry, twisted-lips smile. "I do not seek his flock, I have my hands full with my own. But I certainly would not shun helping out if the Lord told me to do so."

"Will you offer your services?"

The smile again. That you-think-you-can-put-one-over-on-me smile. "Not as such, no. If I am called, I will do my best."

"What do you think this will do to your relative Nielsen ratings?"

"Anybody who knows me knows I don't pay any attention to such things. I've no idea."

"Did your faltering ratings have any bearing on your involvement here?"

"None whatsoever," he said. Then clarified, "I don't agree with your statement about our ratings going down. Ratings had nothing to do with it."

"Will we be able to see the affidavits you spoke of?"

"I'm certain in time they will be released to the press."

"What time? How much time?"

"Well, the church body will have to review them first. Then they'll decide."

It was my turn. It was almost as though the whole event was building to this moment.

"Reverend Banghart," I called him, like I had never before. I was setting him up and I could see a smile of gratitude on Ernie Jo's face. "Did you ever compromise your own marriage vows?"

Now the smile turned to chagrin, but I don't think Ernie Jo realized. "Oh, no, sir," he said, shaking his head as though deep in thought. "I'm clean on that score. Why, I never even kissed anyone but my wife."

By the time the last question was asked and practically answered, the perspiration had built to a trickle down Ernie's fleshy cheeks. I expected to hear an audible "plop" when the drops hit the ground, but that was wishful thinking.

"Does this announcement have anything to do with the Jesus phenomenon out in the California desert?" a woman in front asked.

"No, ma'am, it does not," Ernie Jo said grimly, as though he resented the inference but also could not help but expect it. "Not at all."

"Is it true your ministry is sagging as a result of this person who is, in effect, giving away free what you sell?"

"Why, that is just patently ridiculous. Certainly, there are fluctuations in our good fortune, but this is just the way I look at this—a blip, if you will, on the timeline of the Ernie Jo Banghart Ministries. We are healthy, we are strong. I thank God every day for the tens of thousands of loyal supporters we have—and that's all across the world I'm talking about. No," he shook his head so his moussed hair jiggled, "you don't have to worry none on that score."

"No? But I saw your last television program, where you said you were never more desperate and you needed everyone to give just as much as they could spare."

Ernie Jo stared bullets from an Uzi at his interlocutor. There wasn't any doubt just how Ernie Jo had received that tidbit. I sometimes wondered if he lived in a vacuum bubble where he could say anything he pleased without anyone doubting him or even remembering what he said.

"Are there any more questions about the subject of this press conference?"

"How about that one?" the last reporter shouted.

"That's not a question," Ernie Jo parried, "that's an accusation. I'm here to discuss a particular tragedy—that is, if you want to discuss it. If you have nothing further on that, why, we'll call it a day."

Nobody had anything further. The pall I felt was indicative of a general feeling of sadness in the room—sadness for the sinking of Ernie Jo to this level to try to save his quaking ministry. What would happen to him, I wondered, if he were caught in the act himself? What was going to happen to poor Bobby?

†   †   †

A lot of journalists are lazy. The lot of them at Ernie Jo's press conference were lazy. They took Ernie Jo's spiel as though it were a government handout and ran it pretty much "as is." I decided another slant was in order.

I walked across what Ernie Jo liked to refer to as his "campus" from the TV center, where the press conference was, to the office complex, where Ernie's wife, Emmy Sue, was.

I could tell Emmy Sue was flustered when her secretary told her I was there to see her.

When I was finally ushered into her office, amid protestations that she couldn't possibly have anything interesting to say, I could see she was flattered and pleased by the attention.

She didn't rise from behind her desk, but I was reminded of what a pretty woman she was. Here the ministry was over thirty years old, and she was only in her mid-forties.

She was wearing a white angora sweater that set off her

chestnut hair with a flare.

"To what do I owe this…" she smiled awkwardly—"should I call it a pleasure?"

"It is for me," I said.

I looked across the man-sized desk that divided us and I could see the little girl of fourteen that Ernie Jo had fallen in love with.

"But I can't imagine what you would want with me." (This came out as if in Southern-charm-school talk—"Bud I cain't *imagine* what you would want with li'l ole me.")

"While I was listening to Ernie Jo go on about Bobby," I said, "I thought of you—and how your work here goes unsung."

"Shoot," she said in mild, self-effacing protest, "I don't want any credit—I don't do that much anyway."

"No? Just the entire business end of the ministry."

"But that ain't nothing to what Ernie Jo does. He's the force here. I'm just a bean counter." Her lips gleamed with a touch of moisture as they parted with a modest laugh—"Less to count lately," she said.

"Make a difference—?"

"Well, sure it does."

"I mean to you, personally—in your job? Doesn't it take as much work to keep track of a thousand beans as a million?"

"Well, no, it does not. There are overlaps—sure. It's not proportionally more work, but it *is* more."

I thought I had softened her enough with small talk. "So, Mrs. Banghart—"

"Oh, Emily Sue, please," she looked at me slyly—"Mr. Foxxe."

I smiled as close as I could to an Ernie Jo Banghart smile. "Okay, Emily Sue, if I can be Frankie."

"You can be anything you want."

Damn, she did have a swell smile herself. I could see what sent that young stud Ernie Jo off the deep end. Probably figured if he didn't grab her early, someone else would.

"Emily Sue—you know, that's a pretty name."

"Why, thank you."

"Where'd it come from?"

"My momma and my daddy," she said with a twinkle in her eye. "Where else?"

"I thought it could be after an aunt or a grandmother."

"Nope, just made it up."

"Well, they did a good job."

"Thank you, sir," she said and dipped her upper body in a curtsy motion. If I didn't know any better, I would have said she was flirting with me. I was embarrassed to find myself looking at her chest and the white angora sweater that set off her perky breasts but didn't cling to them the way some cheaper goods might have. But worse, she saw me looking and flashed that damned dazzling smile again. She cocked an eyebrow inquisitively. I felt she wanted me to get to the point, though I had momentarily forgotten what the point was.

"Ah, yes, well, I was just at Ernie Jo's press conference and I thought, he's getting all this attention and you're the power here. You know where all the money is. You probably know what brings it in and what doesn't. Am I right?"

"Well, I have some ideas."

"You think this press conference today was a good idea?"

She frowned, studying my face as if to gauge how much she could tell me.

"Now, Mr.—ah, Frankie," she said. "I don't want to be seeing my name in the papers saying I said thus and so. I'm strictly behind the scenes."

"Well, I do see you onstage for Ernie Jo's services."

"But you don't see me doing anything. I'm not there to distract anybody from Ernie Jo and I don't want to start."

I thought about that a moment. Surely some of the men were distracted. Surely someone had thought about that.

"Did he talk this press conference over with you?" I asked.

"Ernie Jo asks my opinion on things—yes."

"Did you think it was a good idea?"

She squirmed in her high-backed chair. "Now, Frankie—I told you—"

"Off the record, Emily Sue. Just for my own background."

She cocked another eye. "Can I trust you?"

"Certainly—my word is my bond. Ask Ernie Jo. No reporter could last two minutes by breaking his word to sources."

She studied me, then took a deep breath, and I knew I had won her over.

"No, I did not support this press conference idea. Ernie Jo had this notion it would get him attention, and lately, as you well know, that commodity has been hard to come by, what with this Jesus thing in the desert out there. I said you aren't going to make any friends tearing Bobby down—and about something so private as sex." She closed her eyes a moment, as though she were visualizing something distasteful.

"Don't get me wrong," she said. "I don't condone Bobby's actions, but I don't see it particularly helping Ernie Jo, either. People back away from scandal when it has to do with church people."

"You think it could backfire?"

"Backfire? How?"

"You know—Ernie Jo might have some…indiscretion on his part."

"Oh, I wouldn't believe that."

"He said you're the only woman he's ever kissed—you have any reason to doubt that?"

"Well, no, I do not." She was blushing. "My, we are getting awfully personal here, aren't we?"

"Off the record, though. Is your love life with Ernie Jo satisfactory?" I asked, substituting "love" for "sex" at the last moment.

Did I imagine it, or did Emily Sue lean forward to press her assets on the desk when she said, "For Ernie Jo—or for me?"

She threw me with that. "Well, both…each," I fumbled, "one at a time…"

"Goodness," she said. "I'm of a background and a mind-set where we don't talk about such things easily."

"So am I," I offered as encouragement.

"Yes," she said, looking me over for some crack in my facade that might be leaking dark fluids of my soul. "You've never been married, have you, Frankie?"

I didn't ask her how she knew that, I just shook my head.

"You were a priest, weren't you?"

Now she got my attention. "How did you hear that?"

She waved a hand as if to say I didn't have to ask, and I expect that was right. "Rob Houston over at the paper told Ernie Jo," she said.

Of course he would, I thought. No mystery which of us was more important to old Rob.

I said, "I know you can't tell me anything I didn't hear many times over in the confessional. I've had relationships." I don't know why I felt compelled to tell her I played the game.

"Then you know the man usually wants…those things more than the woman."

I thought it over. I knew it was generally true—I also knew it wasn't *always* true. But I needed to keep her talking.

"Remember, I was fourteen when this dashing young man came on to me. Now, I don't know if you have any concept of what that can do to the head of a young girl, but it wasn't long before I came to believe myself a princess. Understand, in our simple lives down here in the Deep South, a preacher is like a god. That's one reason this business with Bobby Candle doesn't set well with me. You don't go bringing down other people's gods. And Ernie Jo was just so handsome—"

"And you are *very* pretty," I interjected.

"Well, thank you." She blushed and seemed to tilt her chest

ever so slightly forward. "So I married him, what *else could* I do? My momma and daddy were terribly conflicted about it. They loved the idea, there was no hiding that. But just as naturally, I guess, they wished for me to get through my childhood before I settled down to be somebody's wife. But Ernie Jo was just so charming and persuasive, they gave in. He talked about doing the Lord's work more effectively with a helpmate. The implication was, if he had a wife to relieve him of certain natural urges, he would be better able to concentrate on the work of the Lord." Emily Sue looked at me through a doubt-cocked eyebrow.

"Did it work?"

"Well," she gave a short laugh, "I wanted to please him, I really did, I just didn't seem to have it in me so much. Then, after Brucie was born—" she lifted her hands in a gesture of hopelessness, "why, I guess my focus changed. I was a mother more than a wife. I figured Ernie Jo was a grown man now—" she giggled—"he was twenty, after all. I was still a teenager. But when it's between a man and an infant, what do you do? The infant needs you more. So I did the natural thing and favored Brucie."

"Do you think Ernie Jo may have ever...well—strayed from his vows?"

"Oh, I don't think so. When would he have time? And he's recognized all over the world. Those things take an investment in time—romance and such—lunches, outings." She shook her head. "No, I don't see it."

I thought myself admirably delicate that I didn't mention the possibility of the professional woman who didn't require any romancing. In whom the time investment was minimal.

"What do you think would happen if he were caught in something...compromising, now that he's made all this fuss?"

"Why, I don't know. I expect his enemies would be merciless. It could cost him dearly."

"His ministry?"

"Oh, I don't know about that. Ernie Jo is strong and resilient."

I thanked her and she stood up, showing me the whole enchilada, you might say. I told her Ernie Jo was a lucky man. She held out her soft hand for me to shake. I took it and she held mine warmly.

"Sometime, we must meet again," she said. "And you can tell me about your sex life."

ANOTHER BLAST FROM GOD'S TROMBONES:

Monks roamed the northern roads, offering papal indulgence of remission of all sins for forty days' service in the holy war. An army of northerners more than 15,000 strong, led by German mercenaries, gathered in Lyon. As religious leader of the crusade, Innocent appointed the abbot Arnald-Amaury, an ambitious fanatic who had no qualms about killing heretics.

In July 1209 the army marched on the ill-prepared town of Beziers…the crusaders burst through the town gates and unleashed a riot of murder and looting. In the middle of the massacre…Arnald Amaury was asked how the soldiers could distinguish heretics from Catholics. "Kill them all," he replied; "God will recognize His own."

—*Jonathan Sumption*
The Albigensian Crusade

Christianity and Islam as well as Judaism...share...the Biblical propensity to conceive of history as one God expressing himself in the world through his choice of One People—a people who get defined against inferior others, with predictably dire consequences.

> — *Lawrence Weschler*
> *"Mayhem and Monotheism"*
> The New Yorker

THE GOSPEL ACCORDING TO

MICHAEL

Things have never gone better for us.

Jack Whitehall said we should be careful or else the bubble might burst and drown us all. Jesus didn't seem concerned. He was the coolest person I'd ever known. I mean, nothing fazed Him.

His message was getting across on TV and radio and He never had to spend a nickel, they just came to Him to beg permission.

Some computer nerd put us on the Internet and the hits on our page crashed the system.

The churches suffered major blows. The poorer churches had been holding on—maybe because the communicative media was slower to reach them, maybe because their churches were more a part of their daily lives—but now they were suffering, too.

My dad was appointed spokesperson for the establishment churches and he was on TV every day. I stopped going on because it freaked him out. It suited him more than me, anyway.

Amos was angling for another meeting with Jesus Christ. He wanted Jesus to go to him because he was afraid if he came up here Sheriff Jessup would kill him because he killed the sheriff's dog. There was even talk that he was afraid I might do something for the way he treated me his last trip, but I couldn't believe he didn't know me better than that.

Jack Whitehall favored a national tour for Jesus. Jack seemed to be wearing down. All this activity was hard on him. We talked about it a lot, but so far, Jesus seemed satisfied to stay.

If anything, Amos looked more serious than ever when he came back to see Jesus. I decided, in spite of his normally jolly face, my father was a tense and basically unhappy man. I had a flash of sympathy for my mother, who had always seemed like such a saint to me.

I didn't want him to come, but I couldn't talk Jesus out of it.

"Try to understand your father. Everybody copes with the stresses and strains of life differently. But wouldn't we be better off if we could all direct our frustrations away from others?"

Amos came at the appointed time. I confess I had slipped

out to the Disciples who were guarding the place to ask them to put the fear of God in Amos. Give him a Devil's Disciples' stare, be extra macho when pressing him for identification. When Amos came into the room, he nodded a curt hello to Jesus, then looked at me. "I see you've virtually disappeared from TV, young man. That's good."

Amos sat facing Jesus. I stood out of the line of sight, in back, like I always did.

Amos put his hands on his knees as he did when he wanted to signal a big event in the offing. It was an obvious gesture, beginning with raising his arms above his head—like he was surrendering the troops to the enemy—then swooping down with an energetic fanning motion.

"Well," Amos exhaled as though he had overexerted himself, "Mr. Jesus, you have created quite a stir."

Jesus smiled but He didn't say anything. "Yes, sir…" Amos said. "And that's why I'm here. Yessss—" the hissing trailed on. "Unlikely as it seems, I have been appointed as spokesperson for the religious community in this matter." He glanced quickly at me, then back to Jesus. "What it comes down to is this: when we see Ernie Jo Banghart's operation hurt—crippled, even—we don't despair. So many unfortunate, trusting, ignorant souls lost to him, why, so much the better. But when it started to hurt the established mainline religions, panic set in. Do you understand, sir, what is happening to our churches?"

I wanted to ask Dad why that should bother him. He was no big believer or anything.

"Now, ordinarily, I wouldn't worry about this kind of thing. My interest is historical, not theological. If there is any good in organized religion at all, it is in helping people cope. Maybe keeping them from killing each other, but historically, that's been far from certain. But it gives them something to believe in. Buy a little peace from the have-nots."

Jesus raised an eyebrow. I couldn't help myself—Jesus

seemed unwilling to talk until Amos stopped, so I said, "Why not believe in Jesus, is there something wrong with that?"

"Wrong?" Amos sneered. "That might be a philosophical question beyond your ken, my boy. Today my interest is in pragmatic matters. Our established churches—the venerable institutions—are teetering on the brink of collapse. Churches never were rock-solid solvent. A lot of them were hand to mouth, able to exist only because the electric company was patient about the bill. In the main it's been a struggle in the best of times."

He paused as though looking for some miracle to see him through. He seemed, as he got closer to the point, to be losing it. As though he had rehearsed the beginning and counted on Jesus to take it from there. "Now, Mr. Jesus, there are a lot of people who have counted on these institutions for centuries for rituals, it's true—baptism, communion, marriage, burial, what have you—but also for psychological and spiritual, if you will, well-being. Now you come along and no one knows what to think anymore. Because, as you know, those churches have been dependent on the financial support of their parishioners, and that support has virtually dried up." A cocked head. "Why, as the saying goes, pay for something you can get for free?"

Jesus seemed to nod in understanding, if not agreement. But He didn't give Amos the satisfaction of filling the dead air.

"So they appointed me—informally, of course, this is no official act—to come and talk to you. See what we could work out." Now Amos turned to gaze at Jesus—it was almost an accusation—and he stopped talking.

Jesus let the silence hang like a hovering vulture, then seemed to think He was being impolite. "Work out?" He asked.

Dad nodded. "Yeah, that's it," he said, as though a rather slow student had finally caught on to a simple concept.

Now Jesus tilted his head, questioning Amos.

Dad didn't like it. "Well," he said, as though admitting defeat, "the consensus is you have built yourself up to such a powerful position, you hold the fate of the churches in your hands. If you don't acknowledge it, you do us all a disservice. I'm used to mass hysteria. I understand it."

"Hysteria?" Jesus said. "Would you call eliminating hate, hysteria?"

Amos blushed. "I didn't come here to make debating points. The simple, and if I may say so, indisputable fact is you have tied this country in knots. I blame it on television. I know you don't use it directly, but the word is spreading."

"Are people being nicer to each other?" Jesus asked.

"Some may be," Amos said. "That's not the point. The point is we have had on this beleaguered earth an institution known as the Church for twenty centuries now. Oh, I don't mean to suggest the Church is autonomous, perhaps I should have said churches, but the Church has been, by and large, I would say, a force for good. Yes, yes, I know about the arguments about the brutality, the crusades, the inquisitions, narrow hatreds, intolerance—" He waved a hand of dismissal. "I'm no fan of these things, and I've had serious doubts about the mythology, but—" he spread his hands—"I'm here to get you to understand the plight of the churches, which have been here for hundreds to thousands of years. While, with the best construct, you have been here maybe thirty years, and—what? a couple months this time?—" With Amos's dour face, we couldn't mistake him for a believer. "And I've no doubt you will disappear again, perhaps as mysteriously as you came. Then the churches will be left to pick up the pieces."

Jesus stepped in. I thought it was about time. "So you'd like me to disappear sooner rather than later—get it over with?"

"That would be ideal, of course," Amos said, "but I told them not to expect miracles." Amos smiled broadly, proud of his wit. "No," he said. "We're looking for some accommodation."

"Accommodation?" Jesus said.

Amos nodded. "I hate to use this analogy, but when the itinerate evangelists came to town, they would have their service, their altar calls, then send their converts to local churches. Of course, I'm the first to admit it wasn't always so productive. The evangelist would show up with a professional-type show, and when he left town, he took the singers and the orchestra with him. These small-town churches were no match for the showmanship—so the salubrious effects of that proselytizing were short-lived."

"I don't understand," Jesus said.

"Well, it's simple, really. You want to do good. So do the churches. If you would encourage your folks who are struggling to overcome hate to go back to their churches, their venerable institutions might survive long enough to pick up the slack when you're gone. Instead of weaning people away from their churches, you could be a force for strengthening the congregations around the world."

Jesus's head was bobbing. "Tell them to keep sending in the money?"

Amos blew. Amos's fuse was never what you'd call long. "No, damnit! This is not about money—not only money. Maybe you'd be on the mark with Ernie Jo Banghart and fellas of that ilk—but that's not what I'm about here. I'm about things like continuity, reliability, day-to-day filling of needs. Not chimera and magic tricks…flash-in-the-pan deities; and naïve, amorphous ideas like unconditional love. It's a nice act, Jesus, but it isn't real, and you know it. It has no staying power. Our churches have proven their staying power over the centuries—twenty of them for the Catholic Church—and the others grew out of that. So you understand, I hope, why we cannot just sit idly by while a flash in the pan puts us out of business," Amos grumbled. He wrestled with an intake of air. "So I am here to talk sense." Amos seemed to soften now. But from experience I knew if he did soften, it was because he calculated that soft would go down better than hard with Jesus.

"Dr. Lovejoy," Jesus said, "you may remember when I walked the earth the first time, I had no 'church.' I was not a representative of any organized religion. Parables, beatitudes, a few miracles was about it. My thing today, as you say, is making the world a better place."

"Pie in the sky," Amos muttered.

"If you say so," Jesus said without anger. "But my focus is on the individual; helping him cope, giving him hope. Nothing could have been further from my mind than large organizations passing collection plates."

"Well, sure," Amos said, "well and good, but people like to congregate—we are, at bottom, social animals. Your pitch is undermining these natural instincts. When you are gone, these venerable institutions will be in hopeless disarray." Amos was pleading. "Couldn't you put a word in for the organization now and then? It wouldn't have to be much."

When Jesus finally spoke, He seemed to be using a lot of care with His words. "I am here to help us all get along with each other. To promote man's humanity to man. The organizations of religion are outside my ken. Tell me you have replaced the hate in your heart with understanding and I will be fulfilled."

Amos seemed to be insulted. "So the answer is no? You won't lift a finger to save our churches?"

"My hands are full," Jesus said, holding out His hands as I had seen in depictions of Him with a flock of children saying, "Suffer the little children to come unto me." "The Church, as you call it, is so many different things to so many people. It is far beyond my grasp."

Amos's eyes narrowed. Amos always believed himself a persuasive guy. Now he would have to return to those who had put their faith in his abilities and he would have to tell them that he had failed. Amos shook his head in sadness like he did so often when I was growing up and had disappointed him.

"I just think..." he began, then seemed to reconsider. "I wonder," he started over—"I fear the 'Church,' as we have been calling it (he wiggled his fingers to show quotes again), has gotten so large and powerful that it is vested with interests so deep that it can't possibly sit idly by and watch its foundations crumble. I fear, yes, I fear, they cannot and will not allow this to happen to them. They sought your voluntary help. You rejected that notion. But I fear they cannot accept that."

"So what can this *they* do about it?" I burst in.

Amos looked over at me, his face showing clearly I had not made him happy with my interruption. "I think it's clear enough," he said with that steely, dead-level certainty of his. "They have no choice but to do whatever it takes to stop him."

I couldn't believe my ears. Is this what religion had come to? "You mean you're going to crucify Him?"

Amos looked at me, then at Jesus, and shrugged his shoulders as if to say it was out of his hands.

Jesus smiled a thin smile—so thin I wasn't sure it was a smile.

Get Your Name on My Wall

A roly-poly reverend who seems a complete stranger to dietary restraint is facing the camera straight on, bathed in after-shave and sincerity.

He presides over a Virginia flock, housed in a Norman Rockwell picture-postcard white clapboard church with a pointy steeple.

His politics are no secret. He has been in the forefront nationally with his anachronistic MOMM— Majority of Moral Mortals. He is a fundamental Christian, believes every word in the Bible and we may therefore conjecture what he speaks only privately in moments of holy levity: that were Jesus alive today he would be a Republican.

Our roly-poly preacher is hawking "For gifts of a hundred dollars or more to build a new wing on our college dormitory I will put your name on the wall, under a brass plaque, which will immortalize the amount of money you send."

He is a half-decent pitchman, the kind you might find on your local television station, plagued by "the largest inventory of fine used cars in our history, and I'm gonna make you the deal of a lifetime, 'cause friends, the boss upstairs says I gotta move these cars…"

The reverend was not of the white-space school of advertising. He believed in filling every moment with sound. Since he was on the air virtually nonstop and he spoke extemporaneously, naturally there was a lot of repetition. Every phrase of his earnest plea was concluded with: "So put your name on the wall till Jesus comes."

—*Frankie Foxxe*
Evangelists as Fundraisers

Many Americans have taken to heart the essential wisdom that if you talk to God you are praying—if God talks to you, you are schizophrenic.

—*Rodney A. Smolla*
Jerry Falwell v. Larry Flynt

THE GOSPEL ACCORDING TO

FRANKIE FOXXE

Well, old Ernie Jo took care of Bobby Candle all right.

Put him right out of business. But if Ernie Jo Banghart expected a dramatic boost in his ratings, he was sorely disappointed. Ratings were down all over the frequencies. Jesus had hit everyone, so the residue from Bobby wasn't worth scraping off the floor.

I called on Ernie to ask him about it and he gave me the usual protest that he didn't air the dirty linen in public to gain ratings or ruin the competition, but rather to cleanse the Body of Christ, blah-blah. He did concede pathetically that if this impostor in the desert ever went up in smoke, there could be—just might be—some small advantage to his ministry and his ratings from the demise of Bobby—"But that day, if it ever comes, is going to be a long way off."

The powers of the church appointed a pastor other than Ernie Jo to shepherd Bobby's flock. Talk of turning that task over to Ernie Jo met with comments like, "That'd be putting the wolf in charge of the sheep."

We didn't have to talk about that. Ernie Jo wasn't dumb.

"Well, listen, Frankie," Ernie Jo said from his regal position behind his aircraft-carrier desk, "I'm glad you come over, I've been meaning to ask you a few things."

I smiled at the subtlety Ernie Jo exuded in turning the tables to interview me.

"I read your piece on this so-called Jesus fellow, and I was, frankly, astonished, yes, I was. In fact, I had to read it twice because I couldn't believe what I read the first time. Do I unnerstand this thing correctly, Frankie? I mean, is this the old Debunker of Myths talking? Are you applying the same standards to this charlatan as you are to the rest of us?"

I couldn't help smiling at that. "The rest of you charlatans, you mean, Ernie Jo?"

"Call us what you will," he said, "it don't matter none to me. I know what I am. Oh, I can't say you rubbing salt in me like you do doesn't get me down now and again, but as I say, I know who Ernie Jo Banghart *is* and I let it run off me like water off a duck's back."

"Well, you may have a point there, Ernie Jo—maybe I do you a disservice—"

"You sure do—"

"—in my pieces because I don't know who you are—"

"Or you misunnerstand me."

"Yeah," I said, my head bouncing up and down, "why don't you set the record straight? Tell me who you really are?"

He looked surprised. "Why, I'm just who I say I am. I don't pretend to be no more, no less. I'm a preacher of the gospel, a poor soul, no better 'n no worse than anybody else. Preaching is my calling—I was called to it by the Lord when I was barely knee-high to a grasshopper, and my little ministry just grew way beyond anything I ever even thought about. So, the thing I just cannot unnerstand is, why is it you so *skeptical* 'bout everything I do, and the next thing I know you are doing this piece on this charlatan? I mean, I could take what you dish out on me if you were consistent, and that's across the board is what I mean—no favoritism. But here it looks like you actually *believe* this man is Jesus."

He bored into me with his jackhammer eyes, begging an explanation. "So what is the difference?" he asked. "We are both trying to do good for the Lord—leastaways, I know I am. I can't rightly speak for this showman on the Coast. But me, I take a pounding from you, and I'd swear to Almighty God that you are writing like you are starting to believe this here other fella, and I'm frank to tell you, Frankie, that just boggles my mind."

I looked at him across the desk and tried to read his soul and his history and fit one with the other. I think I must have been going soft in the head, because I was starting to have strange feelings of— was it sympathy? "The difference, you ask—I'd say it probably comes down to the money. Jesus doesn't ask for it."

He nodded, almost as though he agreed. "I don't expect you'll believe this, but the money just came at me out of nowhere— and I know you aren't going to believe this, either—but I don't *care* about money for myself. 'Course I like nice things, but I have nice things—more 'n I need. I confess to a sinfully good feeling being flown in our plane or even chauffeured in my Lincoln Town Car, and I like my houses, too. But I don't need 'm, Frankie, and that's the God's truth. I'd be just as happy living in a motel room."

An apt choice of options, I thought.

"All I care about—and I mean all—is saving souls for Jesus Christ. And I mean that just as sincerely as anybody can."

He looked me in the eye and I was surprised to find the Debunker of Myths was swallowing what I had always thought was the biggest myth of all.

"I mean, it's in my blood."

"And this is all because God told you to do it?"

"Yessir, I know that you can't believe that neither, but it's the truth—oh, and I'm aware of that saying, how does it go? When you talk to God, it's prayer, and when God talks to you, it's psychosis—or some such. But that's all right—call me a psychotic if you want to, I know what I heard."

"The voice of God?"

"Yessir!" Ernie said, clamping his lips down on the idea as if to prevent it from getting away from him.

It was a further sign I was getting soft that I wanted to believe him. Oh, I didn't believe that "God" talked to him, that was too much for me in any state of gullibility, but sitting there, facing Ernie Jo Banghart, I tried to find some rationale for his beliefs. I dug back into my past for any hint that I might have heard voices, or imagined sounds, from some unseen source. And I had to admit (but only to myself) I had imagined conversations with God in the throes of my religiosity. However I looked at it, I could imagine sincerity on Ernie Jo's part.

Don't get me wrong—I don't think God talks to Ernie Jo Banghart or anyone else. And if she did, I don't figure Ernie Jo for the selection out of six billion. And yet...what or who was God? Perhaps God is our inner voice—telling us what to do, or what we want to hear. I am willing to acknowledge that God can come in many forms—nature, inner voices, the libido, id, ego—an intermediary in our relationships.

Of course, the other side of the coin is just as persuasive. How could she—or maybe even he—possibly service the masses of souls that seem to constantly demand nourishing? Really, the Debunker of Myths is in no position to acknowledge God; the logic just isn't there. And yet—

"You know, Ernie Jo," I said, "some months ago, I would have said you were crazy. Now…" I threw up my hands. "But, okay, let me say I buy what you say about the world's goods. Don't care a fig, one way or the other. Yet, you will have to admit a large percentage of your time is dedicated to filling the collection plate—metaphorically, of course. Then, on the other hand, this guy comes around, says he's Jesus and says, hey, let's just try to make this old world a better place. Let's stop hating people. And, voila! People sit up and listen. They give it a go. And would you believe it? Crime is down, assaults, rapes, way down. I can't account for it myself, but I'm glad it's happening, no matter who gets the credit. And, of course, the kicker is, he never asks for a nickel."

Ernie Jo closed his eyes and shook his head. "Don't have to," he said. "Gets all the free TV time he wants. Nobody gives it to me for free. Nobody ever did. Look, Frankie," he opened his eyes and leaned forward on the desk, confidential-like, "I frankly wonder sometimes how I came to this place in life. I tell you, I was happy as a clam on that sawdust trail, sweating like a pig in those gospel tents, an audience of ten to fifteen people at the start. I loved it, I tell you. There is just nothing like the feeling I get preaching the Lord's Word. I know you don't believe, well, in anything, as far as I can tell—except now I'm beginning to have serious doubts after reading that love letter to Jesus. But, no matter, I'm telling you straight from the heart, I love the Lord with all of my heart; I always did and I always will. Rich or poor, it don't matter none to me."

"That great theater impresario, Billy Rose, once said, 'I've been rich and I've been poor and rich is better,'" I said.

He waved a hand to dismiss that heresy. "Be that as it may, we just got so big without seeing it coming. We were blindsided, you might say, and there was all these people with all these needs and I just could not turn my back on poor souls crying out with spiritual needs. We were reaching people, Frankie—meaningfully. We were touching their souls, and I don't care what you think, I know that's impordand. So you may say money. Yes, I ask for money. Yes, we need it. Do you know we used to employ hunderds of people here? So many, I don't know how many. I used to know everybody's name." He shook his head. "No more. Yes, it's a big business, yes, we need money, but everybody gets good value for their money. We run this operation on a shoestring considering the income we…used to have. I know you were always riding me about our salaries an' all, but if you want to be honest with yourself, you have to admit anybody in a like job in the private sector is making many times more than we are. I could give up the money, easy," Ernie Jo said.

"What couldn't you give up?"

"My love of the Lord. That'll stay with me forever."

"Any idea how Jesus does it?"

"For nothing, you mean? No, I don't, and don't think I haven't agonized over that. He's simply putting us under and you are one of his cheerleaders."

"You got to admit it's a persuasive pitch he gives—'Love thy neighbor as thyself'—and you don't have to pay a dime."

"You don't have to tell me," he said, shaking his head in misery. Ernie Jo pointed to the TV set next to his desk. "And I can't hardly turn that thing on without there he is talking about love instead of hate. How can anyone argue with anyone about brotherhood, motherhood, and apple pie? And I calculate he is on some channel somewhere every minute of the day or night. Why, it's got to be the biggest con ever to come down the pike."

I must have shown my skepticism, because Ernie Jo said, "No, let's test it out. I got all the channels around the world here."

He picked up a remote-control jigger and began pressing buttons until he came to Jesus standing in Jack Whitehall's meadow talking with his soft-toned, soothing voice to a multitude of acolytes.

"See what I mean?" Ernie Jo said, proud of his rectitude. "Now, you just look at that guy and tell me if you don't smell a con man a mile away."

I looked at him, but I didn't smell anything. I shook my head. "I don't see it, Ernie Jo—and I certainly have looked for it from the beginning."

"Oh, no," Ernie Jo insisted, "no way is this possible."

"Why not? You know what attracts people to religion in the first place?"

"Peace, unnerstanding, meaning. A connection to something greater. You take your ordinary person and he don't know what to make of this world. And I can't rightly blame him, I don't know what to make of it myself, sometimes."

"Yes," I said, "and you sell him your version of the solution for his needs and this Jesus—he gives it away. You go down to the corner where there are two apple stands. The apples are identical. One guy is selling them, the other giving them. Where do you go?"

"He's got to be stopped," Ernie Jo said, running his hand down his face at the weariness of it all.

I understood Ernie. I even sympathized. "How you going to do it?"

"Howsoever I can."

"But why? You want to reach people. He's reaching them. You don't have any ego or financial needs, the way you tell it; here is a guy who is doing effortlessly and for free what all the rest of you have been struggling to do all these years."

"Whoa, Frankie. That sounds good, but what do we do after we're in a shambles because this guy has tore through here like a cyclone, then left us in the lurch?"

"Doesn't show much sign of leaving," I said, looking up at his serene but magnetic form on the television screen. "What do they say, Ernie Jo, a thousand-year reign?"

"Well, that's the Bible, but not this—"

"Sure?"

"Sure as I'm sitting here."

We listened to Jesus's simple, straight-from-the-shoulder coaxing to remove hate from our hearts, and I liked it. I'd heard it often enough to convince myself that whoever this guy was, that was all he was after. He didn't play a guitar or sing or write songs or build churches or hospitals or send out prayer cloths dipped in olive oil. He didn't sell Bibles or gold crosses or flowers or putting your name on the wall or promise heavenly rewards, he just said let's get rid of all our hate—we're all brothers and sisters under our skin, we're here for a short spell, every moment spent hating someone is time subtracted from your allotted span.

And he really seemed to have no hidden agendas to his pitch.

Ernie Jo was watching the screen ruefully. "Got to be more 'n meets the eye," he said. "Ain't nothing so goody-goody perfect in this life."

"Not even Jesus?" I asked.

"Jesus," he said. "Jesus? Only two things I'm sure of, Frankie. That's no Jesus—"

"And?"

"Whoever he is, he's got to be stopped."

† † †

I don't know what made me suspicious another trip to Mobile was in the offing, but I just decided to drive off the grounds and hide around the corner of the entrance where I could see Ernie Jo's big Lincoln Town Car roll out of the pearly gates and point east.

I didn't have long to wait.

Driving out to Mobile and thinking about my chat with

Ernie Jo, I realized I think Ernie Jo believes what he says—right down to hearing God talk to him. I don't think he raises money to get richer, but to keep his work at the fevered pitch he's built. The more money he raises, the more people watch him and love him. Doesn't everything come down to ego, anyway? I can see a pile of money paling in comparison to a couple thousand worshipers flailing their arms overhead, and crying, "Yes, Jesus, hallelujah!" right along with you.

In a way, I can see it "just happening," like he says. All the mysterious forces that have gone into making up Ernie Jo Banghart are at work, perhaps without him knowing it. The same goes for poor Bobby Candle and his curious wife, Billie Jean, and for you, me and Abe Lincoln. We are what we are—made by God?—I'm not ready to go that far, but nature is nature. We must do the best with what we are given. Hell's Kitchen can produce Irving Berlin along with its criminals. Ernie Jo is Ernie Jo—Frankie Foxxe is Frankie Foxxe. We all dragged around our frailties—we all wanted to keep them hidden—so why would I, or anybody, want to expose and gloat over the peccadillos of others?

Months ago, B.C.R. (before Christ's return), I would have reveled in the fall of Ernie Jo Banghart. Now I had nothing but sympathy for him. It was the boy-girl thing with its underlying incompatibility of the sexes. Emily Sue gave me a fix on that.

Ernie Jo pulled into the small asphalt apron in front of the Restawyle Motel. I stayed across the street. My camera was in my glove compartment (I wonder when was the last time that compartment was used for gloves?), but that was where I intended it to stay.

Ernie Jo didn't seem to even check the area before he got out and threw open the trunk after releasing it from the inside of the car.

I couldn't see what he was doing right away. I saw some white diaphanous material swirl in the gentle breeze blowing through the Restawyle parking lot. He'd done Theo Roosevelt, so I thought it might be time for Franklin Roosevelt (he could take lessons from Rob Houston, maybe borrow his cigarette holder), or perhaps Ike Eisenhower in uniform. But, no, I saw Ernie Jo twirl the white gauzy stuff around him, then reach into the trunk for a turbanlike concoction, which he put on his head.

Aimee Semple McPherson! A stroke of genius. Though I didn't think Miss Rhonda in room twenty-nine would catch his drift.

Ernie Jo approached the door, struggling to walk on elevated feet, as though he were wearing high heels.

When Rhonda opened the door to room twenty-nine, she exclaimed, "Jesus! Don't tell me—are you Jesus Christ?"

I heard her across the street.

No sooner had the door closed on room twenty-nine, than a car seemed to swoop down on the lot as though a turkey vulture had found a ripe carcass. It parked behind Ernie Jo's Lincoln, bumper to bumper. The doors sprung open and two men bounded out. I instantly recognized one of them. It was Bobby Candle. The other was a hulking, swarthy gentleman whose authority one would be foolish to question.

Bobby went around to the left front tire and let the air out of it. The hulk did the same to the right rear. That completed, they each extracted instruments of incrimination from their car: Bobby a still camera, the hulk a video camera, which they both put to good use.

My heart sank for Ernie Jo. But now my reporter's instinct reared its ugly head and I was on the brink of getting out of the car to get the story from Bobby—I had my hand on the door handle, but suddenly it froze in place and I couldn't move. I decided it wasn't a story I wanted, after all.

I didn't hate Ernie Jo anymore.

I turned the car around and headed back to Gulfport.

ANOTHER TWANG FROM GOD'S GUITAR:

I can't understand how all this can happen. It's enough to make one lose one's faith in God!

> —*Eva Braun, writing from Hitler's bunker during the siege and bombing of Berlin in April, 1945*

THE GOSPEL ACCORDING TO

SHERIFF STONEY JESSUP

I was settling in front of my television for the Ernie Jo Banghart Ministry Hour.

Word was, he was going to tell his side of the story about the mess he got himself into out by Mobile.

I heard the news about it on the television and it was in all the papers. I saw that there tape that Bobby Candle took out by the motel. Far as I could see, it didn't show nothing. Ernie Jo dressed up in a costume like that lady evangelist, Aimee Semple McPherson, going to his car, where he had two flat tires. Bobby let the air out of them. I guess Bobby was mad about that other business, where he was caught with his pants down, so to speak. So he was just getting back at Ernie Jo.

They had these pictures of him coming out of the motel, but that's all. That in and of itself don't say nothing. But there's talk that the church organization is going to censure him. Take some action or other 'bout taking him off the TV, like they done to Bobby Candle. Sauce for the goose, sauce for the gander type of thing.

It's a shame a man like that who can move so many people to Christ has to go through this mess. There was speculation among the newscasters that Ernie Jo was trying to look like Jesus. Someone, I don't know exactly who it was, said, "No, Ernie Jo wouldn't blaspheme—it was Aimee Semple McPherson." They're making a media circus out of it, and it makes me mighty low. I got a lot invested in that man, and now it looks like they gonna take him from me.

I didn't think they had any evidence of nothing to speak of. I mean, it's no sin to just *go* to a motel out by Mobile dressed like a woman. It sure isn't illegal. But now this two-bit hooker gone on TV and talking out of school about Ernie Jo. It's like she's a big celebrity all of a sudden and she can't get enough of it.

They ask her all these personal questions and she just answers them like she's some kinda psychologist or something. I mean, it just makes me sick to my stomach to have a woman of that low caliber bringing down a man of God as great as Ernie Jo Banghart.

Like they ask her, "Do you think Ernie Jo should be preaching the Word of God?" and she says, "No, I don't think he should be preaching."

She never heard, "Judge not, that ye be not also judged"?

It just pains me to see her sitting there on this national network TV show telling everybody how cheap he is. Says she didn't want to say anything, but the media just hounded her to where she got no rest—so she come out with the whole story. Got front page in one of them tabloids. Gonna be in *Penthouse* magazine, I hear, and I can just imagine what that'll do to poor Ernie Jo.

Ernie Jo's program started with them balls spinning in the air. Lord, how that opening thrilled me, no matter how many times I saw it. I guess today was an especially exciting service because of the scandal and all. I'll bet he gets good ratings on this one.

The titles came on over a shot of one of Ernie Jo's really big evangelistical services where the audience goes for miles.

I could hear the orchestra playing the hymn "Just as I Am," and I expected Ernie Jo to come out with his guitar and strum along like he done on all his shows. Then I noticed the chair was missing where it usually was in the front, center of the stage.

The orchestra kept playing while Ernie Jo came out in a dark suit with a plain dark tie. It looked like he was going to a funeral. Usually he favored light suits—tan and light blue—but today was a somber occasion, I guess, and he wanted to dress the part.

You could tell as soon as you saw him that something was weighing heavy on his mind. He had that smile he always brought with him, but it was different somehow—kind of sad, you know, and that was understandable.

"Welcome," Ernie Jo started the proceedings with a crooked smile, like he was saying "I know a lot of you are just here to see me fall on my face, but I can't do anything about that."

"I will get right to it," he said. "I expect you all have seen or read the events of the past week, and you—especially you who have been so generous and loyal to our work—deserve an explanation. Oh, that I didn't have to do this," he said, and I could see his eyes tearing up already. Ernie Jo was a crier and he could cry like nobody's business during a sermon when he got to a real sad part, or even, sometimes, a real happy part.

"This, I'm frank to tell you," Ernie Jo was struggling for words. As always, he didn't use any notes, he just spoke from the heart, like he says. "This has been the roughest period of my life—and I've had many rough spots, like everybody else. And I have prayed to the Almighty harder than I ever prayed before—and I mean morning, noon and night—and I haven't slept hardly at all, neither. I'll tell you in just a moment what the Lord said to me, just after I tell you what I said to the Lord—and I'm gonna say to you:

"I have sinned, oh, Lord, and I beg Your forgiveness. I don't call it a mistake, I don't call it a mendacity, I call it a *sin!*

"I do not ask to be excused, I only ask the Lord for His forgiveness. To wash me in the blood of the Lamb, to make me whole again, and one with the Lord God Almighty—praise God, hallelujah.

"There were times in this work when I would have gladly given up my life if the Lord so willed it. But He told me in no uncertain terms that my work was more impordand than I was—*His* work is the only reason for my being. This *sin* of mine has taken me to the depths with Satan, and the Lord has wanted me to sink to those depths, to lose the battle with Satan and taste the very fires of hell; because only by hitting the bottom could I become a more useful servant in the kingdom of God.

"The Lord said to me, 'Ernie Jo, you can't quit now; you're no quitter. You've got your work cut out for you—and you are ever so much more useful to me now that you have experienced the sin and degradation of the worst of sinners. And you are stronger, too, to fight the forces of evil—now that you have been taken hold of by them yourself.' Heretofore, I had not experienced the abyss of sin firsthand. But now that I have, I am the better person for it.

"And the Lord said to me, 'Ernie Jo, I want you to go right on with your work of winning souls for my kingdom and the kingdom of Jesus Christ. That's all I ever expected of you and you have not ever let me down in that regard. At a time like this, with an

Antichrist on the scene, your work is more impordand than ever.' And, my friends, it is that Antichrist caused this to happen. I cain't say exactly how, but the Lord and I *know*, we just know he is behind it.

"'Yes, Lord, hallelujah,' I said, 'all power and glory be to You, Lord! Hallelujah, amen, Jesus be praised!'

"Oh, I am a miserable sinner, Lord, but with Your help and the help of these generous, forgiving folk that have made up my ministry over these many years, I *will* come back to do Your will. Today begins a new day, a new era in my ministry of the Lord. I am humbled, chastened, chastised, whatever you want to call it, but God has made me whole again, and all I can say is I am raring to go. I am going to put all this behind me—the Lord told me to do so in no uncertain terms. I will devote one hunderd percent of the rest of my life to His work, and if that calling includes directing some not inconsiderable part of my efforts to exposing this fraud Antichrist on the Coast, why, so be it, and thank you, Lord, for giving me the strength to do it."

Ernie Jo looked refreshed by that. I believe he was a new man and I was glad of it. With Fluffy gone, I just couldn't stand to lose another faithful friend.

At times like this, when I was especially lonely, I ached for Fluffy, and it gave me comfort to think he was in a heavenly paradise.

Then the TV filled with the talking heads to give us their take. Like we heard something, sure, but they got to be careful we heard it like they wanted us to. So we don't go off half-cocked with our own ideas on things.

The fellow asking the questions was that there Taylor McCaw, who I could never imagine as a real person, doing real-person things, like going to the bathroom.

It was one of those setups where the interviewer, McCaw, was in a studio in New York and the guest was someplace else, with an earphone to hear what the host of the show was saying. You could always see them concentrating on the question—their minds a thousand miles away, giving them no camera presence whatsoever. But the host always looked good.

They got Bobby Candle right up there first. He was outside, with a white shirt and no collar or tie. His wife, Billie Jean, was right behind him, listening hard to every word.

"Bobby, how do you feel now that Ernie Jo Banghart is suffering the same fate as some said he caused you to suffer?"

"I'm sad. Sad for him, sad for the church. The Lord teaches us to forgive our trespasses and those who sin against us. I have no hate in my heart; I'm not that kind of person."

Bobby was talking real fast and punchy, as though he was afraid they wouldn't give him enough time to say what he wanted. "I don't think he should have said the things he did about me, but he did, for whatever reason—I don't know *what* was in his heart, but I'm not that way. I don't take any pleasure in anybody's misery. I just hope there can be a healing process for all of us."

"Do you think the church will sanction him as they did you?"

"Well, I don't see how they can treat him any different, but I'll leave that up to them. They're the ones charged with that decision and I'm sure they'll make the right one."

"What about this man on the Coast, Bobby, who calls himself Jesus? Do you think he really is Jesus?"

"That's a tough question. I know I like what he is doing. The crowds he's drawing tell you something. He's made me think again about the futility of hate. I'm keeping an open mind—but I like him."

After a commercial, they switched to the West Coast and the man who killed my dog, Fluffy. I had to fight myself to keep from *hating* him.

Amos Lovejoy did not look comfortable. But as soon as he saw the red light aglow, telling him he was on, he worked up a synthetic smile. All we saw was a big closeup of his head.

"Dr. Lovejoy, you heard Ernie Jo Banghart just now with his *mea culpa.* What do you make of it—especially that it comes so close on the heels of his exposé of Bobby Candle?"

"Well, Taylor, I think it started with nothing more than a ploy to pump up Banghart's sagging ministry. I think Ernie Jo went at Bobby to get his share—or what was left of it—of the audience. Bobby, of course, reciprocated, and now we have two evangelists in the stew."

"Will the Board of Pentecostal Churches go easy on him? After all, he does contribute millions to the greater church."

"I don't see how they can—after what they did to Bobby Candle at Ernie Jo's behest."

"What will be the result of all this brouhaha about these evangelists, now that this man called Jesus is taking the country by storm?"

"I expect it will make him even stronger."

"Will that be a good thing?"

"I don't think so," Amos said. "Not only were these TV evangelists hurting, but all our traditional churches are hurting. Unless this mock Jesus can bring his band of religion into the mainstream of religious thought and practice in this country, something's gonna have to give."

"And what do you think that will be?"

"Right now, I don't see any signs of this mock Jesus giving in, but the signs of organized churches weakening are all around us."

McCaw switched to Gulfport, Mississippi.

"Frankie Foxxe, you've been following Ernie Jo Banghart for some years now. You're the self-styled Debunker of Myths. What do you make of Mr. Banghart's performance today? Do you think he's sincere?"

Frankie looked at the camera. "It may surprise you to hear me say I think he was sincere. It's easy for us to criticize, doubt, and debunk a lot about Ernie Jo Banghart— but I've come to the conclusion that he does believe in what he says."

"You think God talks to him?"

"I think *he* thinks so."

"So what is your take on these sex scandals?"

"I'm afraid it would take a lot of your programs to say what I think about that. The sex/religion thing is an anomaly, a conundrum, and a contradiction. Be fruitful and multiply, on the one hand, and be careful and abstain from sex, on the other. If multiplying is so wonderful, why are Catholic nuns and priests expected to be celibate? Sex goes way back, you know. If it didn't, we wouldn't be talking about it. The Church, like everybody else, needs sex to keep its doors open. But it also needs control of it, mainly because of accountability. They want to see that fathers take responsibility for their own."

"Are we more hysterical about sex than we need to be?"

"I'd say so—when you think how simple it is to do, and how many people do it."

"Didn't Ernie Jo Banghart bring this on himself by going after Bobby Candle for the same thing? Said it was a cancer on the Body of Christ that had to be removed."

"Can't deny that," Frankie said. "But I see it more as a tragedy, where Ernie Jo sowed the seeds of his own destruction."

"Let me ask you, Frankie, how is all this tied in with the man called Jesus? Do you think it would have happened if Jesus were not here?"

"Oh, probably. There is a lot at stake in the TV-audience ratings. Ernie Jo was on top, but competitors spring up like weeds. Pressures are great. The evangelists may not start out needing money, but as they get successful and build a following, they usually build with it an institution—or call it an empire—and they are more or less trapped by the beast."

"But do you think this man could be Jesus Christ returned to earth?"

"No, but he made me examine what I believe. I used to be a believer. I mean everything. But with time, I've come to believe there never was a Jesus—he was made up along with the God who is supposed to be in our image. Heaven help God if he is. So, if there was no actual Jesus two thousand years ago, how could this be the man returned? The Resurrection is beyond my ability to believe. But I am opening my mind to other possibilities. Like goodness and truth—beauty—and the possibility that someone, somewhere could be the catalyst for these things. I see this 'Jesus' as such a possibility."

"So, Frankie Foxxe, what do you think is going to happen next—in the big picture of Christianity? Is this the beginning of the thousand-year reign predicted in the Bible, or is it just a pleasant diversion? Will Ernie Jo Banghart survive? Will the churches rebound?"

"Lot of questions there, Taylor," Frankie said. "I'm no seer. I think Christianity and churches have survived much worse in their history. TV evangelism is a lot newer. The stakes are high, and when they are that competitive, you are bound to have victims of ambition. Bobby Candle and Ernie Jo Banghart are the first. I expect there will be more. As for the thousand-year reign, I'm not a believer in the supernatural."

"How do you see all this ending for this—Jesus? Will there be some kind of a showdown?"

Frankie laughed—"At the OK Corral? Could be. Someone goes gunning for Jesus. I've heard the sentiment expressed: it can't go on, it's him or us. Maybe we'll have another crucifixion. And then what, will he rise from the dead?" Frankie shook his head as though he thought that was impossible.

Sitting there in my lonely sheriff's station living quarters, I wasn't so sure.

ANOTHER BLAST FROM GOD'S TROMBONES:

A real-estate developer had improved a hopeless swamp, making a lovely amusement park out of it. For the grand opening, he invited the dean of the local ministers to bless the project.

Before the ceremony, the developer and the minister toured the park. The minister, astonished at the transformation of the primitive unusable land to a thing of natural beauty, said:

"My goodness, God and you have sure done wonders to this swamp."

The developer nodded and said, "You should have seen it when God had it alone."

—*Frankie Foxxe*
Religious Humor: The Oxymoron

We should always be disposed to believe that that which appears to us to be white is really black, if the hierarchy of the Church so decides.

—*Ignatius Loyola*
Exercitia Spiritualia

THE GOSPEL ACCORDING TO

ERNIE JO BANGHART

The board of directors of the church called me in.

They didn't have to, they said, but they wanted me to have the courtesy of a meeting to defend myself. Imagine that! I had to defend myself when I was practically responsible for keeping the denomination afloat with my most generous and sizable contributions.

I flew my plane out—the *Evangelist*—over to Memphis for the powwow. I wanted to remind them how successful my ministry was—not me personally, of course—but now things were changed. It *had* to be personal. Or else they would just say let your ministry run itself if you aren't that important to it.

There wasn't one of the twelve on the board of the main church who had their own airplane. None of them had more than one house. I had three. Last year our ministry sent them three million dollars.

They were all sitting around this big oval table when a secretary ushered me in. It was the nuances that were important in things like this. No board member to greet me like they did when they were begging me for a bigger slice of the pie. No, now just a secretary. And it wasn't lost on me that one of Bobby Candle's transgressions was with a church secretary. Well, no matter what else, they couldn't accuse me of that *lapse* of judgment.

They were all around the table, looking like a meeting of morticians. I won't even name them. I don't want to give them the satisfaction. Suffice it to say, they were all glum and the chairman did most of the talking.

He was a tall, slender, older gentleman, who'd had a modest run as a preacher in some backwater Southern town, and I doubted he could even conceive of a ministry the size of mine. Why, I put more into the church coffers in a year than he brought *in* in a lifetime. But I could tell by his tone he felt holier-than-thou. And thou, and thou, and thou.

The rest of them weren't much different, as far as I could tell. The secretary had led me into the room and indicated with a silent nod the only empty chair—the one nearest the door, in the center of the oval table, facing the chairman. I tried to smile and make eye contact with my judges, but they were as stern and inflexible a bunch as I ever saw.

"Ernie Jo," the chairman began, "it saddens us to have to meet like this over this great sadness."

I'm not surprised he never made it as a preacher, using "saddens" and "sadness" in the same sentence. I looked around the room and saw how sad they all felt.

The chairman asked me if I wanted to make a statement.

"I don't have a statement, really," I said, "but I'll just quote our Lord, Jesus Christ, when He said, 'He that is without sin among you, let him first cast a stone.'"

Well, there was plenty of squirming around the table, I'll tell you, but that didn't put them off the scent more than a couple seconds. I mean, I could tell right away they smelled blood—they were dogs after the fox and I would get no rest until they had eaten me alive.

"That was a very fine sentiment when it was first uttered, Brother Banghart, and it's just as appropriate today. I'm sure no one at this table is feeling they are sitting in judgment on you. We are, rather, carrying out our mission as a church board, in an attempt to set certain behavioral standards for the clergy."

"Well, I could accept that, Reverend," I said, "if when we were finished here my name was not mentioned in connection with anything said here." I talked like a scholar with these yokels. I wasn't giving them the satisfaction of looking down on me like I was a cracker.

The chairman bristled at that. "We have a duty and an obligation to look into these charges against you."

"So, in essence, if you will pardon my saying so, you *are* sitting in judgment." I hadn't intended for that to be argumentative, but that's how he took it. His face flushed and his hands trembled on the papers he had picked up. There was shifting and throat clearing from the silent peanut gallery around the table.

"Brother Banghart, I would respectfully request you not be

contentious. This is not a happy duty for us. You have been our largest financial supporter—yea, far and away. We do not wish you ill. If we could make this go away, we would only too gladly do it. The world is watching us. I must say you have not made it easy for us. If my memory serves me, you started all this sex scandal for bringing certain irregularities to light about our brother, Royce Elliot. Then it was Bobby Candle. It was his anger and retaliation that brought us here today. Am I right so far?"

I nodded. For I soon saw *he* was being contentious and I was heavily outnumbered.

"We have sanctioned Bobby Candle by restricting him not to broadcast for a year. This action, I'm led to understand, was with your wholehearted approval. He was, I believe you referred to him as, a cancer on the Body of Christ and he had to be removed for the good of all concerned. Now, I guess, what this meeting comes down to is a search for some way *not* to treat you the same."

"Well, now, just a minute, if I might. Bobby Candle is an entirely different matter. I mean, the sex was just the frosting on the cake. There's all that business with selling the condos ten times over—and the water slides in Fairyland."

"Playland," the reverend corrected me.

"Whatever you want to call it," I said. "Because any way you want to slice it, it is not the business of winning souls for Christ— *that* is my *only* business, winning souls for Christ."

"We are all individuals in our pursuit of grace," the chairman said. "It is not ours to judge which approach is the most effective."

Here, I thought, you can get some idea what's effective and what's not by the size of the contributions to your coffers by the various churches, but I held my peace.

"Brother Banghart, we want to ask you how you feel about this unfortunate event."

"How do I feel? I imagine just like you'd all feel in the same circumstances."

"And how is that?" He didn't seem in any mood to let up.

"I feel like I've been raped," I said. "I've been misunderstood, abused, ridiculed, you name it, and, Brother, it doesn't feel too good."

"Are you sorry?"

"Am I sorry? What kind of question is that? Of course I'm sorry."

"Sorry it happened or sorry you got caught?"

That frosted me good. I was just steaming inside and it was all I could do to keep my temper.

"Listen," I said. "There wasn't anybody in that room that saw anything. It is nothing but prurient speculations. It's pornographers spreading rumors to bring me down. I'm their enemy since day one. The smut peddlers have it in for me, big time."

"Do you want to tell us what *did* happen in that motel room?"

"No, sir. God has told me in no uncertain terms to keep my mouth shut about that. It only encourages pornographers and Satan's errand boys in their battle to bring me down. I can tell you there was no fornication in there or anywhere—why, I never even kissed anyone but my wife."

"Ah, perhaps, Brother Banghart, but now this woman is going on TV and talking to the tabloids. We are all on the spot."

"And you are taking the word of a whore over a minister of the gospel?"

"We aren't here to take anyone's word. We are here only to try and get at the truth. Can you help us?"

"She lies," I said to this bunch of stone faces, and then it occurred to me—they *were* taking this whore's word for it. No matter she was getting rich throwing mud to the media, who just loved to wallow in it.

I took out a notepad from my inside jacket pocket. I jotted down a number:

$28 million 920 thousand

and handed it to the chairman. I let him look at it so it would sink in, then I gave him another:

Whore $0.

He looked at me inquisitively.

"That's our relative contributions to this church body," I said. "Now whose word do you want to take?"

"Yes," the chairman said. "We certainly are beholden to you for your financial backing. We are very appreciative…"

"You don't mind me saying so, you have a funny way of showing it."

"But this isn't about money…"

"No?" I asked. "Everything is about money."

"We don't think so. That money was directed to us by prior agreement with you. But it comes from your contributors, from the Lord."

Oh, that was it. They were going to belittle my part in it. I could not sit idly by while they robbed me of credit—me who *never* sought any glory for myself. "I don't like to have to say this," I said, "but the Lord and I have given you a sight more than the Lord and others. But you're right; all the glory goes to the Lord."

"We are trying to understand, Brother Banghart, if you have any remorse."

"Remorse?"

"You know what it means?"

"Yes," I said, trying to ignore the insult, "I just don't know what it has to do with me. If you are taking the hooker's word, I don't know where that leaves me."

"You deny her charges?"

"Charges? Was there supposed to be something illegal? Is someone pressing charges?"

"Brother Banghart, you are making it difficult...."

"Am I making it difficult? What are *you* doing?"

"All right, Brother Banghart, what do you recommend we do?"

"Do? Why, nothing," I said. "You tell those pigs in the media that you have only the word of a whore—I guess you can't call her that—maybe you can say prostitute. And you can point to my thirty-three-year career without blemish in saving millions of souls for Christ. I don't expect you'll want to say anything about the millions I gave...the Lord and I gave the church. I mean, what if you expected the worst, what would thirty-three minutes be against thirty-three years of saving souls for our Lord and Savior Jesus Christ?"

"Let me understand, Brother Banghart, are you telling us nothing went on in that motel room?"

"God told me to shut up about it."

"So there was something to 'shut up' about—as you put it?"

"There was *not!*"

"So why did you go into that room dressed as Aimee Semple McPherson?"

"Just a costume—for fun."

"For fun? Was the woman amused?"

I was getting hot under the collar. I was expecting to blow at any moment. "Why not ask her? You seem to be willing to take her word on everything else."

"Brother Banghart, I don't think you are here in the spirit of cooperation."

"Cooperation? And what is *your* spirit? Innuendo, supposition, accusation? You call me *Brother* Banghart, but I don't detect any feelings of brotherhood around this table. I'm sorry, gentlemen, but I've had about all the suspicion I can take. Thirty-three years I labored in the vineyards of the Lord, and you are reacting to lies, deceit, and all kinds of destructive talk. I say destructive because these forces for pornography are out to destroy me. It's a personal vendetta, yes, but these atheists, gentlemen, would love nothing better than to destroy the Almighty's church along with it. Today it may be me. Tomorrow...*you!*" I sat pointing at them all around the table. "So let's get to the point here. What are you proposing to do about these lies? Have you got the guts to go on record standing behind a man who has preached the gospel morning, noon and night, seven days a week, three hunderd sixty-five days a year—three hunderd sixty-six in a leap year? Or are you going to cower to the forces of pornography and the bought-and-paid-for word of some two-bit whore?"

"Please, Brother Banghart, there is no need to get angry."

"Oh, no? Not for you, perhaps. You aren't the one whose reputation is being impugned—you aren't the one whose lifeblood is being drained by Satan."

"Brother Banghart..."

"Just tell me what you want!"

"We want to give you the opportunity to tell your side of the matter first. We will then retire for our deliberations. I expect there will be some sanctions. I don't see how we can treat you much different than we did Bobby Candle."

"That midget!" I stormed, a little more heated than I would have chosen. "Why do you insist on comparing me to that moral pygmy? Why, his ratings never got anywhere near mine. His contributions to this church body have been minuscule next to mine."

"Brother Banghart, please, we aren't using money as a criteria here."

"No—you are sitting around this table and I have a feeling I'm at my last supper and for a handful of silver that whore has betrayed me and you are instruments of Satan to besmirch the Church of Christ—doing his bidding just as sure are you were in his employ."

"Brother Banghart—" They tried to stop me because I was on a rampage and I was hitting too close to home.

"Let me tell you something," I said. "I understand where you're coming from. I may not agree, but I can see it coming a mile away. The godless media has got you in a box—hoodwinked. You feel you have to do something. Well, that's in your hands, gents— you give me a slap on the wrists, okay—I can take that, but you slap me with sanctions that will ruin my ministry *and* the lives of those millions of souls who depend on me for spiritual nourishment, and I won't stand for it."

"You'll break away?"

"You said it, I didn't," I said. "Now, if you are finished with your crucifixion, I'll leave you to your deliberations—" I admit I dragged the word out: dee-libb-ehr-aye-shuns. I wasn't in my best form. Never am when I'm angry.

I shot to my feet like I was a launched rocket.

"Sorry I can't spend more time on this inquisition, but my airplane is waiting. All praise be to Jesus!"

With that, I gave them a curt nod and hightailed it out of that stuffy room. If ever you want an idea of what hell is like, I invite you to pay a visit to that stinking, hot room with the twelve apostles sitting there, their dirty minds working you over silently. I don't know what but under the circumstances, my blowup wasn't modest.

A ride in my plane never felt so good, settin' there thinking of all those ne'er-do-wells who were going to sit in judgment on a thirty-three-year career in the Lord's work based on a thirty-three-minute innuendo.

Naturally, the press, Frankie Foxxe in particular, were there when I landed, cameras blaring as though they were six-shooters in one of them horse operas.

Frankie asked me how it went, my meeting with the bigwigs, was, I believe, how he put it. I don't know why I had this affinity for Frankie Foxxe at that moment. He could have been much more aggressive, but the way he stood there and phrased his question, I honestly thought he might be almost sympathetic—like we were all men under the skin, after all.

"Fine," I said. "I've nothing but respect for the leaders of the church, and I don't envy them their decision. It's in their hands now," I said, and then to emphasize the reality of the matter—"in the hands of the Lord. All praise and glory to the Lord, hallelujah!"

There were more questions, but I didn't answer them.

As the vultures were dispersing, I seen this middle-aged man who looks like an ex-cop, and he comes up to me and says he's got something for me and he hands me this raft of papers he was hiding in his hand behind his back. Anyway, he whips them out from behind him and slashes them at my face, as though he were about to cut me with a knife.

Well, when I read them papers, I would have preferred the knife. They were, the creditors, that is, repossessing my airplane for nonpayment of x dollars and some odd cents. Was God trying to tell me something? Was it just a coincidence that the papers were served on me after my trip to the church-board members in Memphis?

Like, was there any doubt what *they* were going to do with me? As though that weren't enough.

I was relieved to see the Lincoln was still in the airport lot. It hadn't come to that yet, but I expected it was only a matter of time.

It was a long trip back to my headquarters—not in miles, in agony.

† † †

I was sitting in my office with Emmy Sue when I received the call from the Pentecostal Church offices that I was to refrain from preaching the gospel of Jesus Christ and God Almighty on television for a period of one year.

I passed the word on to Emmy Sue. Then Brucie came in and fell into a chair, like the weight of this insane decision just struck him like a blow from a cannon.

There was a long silence while we all thought of what this

would mean to my ministry and to all those many fine souls associated with us, both on our working end and those of our followers who depended on us for their day-in-and-day-out spiritual needs.

Emmy Sue broke the silence. "What are you going to do, Ernie Jo?"

"I don't rightly know, yet," I said. "A year off the air would *kill* this ministry."

"You think they want to kill you?"

"Looks like it," I said.

Brucie spoke up. "You don't have to listen to them, do you?"

"Well, no, I can withdraw from the Pentecostal organization if I want. But there's ramifications."

"Like what?"

"Well, there's the looks of the thing, for starters. Especially with the Bobby Candle business. It'll be like I sanction the restrictions for Bobby Candle but not for myself. People will think I consider myself above the church law—like I'm better than Bobby Candle."

"You *are* better than he is," Brucie said with feeling.

"Be that as it may, we are talking about *appearances*."

"Maybe you should have thought of that when you made those trips to Mobile," Emmy Sue said.

I didn't like the tone of that, but in deference to Brucie, I didn't respond in kind.

"You don't need them, Dad," Brucie said. "You are their star. All the money we send them every month."

"Not so much since we are so far off," Emmy Sue said.

"Well, it won't be nothing if they keep him off the air," Brucie said. "Isn't there any way around it?"

"Breaking away from the organization is the only way. But defying their authority is a big step. I don't know how many of our associates, teachers at the college, for example, would stay with us. They'd consider their futures before their loyalty to any one individual."

"But they owe their jobs to *you*."

I nodded. I was touched by Brucie's loyalty and equally surprised by Emmy Sue's silence. But I realized I shouldn't have been. My father always said, 'Hell hath no fury like a woman scorned.' Quoting Shakespeare, I believe. Well, I could say plenty about that, but I held my tongue in front of Brucie.

"Oh, some of the ministers would stay," I said. "But some of them would protect their own hides. Fair-weather friends. I don't know that I can rightly blame them. They are probably thinking I'm done for, and nobody latches on to a falling star."

"Dad! Your star is not falling."

"No? Ask your mother about the finances. This is absolutely going to kill us—on top of this Jesus thing, I tell you, we've *never* been lower, and that includes when I was just starting and didn't have two nickels to rub together. At least then I didn't have all these people who depended on me—and all these *bills!*"

Emmy Sue was looking at me like I'd let her down or something. And in a way, I expect I'd let everybody down. But certainly, she must have known, or at least suspected, that she might be the cause of it all.

Brucie got up to leave, shaking his head, saying, "It just doesn't seem fair." He went out the door, shaking his head, and the tension built in the room.

"Well!" Emmy Sue said in an exasperated sigh. "You've really done it this time. You just can't keep your fly zipped up, can you?"

"Oh?" I said. "And why do you suppose that is?"

"I expect you're going to blame it on me. I can see it coming a mile away."

"You? Blame it on you? Just because you're the most *frigid* woman that ever walked on God's green earth? Blame it on *you*? Perish the very thought!"

"Oooo!" Emmy Sue was mad, but I couldn't help myself. All the resentments of all the years built up in me just came spilling out. I jumped out of my chair and my anger just propelled me over to Emmy Sue. I stood over her, shaking my fists at her.

"If you had any idea how to please a man and you weren't so stuck on yourself with your fine clothes and big houses and all, I might not have been driven to seek out women in Mobile."

"And God knows where else," she said, cowering down, red in the face now with her own mixture of anger and fear. "I might have known you'd blame it on me. Nothing is ever your fault, is it, Ernie Jo?"

"I'll take my share of the blame. Will you?"

"Me? You are a minister of the gospel. Don't you think you should show some restraint in those matters?"

"Restraint?" I shouted, indignant at her obtuseness. "Abstinence, you mean."

"With you it's all or nothing."

"Yeah, all for you but nothing for me—do you have any idea I wouldn't have strayed if you weren't such a cold bitch?"

"Oooo, you are so uncouth. And now your intemperance has finally brought us all down so far I don't see how we'll ever pick up the pieces. You've ruined all our lives."

"Bitch!" I said, pounding my fist on the arm of Emmy Sue's chair.

She jumped up like I had pushed some parachute ejection button, and stormed out of my office, and I'm frank to say my mind had never been in such a muddle. I literally didn't know where to turn. There could be no thought of a trip to Mobile, but, oh, how I needed that now! I swear, I don't know how I got through the rest of the day. My world was falling in all around me and I prayed hard for the Lord's guidance.

I don't want to say it was in any way directly related to those prayers, but it wasn't but two, three days thereafter that there was this certain party that came to me with a proposition. And that proposition, I don't mind telling you, was directed at solving this problem all the legitimate ministries were having with this so-called, well, I can't call him anything but the impostor he is.

This fellow said he could take care of the problem but it would cost some major money. I told him how our finances were strained at this particular moment in time and he seemed amenable to a reduced rate for, ah, his services.

I don't have to tell anybody I didn't like to be in this position, but circumstances just insisted on it, and it was totally out of my hands.

So I scraped together the down payment, he called it, and it was a lot of money. But I figured it would save my ministry and so many more like it that I thought it would be worth it.

Well, he just plain absconded with the funds. He wasn't the most savory of people, I guess, and I didn't know where to find him. He just left without a trace, and so I had to find another solution.

ANOTHER BLAST FROM GOD'S TROMBONES:

The 900-foot Jesus

*F*riends, I had a dream last night that I want to share with you today." This preacher looks more like a mortician, with his all-purpose long face that might crack a smile only at the Rotary Club when someone tells a really raunchy joke.

He is dead, dead serious today, but you would be, too, if you had overextended your ministry by more than ten million a year. And it's not hard to do. Spend and beg, spend and beg, and it would take a C.E.O. from Harvard's M.B.A. program to figure it all out.

All through his career it was build now—pray later. "I have a vision, the Lord gave me a vision. I see seven hundred and seventy-seven hospital beds and a medical school and a chapel and a university and a basketball team… There's no end to what I see…" And for years it was "Ask and ye shall receive." And he never seemed to tire of asking.

And when the reverend stood before the cameras and exclaimed his visions of the Lord's command, they were usually high-ticket items—and you couldn't plan for the Lord's work, you just did it. And the money kept rolling in. Oh, in the beginning he had to put on the healing show (and it wasn't that difficult to convince the devout unwashed that when they saw the shill drop the crutches or rise out of the wheelchair that the shills felt better—it gave them hope, and when hope is all you have, what is the matter with that?), he had to get yards and yards of muslin and dip it in Mazola oil and send it out to his faithful "partners," AKA contributors, as prayer cloth anointed personally by the reverend with holy oil. It would, he counseled, heal their ills.

Money, money, money—the money kept rolling in from all directions.

But men of vision are often blinded by the horizon. They see many things, but they don't see limits. The only limit to the wondrous works of God, they say, is the imagination of man.

Economic considerations are unfamiliar to them. Things like supply and demand, the elasticity of pricing, recession, depression and debt-to-earnings ratio are foreign to them. There are no limits to God's goodness, His mercy, and His *generosity*. His people deserve no less.

But megareligion is a quintessentially capitalistic endeavor, and capitalistic endeavors are subject to the whims of the marketplace; supply and demand, and the big C word: Competition.

One successful television ministry begets a hundred others. It dilutes the income. You can't get honey from honeydew melon even if God told you you could. And so our long-faced pastor was forced to have wilder and wilder visions.

Oh, he built his university, all right. And his basketball team was top drawer— nationally ranked. And he built his medical school and stuffed it with honest-to-God *medical* doctors, and that ole college honored him for his splendid efforts by cloaking him with an honorary doctor's degree. We could call him doctor. He was legitimate. Never mind the caveats against pride and vanity. His wife and son would follow later as Doctors of Divinity, but, shoot, they earned it. They worked hard.

Long face built a prayer tower. It was one of those ball-and-pin structures you would see at a world's fair or aquatic park. You rode to the pinhead and you could see the whole shebang—all those miracles you and God had wrought below—the university, the basketball pavilion, the worship center, the hospital. You were master of all you surveyed. It was awe inspiring. It was prayer inspiring.

It was there he had his visionary dream of the 900-foot-tall Jesus. Oh, wags made merciless fun of him. Said he was grasping at straws to save his faltering ministry. Drew illustrations in magazines to show the comparative height of the monstrous Jesus in the landscape, and then speculated on the parson's vision, how did he know it was nine hundred feet tall? Could he have been wrong? Was it, say, only 600 feet—or maybe 1500? Was he, they asked, simply hallucinating? There was, after all, considerable stress connected with the constant fundraising that never allowed for the luxury of a letdown.

So he was again in the prayer tower, after the number-crunchers had laid it on the line about the money not rolling in like it had been, heretofore, from all directions. The bottom line, as they loved to say— those financial types—was that he was going to have to close the hospital.

It was a sad day. The faithless were starting to say he was losing it. A 900-foot Jesus, indeed! Did he, in his wildest dreams, think the faithful—those who had sent in ten bucks for the Mazola-oil muslin—would keep bleeding dollars for a 900-foot Jesus? The giant statue was suddenly relegated to the back burner, where it quickly melted from memory.

Next came his *pièce de résistance*, his *coup de grace*. It was his vision in the prayer tower, where he was holed up, weak from fasting, that God was going to call him home if he didn't collect five million by the end of the month to muzzle his barking creditors.

At the eleventh hour, a dog-racing impresario came forth to pick up some three million in slack. He was a man who made his shekels from the same respectable poor that the parson tapped. For verily, the dog racer had learned the lesson of economics better than the reverend had: when you are investing in hope, diversify.

—*Frankie Foxxe*
Evangelists as Fundraisers

Religion is a real estate scam. The difference between a cult and a religion is the cult has no real estate.

—*Frank Zappa*
Creator of Zappa
on the Crappa

THE GOSPEL ACCORDING TO

SHERIFF
STONEY JESSUP

I never did see a house like that before.

It was two stories and ran all over the place in Palm Springs, California, just down the hill a piece from Glory Pines. It was one of those things you might expect to see in Santa Fe, New Mexico. He had Indian rugs all over the place, even on the walls. I looked but I didn't see any pictures of Jesus anywhere. The floor was this tile that looked like adobe blocks and the walls were white plaster, and you could tell some effort was made to texture them.

The living room, where we sat, was a sight for sore eyes. Coulda played the Super Bowl right there and nobody woulda felt crowded.

Well, Ernie Jo greeted me like a king and I was surprised—me being only a small-town sheriff and all.

I have to admit I was a little nervous at first in the presence of this Christian celebrity. But Ernie Jo had a way of putting you at ease and I calmed down just listening to his sweet voice.

First thing he asked when I sat down was did I want anything to drink, and I said, "No, thanks, I don't drink."

"Me neither," he said. Then he looked at me funny like and said, "'Course, our Lord took a spot of wine now and then, and I find it does calm the nerves somewhat. Mind if I do?"

I said I didn't mind and Ernie Jo went over to this refreshment stand and opened a cabinet that was all full of bottles. He took out a wine bottle and poured a glassful. It looked like a reddish grape juice to me. I'm not a drinker, so you couldn't prove anything by me.

Ernie Jo sat down facing me in this sunken section of the room in front of its huge fireplace. The seats were soft in this long, U-shaped, white sectional couch. So we were sitting at right angles, I guess you'd call it.

I don't know how this slipped out of my mouth, but I said, "I didn't know you imbibed."

Ernie Jo took it real well. He gave me one of his down-home smiles and said, "Shoot, I don't hardly call it drinking—a taste of wine now and then. If you're wondering about them bottles, why, I have them for the heavy entertaining we do to encourage support for our ministry." Then he leaned forward and spoke as though in confidence—"And, believe it or not, some of those rich people like their cocktails—can't hardly live without them."

I smiled. I didn't know what else to do.

"Now, Sheriff," Ernie Jo said, sitting back in the horseshoe sectional, "you may not know this, but I think very highly of you. So does everybody in the ministry. That's why I had handpicked you from our tens of thousands of prayer partners for this task. And, right up front, I have to tell you that this is no easy task. It is not something just anyone can do. It takes a very special person, and that's what brings us to you.

"I don't know if you notice it or not, since you've never been here before, but I'm alone in the house. No servants, not my wife and son, even, and that's unusual, too—and in a moment, I expect the reason for that will be made perfectly clear to you. So, before I start in, we have to agree that what I have to say to you will go no further than this room."

I nodded, perplexed at what could be so top-secret.

"Good! I know I can trust you, that's why I asked you here to this private meeting between a minister of God and a sheriff." (I thought he was telling me how privileged I should feel.)

"First off, I picked you because I feel in my heart your loyalty to my ministry."

That impressed me. My eyes started to mist up.

"Am I wrong in that assumption?"

"Oh, no, sir. Your ministry's been the most important thing in my life. Why, I watch your programs over and over and you are a real inspiration."

"Thank you kindly, Sheriff." I could tell Ernie Jo was pleased, there was no gainsaying that.

"What I'm going to say may seem a little unusual to you," Ernie Jo said. "So I'm going to give you a little background. You know the Ernie Jo Banghart Ministries have as their mission saving souls for Christ."

"Yessir."

"And that's all we do. We don't build water slides, and houses for terminal midgets, or nine-hunderd-foot Jesuses. Souls for Jesus, that's it!" He slapped his fist on his other hand.

"Amen!"

"Now, I'm talking, of course, about the *real* Jesus, not the impostor up there in your mountains."

"I understand."

"I'm glad you do, for that man is set to ruin us."

"Oh, I expect you can withstand anything he throws at you. Television is a powerful medium, and there ain't nothing on TV better than you…"

"Ah, but, no, that's just it. The powers that be have decreed I stay off the air for a year. Even if I ignored 'em, TV costs money and the money is drying up. That impostor makes it look like we are all moneygrubbers. Take this house, for example, if you will. Like I was telling you about those big-moneyed people who'd come here and be so very generous towards the ministry." He shook his head. "No more. They don't return my calls. Those that do want to wait and see if this is really Jesus. Now, just between us, I'm about to lose this house and a lot of other so-called possessions. To be perfectly honest with you, they have just repossessed my airplane. But that's neither here nor there.

"Now, I'll bet, Sheriff, if I told you my meeting here today with you was the most impordand in the history of my ministry — why, I bet you wouldn't believe it."

"Well," I shifted my weight, "no, I…"

"But by the time I finish explaining, I bet you'll agree. First, I have something to show you," Ernie Jo said, and he produced a folder from the dining-room table — a glass-topped thing that must have cost a fortune.

He opened the folder and there I was — a full picture of Prayer Partner Sheriff Stoney Jessup. It was one of those paste-up jobs they do to layout a magazine. Well, I got a thrill out of seeing myself there. And he had given me a *full* page, not a half like that policeman down in Pensacola, Florida.

"Looks mighty dashing," Ernie Jo said. "Looked so good we went to a full page."

I was starting to swell up, when he said, "I only hope we can find the finances to put out this issue. Well, if we are successful with this plan we have in mind, why, we'll bounce back in no time. And," he looked holes through me, "it's all up to you, Sheriff."

"Me?"

He nodded like he was about to launch into some pretty serious business.

"There is an expression, I believe, in your line of work, Sheriff, correct me if I'm wrong, 'Take him out'?"

Well, my eyes like to fell out of my head. Did he...? No, he couldn't have! Surely he misunderstood the expression. I sought clarification. "You mean...?"

Ernie Jo nodded like he lost his last friend. "Believe me, Sheriff," he said. "I wouldn't even dream of anything so drastic if I didn't think it was absolutely necessary." He shook his head sadly. "This man is out to destroy religion as we know it. He is succeeding beyond his wildest imagination, I'm sure. Now, Sheriff, this isn't a decision I came to lightly. I have been praying over this for many weeks. I asked the Lord what to do. Should I just fold my tent and pass all the souls over to this, this...circus pitchman? Should I just give up everything I done all these years? What do you think He answered me, Sheriff?"

I shrugged. I didn't know what to say. "Well, no..." I said. "Of course you shouldn't give up."

"Aha," he said. "But I've no choice in the matter. It takes a lot of money to do what I've done. Oh, maybe if I'da done it on the cheap from the beginning, why, it wouldn't be such a strain now. But with all this organization grinding us down, it's just an impossibility to work without money. It don't come cheap, Sheriff, I expect you know that. Frankie Foxxe makes a big fuss about me taking in one hunderd fifty a year, but he doesn't talk about all the good work we are doing the world over, and I don't imagine there's too many who realize we got expenses. I don't pocket any percentage of that one hunderd fifty million. We spend it on the work of the Lord. All of it!"

"Wow," I said. "That's a lot of money."

"But there's the rub, Sheriff, there's the rub. Our income has stopped to a trickle, but those expenses just keep on grinding me down, day after day. We've already lost dozens of TV stations who just can't wait any longer for their money. I can't say I blame them. They have to eat just like the rest of us. I can't tell you how it pains me to lay off so many people dependent on us for their livelihoods. But believe me, Sheriff, we are down to the *bone!* We are restricted to running reruns of revival meetings, and I don't have to tell you how that cramps my style. I tried everything I know'd, I prayed like I've never prayed before, and I just can't find another solution. You watch my progrum. You know I've begged for money just to keep us going until this apparition blows over. Yessir, that's what I calls him, an apparition."

He looked at me with those eyes that burn right through you. "He's *got* to be stopped," he said, and I swear the voice of Satan was upon him. Then a calm seemed to come over him and he said, "Now, the question is, are you for us or against us, Sheriff?"

Well, I faltered some. Ernie Jo was a man I admired more than any living being, but what he was asking, well, it just wasn't right.

"I dunno, Reverend Banghart—I don't think I can just go killing anyone."

"It's not *anyone.* It's the Antichrist."

"Anti…?"

"You heard me right, Sheriff. That's what he is, pure and simple, and just like the Bible says, many impostors will come in my name, that's exactly what is happening here—and, oh, Lordy Jesus, the people aren't recognizing him for what he is. Look at it this way, Sheriff, if I had given you the opportunity to assassinate Hitler before he began his world conquest, would you have taken it? How about Stalin? Think of the grief you would have saved the world. You would have gone down in history as a savior yourself."

He was getting agitated again. I wanted to calm him down, but I didn't want to kill anybody.

"Well, Reverend Banghart, I certainly am flattered at the confidence you have in me, taking me into your confidence like this, but I don't think I am able to kill a man to save my soul."

"Well, that's exactly what I'm talking about. Saving our souls and the souls of *all* our fellow Christians the world over. This Antichrist will destroy Christianity—all our work, our blood, sweat and tears over the years will have been for naught." He shook his head again. "I shudder to think what this world would be like without Christianity to keep it on an even keel. Well, you think about it, Sheriff, pray on it. If you pray to the same Jesus I do, you know it is not this fella who's riding this hobbyhorse about hate. If that was all Christianity was about, we'd all be up a creek without a paddle. I know it, and you know it."

"He says it's a start..." I offered, without meaning to rile him.

"Start!" he shouted. "That's all this is to him. It's a gimmick, don't you see that, Sheriff? He's mocking us. Belittling real religion. Look, I can unnerstand your shock." He was looking me right in the eye now, turning sincere, like he did on television, and when he did that, I was in thrall. Here was this big celebrity talking to me, one-on-one in his palatial Palm Springs mansion—me, the sheriff of Glory Pines—just like I was his equal. It was enthralling stuff, I had to admit.

"I'm not asking you to put a gun to his head in front of a thousand witnesses. No, I'm asking for more finesse. Maybe you lock him up again for disturbing the peace or something. Only this time he has an accident."

"Accident? What kinda accident?"

"That's where I'm asking you to use your discretion. Maybe he pulled your gun on you and you turned it on him in self-defense. I leave that part up to you. Police often rid the world of undesirables. All on the Q.T. Nobody needs to know about it."

"Maybe these incidents you're talking about happen to unknown criminals. This man has made a name for himself and he hasn't done anything wrong."

"And that's why he must be stopped." From the look in his eyes Ernie Jo meant what he was saying. "I can see you are still a skeptic," Ernie Jo said, and I didn't like the way he said that skeptic, as though I was a heretic or something. "Let me read you something from the Bible. The holy, unaltered Word of God. If that don't convince you, why, I'll pray for your soul, Sheriff." He picked up the closest Bible off the sideboard. He had the Good Book everywhere.

"Now, Sheriff, here is what it says right in the Bible." And he flipped the pages like a Mix Master. "'Every spirit that confesseth that Jesus Christ is come in the flesh is of God: And every spirit that confesseth not that Jesus Christ is come in the flesh is not of God: and this is that spirit of antichrist, whereof ye have heard that it should come; *and even now already is it in the world*'! There it is, Sheriff, it's just as clear as can be."

Then it came out—what was on my mind practically through the whole conversation. "But suppose he's the real thing? He really is our Lord Jesus Christ?"

Ernie Jo shook with laughter. When he pulled himself under control with what seemed like a whole lot of effort, he said, "Then He'll come back from the dead and you'll know for sure."

On my way out, he put his hand on my shoulder and said, "Remember, Sheriff, the future of our ministry—and, indeed, the future of Christianity itself—rests on your shoulders—and I am glad to see they are broad enough to bear the burden."

I wasn't so sure.

I don't know exactly why I was considering Ernie Jo's proposal. I was a law-enforcement officer, after all, and a law-abiding citizen on top of it. But I was wanting to do something for Ernie Jo for all the good he'd done for others. Why, when I think of it, he was almost my whole life outside Fluffy for a while there.

Ernie Jo was a man of persuasion. You don't win so many souls for Christ without you are a good persuader. And, I guess, well, he persuaded me that on top of all his other problems was this Jesus business, which was a thorn in the side of Glory Pines, anyway.

I had about talked myself into it. If he was who he said he was, why, he'd be resurrected in no time. And if he wasn't, why, he didn't deserve to live because he was probably the Antichrist. "Many shall come in my name," sayeth the Lord. Though I couldn't see what harm he was doing generally, he sure was harming Ernie Jo Banghart and his ministries specifically, not to say anything about our poor Glory Pines. Sure, people were nicer to one another, but that didn't help the traffic none.

The thought that held me back was I knew I would be killed on the spot if I done in Jesus. I wasn't sure I was ready to check out, though life had been pretty glum without Fluffy. I thought about suicide more than once.

Ernie Jo was on the TV, celebrating thirty-three years of ministry. The Pentecostals let him on one more time to tell the folks there would be substitute preachers for a while, but the work would go on. Ernie Jo was saying things were getting better. He was beginning to be able to pay some bills—*new* bills, he emphasized. He still didn't have enough money to pay the old ones. And he was talking about going all over the world on missions to save souls for Christ, and how he could do that on a million a week.

But I don't know. There was something about it that didn't strike me right. Like Ernie Jo was putting a good face on a disaster.

After the program was on, I called Gulfport to verify the straight scoop from the man himself.

Ernie Jo came right to the phone. "Sheriff Jessup, it's so

good to hear from you. I enjoyed seeing you in Palm Springs. Have you considered our little plan?"

"Yessir," I said. "I been thinking of nothing else these past few days."

"Good."

"What I was wondering, Reverend Banghart, I saw your program just now, and it sounds like things are so much better—I just thought what we talked about wouldn't be necessary."

"Not at all that way, Sheriff Jessup, not at all." Ernie Jo dropped his voice so I couldn't hardly hear what he was saying. I mean, it was a strain on me.

"Just trying a different approach, Sheriff. We paid a few bills, but nothing next to what we owe. I been crying poor so long and it didn't do diddly. Emmy Sue suggested people like to belong to something successful, so I should tell them how good we were having it."

"Not true?"

"Not strictly, no. But we're hoping saying it will make it so."

I didn't know what to say. My idol was admitting to me he was lying to folks about his finances.

"I know what you're thinking, Sheriff," he said. "Believe me, it pains me to have to resort to these tactics, but the Lord has told me He put me here to do His work, and I must use any means at my disposal to carry out His wishes. But between us, this mock Jesus is killing us—not *only* us, but every other legitimate ministry on the face of Christendom. I'm telling you, Sheriff, our plan is more vital now than ever before. Trust me, I tell you the truth. God has told me in no uncertain terms this plan *must* be carried out—and there will be a special place in heaven for the one who does it. Trust me, Sheriff, that's God's truth."

Put that way, he didn't give me any choice.

…belief is the cradle of myth. I think myth and imagination are, in fact, nearly interchangeable concepts, and that belief is the wellspring of both.

—*Stephen King*
The New Yorker

THE GOSPEL ACCORDING TO
MICHAEL

Mary and I were together twenty-four-seven.

I was so totally in love, I didn't know how to talk about it. I knew I'd never felt more excellent and she said the same. But the weird thing was that wherever you went, you got the same feeling—people were much nicer to each other. Nowhere was this more true than on the road. Road rage used to be all the, well, rage; suddenly, people were letting you in front of them, and waving to you—it was like, Mary and I drove over to Palm Springs and we noticed how no one seemed to be in any angry hurry like they always seemed to be. I wasn't cussing guys out for cutting me off—for not looking where they were going.

Jesus came back into the house after one of His inspirational strolls through the fields of followers who were always camped out around Jack's place. Like He often did, He came back full of ideas about making the world a better place.

He had this one idea that was so awesome and so simple I was sorry I didn't think of it myself. I didn't mind that He put me in charge of getting it. It would be a nice trip for Mary and me. It wouldn't be easy, but if we pulled it off, the sheriff was going to be fully stoked. Jesus remembered Sheriff Jessup telling Him where he got his dog. Jack gave us some cash and let Mary and me use his car for a scouting trip.

Jesus had always been reserved about taking His little meetings on the road. There was a lot of pressure to get Him to go to big stadiums like the Coliseum or the Rose Bowl in Los Angeles, but He said that was showy and His message was too simple for such grand places.

It was a week or so later, and after, I might brag, a highly successful trip to Hemet's great Doggie Dog, and another overflow crowd in Jack's meadow, that Jack became more insistent. We were winding down in his living room when Jack said, "Jesus, I think it's time we look for a more appropriate place for Your meetings."

Jesus smiled. "The honeymoon is over?"

I was thinking Jack was not suitably grateful for all Jesus had done for him—especially for saving his life.

"No, darnit. You've got me hooked for life. I don't see any way You could be an impostor. Anyway, You are doing nothing but good around here, but the facilities are bursting. The roads are more clogged than ever. So, I had this idea," Jack said, trailing off.

"Is your idea to get me out of your hair?"

"Now, You must know that's the last thing I'd ever want to do. I owe You my life—and my wife—Stephanie is coming back," he said, glowing. "She just called to say she's been watching You and she doesn't hate me anymore."

"Good!" Jesus said.

"But, Jesus, we are bursting at the seams in poor little Glory Pines. You are an L.A. Coliseum person. Holds more than five times what we do."

"I'm satisfied," Jesus said.

"Jesus—" Jack said—"are You telling me You'd refuse to go?"

"Refuse, Jack? I'd never refuse you. I'm here at your sufferance. I'm your guest and you have treated me royally."

Divinely would have been a better word, I thought.

"Then You'll let me look into it?"

"Look into what?"

"Renting out the Coliseum."

"Renting? Money? Charging admission to pay it? Passing around the collection plate?"

"Jesus, sooner or later You're going to have to face reality—it takes money..."

"Then it'll be later. It's the first step on the slope to hell—putting your hand out for money."

"But it's the twenty-first century, Jesus—not the first. Things are different."

Jesus smiled. "But I'm the same."

"At least let me look into it. Maybe I can get it donated."

Jesus's eyebrows went up. "Isn't that like a contribution?"

"If they let You speak free? I don't think so. We wouldn't

have to pay the city. It would be a pro-bono kind of thing."

"Can you do that?" I asked.

"Gonna give it my best shot."

"But I'm content here," Jesus said.

"Glory Pines is small potatoes. It's time to go national."

"Our thoughts are universal. It doesn't matter where we say them."

That's the kind of thing we were up against. Anytime anyone asked Jesus about any kind of expansion project, He was dead set against asking for money, no matter how harmless it seemed to the rest of us.

But with no more encouragement than that, Jack went at it with the Coliseum people and they agreed to let Jesus speak there once without charge. One hundred thousand people! More on the playing field. I guess it was not for nothing that in his prime, Jack was one of the all-time great insurance salesmen.

Now all he had to do was sell Jesus on the idea.

The phone rang. Jack answered it. When he hung up he looked confused. His brow was furrowed, his eyes pinched.

"That was Sheriff Jessup," he said. "He's coming over to see Jesus. Boy, did he sound strange."

ANOTHER BLAST FROM GOD'S TROMBONES:

A high-end desert resort. A family of four at an outdoor restaurant table. The father is well-proportioned, with a foreign aristocratic bearing. The mother is a burn victim—jaw, neck and arms are poorly patched together with skin grafts.

The girl is six or seven, the boy four or five.

It is the boy who bursts into song, bouncing happily on his chair:

> The Lord is good to me
> and so I thank the Lord
> for giving me
> the things I need,
> the sun and moon
> and the apple seed.
> The Lord is good to...

Whack! The father clobbers the child on the back of his neck with a loud crack. "Settle down!" he commands. The boy does not say, "Achtung."

The father spends the next five minutes trying to get the boy to stop crying.

—*Frankie Foxxe*
The Uses and Abuses of Religion

But Jesus said unto them,
A prophet is not without honour,
but in his own country,
and among his own kin,
and in his own house.

     —Mark 6:4

THE GOSPEL ACCORDING TO

SHERIFF STONEY JESSUP

I oiled my service revolver, polished it and got it in generally good shape for the job I had to do.

The Lord had always looked out for me, and the least I could do was look out for the Lord in return. This Antichrist, who let my dog, Fluffy, die and didn't even try to bring him back from the dead, had to be eliminated for the good of the Lord. I was pretty well convinced of it. Ernie Jo Banghart was sure that was the way it was, and if for no other reason, that was good enough for me. Ernie Jo Banghart had meant everything in my life heretofore, and it wasn't fair that he should suffer so. I mean, his financial troubles as *well* as his church-organization troubles and all that mess with that woman of the streets. I can see how this strain put on him by this Jesus character could drive a man to drink, adultery, whatever.

I wasn't taking this assignment lightly. I prayed on it day and night, just like Ernie Jo would do. I finally heard the voice of God telling me this is what I had to do. Even though it would probably mean I'd lose my life. I'd be a martyr to the cause, Ernie Jo told me. My name would go down in history.

The thing was, I wasn't so sure if I should shoot myself, let someone else shoot me or surrender and live out my days in jail — up to the electric chair or just life in prison without parole or whatever they decided would be my fate.

Faced with the possibility of imminent death, I had to tend to the appearances of my place.

I thought perhaps I should arrange for an orderly transition to some other peace officer, but since that would have been too painful for me, I decided that was better attended to by others after I was gone. To show I was a Christian gentleman of faith, I left my Bible out, open to the Twenty-third Psalm — "The Lord is my shepherd; I shall not want…"

I washed my dishes and put them neatly away on the shelves above my sink.

I put these notes I've been jotting down in a neat pile on my desk in my sheriff's office. I expect they will be found and will tell my story from my point of view, anyway. I should probably spruce them up — correct the spelling and such, but it would sidetrack me from my appointed task.

I thought about leaving a note, but the more I thought about it, the more trouble I had with what to say. Then I had a divinely inspired idea and wrote it out simply on a piece of my sheriff's stationery:

GOD IS LOVE

I decided to go out in my uniform. I prayed over this many times and when the Lord spoke it was loud and clear. I had given my best to my profession and it was something I should be proud of. No hiding-my-light-under-a-barrel kind of thing.

Sure, I had second thoughts and reservations. Especially, I'll admit, because I was just about sure that the first reaction was going to be someone would up and kill me. I'd be defenseless with a mob, I knew that.

But then I thought: You never know what could happen to you. I could be run over by a car tomorrow. God knows there are enough of them around here.

Or a meteor could crash to earth and squash this whole town. I mean, you just never know. I might be doing everybody a favor with this action.

Sure, those things were long shots and what I was doing was about as certain as you can get; still, thinking about those long shots bucked up my courage.

Ernie Jo's done so much for so many people. This mission was my way of saying thanks to him for all he'd done for so many.

But how was I going to do it? An ambush? Hiding in some trees? From a rooftop—a drive-by shooting? Those were cowards' ways, though it would buy me more time. Sometimes, I even thought, I might get away with it. Who would chase me? Jack Whitehall? Michael? How would they catch me? I happened to know there were no guns at Jack's place—and *I* was the law-enforcement officer around here. But all they would have to do is call 911, and tell them which way I went, and my goose would be cooked.

I wouldn't shoot any man in the back. That wouldn't have any style. The statement I hoped to make would be lost. I would face him down—face to face—so he'd know what was happening and why. I owed him that. I owed anybody that.

Then I thought I might call Ernie Jo Banghart to tell him I was about to embark on his mission. But why? Did I want the credit before I deserved it? Lots could go wrong, then I'd look like a fool. Besides, when you did something because it was right, you didn't need any credit. The Lord would know.

There was always a crowd at Jack Whitehall's place, up the hill from my department headquarters. We'd become used to it around Glory Pines: all them milling about his meadow, sitting around doing nothing, all waiting for a glimpse of Jesus—that is, the guy who said he was Jesus, and as far as I could see, everybody believed him but a few of us who knew better.

I called ahead. It was my intention to go to the door, ask for Jesus, and, wham! hit him with a bullet. But the huge crowd gave me cold feet. I reasoned I should think on it a bit more, to set me up at the ideal spot to do the job.

Every so often, Jesus would come out and wander around, talking to little groups. Mostly, he didn't make big speeches except on weekends, and mostly, he talked about not hating people. I thought maybe it'd best be done out in all those people. More confusion.

So, I'm there, waiting around in my uniform, like I'm keeping the peace, and those Devil's Disciples that are always around look at me funny, like I'm an unwelcome intruder or something. But when Jesus comes out of Jack's house and comes between the piles of people, who separate to make a path for him, he comes right for me and says, "Sheriff Jessup, good to see you again. Welcome," and he spreads his hands from his sides, as though he's offering me Jack's meadow as my very own. "I trust all is well with you, Sheriff," he says and my piece feels hot against my thigh. I am momentarily thrown off my path, he is so nice to me. Well, I could feel the new respect I got from the Devil's Disciples and all the rest of them.

My heart was pounding when I thought about *doing* what I had to do. The planning was hard enough, but faced with a living, breathing person I was going to waste, it got a lot stickier. And I never was one who favored violence. I always thought it should be a last resort. But Ernie Jo Banghart had convinced me this *was* the last resort and my work was cut out for me.

Jesus went over by a little group of believers who were sitting around in a haphazard circle outside some tents, and I heard him saying, "The human mind is capable of so many things, many more than it is ever used for.

"It is a relatively simple matter to convince ourselves that hate is destructive, antisocial, counterproductive and self-destroying. And after that, another simple matter to remove that hate from our hearts and minds.

"We are all children of God, with goodness in all of us. Look for the good."

Then Jesus looked over at me again and smiled. It was eerie, like he was reading my mind or something, and saying go ahead and shoot. Then, as though I'd had my chance, he turned his back and went in the house.

How I know he was reading my mind was he didn't stay out long at all. Usually, it was much longer. But now it was like he was getting away from me to save his life.

That made me think he wasn't the real Jesus. The real Jesus was immortal.

I'd do it the next time he came out.

Vanity of vanities,
saith the Preacher,
vanity of vanities;
all is vanity.
What profit hath a man of all his labour
which he taketh under the sun?
One generation passeth away,
and another generation cometh:
but the earth abideth for ever.

—Ecclesiastes 1:2-4

THE GOSPEL ACCORDING TO

ERNIE JO BANGHART

I was sitting at my desk with Emmy Sue and Brucie across and we was struggling with what to do.

The stuff was really hitting the fan. We were faced with bankruptcy, but I couldn't bring myself to consider it. The symbolism was just too repugnant—a ministry of the Lord, bankrupt? Moral bankruptcy? A bankruptcy of faith?

"It is just counter to everything I've ever stood for," I told my wife and son. I've always said the Lord had never blessed a man with a better helpmate than Emmy Sue, but she was starting to take on an attitude that was working its way under my skin. *Way* under. I could just see in her expression that she blamed it all on me. She wasn't allowing any slack for this Jesus character, either.

"I know what you're thinking," I said to Emmy Sue, "and be that as it may, the problem is in the here and now, and the question is what are we going to do about it?"

"I don't see there is anything else *to* do," she said. "I think you've about done all you could already."

That was a double-edged sword, that one.

"Money," I said. "It all comes down to money."

"Yeah," she said, "not enough of it."

"We need a break," Brucie said. He was not the sharpest arrow in the quiver, but he had a good heart and he was foursquare behind me all the way and I loved him for it.

"Well, we sure can't get the money we need with this television restriction the Pentecostals put on us. I'm afraid we have no choice—"

"You mean there *is* another choice?" Emmy Sue said.

"I mean it's been three weeks and miracles are not happening. You just can't hold on to a following without access to them. I'm afraid the time has come."

"For what?" Emmy Sue asked.

"To go our own way."

"Split from the church?"

"I don't see any other way, do you?"

"That's suicide, Ernie Jo," Emmy Sue said, and I honestly couldn't tell if she was disappointed or not.

"What do you think it is to do nothing? How long before some other ministry picks up our pieces?"

"If there were anything to pick up after this Jesus has swept every Christian away from his church."

"Think about it," I said, "how many of our followers care about the Pentecostal Church? I mean, is that why we have them?"

"No, it's because of you, Dad," Brucie said.

"Thank you, Brucie," I said. I was thinking along similar lines. "There are a lot of Pentecostal preachers. If it was just the church they were after, why, we'd all have identical ratings."

"There's no one like you, Dad," Brucie said.

"That's the trouble," Emmy Sue said under her breath, but I can't believe she didn't expect Brucie and me to hear it.

I looked Emmy Sue in the eyes. "So you want me to stay with the folks trying to destroy me? For the whole year? Sit it out and hope for the best?"

"Maybe there are other alternatives," she said.

"Oh? You think we may have missed something? They got the airplane already, the foreclosure papers are filed on the Palm Springs house as well as the Palm Beach place. We're a hairsbreadth from losing our Gulfport home. And believe me, I have looked seventeen ways to Sunday to find a solution."

"Could Mom take over in the meantime?" Brucie asked. That set my teeth on edge.

"Mom?" I asked. "The TV ministry?"

"Well, it'd only be temporary so we wouldn't lose everything."

I just looked at him, dumbfounded. Emmy Sue is a nice enough person, I thought, and good-looking, but there was just no way. She was no public speaker.

"Brucie," I said, "that's a nice idea. What do you think, Emmy Sue?"

"Oh, gosh, no," she said. "I could never do half what you do."

"Maybe a quarter's better'n nothing," Brucie said. And that's just what I mean about him not being no Einstein or anything.

I looked at Emmy Sue to try and see if this was a put-up job. Emmy Sue looked at me as though she was just as surprised at Brucie's suggestion as I was, which made me *more* suspicious. Were they plotting to take over—sweep me under the rug someplace? If they were, it was all Emmy Sue's doing. Brucie would *never* knife me in the back.

All the same, I decided I'd better keep my eyes open and my back to the wall.

I still had hopes my problems would be solved by that rotund sheriff out in Glory Pines. Removing that cardboard Jesus would go a long way to getting me back on my feet.

THE GOSPEL ACCORDING TO

SHERIFF
STONEY JESSUP

At that particular time, I
wished I could have con-
trolled my nerves better.

The last thing I wanted to do was aim at Jesus and hit someone else by mistake. My heart was pounding, my palms were sweaty, and I knew it was now or never. I just didn't have a lot of faith I could steady my aim. I started taking gulps of breath and sucking in my gut, but if it did much good, I didn't notice it.

The crowd always had an expectant feel to it—like something wonderful was going to happen.

They were in for a surprise. If I could keep my hand steady. I decided, finally, I would have to shoot him point-blank, I just could not trust my aim or my trembling hand. I wouldn't have any trouble getting close to him—he'd smile again and say, "Hi, Sheriff, how's it going?" or something friendlylike—just to make it harder for me. But I was going to do it. My mind was made up to that; what I'd do after, I wasn't so set on. It would depend on the reaction. If they came at me like a crazy mob, maybe I'd just turn the gun on myself. I sure couldn't hold off any mob with a pistol.

I expect the Devil's Disciples would rush me, probably strangle me or cut me up or something, maybe even turn my gun on me. So maybe I should save them the trouble.

I thought of Fluffy and had the funny feeling that I shouldn't do it to myself—he wouldn't approve. But that was silly. Fluffy was gone, and I was at loose ends, I hardly knew what to do with myself. Getting through the day was not any kind of picnic anymore.

Then there was always the chance we'd be reunited in heaven. Me and Fluffy. That would be a great day.

I was at the crossroads, no question about that. Would I go down in history as a martyr to the cause of the true Christ? Or would that detail be lost in the shuffle and this be considered just another murder? Or could it even develop that I *had* made a mistake? Well, if it's going to be that, Lord, send me a sign, because now I'm going with Ernie Jo.

Jesus came out the door of Jack's place and had a very pleasant look on his face, which I doubt he would have had there if he knew what was coming to him. He seemed to be looking for something, then his eyes lit up as they landed on me. There were thousands of people there and he was seeking *me* out.

I couldn't hate him. I thought my job would be a lot easier if I could. But I knew I had to do it, and now it was as though he knew it, too, and he was coming towards me to make it easier on me. I had to be close to him. I knew that. I was shaking so.

But it was just as Ernie Jo said it would be. The Antichrist would fool us into believing he was the real thing.

I sucked in my breath and my right hand just sort of floated to my holster as Jesus came closer. All the eyes of the crowd were on him, so nobody saw me reach for my piece.

Jesus was still smiling at me when I pulled the heat from its leather holster and drew the gun up until I had pointed it at his middle. In that moment, I had the strange feeling that I was doing this not for me or Ernie Jo, but for Fluffy. I don't know why.

The funny thing was, when Jesus saw my piece and must have known what I was doing, his smile didn't even fade that I could tell. And he just kept coming towards me, as though he had an urgent message for me or something.

That smile got to me, all right. It was eerie, like he could smile me out of what I had to do. But I wasn't falling for that. This was the time for action, not philosophy.

I often say the Twenty-third Psalm to myself when I have fears for my life. I've never had them as bad as when I saw Jesus coming closer to me, getting within easy firing range. I said it real fast:

> The Lord is my shepherd;
> I shall not want.
> He maketh me to lie down in green pastures:
> he leadeth me beside the still waters.
> He restoreth my soul:
> he leadeth me in the paths of righteousness

For his name's sake.
Yea, though I walk through the valley
of the shadow of death,
I will fear no evil:
for thou art with me;
thy rod and thy staff
they comfort me.
Thou preparest a table before me
in the presence of mine enemies:
thou anointest my head with oil;
my cup runneth over.
Surely goodness and mercy shall follow me
all the days of my life:
and I will dwell in the house of the Lord
for ever.

I took a deep breath. The trigger of my piece was cold on my finger.

Then what happened was partly a blur and partly so clear I will never forget it as long as I live. At first it was like an apparition, a ghost from the past, and I know folks will think I'm crazy when I tell them that when I squeezed the trigger—at that very instant—my dog, Fluffy, jumped up at me and deflected the shot into the heavens above.

I thought it was a dream and God was sending me a sign that maybe this was His son. Then, just as quickly, I felt this dog licking my face. This dog in my arms—I don't know how he got there—was kissing me just like Fluffy used to—and I must have yelled "Fluffy!" for he wiggled his little tail in response, so I knew for all the world, this was my dog, Fluffy, and he must have been resurrected, for there was just no other explanation for it.

ANOTHER BLAST FROM GOD'S TROMBONES:

More Spontaneous Eruptions

*J*esus Christ, as portrayed in some New Testament passages, is "narrow-minded" and "vindictive." The Gospel writers "twisted" the facts concerning Jesus' resurrection, which was never meant to be taken literally. The virgin birth of Christ is an unthinkable notion, and there is not much value in the doctrine of the Trinity, or in the belief that Jesus Christ was sent to save fallen humanity from sin. St. Paul, the missionary of Christianity to the Gentiles, was a repressed and "self-loathing" homosexual. As for the Old Testament, it contains a "vicious tribal code of ethics" attributed to a "sadistic" God. The idea that Yahweh bestowed the Promised Land upon the Israelites is "arrogance."

Excerpts from a tract by a staunch atheist? On the contrary, those are assertions offered by a bishop of America's Episcopal Church, John Spong of Newark, in his new book, Rescuing the Bible from Fundamentalism.

The provocative prelate also has Roman Catholics fuming. A task force in his Newark diocese has just declared that Catholicism's view of women is "so insulting, so retrograde that we can respond only by saying that women should, for the sake of their own humanity, leave that communion."

—*Richard N. Ostling*
Time *magazine, February 18, 1991*

Blaming Eve

You are the devil's gateway; you are
the unsealer of that forbidden tree; you
are the first deserter of the divine law;
you are she who persuaded him whom
the devil was not valiant enough to
attack: you destroyed so easily God's
image, man. On account of your
desert—that is, death, even the Son of
Man had to die.

—*Tertullian*

THE GOSPEL ACCORDING TO

FRANKIE FOXXE

Things had come, as they
say, to a pretty pass.

Well, not that pretty, actually.

Though I wasn't there to see it, I'd heard a rumor Sheriff Jessup took a shot at Jesus, but missed because a dog jumped at him. There is talk the sheriff swears it is his dead dog resurrected.

At any rate, Jesus didn't press charges. Said the sheriff was so surprised by the dog that his gun went off.

The sheriff is apparently one of Jesus's acolytes now.

Jesus was riding higher than ever. The media had gone overboard with the announcement that Jesus would speak at the Coliseum, guaranteeing an overflow crowd at least as large as the Coliseum itself.

The same media had had a field day with poor Ernie Jo Banghart and his sexual predicament.

Perhaps in time, people would understand that the biological needs put in us by the creator would have to be met one way or another.

But Ernie Jo had railed against those very urges he himself was not immune to, and so it was very easy to cry "Hypocrite!"

Ruination seemed, at this juncture, a foregone conclusion. If he obeyed the church fathers, his congregation would dwindle to nothing. Emily Sue couldn't keep it going. Brucie was out of the question. If he bucked the church authority, his professional staff would collapse, them having to look out for their own futures in the church.

There was a ton of hype about Ernie Jo's Sunday show. Touted as an historical, epic, epochal event, with so much media coverage, I thought Ernie Jo must have robbed Fort Knox.

I knew there was no way the show could live up to its billing. I always thought if you'd seen one Ernie Jo show, you'd seen them all—the excessive repetition of musical verse, Ernie Jo strumming his guitar along with the band, the scrubbed, healthy quartet with handsome young men and homely young women. The potted palms. You could also count on Bible-waving, hunkering close to the stage, the little jig dance, speaking gibberish ("in tongues") and the pop poetry about the great waters washing you free of sin.

The program opened with the usual pyrotechnic titles, the balls of fire burning across the screen—"Great Gospel Gathering" in hunking big letters disappeared from the screen and the long shot of the stage, that usually included a standing-room-only audience, was a tighter shot of the stage alone.

Ernie Jo came out and picked up a hand mike from a folding chair. His guitar was nowhere in sight. The camera dollied in for a closeup of Ernie Jo's head and shoulders.

There was devastation in his face. I knew why, we all knew why.

He began speaking without further fanfare, though I thought he might break out into tears at any moment.

"Friends, I want you to listen very closely to what I have to say this morning. It's gonna be the most impordand announcement of my ministry."

Sitting behind him on the stage were the usual suspects: his wife, Emily Sue, who was checking the flounce of her hairdo and looking like Ernie Jo's announcement was nothing more than the inevitable pitch for funds. Ernie Jo's son, Brucie, was chewing gum and trying to look rapt, but his eyes just had a faraway look like there had to be somewhere else his time could be more profitably spent.

The grandbabies, as Ernie Jo referred to them, were swinging their legs under the chairs they were obliged to sit on, perches inadequate for their feet to touch the floor. Their mother, next to them, also seemed oddly disengaged from the proceedings and her children, as though her mind were on a sunny meadow somewhere with a blanket thrown on the tall grass and a drummer beside her, touching her skin.

"I don't have to tell you what a toll these events of the last few weeks have taken on this ministry," Ernie Jo said. "The Lord has told me *He* has forgiven me and I should just shut my mouth about it. I can tell you that what is being said is totally false and it is just amazing to me to hear the scurrilous lies that people—even other ministers of the gospel—tell about me.

"Be that as it may, I have put all that behind me, just as the Lord told me to do.

"What I want to say to you today from the bottom of my heart is the most impordand announcement of my life and my work in the vineyards of the Lord, our Father who art in heaven—*Hallowed be Thy name!*"

Ernie Jo shouted this line, and normally there would have been a roaring, ricocheting, response from the audience, but now it was so scant there was only a small sound that sounded like a groan.

But Ernie Jo wasn't discouraged. I had to give him that. He had been through the fires of hell and he was still on his feet.

What he said next was so convoluted and abstract it was difficult to decipher his meaning. What I gathered he was saying was he was not going to be saddled any longer with the strictures of the church. The edict that he stay off TV for one year was unrealistic. He had asked the Lord's forgiveness and gotten it and his work on this earth was far too important for him to crawl under a rock.

"This is not about *me*, friends, this is about the Lord's work, and you can take my word *for* it, there is nothing on God's green earth more impordand. And now it seems I am to be His right arm on this earth for a thousand years.

"I did not seek this, I cannot say I even wanted it, but you well know there has been a lot of turmoil on this earth since this man appeared and told everyone he was Jesus Christ.

"Well, I had my doubts right off, and I prayed the Lord for guidance in how to handle this—person.

"Oh, verily it is said, the truth shall make you free, and, friends, no truer words were ever spoken. I have seen the light, I have seen the truth, and it has made me free. And it will make you free as well—and you and you and you," he said, pointing to the corners of his nearly empty auditorium.

"I can honestly say I have never been closer to our Lord in my life; these last few weeks where events have been so out of control my head was spinning.

"I didn't give up, but I prayed like I never did before for a sign, anything, any crumb to tell me what to do. I promised myself if the Lord said for me to give up, why, that was what I would do. If the Lord had said, 'This intruder is my Son, Jesus Christ,' I would have honored the ground He walked on. I would have given up my ministry gladly, and followed Him to the ends of the earth. And I'm talking about thirty-three years of saving souls for Jesus—thirty-three years! Glory, hallelujah—all glory and praise be to God Almighty!"

Again, a rumble from the faithful.

"But God spoke to me in the night and He didn't say, 'Follow this man,' He didn't say, 'This man is the true Christ, the Savior I sent into the world to save mankind for eternal life.' No! He said, 'This is *not*, repeat *not*, the man I have sent to save the world. This man is the Antichrist I have warned you about and must be stopped at all costs—' all costs, my friends, or else this world as we know it will be lost to Satan for all time.

"I had my marching orders, and I tried to stop him. I tried to preach the true Word of the Lord in the face of this charade against the Holy Spirit.

"But the power of Satan is awesome, indeed. That was why these pornographers and what have you were able to smear me in the media. It was all a part of the Devil's same nefarious plan. Why, if you don't believe me, just think how the bodyguards of this Antichrist who calls himself Jesus are called the Devil's Disciples.

"Yes, the Lord said, 'There will be many who falsely come in my name, but there is only one true Christ'—and, as I said, I tried every avenue open to me to bring this man down, and now I hear talk he has booked the Coliseum in Los Angeles.

"I can tell you firsthand that place don't come cheap. I been telling you all till I'm blue in the face that impostor has some powerful rich people behind him. It's the pornographers who been at me since the beginning.

"He's going to the Coliseum to spread his heresies to throw

people off the track to the true Jesus.

"None of my best-laid plans came to fruition. Weak souls crumbled when faced with the moment of truth. But the Lord told me to be strong in the face of adversity and I dug in my heels in His name. And the more I prayed, the more I seen the light. I mean, it got so bright, it was blinding.

"Then, finally, one Sunday morning I was out in my driveway of my home for over fourteen years that I'm losing to foreclosure—out in my driveway. I'll never forget it for as long as I live. It was there—six-ten in the morning, I looked at my watch because I want to remember this moment forever—and there—I mean, it was hardly light yet—and there, right in the middle of my driveway, which wasn't going to be mine much longer—I had this vision—it was in the middle of this flash of light—I mean, I heard the voice of God before, but I never *seen* Him—till now. I mean, honestly, there He was, as clear as the nose on your face, and here's what I been leading up to— here's the earthshaking news. God says to me—and I mean He was clear: 'Ernie Jo, you've been doing my work for thirty-three years, and thirty-three years is precisely what it was that Jesus did for me the first time. You want to know why that is? Why I speak to you this particular time? I'll tell you. The time is at hand to stop Satan in his tracks—to put an end to this blasphemous Antichrist. The only way I can do that is to reveal to the world the true Christ...'"

Ernie Jo paused dramatically and you could hear a pin drop.

"'And I have tested you in the fires of hell and the peaks of heaven. You have passed my tests, Ernie Jo—because you are Jesus Christ incarnate. I have put you back on earth to save the world from the Antichrist.'"

Here Ernie Jo shook his Bible in the air over his head, did a little shaking dance, and shouted, "Yes, Lord! I'm ready, all glory and praise to You almighty, all-knowing Father in heaven above!"

The audience was stone quiet now. Their faces on the TV camera were astonished.

I'd have said it was funny if it weren't so pathetic. Ernie Jo was a human being and Jesus taught us to love our brothers and I simply wasn't going to hate him, no matter how outrageous he had become.

The next time I saw him, he was wearing white robes and sandals.

†   †   †

Emily Sue Banghart called me, alarms popping off in her voice like firecrackers: "I think Ernie Jo is planning something terrible," she said. "He's got it in his head somehow that he really is Jesus Christ and it really is his duty to do something about this 'Antichrist,' he calls him." Her mellifluous Southern tones were blunted in her excitement. "Frankie, I'm worried. He's got a gun and he's not himself."

"Did you call the Los Angeles police?"

"Oh," she said. "Sure." Then she paused. I suppose I should have known the rest of it.

"And?"

"He—the officer—said lots of people have guns—way more than there are cops to watch them. He also said lots of people dress up like Jesus and there isn't room in the lockup for them, even if it was against the law, which it isn't."

"I'm sorry," I said, and I was. "I just don't know what I can do about it."

"Can you talk to him? Try to stop him—something?" She broke down and I could hear the gut-wrenching sobs through the phone.

"Where is he?"

"Oh, Lord, he's on his way to Los Angeles. We don't have a plane anymore, so he's flying commercial. I think he's planning to…do it…at the Coliseum, in front of all those people. Please,

Frankie, I don't know where to turn. Me and Brucie lost everything but our dignity. Now we'll lose that, too."

I told her I'd try to find him, but they expected a couple hundred thousand people at the Coliseum for Jesus, so I didn't know if I'd even *see* him. Besides, I had no thought of stepping in front of a bullet to save anyone. If he's really Jesus, he'll be resurrected anyway.

I talked it over with Rachel. "You're crazy," she said.

It was not an original thought, and, crazy or not, she wanted to go along with me to L.A.

She was already salting our conversation with unsubtle references to the matrimonial state, as though she were taking it all for granted, and I was finding my resistance dissolving.

We flew to L.A. in a cramped tourist section. Rachel said it might be fun to fly first class sometime.

"Marry rich," I advised. "The accumulation of wealth has not heretofore been my forte."

As soon as we landed we drove our rental car—the last one at the airport, I was told—out to the Coliseum in Exposition Park, adjacent to the USC campus. A lot of their football greats had torn up the turf on this Coliseum field.

As I looked down on the field from the stands midway up at about the twenty-yard line, I could visualize the teams suited up and going at each other. Through the ages we have all had our circuses.

A bunch of Devil's Disciples were roaming around the place. I expected to get a fix on the best possibilities for security. I asked if any of them had seen Sheriff Jessup, and, sure enough, I followed a pointed finger to see the sheriff, his fluffy dog in his arms, talking to a gaggle of Disciples. I followed the finger to the Glory Pines lawman, who seemed in good spirits, and not too out of his element in this huge arena.

"You in charge of security for tomorrow?"

"Well, personal. They's gonna be a jillion of L.A.'s finest on the premises to keep the peace. Jesus just wanted me and the boys to take part, so we are monitoring crowd control, safety and securi-ty." The sheriff spoke as though he were reading from a manual.

I gave him my news about Ernie Jo Banghart. The sheriff smacked his lips and said, "Thank you. We'll keep an eye out for him." Then he shook his head. "The man used to be the greatest. What do you suppose's gotten into him?"

"Well, for starters," I said, "he thinks *he* is the real Jesus."

The sheriff nodded sadly. I saw the dashed hopes of a life-time in that dipping of his pointy head.

Ye shall not go after other gods,
of the gods of the people
which are round about you;
(For the Lord thy God
Is a jealous God among you)
lest the anger of the Lord thy God
be kindled against thee,
and destroy thee
from off the face of the earth.

—Deuteronomy 6:14-15

THE GOSPEL ACCORDING TO

ERNIE JO BANGHART

I had my marching orders
in the army of the Lord.

My first battle, and, I'd hoped, the decisive one, would be fought on the floor of the Coliseum, which was fitting since the Christians had it out with the lions in the historical Colosseum in Rome, Italy.

Because of this revelation put on me by our Lord in heaven, there have been several changes in my life. First, it was apparently me who said, the first time around, you should leave your family and go with me. So I was leaving Emmy Sue and Brucie behind on this errand.

I had this little pistol given to me by a parishioner a while back. She thought I needed protection. She suffered from an acute sort of paranoia, and I took it, bullets and all, and promised to keep it around me at all times. I never felt the need, but now it was going to come in mighty handy. And it would fit nicely under my robes.

I'd forgotten what a hassle it was to fly commercial. Lot of people gave me the eye in my robes. Some of them knew me from before; some were friendly, some openly skeptical. When you do the Lord's work, you open yourself to all kinds of criticism.

But checking bags and waiting to pick them up was a real pain. I had people to do that when I had my own plane, but now things were different. First off, a lot of people who were just as loyal as they could be when the money was rolling in gave me the cold shoulder now. Left me for greener pastures. I was, frankly, surprised at how little difference it made to most of them when I discovered I really was Jesus Christ returned to earth. Well, actually, I'd been here all the time—that is, well over forty years—God just waited, until He had no other choice, to let me know about it.

And there weren't any people falling all over themselves to help me, either. That was okay by me because I knew who I was, even if they didn't.

When I thought about it, it all made perfect sense. Why, when I was no bigger than knee-high to a grasshopper I was preaching the Word—just like Jesus. Then there was a thirty-year hiatus when Jesus was incognito—some say He was a carpenter, but we don't really know. I was steadfastly preaching the Word for those number of years. Now I was out in the open, just as Jesus was, recognized as the Son of God, by God Hisself, if not by ignorant mortals.

But no matter. I had no doubt at all that as soon as my mission was complete— that is, the eradication once and for all of this Antichrist menace—I would be finally recognized as the true Christ.

Rooms in Los Angeles were as scarce as hens' teeth, what with all the fuss about this Jesus impostor character. There was no room in the inn, so to speak. I looked around for a barn because of the symbolism of the thing, but barns in the city of Los Angeles these days are in very short supply. But I found a place called Rancho something, and it was pret' near in another county, and their restaurant was called the Farmhouse. I thought that was pretty meaningful.

Good thing I got me a rental car, because Los Angeles is not pedestrian-friendly. In spite of all the walking I must have done in a former life, I was glad to have this set of wheels to get around in, because otherwise I never would have made it anywhere near the Coliseum.

I headed out there, first thing, to scope out the territory. Get a look-see at the stage and how he'd be coming in. Kind of plot my strategy.

I got out to the Coliseum after fighting the most Byzantine traffic you ever have seen. I was wearing my robes because this errand was directed by the Lord Himself and I didn't see any need to hide my true identity from anybody.

Though I saw many looking at me funny, I kept my head up. They didn't look at the Antichrist funny and he was dressed exactly as I was.

Well, there was no sign of the impostor out at the Coliseum. I wasn't surprised. There were already hundreds of people—maybe thousands, I didn't rightly know—waiting to get into the arena, even though the event was still more than twenty-four hours away. They had sleeping bags, chairs and tables, like it was old-home week down by the river. I could have told them they were waiting on the wrong man, but I'd let them discover that for themselves.

I got a good idea of what was coming down by walking around the place. The field was already being set up with chairs and a stage in the center. The thing was a perfect oval and it completely surrounded the stage, which was dwarfed by the vast seating and the distance those in the highest seats would be from the speaker.

I made no secret of the fact that I intended that speaker to be yours truly when the dust cleared and everyone present was expecting to hear an explanation from me. I had no intention of disappointing them. I was already working on my speech. It was going to be a doozie.

So I saw the tunnel where the football teams made their entrances and I was thinking the fake Jesus would have to come from there also, as there was really no other alternative. I figured I would stand there and when he came out, whip the pistol from my robes and shoot him point-blank. I expected some shock would register with the crowd at first, but when I got across who I really was, I expected they would hoist me on their shoulders and sweep me to the platform. They came to hear Jesus, they would say, and how much better it is to hear the *real* Jesus than the fake.

It was a good thing I left my motel bright and early the next morning, because the traffic jam-ups just boggled the mind. The closer I got to the Coliseum, the slower it went. Didn't all these people know I was going to be there to save them from this Antichrist?

I had to park on the far side of the Shrine Auditorium—my old stomping grounds—and I was lucky to get the space. But I had to walk over a mile through the USC campus, where quite a few students of every stripe noticed me, some few with appropriate reverence, more with the snickers of heathens.

When I finally made it to the Coliseum gates, I was so drowned in a mass of people, I hardly knew where I was at. I mean, just about all you could see in that mob was people, and I finally sensed that this crowd was angry because they weren't being let inside the arena. Quickly I picked up on the scuttlebutt that it was already full inside, and there were a good four to five hours before it was to begin. That was okay by me, I didn't need a seat, but I did need to get in to carry out my assignment from the Lord.

It wasn't easy, but I finally worked my way up to the fence, where I caught the attention of one of them awful Devil's Disciples. "Say there, fella," I said. "Who's in charge here?"

He gimme one of them peculiar smiles, showing all his bad teeth to maximum disadvantage, and I didn't catch on at first, but he was laughing at me.

"I know who you are," he said. He had this walkie-talkie in his hand and he said something in it like he was a bomber pilot— "Over and out."

"Look here, fella," I said. "I've got to get in here."

"Sorry, all full up. Busting at the seams."

"But...but I'm Jesus," I told him, thinking it would sober him up to open the gate.

"Well..." he drawled. "There's some disagreement there."

"Just get me the sheriff," I snapped. He was making me hot under the collar, which I didn't have in these robes.

He looked cross but he said, "Roger, do you read me?" into that walkie-talkie thing, and I guess Roger read him, because he told me he had passed my request along to the boss, whoever that was, and I expected some positive response before you knew it.

Well, it didn't work out quite that way. Must have been a good half-hour before I saw Sheriff Stoney Jessup sauntering up toward me, like he had all the time in the world. Man might cut a more imposing figure if he lost some weight, but I didn't think it was my place to tell him so at this particular time in the history of the world.

"Well, Sheriff, good to see you. I guess you're surprised at the turn of events—at who I really am. I'll bet you wish you had kept our little agreement, because now salvation doesn't look that promising for you. Well, I'm here to tell you it's not too late. 'Forgiveness is mine,' sayeth the Lord. You just go and complete the job and I'll forgive you. Yessir, take you right up to heaven...when your time comes."

The sheriff, he didn't seem to be at all connecting to what I was saying.

"I'm sorry, Ernie Jo," he said. "I can't let you in here."

"Why not?"

"You know why not. You intend on carrying out the mission yourself—the one I didn't do."

"Now, Sheriff, it has to be done. I don't want to do it. If only this cup could pass from my lips, but it can't. No, sir, I'm made responsible to save the world from this impostor—put in charge by God Himself."

He nodded smuglike, with his lips pressed together like he was trying to squeeze the juice out of a leechee nut.

So Sheriff Jessup whispered something to his cohort there and the fella nodded grimly and he didn't take his eyes off me. Finally the sheriff said, "You can watch the program out here. We're setting up TV screens all over so all these people won't be too disappointed. Sorry, Ernie Jo, but my hands are tied."

I started to tell him who I was, but he had already turned his fat back on me.

This was going to take some heavy praying on my part.

I could see it wouldn't do me no good to stay there with this guy's fish eyes on me, so I wormed my way back out of the crowd to look for a better vantage point from which to erase this scourge from the face of the earth.

Then I began to wonder how in the world they were going to get him in there. It would probably be a helicopter, and how was he going to pay for that without taking money? More hypocrisy! But a helicopter sure would be out of range of my little pistol.

So I fought my way out of there and back to my car. I

thought it would be better to have some substantial armor around me for my task.

I was surprised at how little attention I got working my way out of that mob. I mean, you'd have thought I was just another of God's creatures instead of His only begotten Son.

On my way back to my car, I looked up from my thoughts and saw the Shrine Auditorium looming large on the landscape in front of me. It brought back memories, all right.

When I walked by, I noticed the stage door was ajar. I poked it open and peered inside into the darkness.

Now I look through a glass darkly, then face to face. I was reminded of that from the Good Book.

I had some time to kill before I could get back to the task at hand. There didn't seem to be anyone around, so I went inside and stood in the wings, looking at the empty stage. There was only the light from the open back door, and that old barn of a place looked dusty, like one of those rooms that's been shut up for the season.

My eyes grew accustomed to the darkness and I could actually make out some lines, like the edge of the stage and the tops of the seats. It wasn't long before I was picturing myself right there making my entrance to center stage from stage left while the music was playing, so no one would feel obliged to applaud or anything like that.

Oh, those were the days, all right. I knew I had it good, but I didn't know how good I had it. Back when I was in the service of the Lord, and not the Lord Hisself.

I was thinking of my last stand here at the Shrine. That was after this so-called Jesus had made his first splash and my audience suffered proportionally. But I didn't let up just because the house was disappointing. I didn't *ever* let up. Why, I swear I gave some of my best sermons to eight or ten people back in the glory days on the sawdust trail.

Thinking back like that was starting to choke me up. A few sniffles came upon me and I found myself wandering onto the stage like I would do before the Pentecostals ruined me and took away my TV—they knew there was no way I could survive that. No one could. I'd even hedge my bets about Jesus.

I swear I didn't know what these people wanted. I gave them everything I got and it wasn't good enough. They wanted showmanship, I gave it; they wanted music, I gave it; they wanted preaching, I gave it all I got. They wanted everything—perfection—everything, and I gave 'em all I got. They wanted me to be Jesus Christ. I *was* Jesus Christ. And still I didn't get through.

Out there, front and center, I saw myself pick up my guitar and start strumming along with the band. When we finished the number and everyone was on their feet, singing their hearts out, I said, "Let's sing it one more time." I did that four or five times till they were in a frenzy. Then when I sensed there was just no more in anybody, I laid down my guitar on my chair where I was resting my foot to support my guitar on my leg and I picked up my microphone from the piano. While I was doing that, the crowd settled down until you could hear a pin drop while they waited for me to talk.

Then I found myself talking to the empty house there just like it was full.

"Oh, that music," I said. "They just ain't nothing like it in this world. No, sir, you got to get into heaven afore you can find anything to compete. And through the grace of our Lord Jesus Christ may you *all* meet on those heavenly shores when we cross over—hallelujah, glory, Jesus, all glory to ah—Jesus, hallelujah."

And the shouts of "Hallelujah" and "Praise God" would sweep back at me.

As I stood there on the stage of the Shrine, between the camels on either side of me, I prayed for a sign to help me through these rough moments I hadn't bargained for. And God sent waters down—as strong and fertile as the wide Mississippi River—and those waters cleansed me—I mean, they wiped me clean of all my impurities and the voice of the Lord spoke loud and clear:

"You are my only begotten Son. Go out in the world and save it from those who would destroy us."

I mean, He was just about as clear as if He had been onstage with me. I mean, I may have seen it as an impossible task—I may have seen it as an unpleasant assignment—but there was just no doubt in the world about what He wanted done and who He wanted to do it.

My hands were tied. I was on the road to Calvary.

†   †   †

I suppose if I wanted to disappear in the crowd at the Coliseum, I would have worn everyday sport clothes instead of my robes. Made the job a lot easier. Escape, too, though I wasn't thinking about that. But I wasn't going to take the easy way. I had a statement to make—I was Jesus—and I didn't want to hide it.

So I walked back there, like I must have walked the first time, two thousand years before. There was derision again, but I was used to that, and I swear I saw awe on many of those faces.

The Coliseum grounds were still wall-to-wall people. I moved around the edges till I came to the automotive entrance, where cars could get into the tunnel. I stepped behind a fat-trunked tree and waited for him to come.

I waited there a good long time and no one came. By my watch, there were only minutes till they were to begin and I saw no sign of anything.

Three things came to mind:

One, he was already in there.

Two, he was delayed.

Three, he was going in some other way.

Then the best thought occurred—someone else had gotten him, saving me the trouble and agony.

Suddenly, I heard a rumbling and I thought I should have

stayed out of this earthquake country, because it felt like a big one.

It swept over me like an out-of-control tidal wave.

The cheers from the mob inside and outside of the Coliseum were deafening. The sound levels absolutely put rock music to shame.

Somehow I'd missed him. I looked around to see if there wasn't some way for me to get inside the arena. But, number one, you could hardly move around there — and, two, the security was as tight as a drum.

The irony didn't escape me. This impostor was getting millions of followers right out of the starting gate and I wasn't even at the table.

I was, as they say, a prophet without honor in his own country. So I wasn't going to give up. He'd have to come out somewhere, sometime, and he wasn't going to do it anonymously.

That's when I'd get him.

All glory and praise to the Lord. Hallelujah!

I felt for the pistol where I had it strapped around my middle. It felt cold, but it was still there, offering me a kind of isolated security and hope.

Now all I needed was the opportunity to use it.

Slave to a God whose sole known verb
is *Flatter!*
His world a spectre and his soul a
wraith
Astray in the illusion he called *Matter,*
He got religion when he lost his faith.

　　　　—Howard Nemerov
　　　　HE

THE GOSPEL ACCORDING TO

FRANKIE FOXXE

Jesus rejected the helicopter idea as being too ostentatious.

I guess a donkey was about His speed, though He didn't seem to object to automobile travel. So we got Him into the Coliseum in a bread truck. I thought it was poignantly symbolic.

I'm not sure what was happening to me wasn't being dictated by some nefarious sorcerer somewhere. Things were piling up on the old Debunker of Myths. First, I hear Andi Lovejoy's arthritis is cured by this Jesus, and then Jack Whitehall virtually comes back from the dead with Jesus standing over him. I'm worn to a frazzle waiting for those fissures I so cavalierly spoke of to turn into an earthquake.

The observant reader will have noted that I have been capitalizing the pronouns referring to this Jesus when used by those who believed He was the genuine article. The skeptics among us have settled for lowercase. For consistency, if nothing else, I will henceforth capitalize my pronouns when referring to this Jesus, though I would not be too quick to jump to any conclusions relative to my beliefs.

One of the astonishing things about Jesus's talk was how it didn't change with the size of the audience. If any situation called for, or at least excused, flights of oratory, one hundred thousand or so in the Coliseum, and as many outside, was surely it. But He kept the message on its low, even keel—love thy neighbor as thyself, and keep spreading the love that eradicates hate.

The more the crowd roared its approval, the more Jesus seemed to scale back His tone and emotion. But the longer He talked, the louder they roared.

While all this unseemly adulation was going on, I kept thinking of my call from Emily Sue Banghart and wondering how they were going to get Jesus out of here alive. It is one thing to sneak Jesus in in a bread truck when no one knew when He was coming or where He was coming from, but it was quite another to sneak Him out when over one hundred thousand folks inside the arena could watch His every move. They should have consulted some magician—perhaps a trapdoor in the stage, leading to a tunnel somewhere. But it was too late.

Besides, Jack Whitehall told me Jesus didn't want to be hidden from the people like some South American despot. But if Ernie Jo Banghart had become so deranged he wanted to kill Jesus, how many other potential assassins might be hovering in our midst?

As I sensed the speech coming to an end, I thought back over the phenomenon of this man. He did seem to have a gentle, almost feminine side. Love thy neighbor and cut out hate were feminine ideas—sad, but true. Perhaps the remarkable thing was not the speech itself, for that, in the cold light of print, would seem unremarkable indeed. No, the remarkable thing was that it was so *unre*markable and still moved so many people as it did. His followers had grown exponentially, He was a megacelebrity. His name topped every survey of the most admired personages. It was as though all these people, whose lives heretofore were concerned only with minutiae, had been dramatically infused with sudden meaning.

I was embarrassed to admit that the old Debunker of Myths was turning to jelly. Whether or not I could swallow the theology of the phenomenon, I couldn't escape or ignore the fact that it was doing so much good. And good was what I thought drew me to the priesthood. I found myself wrapped up in getting Jesus out of there alive. Michael and Mary and Jack Whitehall had brought Him in with the sheriff and a couple of Devil's Disciples. It was going to take more than that to get Him out. The Los Angeles police were cooperating and my hope was we could overpower any lone crackpots out there, including, but not limited to, Ernie Jo Banghart.

But power was not everything when dealing with lone cranks. And I had told the sheriff to keep Ernie Jo covered.

As to Jesus of Nazareth, I think His system of morals and His religion, as He left them to us, the best the world ever saw or is like to see; but I apprehend it has received various corrupting changes, and I have, with most of the present dissenters in England, some doubts as to His divinity.

> —*Benjamin Franklin*
> *Letter to President Stiles of*
> *Yale, 1789*

THE GOSPEL ACCORDING TO

ERNIE JO BANGHART

I finally realized I would never get anywhere with my mission in these robes.

I was standing out like a sore thumb. I needed to melt into the crowd and I couldn't do that in my new persona of Jesus Christ. So I made my way to a bathroom and there, inside one of the stalls, I took off the robes. Underneath, I was wearing a pair of shorts and a plain tee shirt—no slogans; I hadn't thought it would be appropriate for Jesus, though there certainly are some clever ones. There's one that says, "Jesus is coming, look busy." I seen that on a bumper sticker someplace—and another I thought of buying says, "If a man speaks alone in the forest where no woman can hear him, is he still wrong?" I got a big kick out of that one.

Anyway, I rolled up the robes, and outside, in a trash bin, I found a McDonald's bag. I emptied it out and pushed the robes inside. I noticed a bunch of people watching me rummaging through the trash. Well, if they thought I was a street person, so much the better.

I thought the service inside the Coliseum would never end. From deafening cheers and the roars that rolled out of that giant arena, I'da thought there was a championship football game going on inside.

It was up to me to carry out my task, and there, among multitudes, I realized how ill-equipped I was.

I didn't have a rifle with a telescopic sight so I could pick him off like a real assassin. I did not have access to the man himself so I could pull my trigger at the required point-blank range. All I had going for me was God was on my side—and as the song says— If *He* be for you, who could be against you?

As it turned out, quite a few persons seemed to be against me.

Throughout the grounds outside the Coliseum, vendors were set up, selling memorabilia of the event. There were crucifixes and plaster statues of Jesus, looking more like the man inside than some we have seen. There were tee shirts with his picture and "God is Love," "Jesus Saves" and the international "No" signal, the red circle with the diagonal through it, stamped over the word

I was looking for a disguise, so while everybody was watching the big TV screens that were set up outside the arena, I bought a baseball cap that said "He's Back" in yellow letters on maroon in front and "HATE" in back.

I put it on and pulled it down to hide the top half of my face. Nobody paid me no mind.

These big TV screens were symbolic of the great wealth behind this event. No one was going to tell me that was all done in the name of brotherly love and free of charge. As I've said, I expected it was the pornographers and folks of that ilk who were bankrolling this show, though I couldn't prove it. I knew it was *some* deep pocket or other, and the thing that surprised me, made me mad, frankly, was that no one seemed to care. This guy had so bamboozled the public with his holier-than-thou charade about not taking money from anyone, they couldn't hope to see the inconsistency of his argument. Taking donations from huge corporations was no better than taking them from various individuals. Worse, actually, because you were more beholden to a larger entity that gave the larger donation.

And what about these vendors? They certainly weren't allowed to operate free. I expect they were rendering unto Caesar what was Caesar's, with a nice piece of the pie left over for the charlatan.

Anyway, I could worry about that later. I roamed the edge of the crowd around the tall chain-link fence they had erected to keep the gate-crashers out. I was looking for a weak spot in their cast-iron security.

There was room to roam on the fence side of the mob because most people were watching this image of Big Brother on these big screens which were high up on the fence, so if you were too close to the fence, you couldn't see anything.

By law they couldn't lock the gates—in case of fire or the need to evacuate quickly. So they had people standing at each gate to keep the riffraff out.

I tugged my hat to bring it as low as I could over my eyes and still see where I was going. I made a circle around the fences, looking for a breach in security.

The hat was really helping me out. "He's Back" on the front and "HATE" on the back pegged me as a true believer. Once the cops saw the hat, they hardly gave me a second look.

R.I.P.

Finally it just got to be too much. The persecution and the lies, the reviling of the faith and the faithful.

You always had soldiers who wanted to break ranks. It was the duty of a good commander to see that didn't happen.

It seemed that the nerve of the authorities was beyond endurance. Why, they sent a congressman after the preacher and his congregation, down in this South American hot place. Snooping they were. Heard reports of people kept against their will from leaving.

Well, of course that had to be dealt with. What were the alternatives? The church was supposed to be immune to the state, but here they were, a whole posse of them, making a media-event fact-finding mission out of a little boondoggling with a nice winter trip to the sunny climes.

There was no end to that kind of thing. First an obscure member of the House of Representatives, and the next thing you know you'll have a whole jumbo jetful of senators landing on you.

There was talk of the Russians making place for them. Giving them asylum. But the talk faded. But one thing was certain, the preacher said. They had to get off the dime. They couldn't stay there and have all this insufferable scrutiny and interference with their religious freedom, guaranteed by the U.S. Constitution. And they weren't even *in* the U.S.

There wasn't any option he saw besides the

poison. They'd had enough poison drills, so most of the pious capitalist-hating socialists would swallow their religion with their existence in one gulp.

Meager arguments were made. The man with the hair black as a raven, the man who said he wanted to be a nigger, beat them down. That's why he was their father. He made the decisions. He'd kept them free from all their worries, and he was making the decision now to end it. He promised them it would be quick and painless, but it wasn't the first time he had lied to them. But it would be the last.

"Give it to your babies first," he said. "Be strong, don't go like some sniveling baby. There is just no other way, believe me. I tried everything."

And they came up to the paintless wooden table with the punch bowl full of Kool-Aid with a cyanide kicker and they drank their slow, miserable, burning death and it turned the bodies of the whites black and the blacks stayed black.

The implication was strong that the reverend was going to drink of the same cup. But those who listened closely must have realized it was only an implication.

One by one the preacher's girlfriends took the bitter dose, and finally his wife, that long-suffering, neglected woman, went down with those who enjoyed her husband's favors.

But maybe she had the last laugh. Maybe she understood finally just how little there was to enjoy. And after all, it was she who was married to god the father. And there was no stigma of divorce. They stayed married right to the end.

And wasn't it a noble experiment? A colorless society where blacks and whites ate, slept and worshiped together. Where rich and poor could get along as brothers. He had given them meaning, he had given the purposeless purpose, and who could ask for more than that?

When they cleared the human wreckage of the 900-plus bodies of the mass suicide, they discovered that it was difficult to tell blacks from the whites, because the poison used turned the whites black.

Their leader didn't partake of the poison. He instead died of a gunshot wound. The gun was found, thirty feet from him, without his fingerprints on it, making suicide seem problematical.

And so it was that this spiritual leader to hundreds, who always proclaimed he wanted to be black, was the only victim of the massacre who was white as a ghost.

—*Frankie Foxxe*
The Underbelly of Fringe Religion

Blessed are ye,
when men shall revile you,
and persecute you,
and shall say all manner of evil
against you falsely,
for my sake.
Rejoice,
and be exceeding glad:
for great is your reward in heaven:
for so persecuted they
the prophets which were before you.

—Matthew 5:11-12

THE GOSPEL ACCORDING TO

SHERIFF
STONEY JESSUP

Larry LaRue, the Disciple assigned to watch Ernie Jo came to me all agitated.

He was short on breath when he told me about it. I was on the field of the Coliseum when he come running as fast as he could, considering all the folks was down there.

"Sheriff," he puffed. "Sheriff, I lost him!"

It hit me right away. I mean, there was no delayed reaction or anything. "Ernie Jo?"

"Ernie Jo," he said. "He went into a bathroom and never came out. When I went in, he was not there. Nobody seemed to have seen anything. I went in there, checked the stalls—" He shook his head. It was enough to make you believe in miracles...for the other side.

We mobilized a good-sized posse and fanned out over the grounds, inside and out, with special attention to all the gates. I quickly realized we didn't have the manpower to do a decent job of it. The unspoken question after I briefed them all was who among us would take a bullet to save the Savior? I wouldn't expect anyone with a family to do it—unless there was no alternative. I wondered if Fluffy would be considered family. I was convinced it was the same dog—he had mannerisms just like he did before he was taken from me. Like the way he dug his nose into my shoulder and jumped up to see me after I'd been gone. I finally had something to live for again. I wasn't going to take him for granted this time like I did before.

After the troops fanned out, I sought out Michael. I found him just beside the stage. I told him what happened, then suggested we form a cordon when Jesus left the arena—protect Him from *any* old assassin.

"Good idea," Michael said. "But He won't go for it. We tried to get Him in a helicopter, an armored car—anything that offered the slightest protection. He wouldn't go for any of it. Called it elitist, and He wanted to be among His people."

"But, reason with Him, will you, Michael? We have an armed assassin on the loose. We had him in our sights, but we lost him. We are afraid for Jesus's safety."

"I'll talk to Jack, but I'm not optimistic." The speech was winding down and we'd have to do something fast.

For God so loved the world,
that he gave his only begotten Son,
that whosoever believeth in him
should not perish,
but have everlasting life.

—John 3:16

THE GOSPEL ACCORDING TO

ERNIE JO BANGHART

Quite honestly, I was getting nervous.

His preaching couldn't last forever and I was no closer to being inside than I was when I got there. It's a good thing I was so alert or I would have missed my opportunity.

On my second circumnabulation of the oval Coliseum fence, I saw a commotion up ahead. People were beginning to leave; I suppose they sensed it was almost over and they were trying to beat the crowds and traffic. From outside the fence, a bunch of paramedics were charging into the arena with a stretcher rolled up so it looked like two poles with a white canvas wrapped around them. The young guard was momentarily confused when the paramedics, who wanted to get in, bumped into people going out. Someone, I think one of the paramedics, yelled something and the gate guard turned to say something to the people exiting. I think he was telling them to make room. "Emergency," I heard someone shout, then others picked it up, and finally, I started yelling "Emergency!" as though I was part of the crowd.

I was almost in when the guard stopped me. "Where do you think you're going?" he said.

"I left something inside. I gotta get it."

"Left what inside?" he asked. It was clear he didn't believe me.

"Coupla tee shirts I bought for my grandbabies," I said, keeping my head down so he had a good view of "He's Back" on my hat. "I just remembered when I saw that vendor stand over there—" He turned to look at it.

I darted to the tunnel.

"Hey!" he yelled.

"I'll be back in a minute," I said, and disappeared into the tunnel.

Inside, I stepped down to the ground level. The place was swarming with cops and these Devil's Disciples fellas, and I had many an anxious moment when I thought I was getting the fish eye from one or another of them. Quickly I disappeared into the hordes of standees down on the ground. The fake was riding his hobby horse to wipe out hate, and I was relieved I had the symbol on the back of my hat.

I inched my way towards the stage, meeting with surprisingly little grumbling on the way. I was polite, whispering "Excuse me," as I went. "Pardon me," in hushed tones. The crowd was so rapt in their attention, I don't honestly believe anyone noticed me.

I got as close as I could. The stage was surrounded with police and Devil's Disciples and I didn't trust the little gun in my pocket to shoot that far with any kind of accuracy. So I had to count on the mass confusion at the end, when I expected him to be mobbed by the mob.

The speech ended and I expected music or something to wind down the proceedings, but nothing came except an enormous roar from the crowd. He didn't even have music to warm them up or give them a break from the preaching. How he got away with it, I'll never know.

There wasn't any altar call at the end of the service, either. In my experience, he was missing a good bet to win and hold souls for Jesus, but that was his doing, not mine.

As though God was scripting this event for me (and why shouldn't He? I was doing *His* bidding, after all), the crowd seemed to push toward the stage, as though they all had to simply touch him or they would go mad.

He smiled with fake modesty and looked like he was surprised at the reaction and didn't know what to do next. Sheriff Jessup pushed his way onto the stage and came face to face with the Antichrist. My immediate thought was that Sheriff Jessup was going to carry out the mission as he agreed upon in the first place.

But he was only telling him something. Probably to be careful—probably that the cops were going to surround him to get him out of there. When I realized Sheriff Jessup was not coming back to the side of the angels, I pulled my cap down and dropped my head. The last thing I wanted was for the sheriff to recognize me.

When I was fairly sure he hadn't seen me, I tried to move to where I could get a clear shot. The sheriff was so big, he was block-ing the target. If only I had the time and skill to get them both. But I realized I had to be content with bagging the prize.

Shooting from this range, I realized, was a crapshoot, not worth the chance. I had to watch the Antichrist's every move so I could gauge which way he would leave the stage. I had made it to between the stage and the tunnel where cars and trucks came through, but I knew he could fool me and go out any of the many exits around the Coliseum—even up the peristyle end, opposite the tunnel. That way would keep him from the protection of a car. I didn't see a car at first. Movement was severely restricted in the area, what with all the folks pushing toward the stage. It was almost as though they expected an altar call, and when he didn't offer one, they decided to have one of their own.

I heard one of the cops shout, "Clear a path for the car! Move it!"

There was more commotion and the Antichrist and Sheriff Jessup turned toward the tunnel; I suppose to get in a car that was coming towards them, but I didn't honestly see how it could be moving more than an inch at a time.

Everyone down there was angling to get closer to the man onstage. I was feeling the pressure of the mob and was simply pushed in the direction I wanted to go. The ribbon of blue-uni-formed cops was helpless and I was afraid we would all be crushed to death.

Somehow, I'll never know exactly how, I got carried on the wave of humanity in the direction of the Antichrist and I found myself washed between the stage and the frustrated car, which now had a bevy of cops in front of it, trying to move it in closer.

I'll tell you honestly, the way the crowd was pushing and shoving, I'da been nowhere if God hadn't been urging me on.

"Go on, go on," He kept saying, and I thought, that's easy for You to say, but I cannot move. Show me Your power by clearing a path.

And God took up the challenge, because the next thing I knew, I was pushed up with the crowd in front of where the fake was heading toward the big black Cadillac that was inching its way toward the platform.

Suddenly, I saw him. God said, *"There he is. Get him."* I tried to move closer, but I was rooted by the folks around me. My eyes were on the Antichrist. There was a young man and an older one who seemed to be in charge. There was a pretty girl with the young man—a girl I could have had some thoughts about were the situation different. Then I saw the back of Sheriff Stoney Jessup—trying to maneuver the crowd out of the way. He was in the way of my target. I knew I only had one chance and I'd rather not shoot than take the chance of missing.

There was such a noise in the place and it seemed to be magnified by the walls of the Coliseum. I looked up to see how I could get closer and I caught the eye of Frankie Foxxe. He looked distraught when he saw me, but he was too far away to do much about it. I will say, he did seem to know what I was about, from the look on his face. He started yelling something but no one heard it. There was just too much noise. He was flailing his arms and fighting to get closer to me, but he just didn't have the belief, I mean, the strength, to move any faster than the crowd would let him, and by now, there was no movement at all. No one was leaving, they all wanted a piece of the man they thought was Jesus, and *none* of them seemed to realize I was the *real* Jesus. I knew, from my conversations with God, that would all change as soon as I fired the shot.

We were all pushing—the crowd trying to get closer to the Jesus impostor and him and his entourage trying to get to the car, which wasn't hardly any closer than before.

Then God gave me my opportunity. Just when I thought I was about to suffocate, somehow the pushers in front of me pressed back to make room for this fake Jesus to move forward, towards me. Sheriff Stoney Jessup turned around at that moment and Frankie Foxxe must have gotten his attention, for he looked around as though looking for something specific, then he saw me. It must have been instinct that caused him to block the fake Jesus from me, because he pressed his enormous bulk as close to covering him as he could. That wasn't a perfect cover, owing to the crowd and all, but I was afraid to take the shot, just the same.

But here is where God came in on my side. I was getting so close, I slid my hand into my pocket and felt the chilling metal of my pistol. I had to be ready to draw it at any moment.

"*Go for it*," God was saying, but at that time, my target was barely visible. Suddenly, things began to happen. There was still a lot of pushing and shoving and I was pushed closer to the Antichrist, who was advancing slowly, but now, somehow, Sheriff Jessup was pushed out of the way and I was in range.

The Antichrist saw me and had this smile on his face when he said, "Hello, Ernie Jo, it was nice of you to come." That set me back a moment. Here he was, picking me out of these tens of thousands and saying hello. But God said, "*Do it!*" and there was no mistaking that command.

It all happened so fast I'm not sure I remember it right, but I pulled out the gun and everybody seemed to be frozen in place as I pulled the trigger—once at his forehead, once at his heart and once at his stomach.

Then everybody seemed to lunge at me and I went down on the bottom of the pile, and I heard the Antichrist say in this squealy, little-girl's kind of voice, "Father, forgive him, for he knows not what...he..." Then he was silent and I was about to suffocate. Hands were reaching for my pistol, but I'm just as sure as I am of anything that if they had shot me, I wouldn't have died.

"Gods don't die," I said aloud, not that too many were close enough to hear through that pile of humanity atop me.

Then someone got ahold of the pistol. I didn't fight him. God was on my side. Then I heard a distant voice say, "Don't hate him. Jesus said we aren't supposed to hate," and I couldn't swear to it, but I thought it was the voice of Frankie Foxxe. Then I felt a loosening of muscles on the men on top of me—a relaxing of their hold. I could see through the crowd of wrestlers, who were parting, the faces of many who looked like they were ready to kill me, but were frozen somehow, as though the Almighty had poured hot bronze over them.

Apparently, God had told them I was the real Jesus, because they released me. That's what I thought, anyway, but it turned out they were just making room for the men in blue—Pharisees they were, because they hauled me away to jail. Nobody lifted a hand to harm me, so that was a lucky fringe benefit of the Antichrist's teaching.

When I looked up, I saw the entourage watching me, with tears in their eyes. Tears of remorse, I'd say, not hate.

The crowd seemed relaxed to numbness and somehow Frankie Foxxe was standing by me when they put me into a cop car that I suppose was to be used to escort the Antichrist to further glorious shams.

Frankie Foxxe looked me in the eye like he really felt sorry for me. He was the Debunker of Myths, after all, so it was natural he would be skeptical about me.

But I noticed a funny thing about him. He had tears in his eyes, too.

ANOTHER BLAST FROM GOD'S TROMBONES:

Everybody is a bit right; nobody is completely right or completely wrong. The prevalence of this point of view among all decent people nearly always has the same dreadful result for, according to their doctrine, every time a contemporary is quite right, he must be crucified. They can never forgive him because he denies their dogma; worse still, he reveals that they hold another dogma which they conceal. The unavowed dogma of these diffusionists runs as follows. The truth is everywhere and nowhere; it evolves itself without anyone knowing it, as if, in the end, Judas is just as right as Jesus. One can read that Jesus incited Judas, according to the maxim: "It is not the murderer but his victim who is guilty." Judas and Jesus must be "synthesized"; both are "only" human: all men are swine.

— *Eugen Rosenstock-Huessy*

And there are also many other things
which Jesus did,
the which,
if they should be written every one,
I suppose that even the world itself
could not contain
the books that should be written.
Amen.

—John 21:25

THE GOSPEL ACCORDING TO

FRANKIE FOXXE

Of course, the thought I
had failed would plague
me for all eternity.

I knew Ernie Jo might assassinate Jesus and I did the best I knew, but it wasn't enough. What more could I have done? Hired more guards? Jesus was not happy about having so many. Insisted on a helicopter for His exit? Insisting didn't move Jesus. Jesus wanted to be with the people.

By the time the paramedics got to Jesus, it was too late. The three bullets lodged in Jesus's brain, heart and stomach had done their work. A reporter more cynical than I am (if such exists) might have called them the Father, Son and the Holy Ghost—the Trinity shots. Even if the paramedic crew had been able to part the crowd instead of clearing the crush of humanity at a snail's pace, it would have been too late.

The news from these paramedics was the surprise of the millennium. It set all believers on their ears. I'm not sure what my initial reaction was, but now that I think of it, it has a certain sweet logic to it.

I was hanging around the paramedic wagon onto which Jesus had been loaded. I was simply playing reporter, waiting for my story amidst the pandemonium of the crowd.

I suppose some of us were waiting for the announcement of a miracle. A resurrection of sorts. Instead, this redheaded, burly guy comes out, a mixture of macho and childish wonder.

He says, sputtering like he can't believe what he is saying, "Jesus, I mean, that is, this person we thought was Jesus, well, He is a...woman—a She."

There was a flurry of questions, pointed disbelief all around me. It was something I could feel. Nobody had to say anything, it was just in the air I was breathing. The redheaded paramedic shook his head, pursed his lips, and held his ground.

"There ain't no doubt," he said. "Flat-chested, sure, and I can't explain any of it; how we could have been fooled, anything. It just...is."

It was an hour later before I got reunited with Rachel, who had disappeared to the bathroom at an inauspicious moment. Her excited smile was the size of the Coliseum itself when she heard the news. She looked at me, not so much straight in the eye as straight down my gullet.

"So! A *female*," Rachel said, not only laying on the first syllable like a ton of bricks, but dragging it out like a Greek Orthodox wedding. "Didn't you say that's all it would take to get you to believe? The asexual turkeys in New Jersey—remember? So I guess this does it. You're a believer!"

She was having the time of her life and I didn't want to be a wet blanket—but I didn't fall into her trap, either. So I muttered, "I didn't say that was *all* it would take."

"Cop-out, Father Frankie," she said, "cop-out."

My first thought on hearing this startling sex news should have been to dive for a phone, file my story, but it wasn't. Instead, I dragged myself away from the paramedics' wagon and back over to the stage, where I looked up to where He, or She, had been standing, speaking to the multitudes, admonishing all of us to turn our backs on hate. Then I wondered, why do we always kill the best among us? If you are a believer, it happened two thousand years ago. If it is mythology, it is still a good story, and the point of the story, to me, is we sacrifice the ideal for the mundane. There is a strong pull in society toward the norm. Mavericks are shunned, avoided, ignored, fought until they disappear or conform.

To think that a man like Ernie Jo Banghart, not the best among us, could bring down a Jesus Christ, or a Jesus Christ lookalike, depending on your persuasion, is almost unthinkable. Just as the heathen Roman soldiers, the unlawful Sanhedrin and the wimpy Pilate brought down the God-figure Jesus Christ, Ernie Jo Banghart and all the doubters brought down the closest thing we've seen to goodness. If we can't be good, why would we suffer others to show us up?

Eventually, Rachel and I left the Coliseum. I don't have any memory of how I got out of there. I filed the story. I wasn't first, but then J. S. Bach wasn't the first baroque composer, either.

As for Jesus, we laid Her in a tomb with stones around it. Not big boulders so heavy even God couldn't move them, but hefty, symbolic stones. We were trying to give Her the benefit of the doubt.

It was during this undertaking at Jack Whitehall's meadow in Glory Pines that I got to know my fellow mourners who had been so important to the brief ministry of this woman, whoever She was. And I got interested enough to keep tabs on them.

Michael and Mary married and moved to Ventura, where he works in a hardware store and she at the outlet for Ralph Lauren seconds. My latest intelligence on the Michael Lovejoys is that she is a little bit pregnant. Mom and Dad Lovejoy, Amos and Andi to their close friends, are treading the status quo. Though he doesn't broadcast it, Amos was not distraught over the demise of Jesus. Jack Whitehall was a happy new man with his wife's return. As far as I know, they are living happily ever after. He still does a little healing when he feels the Spirit of the Lord upon him.

The Devil's Disciples scattered to the four winds, and if my sources are correct, never gave up their crusade against hate.

Millie Brosky, the abused waitress from the Easy Eats diner, was released from the mental hospital the day Jesus was shot. She decided not to go back to the waitress trade, and took a job instead in a discount store. She thought it would be less dangerous.

Sheriff Stoney Jessup retired from peacekeeping with his dog, Fluffy, without seeing his picture in Ernie Jo's magazine, *God's Guitar*. The Ernie Jo Banghart Ministries went belly up, officially when he went to jail, but really when he said he was Jesus Christ. It was more than the faithful could believe. Sheriff Jessup's retirement wasn't exactly a decision made with malice aforethought. He was beginning to outgrow his uniform and he went to the tailor to have it let out, whereupon he was told it had been let out to its limit. The only way he could get a uniform to fit was buy a new one or go on a diet.

Neither option lit any fires in the sheriff's heart. So he took early retirement. He made some tapes of Jesus when the TV crews filmed Her talks, and he passed the time with Fluffy watching them. He did occasional work as a security guard for minimum wage. Every once in a while he'd watch an old Ernie Jo Banghart tape and marvel at the talent of the man. He never got a tape of his own speech on the steps of the jailhouse while he was holding "a black male" incarcerated.

Sheriff Jessup moved down the street to Mary's shack behind Filmore's place, and there he and Fluffy lived in peace and harmony with their landlord, who, magically, had gotten the hate out of his system.

Rachel Brighton is making noises about tying me down with a nuptial knot and I seem to be shedding my thick, slick, defensive coat that protected me heretofore.

If I succumb, Rob Houston will not be in attendance for the festivities. I have taken a job with the *Los Angeles Times*, where they let me work for months on my feature stories. Rob himself has become a candidate for carbon-dating.

Just after editor Rob Houston passed the word he owned the *Gulfport Riptide* (false), it fell into bankruptcy owing to the bloodletting caused by the demise of the Ernie Jo Banghart Ministries.

I wrote Rob a letter of condolence, and he wrote me back that the bankruptcy was a bookkeeping thing, and he had just cleared it up with a million bucks of his own money. "But what the heck," he wrote. "You can't take it with you."

Especially if you don't have it, and he didn't. The chain that bailed the *Riptide* out of bankruptcy put Rob Houston out to pasture, making me think there might be a God, after all.

Ernie Jo Banghart is not languishing in jail, he is thriving there. He is converting prisoners to Jesus left and right. It is a captive, and surprisingly receptive audience. Every now and then, perhaps in spite of himself, Ernie Jo sprinkles his preaching with a bit about love thy neighbor as thyself, and now and then he takes off on a tirade against hate, but no one considers it unusual.

Emily Sue Banghart divorced Ernie Jo and married Bobby Candle, after his wife left him for the contractor who built the water slides in their Jesus playground. Bobby and Emily Sue have a television program where they appear at the top of the aisle, holding hands, and come down to the stage so joined. There, in a comfortable living-room setting, they field spiritual questions from the audience. My favorite from the most recent show was: "I just lost my dog, is there a chance he will be resurrected?" The consensus of the Candles, who seemed to be burning at both ends, was, in all probability, not.

Brucie Banghart, heartbroken still, visits his father faithfully in the slammer. He has taken a job as a telephone order taker on Christian television. He will not comment publicly on whether or not he believes his dad is really Jesus Christ.

Does Ernie Jo still think he is Jesus? I visited him in prison and was not really surprised that he did. He was still an imposing presence in his prison garb, and he told me it was all going according to God's plan. He was reviled and incarcerated the first time around. Misunderstood. A prophet without honor in his own land. You know the rest. Any day, he was expecting the hand of God to pluck him from that jailhouse and set him free to spread the Word. Why, at that very moment, he was working on a plan to have his Sunday exhortations televised from prison. He was conversing with God daily about it.

There was speculation God sent a woman this time to even the score. But some were convinced it had been a woman the first time but the chauvinists purposely deceived the multitudes. It could explain a lot of things, like Jesus's apparent sexual indifference to women.

Still others thought it was a big put-on. A smallish minority believed it didn't happen at all—it was pure mythology.

All of which goes to prove, in the end, we believe what we want to believe.

Did the message survive the brief appearance of the mysterious Jesus? Well, human nature being what it is, all I can say is that it was fun while it lasted. It was not so amazing to me, the original Debunker of Myths, how quickly and easily people slipped back into their old ways. Hating those different than we are was part of the nature of man—woven into the fabric of society, as well as the genetic coding.

I will admit that the thought of a hate-free world intrigued me. As I saw strides being made, I couldn't believe it was possible. I guess I was right to be skeptical. Skepticism, I've found, is always a safe bet if you want to be right.

As for Jesus, there was some evidence of graverobbing when She disappeared from Her tomb. And a number of people claimed to have seen Her on the road to Emmaus and elsewhere.

But no one could be sure.

THE GOSPEL ACCORDING TO

GOD

A Conversation with Theodore Gardner
author of *He's Back*

What inspired you to write a book about Jesus returning to earth?

Some decades ago, I had a philosophy professor at USC who said, "Millions of people think Jesus Christ is going to return to earth. What would happen if a man in white robes and sandals got off a plane in Los Angeles and said he was Jesus Christ returned to earth? They'd lock him up.' I have been ruminating and writing *He's Back* ever since. It is the book of my lifetime.

What happens to the stranger?

He claims to be Jesus returned with the immediate purpose of eliminating hate from the world. He refuses donations and a $150 million TV contract. An ex-priest who styles himself as a Debunker of Myths goes at the stranger with surprising results. Jesus is celebrated by the people who have been rejected by the establishment. He captures the hardest hearts without any institution validating him.

How did you research the topic?

A lifetime of religious training, observation and reading. I studied the leading TV evangelist, watched his TV shows, read his magazine, even attended one of his revival services. Other characters and stories are loosely based on people I know.

What is the meaning and symbolism of the format you chose for this novel (the gospels, the blasts, twangs, etc)?

I was attempting to give a broad brush background to Christianity in the U.S. in the "Blasts from God's Trombones" —not unlike the news reels in John Dos Passos's *U.S.A. Trilogy*. The biblical quotes and secular "Twangs from God's Guitar" relate these sources to the content of the chapter. A blast from the trombone, is, of course, louder than a twang from a guitar.

What are the significant changes each character undergoes in the story?

Well, if you don't mind, I'd rather not give the story away. Suffice it to say there are many transformations of the characters. Some make complete reversals, but all are affected in some way by this simple stranger who asks so little.

Would you characterize this novel as contemporary fiction, fable, or epic? Why?

I think all of these labels could easily apply—you might even add allegory. But I would defer to the opinion of the reader.

What was your writing process for this book? Revisions? Was the story formed in your head prior to writing it?

The story is always formed in my head before writing. I always say the writing is easy, the thinking is hard; but as you write, ideas beget other ideas, and chapters are added, omitted, viewpoints change and change back again. I suspect this book has gone through more than ten drafts.

Other Books by Theodore Roosevelt Gardner II

The Paper Dynasty
The true and explosive story of the most remarkable family in America inspired *The Paper Dynasty*. $23.45

The Real Sleeper
An enchanting May-to-December romance. $14.95
Free booklet of excerpts available for this title, call (800) 777-7623

Give Gravity A Chance : A Love Story
The *Pygmalion* for the millennium. $20.00

Flip Side: A Novel of Suspense
Can a murder trial really have two such conflicting perspectives? *Flip Side* gives us two heart-stopping versions of the same high-profile multiple-murder case. $22.00

Something Nice to See
A delightful children's story about tolerance, set during the creation of the awe-inspiring Watts Towers. $15.95

Order from your favorite bookstore, library or from Allen A. Knoll, Publishers at (800) 777-7623. Or send a check for the amount of the book, plus $3.00 shipping and handling for the first book, $1.50 for each additional book (plus 7 ¾% tax for California residents) to:

Allen A. Knoll, Publishers
200 West Victoria Street
Santa Barbara, CA 93101-3627

Credit cards also accepted.
Please contact us if you have any questions, would like to receive a free Knoll Publishers catalog, or a reading guide for *He's Back*.
(800) 777-7623
email: bookinfo@knollpublishers.com

Visit our website at www.knollpublishers.com